GUMSHOE
FOR TWO

Also by Rob Leininger

The Mortimer Angel Mysteries

Gumshoe

Gumshoe on the Loose

Other Books

Richter Ten

Sunspot

Killing Suki Flood

Maxwell's Demon

January Cold Kill (A Gabrielle Johns Mystery)

Olongapo Liberty

GUMSHOE
FOR TWO

A Mortimer Angel Novel

ROB LEININGER

OCEANVIEW  PUBLISHING

SARASOTA, FLORIDA

ISBN 978-1-60809-280-2

Published in the United States of America by Oceanview Publishing
Longboat Key, Florida
www.oceanviewpub.com

10 9 8 7 6 5 4 3 2

PRINTED IN THE UNITED STATES OF AMERICA

For everyone who read GUMSHOE.
This one's for you.

Acknowledgments

MANY THANKS TO my "readers" who spotted numerous errors and typos in the next-to-final draft: Madelon Martin (who loves to spot errors); Tracy Ellis; and my wife, Pat. You guys chuckle at me almost silently, but keep me from being laughed at out loud. A special thanks to Tracy Ellis who believed in the first novel, *Gumshoe*, told a friend about it, who told someone at Oceanview Publishing and got this snowball rolling downhill.

I am further indebted to the people at Oceanview Publishing: Bob and Pat Gussin, Lee Randall, Lisa Daily, and Emily Baar. Your expertise and professionalism makes it all happen.

Finally, to John Lescroart (pronounced "Les-kwah"), incredible friend and *New York Times* best-selling author of the Dismas Hardy novels, thank you for believing in me as I believe in you. And may we, and our wives, meet again in Banff for more good food and talk. Or at Bouchercon. Bouchercon would be nice.

GUMSHOE
FOR TWO

CHAPTER ONE

"SHAKE THE HAND of an honest politician."

Harold J. Reinhart, senior U.S. senator from the great state of Nevada, had found himself a battle cry that apparently resonated with voters. Enough of them, anyway, that his polling numbers were up 5 percent in the past month. If you thought political polls had the slightest bearing on reality—never a good idea—this proved you could fool some of the people all of the time. But when you head out to conquer the world with an unbeatable oxymoron like that, it's like playing chicken with the devil.

"Omigod," Jeri said, grimacing at the television above the bar. "Can't we turn him off?"

"You kidding?" I said. "Brilliant orator like that?"

"Uncle Harry," sixty-two years old, was making a bid for the presidency. With numbers in his own party trolling below 15 percent, it wasn't as if the guy was on fire. But he was in the news, front page above the fold in the *Gazette-Journal*, second story on television behind a hotel fire in Vegas. He'd missed a noon rally at Wingfield Park on Saturday where he was scheduled to shake hands with an estimated two thousand supporters—good luck rounding up fifty warm bodies, I thought—and hadn't been seen in three days.

Tuesday night, 11:06 p.m., Jeri and I were sitting at the bar in the Green Room of the Golden Goose Casino watching a week-old clip of our very own lying senator on Channel 8 as he delivered his now-famous campaign slogan, when—

"Omigawd, lads, we have found paradise!"

Six drunken Shriners tumbled into the room like moonshine sloshing out of a Mason jar, turning what had been a reasonably pleasant atmosphere into a 90-proof circus. I heard them coming ten seconds before I saw them.

A Shriner convention was loose in Reno. This piece had broken free of the larger mass and discovered the Green Room. I'd always thought of the place, tucked into an odd corner of the Golden Goose Casino, as the city's "best kept secret," but maybe it was the track lighting that turns skin and teeth an unsettling shade of green that kept the hordes away. If a guy was hoping to get lucky, this was the last place to bring a date. Green is an easy skin tone to overdo.

Jeri DiFrazzia was my boss, business partner, friend, lover, and fiancée. This was only the third time she'd been in the place. For me it was something of a second home, especially nearing the end of baseball season. This evening the Cubs had whipped the Pirates six to five in extra innings, just in time for News at Eleven.

Mid-September, Jeri and I were using free-drink coupons the bartender, Patrick O'Roarke, had given me five weeks ago when I was in the hospital recovering from fencing wounds. A gorgeous but unfortunately psychotic twenty-year-old girl half my size had run a foil through my chest and out my back, missing my subclavian artery by a quarter inch. Up till then I didn't even know I had a subclavian artery. She'd also stabbed my foot and slashed my face. For the rest of my life, I would have a scar across the bridge of my nose and my left cheek, an inch below my eye. If I'd still been working for the IRS, the enhanced intimidation factor would have been worth a nice raise. The various holes and slashes were the first fencing wounds reported in the state of Nevada since it was admitted to the Union in 1864, but the national celebrity I'd received was for locating Reno's missing mayor and district attorney, not the puncture wounds. That near-death experience had taken place the first week of August. Since then I'd been in recovery mode, taking it easy. Jogging still put twinges in my chest.

My name is Mort Angel. Not Mortimer—although that mistake was made forty-one years ago on my birth certificate and was never corrected, causing me no end of embarrassment and trouble. Mom is still on my shit list for that.

Jeri DiFrazzia and I investigate—privately. Well, she does. It says so on the door to her house-office. I'm a PI-in-training, having quit a thankless IRS job the first week of July in order to prowl dark alleyways and dodge bullets. I hadn't counted on sword fights. In Nevada it takes ten thousand hours to become a licensed PI. Ten thousand freakin' hours—a requirement that weeds out the wannabes by the truckload. Five *years* of training. Currently I was 6 percent of the way through that thicket of bullshit. Bet Spade and Hammer didn't have to slog through any of that. I figured it took them about as long as it took to pound a nail and hang a shingle. I know McGee—Travis—hadn't gone that route.

Jeri was working on an End Wrench with a twist of lime and a cherry. I had abandoned my usual—Pete's Wicked Ale—and had a longneck of Moose Drool brown ale in front of me. An End Wrench, I'd learned, was orange juice and tonic water, something I wouldn't put down my throat to win a bet under a hundred bucks. But Jeri was in training. She had a national competition coming up in three days in Atlantic City. She had a flight out on Southwest at 8:35 in the morning. My job, starting at 8:36, would be to hold down the fort and keep out of trouble while she was away, which was going to be a while since she was meeting her brother Ron and his wife the following Monday. Ron was competing in the Pan American Judo Championships the following week in Manhattan. The whole family was type-A like that. I'm more B-minus, but I compensate with luck. Jeri would be gone for twelve days, the longest we'd been apart since she'd taken me on as an investigator-in-training midsummer at the urging of my ex, Dallas, who'd probably wanted a good laugh.

Back to our lying senator. His absence had become bigger news than his poll numbers, so ditching that rally at Wingfield might've been a way to get even more attention, though that might just be my churlish take on politics in general. Reinhart's absence was made more ominous when his chief of staff, Jayson Wexel, was killed in a house fire two days ago. The fire started in a fireplace, no surprise, except the daytime high temperature was eighty-five—and when the place had cooled, investigators found Jayson, age forty-nine, burned to a crisp. It looked like an accident, but . . . maybe not. Police were looking into it and "no comments" were being flung at reporters by lawmen as they entered buildings and climbed into cars, so it made for dry viewing and languid ratings, even with Senator Reinhart's disappearance.

Jeri nodded at Reinhart on TV. "You oughta find that guy while I'm gone."

"I'll get right on that."

"Last August I wouldn't have put it past you. You and Kayla."

A neat little dig there. Kayla, the missing mayor's beautiful daughter, and I had gone off to Austin in the middle of Nevada, ignoring Jeri's suggestion—okay, order—not to "horse around" with the investigation until she got back.

"My forte is decapitations," I said. "Not missing dimwits."

She smiled and sipped her drink. "Senator Dimwit would put you back in the spotlight again. That's something."

"No need, I'm still hot on Google. And our missing politician is probably in disguise in Puerto Vallarta boffing senoritas, trying to boost his numbers by getting himself in the news."

"*Boffing?*"

"It's in the dictionary. Look it up."

"With that guy Wexel dead, Reinhart might not be laughing it up in Puerto Vallarta."

"Right. He might be in Cancún."

"Mort—"

That was when the Shriners rolled in. To a pile of drunks in red bucket hats, too-white shirts and red vests loaded down with merit badges, pins, and whatnot, half-blind as they were, it's surprising Jeri ended up on the big Shriner's radar, but she did. Fast, too, so the old guy had an eye. But maybe not so surprising. As usual, Jeri was looking good, dressed in tight-fitting plum pants and a long-sleeve ivory shirt. She had a face that drew stares, she's that beautiful. She's not much into jewelry—rings interfere with judo, karate, and aikido—but that night she was wearing gold hoop earrings that gave her a subtle gypsy look, especially with her dark hair cut in a feathery layered style. The reddish highlights, of course, were invisible in the green lighting, but the big guy didn't know that.

In his funky fez, he looked about seven feet tall. In fact, he ran six foot six, an inch taller than the bartender, O'Roarke, two inches taller than me. Bunch of big guys in that bar, except that the rest of the Shriners were shrimps, all of them six feet or less.

Man Mountain passed by Jeri then hung a sloppy U-turn and sidled up to her on the side opposite me. He stuck an elbow on the bar, leaned in close, and stared at her. "Man oh man, you are some kinda hellacious pretty, sugar."

Jeri leaned away from his breath. A lit match might have blown Bigfoot's head off. "Yeah, thanks," she said.

The two hints—Jeri's body language and the arm's-length voice—didn't take, and things proceeded from there.

"You an' me, little lady, we oughta dance."

"I'm pretty sure we oughtn't."

"Y'all don't dance with strangers? Well, allow me to fix that apace. The name's Earl. Earl Eberhard."

"You sure?"

Earl didn't know what to say to that. He blinked a few times, squinted at her, then said, "Hah?"

Jeri stared at her drink. "Is it just me, or did it get a whole lot stupider in here in the last thirty seconds?"

I put a hand on her arm. "Whoa, there, little lady."

She gave me a look that could have etched glass, an industrial process involving hydrofluoric acid, then she caught my meaning and nodded. Some of the tension went out of her. This gaggle of fools wasn't mean, just drunk. Happy drunk, actually. The big guy was away from the ol' ball and chain, whooping it up a bit, and he'd stumbled across something that got his man-circuitry galloping, couldn't turn it off.

"Earl," I said. "How 'bout I buy you a drink?"

"Maybe later," Earl said, not looking at me. "Right now I got me a date with this purdy lil' gal. We gonna dance."

"How about tomorrow?" I said.

Finally, he squinted at me. "Who're you, an' wuzzit to ya?"

"The name's Mort, and this purdy lil' gal and I are engaged, that's wuzzit to me."

"Well, then, you're some kinda lucky, stud. But that mean she can't dance?"

"How about you leave that up to her?"

Earl sized me up with bleary eyes. He had me by fifty pounds, but they weren't good pounds. Mine were better even though I was still convalescing, not yet at a hundred percent. He didn't get that, however, because he pushed back into Jeri's space. "Man, y'all're some kinda gorgeous, gorgeous."

"And you're some kinda—"

"*Maybe*," I said before Jeri could say whatever incendiary thing she was about to say, "you two oughta arm wrestle for it."

Well, it just popped out. That's my excuse. My mouth has a mind of its own, an entire inner life independent of mine. Thing is, something like that can take on a life independent of the mouth. This one did.

Jeri turned and stared at me.

Earl, however, roared with laughter. I think that's what really did it. His belly shook. In a beard, a red suit, and a button nose he'd make a jolly old elf. Trouble was, his nose looked like a pickled cucumber and it was only September.

"Arm rassle?" he howled. "Har, har, har." His laugh was one of those. It dug into your brain and loosened neurons.

"C'mon, Earl," said one of his buddies, five-ten and as bald as an egg.

Baldie wasn't nearly as drunk as Earl. Or the rest of them, for that matter. I figured him for the designated Shriner With A Brain. His job might have been to keep Earl out of jail. The other four were staggering in place, trying to keep up with all this, but they looked like harmless souls, just wanting to down a few more shots or shooters, turn their brainpans into happy comatose oatmeal, then head off to a room and crash. The Designated Brain's name turned out to be Barry Flynn.

Earl looked at Barry with tears in his eyes. Real tears. He had to wipe them away with the back of his hand. "Arm rassle, Barry. 'Magine me rasslin' Missy 'Merica here? Har, har, har." He sucked in another breath. "Har, har, har, har."

Jeri popped off the barstool, all five feet three and a half inches of her. At the sight, Earl doubled over with laughter. The top of her head didn't reach his shoulders.

Barry gave us an apologetic shrug.

Jeri, however, gave Earl a look that could freeze a yak. She was facing away from me, but I caught her look in the mirror behind the bar. Type-A, like I said. That "Missy" thing had fired her rocket. Earl's "har, har, har" was just the cherry on top.

Jeri poked him in the belly, hard. "Bring it on, wiseass."

For a moment, time stopped. Stopped so dead it seemed the earth had quit rotating—which would've thrown off all the clocks and pissed off untold billions of people.

I stared at Jeri.

Earl quit haring and stared at her.

The rest of the Shriner pack stared at her, including Barry, as the world held its collective breath—

* * *

—which makes this a perfect time to mention that in late August, when I was finally up to it, Jeri decided she wanted to meet my mom, Dori Angel, a lady so rich she sometimes finds hundred-dollar bills in her hair. She also shacks up with guys half her age as long as they're "pretty," which means tan, over six feet tall, well-muscled, and dumb—dumb evidently being an attractive feature in a sex object. She goes through three or four a year. My father has been out of the picture for quite a while, having died in a golfing accident of his own making.

The trip was a huge success. I got a tan, and Dori and Jeri bonded, possibly because their names both end in the letter "i." At least that was my theory. No other way to explain it.

* * *

Okay, back to the wrestling match.

"Let's do 'er," Earl said.

Jeri rolled her shoulders and shook out her arms, which might have told Earl something, but he was too busy chuckling as he finished off a Kamikaze: Smirnoff Red Label vodka, triple sec, and lime juice. The drink had been ordered for him by one of the other guys, Gill, which indicated that this was not a Mensa convention.

I stood next to Barry.

"This probably isn't a good idea," he said.

"It just popped out," I offered by way of explanation.

"Uh-huh."

"My mouth says things when my back is turned."

He looked at me. "That right? I got a cousin used to do that. He's in prison now." He turned his attention back to Earl and his Kamikaze. "Earl ain't a bad guy. Just kind of a sloppy drunk, you know what I mean."

"Yup. Been there."

We watched Jeri and Earl a moment longer, then my mouth had its second bright idea of the evening.

"Side bets, anyone?" I said, loud enough to cut through the chatter.

All eyes turned to me. Jeri gave me a look. "Might's well pick up a little extra traveling money," I told her.

That got another round of baritone "hars" out of Earl. Not knowing how dangerous it was, he patted the top of Jeri's head. "Whatdda you weigh, sweetheart? One-ten?"

In his defense, he hadn't seen her in gym shorts and a halter top. First ten seconds I'd seen her, in a loose cotton shirt and sultan pants, I had her pegged at one-fifteen and I wasn't drunk off my ass at the time.

Jeri gave him a smile with a lot of teeth in it.

About that time, Shriner Jim-Bob was waving a twenty-dollar bill at me. "Twenty on Earl."

"Slow down," I said. "Lookit the size of that guy. We're gonna need some decent odds here."

"Five to one," Jim-Bob said.

I laughed. "How 'bout ten to one?"

"You're on."

And we were. Jim-Bob, Barry, and Al were in for a hundred each. Pretty sporting, considering they'd only get ten bucks out of it if Earl won. Gill was in for two hundred. At that point Jeri and I were only in for fifty. Then Earl said, "Hundred to one, girlie. My ten grand against your hundred."

Whoa. The world slammed to another halt, then started to spin again, slowly. The air in the room changed.

Barry said, "Earl, no."

I said, "No."

Jeri said, "No."

Earl stared at Jeri, eyes bright. "Or," he said, "maybe we could mud rassle, honey bun. Win or lose, that'd be worth ten grand."

Honey bun? Mud wrestle? I took a step closer to save Earl a month in traction, but Jeri reined herself in and said, "Arm wrestle, buster. Our hundred bucks against your ten Gs."

Buster. I liked that. Made me proud of her. Even working for the IRS I'd never called anyone "buster."

"You're on, sweet cheeks," Earl said.

I drew Barry aside. "Any way to stop this stagecoach before it sails off a cliff?"

"Double shot of fast-acting Valium for both of 'em?"

"Got any on you?"

"Nope."

"Not sure why you brought it up, then." I put my hands in my pockets. "Guy's a bulldog-terrier mix, huh?"

"Been that way long's I've known him."

"So's she."

"Yep, got that, too." He looked at Jeri and pursed his lips. "I ever seen her before?"

"I wouldn't know."

"I sell insurance. I'm usually pretty good with faces."

"Uh-huh. So—is Earl good for that kind of money or is this just talk?"

"Why? Think he'll need it?"

"One never knows."

"He's good for it. Owns a company in East Texas that makes specialty valves."

"Valves?"

"Gate valves, ball valves, valves for acids, sodium hydroxide, you name it, high-temperature and cryogenic stuff."

"Rich dude."

"You got it. More money than sense, 'specially stewed, out on the town like this."

"You probably still oughta rein this guy in."

"Trust me, that's not happenin'. You shoulda seen what he did in Chicago two years ago. There's a big-chain hotel there that won't take Shriners anymore."

Jeri touched her toes. Earl watched her for a moment, then "harred" and drained another Kamikaze, courtesy of Gill, their resident genius.

"Let's have the barkeep hold the money," Jim-Bob suggested.

Wallets emptied—five hundred bucks landed on the bar. Earl quit chuckling long enough to write a check for ten grand, signed it, left the pay-to line blank. O'Roarke put all of it out of sight and out of reach behind the bar.

Earl sat at a table. Jeri took a chair opposite him. Earl had a smile on his face the size of . . . well, Texas, but his eyes looked like ball bearings since his manhood was on the line. He plopped an elbow down on the table, arm up, waiting. Jeri put her arm up. Too short by five inches. She took his wrist, not his palm.

"Bad leverage for the lady," Barry observed. "Might want to do something about that. Put a telephone book or something under her arm."

"Yeah, well, Earl's drunk. Let's call it even," I said. Fact is, I didn't want Earl's ten Gs or the five hundred. I figured we could afford a hundred fifty bucks if it came to that.

Barry shrugged.

O'Roarke put his hand on Earl's. "Sudden slam don't count," he said. "Start slow or forfeit." He looked over at me with a question in his eyes.

I gave him a head tilt, then said to Jeri, "Go get 'im, honey bun." She shot me a look and I knew I'd catch hell later that night.

Earl grinned at Jeri. "Maybe you oughta roll up your sleeves, little lady."

"Why? There's only one of you."

"Har, har, har."

O'Roarke gave me another look, then took his hand away and said, "Okay, then. Go get 'em."

Earl put on a little pressure and Jeri held him. Earl bore down a little harder. Jeri yawned. Earl's eyes widened. Jeri smiled. Sweat glistened on Earl's forehead. Jeri yawned again, audibly. Earl put his weight into it, then Jeri slammed his arm down so hard that Earl tumbled out of his chair and landed on the floor.

Hard.

A moment of silence ensued for the dearly departed.

Money, that is.

Then the groans started, and someone said, "What the hell, Earl, you shithead."

Earl lay on the floor for a moment, then slowly got to his feet. Jeri went back to her barstool. "Another End Wrench, Patrick," she said as O'Roarke went behind the bar.

"Third place," Barry said to me. "Or was it fourth?"

"Huh?"

"Just remembered where I saw her. National power lifting championships last year in Miami, New York, someplace. She took third, right?"

"Fourth," I said. "In her weight class. But she's stronger now and Nationals are this weekend in Atlantic City. I'm thinking she'll take it all."

"Hell." He looked at me. "You two're engaged?"

"Uh-huh. Three weeks ago."

"Well . . . good luck, man. Don't ever piss her off."

Earl didn't have much to say once he was on his feet. He was too busy being called a shithead and a pussy and other terms of endearment by his fellow Shriners. I got the folding money from O'Roarke. Our fifty, their five hundred, gave O'Roarke a hundred, then Jeri grabbed Earl's check and tore it up.

"Hey, hey, hey," Earl said, sounding like Fat Albert. "You won that money fair an' square, sugar plum."

Okay, some guys are naturally slow learners, like me most of the time. To her credit, Jeri didn't pick him up and body slam him. In fact, she said, "How 'bout that dance, Earl?"

For a moment his eyes got bright and happy, then they shut down. "Guess not. So, little lady, what's your name?"

She smiled. "Jeri."

"Jerry? Man, they're doin' wonders with that sex change stuff nowadays, ain't they?"

I shut my eyes. Earl's life passed before my eyes, which was eerie, but Jeri just patted his cheek, maybe a little hard, and said, "Let's dance. I'll let you lead."

Earl shook his head. "Not till you take my money. You stay right there and hang fire for a few."

He went out the door, came back five minutes later with ten casino chips worth a thousand each, put them in Jeri's hand, and folded her fingers over them. "Don't tear 'em up, sugar plum. Now, if y'all're still willin', I guess I wouldn't mind that dance."

* * *

Jeri and I were at Reno-Tahoe International Airport at seven forty the next morning. At under five-four, a hundred thirty pounds, white and female, Jeri profiled out as a likely terrorist so they gave her the full treatment, checking her shoes—sandals—for C-4, going through her purse to find bottles of exploding lotion. They look for the most unlikely things, then miss automatic weapons when FBI agents test airport security by sneaking Glocks and Uzis through. Granny can't get through unmolested, but profiling Middle Eastern males with "Allahu Akbar" beards isn't PC so they're waved on through.

Before entering the security obstacle course, Jeri kissed me, long and hard. We drew envious stares.

"Go get 'em, tiger," I said once we came up for air.

"Will do."

"Got everything you need? Toothbrush, toothpaste, spare bottle of hydraulic fluid?"

"I usually stock up on fluid after I get there."

"Good idea. Have fun in security. They're waitin' for you."

"Yup. Love those strip searches."

She gave me another quick kiss, then she was gone, into the red-hot security vortex that keeps our nation's air travel safe. Like the IRS, of which I was no longer a part, it was a government-run operation.

Food for thought.

CHAPTER TWO

I SPENT THAT morning and early afternoon camped out a hundred feet down the block from Western Pacific Bank on Wells Avenue, waiting for one William Aaron Dryer, chief loan officer, to make an appearance. His wife suspected Billy-boy of cheating and Jeri had assigned me the task of watching the bank from eleven to four, for which she charged said wife two hundred fifty dollars. Easy money, boring, but I was still convalescing so I didn't complain. The hours added up, even these. I had accumulated six hundred of the ten thousand hours it takes to become a licensed PI in Nevada. I was hoping to make it before I turned fifty.

At two forty-five, there was Billy in a blow-dry haircut, exiting a side parking lot onto a side street in a metallic blue Cadillac ATS-V coupe, the one with 464 horsepower and an eight-speed automatic transmission, not a hard car to follow in a helicopter or a rocket, but I was in my Toyota, a sorry, undernourished thing without air-conditioning or intermittent wipers.

But we only went half a mile so he was just a quarter mile away when he pulled into a driveway on Elm. I caught up as the garage door went down, concealing the Caddy, then all was quiet. Got the address off the house and put it into an iPad with Jeri's PI authorization, found that Billy was entertaining a Mrs. Percival Yates—Yolanda. Initials YY. Or Percival himself, but I doubted it.

Percival. Christ, I wouldn't trade my Mortimer for his Percival, the poor son of a bitch. The things parents do to their offspring. No wonder Yolanda was on the move.

I got an angle on the garage and parked across the street, put a camera with a 350 mm lens on the dash aimed at the garage, then settled in to see what would happen. I didn't think Billy would leave the bank for long, so this ought to be a quickie.

Which, best guess, it was.

When the garage door started back up, I sank down further and watched the action on the screen of the digital camera, got thirteen shots off as Billy got a good-bye kiss in the garage and climbed into the Caddy, backed out, Percival's wife giving him a wave as he drove off, and I got a good shot of that, too.

Which probably meant this job was over, and it was a stinky damn job. Not like the IRS, but it smelled all the same. It just didn't have the patina of criminal activity that taints the IRS.

So I went home and took a long hot shower.

* * *

I was back in the Green Room at the Golden Goose watching a Padres game when the hooker, Holiday Breeze, strolled in and looked around. It was seven forty-five p.m., early for her, but she was perky and fresh, light blond hair in a casually tousled style, blue eyes clear and bright, looking good. As usual, the place was almost empty, and, as usual, she took a barstool next to mine. This of course was a cosmic, preordained thing linked in some mysterious way to me being a gumshoe and her being gorgeous. I hadn't seen her in a month and a half. Since then, I'd gotten a concussion and that sword run through my chest, neither of which was her fault so I wasn't unhappy to see her.

According to her, her name really was Holiday Breeze. But like lawyers and politicians, hookers lie for professional reasons, so I wasn't buying it. I took a hit of Pete's Wicked Ale and waited for her opening gambit, wondering if she'd upgraded her spiel from the last time I'd heard it.

She was still aerobicized and curvy, evidently trying out a new look: three-inch heels, tight black jeans, an emerald silk top with a deep plunge that revealed an expensive artificial tan the color of honey. Her shoulders were bare. Two inches of tight tummy and a very nice navel were exposed. Only two buttons held her top closed, which looked risky. A narrow band of material around her neck held the top up. A brisk wind might have gotten her arrested.

I figured her for twenty-one, no more than twenty-two, so I had twenty years on her. Which didn't matter, at least not to me. She was an adult. Very.

About that time, however, I was starting to wonder if the girl had a brain. Last time we met, right here, same barstools, Holiday had stormed out in a major-league huff. I didn't know how she could have forgotten that treasured moment. Time to remind her.

I turned toward her. "About that mirror on my car—"

"Stuff your mirror, Mortimer."

Okay, that set me back. Mortimer? But, as one of the premier gumshoes in the Western Hemisphere—though I tend to specialize in missing persons—I gave her comment a few seconds' thought.

Finally, I said, "You have cable."

"Huh?"

"Television. You keep up with the news."

She smiled, sort of. "You're good, Mortimer." Then, showing off, she added, "Angel."

I grimaced. "Mort."

"If you like. And I'm—"

"Holiday. Which one, by the way?"

"Huh?"

"Doc, or Fourth of July?"

"Okay, could we talk like normal people here?"

Not my specialty, and not with a hooker, but I was willing to give it a try, so I said, "Let's go back to that 'stuff your mirror' comment."

Late July she'd told me to glue a rat to the sonofabitch, which might require some explanation. The side mirror of my Toyota, vintage 1994 and the color of a urine specimen, yodels, up around sixty miles an hour. This is one of the finest imaginable conversation pieces if you want to drink alone, as I found out with Holiday a week or so before my stay in the hospital with its drips, catheters, and burly nurses who really hate the IRS.

The mirror, designed by Toyota's acoustic engineers, whistles—rather atonally—so how good those engineers are is open to question. During our second encounter, and before she stalked out in the second of two huffs, Holiday suggested that I glue a rat to the mirror. No explanation, of course, but the bartender—O'Rourke—and I eventually concluded that her suggestion was based on the sort of applied physics one doesn't normally expect of a high-end call girl. Gluing a rat to the mirror would alter the air flow, thereby defeating one of Toyota's finest engineering achievements.

"I'm not here to talk about your mirror," she said. I thought I heard that huff working its way to the surface again.

"Yeah? What *are* you here for?"

"You . . . you're a private detective, right?"

"One of North America's finest." It never hurts to advertise.

She gave me the look I often get from Jeri as well as Dallas, my ex—one of pity mixed with a dash of incredulity and a pinch of weariness.

Then she sighed. Her shoulders sagged.

"Buy you a drink?" I said.

"Sure. Why not? What the hell."

Don't get too excited, I thought. "Tequila Sunrise?"

She smiled. "Hey, you remembered." Just then her cell phone rang.

Her smile gave me a tingle that went all the way to my toes. Did I mention that I'm a pig? Man, she was a good-lookin' kid. She let the call go to voice mail. Probably a hooker thing, when they're with a prospective client. Hard to believe she was still working on me, though, after what we'd been through last month.

"When I was an agent with the IRS," I said, "I remembered all kinds of minutiae, which made me both invaluable and feared."

A frown replaced her smile. "The IRS?"

I thought that might get her attention. Most people lose their tan the moment they realize they're in the presence of our nation's Gestapo. But that didn't happen. She was a nice light brown, what I could see of her, which was a lot. Maybe spray-on tans weren't susceptible.

I nodded, then added, "Internal Revenue," in case the acronym hadn't struck home with enough force.

She gave me a squint. "But you're not still . . . ?"

"Nope."

"How long ago'd you quit, or whatever?"

"Three months, give or take. But I had to give it up. Turns out I discovered I had a soul."

"Do you still have friends in the . . . the business?"

"The racket, you mean? IRS agents don't have friends. They even hate and fear each other."

Her smile returned. "Well, that's a relief."

"Ain't it, though? You should've seen our Christmas parties. Punch was spiked with antifreeze."

O'Roarke arrived with her drink. I paid for it with a free-drink coupon. He's a lean whip of a guy, slightly stooped, balding, with a red Yosemite Sam moustache. Best bartender ever. Even better after I gave him that hundred bucks the other night.

Holiday turned toward me and rewound our conversation of a minute or two ago. "You're a detective."

"Yes I am." I don't mention that I'm in training since it plays hell with my gravitas.

"You found Mayor Sjorgen."

"Yes I did." Just his head, but it was in the trunk of my ex-wife's Mercedes, which made it fun.

"And the DA."

"Guilty as charged, ma'am."

She put a hand on my arm. I think it might have sizzled. Man, she was beautiful, even if she was a hooker.

"So you're pretty good," she said. She picked up her cell phone and swiped the screen—multitasking efficiently, which caused me to up the estimate of her income by forty thousand a year.

"You have *no* idea, kiddo."

A slow smile. "Kiddo," she said. "I like that." She would, of course. Hookers like everything. Tell them you like sugar in your gas tank, and they'll tell you they like it too. She put the phone to her ear and listened. Five seconds later I had my answer to that "tan" question—spray-on *can* lighten significantly if the underlying skin tone goes pasty white.

"Allie," she said into the phone, eyes wild. "*Allie!*" She stared at the glowing screen. "Omigod. Omigod."

One "Omigod" was someone telling her she'd left her front door wide open when she left home. Two "Omigods" was trouble of an entirely different stripe.

She hit call back and listened, got no answer.

She grabbed my arm and almost pulled me off the barstool. "Oh, jeez, c'mon."

"What's up?" I asked, bracing myself.

"I . . . I need . . . I want you to . . . please. C'mon."

Well, yeah. A hooker wanting to hire me. Beautiful one, too. And desperate. I figured something like this was only a matter of time. If he weren't fictional and therefore technically impotent, Sam Spade would be eating his heart out.

"Hire me?"

"Yeah, I . . . I guess so. Right *now.*" She tugged harder.

"Well, sure," I said. "Why not?"

This was great, just great. I couldn't wait to tell Jeri. A hooker offering *me* money? Maybe I was already an urban legend. I said as much to Holiday.

She turned loose of my arm, backed off an inch, and gave me The Look. "Jesus, Mort."

"What?"

"Talking with you is like . . . I don't know."

"Fun? Interesting? Educational?"

"None of those."

"Well then, drink up. Booze produces adjectives."

She pushed her Tequila Sunrise away. "No time. Let's go."

Huh? We? She was *serious* about hiring me? "Where to?" I gave the television a nod. "Game isn't over yet. Padres are up by two, and I've got twenty bucks on the other guys."

"I . . . I really need your help. Right *now.*"

"Slow down, hon. I haven't seen any money yet."

"We'll work it out. C'mon." She grabbed my arm again and finally succeeded in dislodging me from the stool.

I looked back at O'Roarke. "Remember this moment."

He lifted an eyebrow at me. Holiday hadn't touched her drink and here we were, headed for the door.

Outside, the sun was behind the Sierras, clouds lit up in red and gold, starting to lose color. The temperature was into the seventies, down from a high of eighty-four.

I yanked her to a halt on the sidewalk. "What's this all about? Who was that on the phone?"

"You find missing persons. I mean, you're good at it?"

"I am, yes." Although luck had played a part, and every one of those people had ended up dead, so there was that.

"And detectives are, well, tough."

Jeri was. I wasn't. "Some of 'em, yeah," I said, not particularly liking the direction the conversation was headed.

"Okay, then. C'mon." She tucked my arm against her waist and led me to a nearby parking garage at a trot that made conversation difficult. I went, of course, since my arm felt cold and the warmth and the feel of her waist were making it happy.

In the garage she hit a remote and a new Audi A3 Prestige convertible answered with a chirp and flashing lights, putting my Toyota to shame. The car was fire-engine red and sleek, not top-of-the-line, but damn nice, and I guessed its mirror didn't howl. We got in. "Nice heap," I said before she fired up the engine.

She stared at me. "Please tell me you didn't say that."

"I didn't say that."

"You—you're *still* impossible to talk to. Heap? You called my great little car a heap?"

"For you, I'll up it to jalopy."

"Unbelievable." She started the engine and backed out.

It didn't howl, at least not at forty miles an hour, which is what we did up Virginia Street to University Terrace, then over to Ralston Street where I live, tires complaining at the corners.

She slowed near my house while I was still chewing on that "detectives are tough" comment that implied I might have to be tough sometime soon. I stared at her. "How do you know where I live?"

She shrugged. "Research?"

Which didn't answer the question, but she had me worried. The only thing in my house a hooker might use that required me to be tough was my bed, and that wasn't going to happen. She turned into my driveway, stopped two feet from my Toyota's rear bumper, and said, "Go get your gun."

I felt my eyes bug out. "My gun?"

"I'm sorry, I didn't mean to slur my words like that."

"How the *hell* do you know I've got a gun?"

"Seriously? You're a private eye and you've got testosterone oozing out of your pores. No way you don't have a gun."

Okay, she was holding her own. She was a hooker with a brain. I mentally bumped her IQ up another ten points. "So I've got a gun. Why am I going to need it?"

"Well, I hope you *won't*, but the point is you never know, so go get it, okay?"

Which was actually a good answer, given that I didn't have the slightest idea what was going on. When in doubt, go armed. You don't have to fire a gun just because you've got one.

"Okay, slow down," I said. "I'm not gonna get a gun unless you tell me what the fuck is going on."

I guess the intensifier didn't take because she leaned across me, unlocked my door, and shoved it open.

"Go," she said. "I'll explain later, I promise."

"I get fifty bucks an hour." But as my boss, Jeri gets thirty-five and I get fifteen. That's the deal. I was going to renegotiate after we were married and I had more clout. I'm worth sixteen an hour, easy. Of course, she has overhead—home office, phone, Xerox, wear and tear on the Porsche, contributions to my 401(k).

"Fine. Go."

So I went. In the house I got a .357 Magnum off a shelf in my bedroom closet, not the flyweight S&W Magnum I'd had earlier that year. I grabbed the Ruger since it has more heft. At the firing range a week ago that damn flyweight kicked more than I'd remembered. I wanted something I could fire more than once without having to haul it back down between shots. You never know when you'll need more than one hunk of flying lead to get the job done.

For a moment I stood there, gun in hand, testosterone oozing out of my pores, wondering what I was getting into, then I put on a shoulder holster, snugged the gun in place, donned a windbreaker to hide it, and left.

Coming out the front door, I noticed a package off to one side. FedEx. That would be another book from my mom. She often sends me books with anti-IRS themes. The first was *Let Us Prey* by Bill Branon, then it was *IRS Whistleblower* by Richard Schickel. Others followed. Mom took great delight in denigrating my former career, and she has a sense of humor like a steam shovel. I grabbed the package and went back to Holiday's Audi, tossed the package in back, got settled in the passenger seat, and patted the Ruger in its shoulder holster. "You should know I'm not gonna fire this thing at just anyone. What the hell's going on?"

"It's my sister." Holiday chirped the tires backing out, which jerked my head forward.

"That call you got. That was your sister?" said Mr. Swifty.

"Uh-huh. Allie." The tires squealed again as she headed south, toward I-80. Nice. Wish my Toyota could do that.

"This's a pretty powerful gun. What'd she do to you when you were growing up?"

I guess that didn't warrant a response because Holiday glanced at me, then back at the road. "What's in the package?"

"Who knows? My mom has a lethal sense of humor."

Which earned me a faint smile but no comment.

"So, where to?" I asked. I had visions of more hours spent in one of RPD's interrogation rooms, once again explaining things to my favorite detective, Russell Fairchild. Last time I'd seen him he'd given me the finger in the hospital, a few days after I'd solved Reno's biggest case for him, biggest pile of related felonies the city had seen in a hundred years. Which was gratitude for you.

Holiday took more corners too fast, and for a moment I slowed things down by considering what had happened in the past twenty minutes. In effect, I'd been hijacked by one of Reno's most beautiful girls, even if she was a roundheel. My being an impressionable pig gave her an almost insurmountable advantage, but Jeri probably wouldn't accept that as an excuse. I looked at her as she took us down a ramp and onto Interstate 80, headed east. The top of the convertible was down. Wind whipped at Holiday's silk blouse as she took the car up to seventy miles an hour. Her hair whipped around, too, its frizzy style getting more frizzed than usual. I could think of worse things than being hauled out of a bar by a girl this great-looking, but when we passed the last exit in Sparks and headed into the empty desert east of Reno, I decided I'd had enough. Another minute and I was going to pull my gun and get a few answers.

"Okay," I said. "This's fun, but where are we goin'?"

She dug the cell phone out of her purse, hit the screen a few times at eighty miles an hour, and handed it to me. "Listen."

I listened. A girl's voice said, "Sarah, it's me. I'm in Gerlach. I got some money, a *lot*, so maybe I can—" *squawk*. "Hey, what—?" then the call ended.

I listened to it two more times, then handed the phone back to her. "Who's Sarah?"

"Me."

"Uh-huh. What about Holiday?"

"Just a name I was using."

"Right. I should've known."

I waited for more. Venus was becoming visible in a sky going dark as we passed through a cut in the surrounding hills. Holiday-Sarah remained silent, concentrating on the highway, so I pulled my gun, aimed the muzzle at the sky.

"Hey!" she yelped.

"Hey yourself."

"Jesus. What're you doin'?"

"Getting answers. Slow it down to seventy and start talking or let me out. And you owe me twenty-five bucks for the past half hour."

She didn't say anything for several seconds, then she let up on the gas. "My name is Sarah Dellario and I'm not a hooker."

Dellario. Figuring I wouldn't have to shoot her right away, I holstered the gun. "Yeah? So what are you?"

"A student. Civil engineering at UNR. I'll graduate next year if I can keep it together in all of this."

Aw, shit. *Engineering* of all things. Right then I knew I was going to have to glue a rat to that mirror on my Toyota. If I didn't, Holiday was going to make my life a living hell.

Not *Holiday*, Great Gumshoe.

Sarah.

Dellario.

CHAPTER THREE

GOOD NEWS, BAD news. Good, she wasn't a hooker—bad, she probably knew more math than I did. But she was dressed in full hooker garb—meaning half-dressed, ready for action—and I was in her car, headed out of Reno into darkness and the unknown. No doubt Jeri would be thrilled.

"If you're not a hooker," I said, "what's with the outfit?"

She glanced down at herself, then at me. "Pretty great top, huh? Great as in awful."

"Depends on your point of view. I'm good."

She smiled, said, "Thanks," which was interesting. Headlights came toward us on the divided highway, interstate traffic headed west into the city. "I've got a few things like this. I bought some at Victoria's Secret, some on the Internet. I had to play the part."

"Of a hooker? Why?"

"I've been trying to find my sister."

"The voice on the phone."

"Uh-huh. Allie. Allison. She's been missing for two months. A little more, actually."

Ah-hah. "And I find missing persons."

Her eyes darted toward me, then she looked back at the road. "Early July, I hadn't seen her in a week and her car was still at her apartment. I have a key to her place. She wasn't feeding her goldfish. So I filed a missing person report with the police, but they checked out her apartment then pretty much blew it off. A week later I hired a private detective. Fifteen hundred dollars later he hadn't found anything, so I had to pull the plug on that. Then I didn't know what to do, so I did my own thing, making the rounds of casino bars pretending to be a hooker, see if I could get any hint of her or what might have happened to her. The police wouldn't do that, or that investigator guy."

Or me, I didn't tell her. I look dreadful in a dress.

"I started hitting the bars around the middle of July. School was out, which made it easy. Now I'm juggling school and bars, which isn't. It was creepy at first, trying to act like a hooker. I didn't know what I was doing. After a while, though, it got to be . . . well, interesting. Fun, actually. I remember you, that time you told me you knew a Mexican girl in Tijuana—"

"El Paso."

"Right, El Paso. A girl who could blow square smoke rings— which, by the way, is impossible—and then that idiotic story about the mirror howling on your car."

"*Idiotic?* At sixty, that mirror sounds like Madonna."

"I'll have to hear it sometime. Anyway, the mayor and district attorney were missing for over a week and the police weren't getting anywhere—like with Allie. Then you found them. You were all over television. Then, half an hour ago, Allie phoned. It was like, I don't know, some sort of weird serendipity, you being there right when she called. So I thought it must mean something, that this was the best chance I would ever get, if you would help."

"Not that I was given a chance to say no."

She looked at me. "You can still say no. If you want. I hope you don't, though."

"I'll keep it in mind. But none of that answers the big question—which is *why* you were posing as a hooker, of all things."

"Oh, sorry. That's what Allie was doing." Her voice took on a sad note. "Hooking, except she was doing it for real." She was silent for a while, then, "Allie was always the dark sheep of the family. I tried to talk her out of it, but she said she was making way too much money, that she'd quit in like a year or two. That's the kind of thing that happens in other families, not mine. I thought it was crazy. Allie *couldn't* be doing that, but she was. Anyway, I knew it was a long shot, me going out like that, sort of following in her footsteps to see if I could find out anything, but I had to try."

"More than a long shot. It was dangerous and had zero chance of success," said Mother Mort.

"Hopeless, maybe, but not all that dangerous. All I did was talk to guys, try to steer the conversation in a direction that might point toward Allie. I never left the bars, the casinos, with any of them, ever. The federal government doesn't have that much money."

Probably a subtle dig at my failed IRS career. Sonofabitch.

We passed the power station at Tracy, fifteen miles east of Sparks, cooling towers laying down a skein of fog between the hills. The lights of the station were bright spots in the growing darkness.

"And . . ." Sarah said quietly, then looked out her side window, away from me.

"And?"

Her fingers flexed on the steering wheel. "I have a three point eight five grade point average. I even took extra classes in calculus and diffy-q— that's differential equations—that weren't required by my major."

"Meaning—you're a serious student."

"Yes. I am."

"And something of a nerd?"

She looked at me, then back at the road. "It's a time-honored engineering curse. Pretty much true, though. You should see some of the guys in my classes, how they dress and how they talk—then they wonder why they can't find girlfriends."

Great, just like IRS agents.

"You said it got to be interesting—pretending to be a hooker. How's that work? Cut you loose from all that serious study, set you free for a while?"

"I guess. At first it was scary. I didn't know what I was doing. After a while, though, yeah, it was fun, going out in clothes like this, having guys look at me. For a few hours I was someone else. But I still really want to find my sister."

"Which is why we're headed to Gerlach."

She glanced at me. "Wow, you're really good at this."

"You have no idea."

She laughed quietly. "You're funny. And . . . well, nice."

"And engaged."

She shook her head. "Don't worry. I'm not . . . you know. After anything like that."

"Uh-huh. Just trying to find your sister."

"That's all, yes."

"Mind if I point out that the top is down on this car and it's getting kinda chilly? Dressed like that, I don't know how you're not freezing."

"I run pretty hot."

I smiled. I would've cracked my knuckles in a gesture of placid indifference, if I'd known how.

She gave me a look. "Oh, uh, I didn't mean that . . . not the way it sounded."

"I forgive you. You're an engineering student."

She grimaced. "Socially inept. A dork."

"I didn't say that."

"Well, I guess it's pretty much true. Was, anyway. It still is when I've got a textbook open. I can concentrate for hours. It's been harder this semester, but I go out and do the bars when I have a little free time. I still can't believe I was with you when Allie called."

"Yep. Lucky us. Actually it's a cosmic thing—maybe I'll explain later. So how about we put the top up on this thing? My sword wound's starting to ache."

"Sword wound?"

"You didn't hear about that?"

"Guess not. Whatever a sword wound is."

"It's when a sword—foil, actually—is run through your chest. Tell you about that later, too. There's a place up ahead you can stop."

A minute later she pulled into a scenic view turnoff, not much to see at night. She punched a button and the top snugged down.

"I don't suppose you've got anything else to put on?" I said as she pulled back onto the interstate. She wouldn't, of course. It was that Spade-Hammer thing, operating in high gear.

She looked down at herself. "No. Sorry. I wasn't thinking the evening would turn out this way. I hope this doesn't bother you."

"The second it does, I'll let you know."

Her lips lifted in a faint smile. "It's been so weird, dressing like this, pretending to be something I'm not, being stared at. At first, anyway. It took a while to wear off, the strangeness I mean."

I didn't know what to say to that, so I let her talk.

"The first time, it was like an out-of-body experience, like it wasn't real, like I was in a dream. I would look in a mirror and see someone else. But then . . ."

I waited her out.

"Then," she went on, "after a while, it started to feel good."

"Good, huh?"

She kept her eyes on the road. "Being looked at. Noticed."

This was the kind of girl who would be noticed everywhere she went. I told her that.

"Not like in the bars," she said. "Not in clothes like this. No one wears anything like this around campus. But really, I'm a very serious student. I get A's in engineering classes. It's the English and sociology and stuff like that where I sometimes get B's. So getting out like this was . . . well, like stepping outside of myself, out of a shell. In sexy clothes I was someone else, someone fun. As Holiday, guys would look at me and, well . . . it just felt good."

"Little hint of exhibitionism there?"

Her mouth turned down. "That's a word I really dislike. It has such a negative connotation." She glanced at me. "Do you think it's wrong, me wearing things like this?"

"Nope. Don't see it as a problem, kiddo. Fifty million women in the country would hate and envy you. Millions would do what you're doing if they could. A lot of women do. That's how Victoria's Secret stays in business."

"Not sure what to say to that, except thanks." She turned the heater up a notch.

"*De nada.*"

We went a few miles in silence, then I asked, "How old are you, Sarah?"

She gave me a look. "Old enough."

"Humor me."

She sighed softly. "I'll be twenty-five in a few months. First week in December."

Jesus, I was lousy with ages.

"How old is Allie?"

"She'll be twenty-one in May."

"Not yet twenty-one, and she's been hooking in casino bars?"

"She had a fake ID. And she's pretty and has a great figure. She told me she was making something like twelve thousand dollars a month. Trying to talk her out of that was like talking to a wall. She got mostly D's in high school, barely got her diploma."

Trying to keep up with her hyper-studious, white-sheep perfect sister, she'd fallen flat on her face. But she was beautiful, too, like Sarah, and she'd ended up making more than a civil engineer with ten years' experience. Probably rubbed Sarah's nose in it, too. I could've been wrong about that, I usually am, but I wouldn't have wanted to walk in Sarah's footsteps either. In college I barely eked out a C in business calculus, which is like real calculus on training wheels.

"I've probably talked to two hundred guys since I started looking for her," Sarah said. "All ages, all types. I didn't know what I was looking for."

"Didn't catch a whiff of Allie in all that time?"

"No."

"And you didn't go out with any of the men?"

She gave me a sharp look. "*No,* I didn't. That's not me. I mean, I guess I looked the part, even acted it, sort of—at least I think so, after I got the hang of it, but that's as far as it went, ever. I wasn't there for that."

"All I'm doing is gathering information. I do this every time I get shanghaied."

"Well, I thought I'd made it perfectly clear already."

We reached the turnoff to Gerlach a few miles before Fernley. Sarah gave me her phone as she swung the Audi onto Highway 447 and headed north on a midnight-black, two-lane road beneath a sky studded with stars. "Hit call back," she said. "See if you can reach that phone she called from."

Ah, a challenge to my technical prowess. Just what I needed. Great Gumshoe fumbled with the damn thing for a few minutes, then said, "I'll steer. You work the phone."

She grabbed the phone, I grabbed the wheel. Good thing the road was a straight shot, empty, aimed right at Polaris.

A minute later Sarah put the phone down and took control of the wheel again. "Same thing," she said. "It didn't even go to voice mail, which is strange." Her voice was tight.

I looked over at her again.

Stunningly beautiful. Curvy as hell. Not a hooker. Studious and repressed, then she'd stumbled on a way to cut loose . . . sort of.

And here I was, headed north in her car. That old PI magic was still in overdrive, big-time. Man, I wished I knew how to crack my knuckles.

We traveled in silence for ten miles. Finally, I said, "So what's the plan here?"

"I don't have one. You're the PI."

Great. Now was not the time to tell her I was in training, still working on my first thousand hours. There never seems to be a good time to bring that up.

"Gerlach's a little place," I offered.

"Uh-huh. I've been through it a couple of times."

"Why would she phone from there? You know anyone up that way? Friends, family?"

"No. No one. She might know someone, though. It's not like we've been super close lately."

I shrugged. "So we'll go up and look around, see if there's any sign of her." Hell of a plan.

Sarah didn't say anything.

I said, "She indicated she has money. A lot of it."

"She's been hooking for nearly a year. She might have a hundred thousand dollars saved up."

"I got a different impression. She was cut off. She was about to say more, then it's like someone took the phone away. Which pretty much means she's with someone. Someone who didn't want her talking to you, or maybe to anyone."

"I know. That has me worried more than anything."

"Any idea who she might be with?"

"She's been gone a long time. Two months. I haven't heard a word from her in all that time. And given what she was doing . . . I really wouldn't have a clue."

I did, sort of. Girl tries to phone her sister, gets cut off. That was a clue. Not a happy one, either.

So here we were, headed for Gerlach, a town with a population of maybe two hundred. The place was littered with hot springs, some of which were lethal. In the past, people had died jumping into hundred-eighty-degree water, which gave me the willies. It was also the only town in the region, about as isolated as any place in Nevada. Hunters would stay at Corti's Motel, eat at the restaurant in Corti's Casino. I'd been through the town a few times on IRS field audits. It wasn't the kind of place you hankered to go to unless you wanted to get away from it all and vegetate for a while, maybe regroup. During the Burning Man Festival, however, the population nearby in the desert would run into the tens of thousands. Then it was a place to avoid, although it did have unclothed girls running hot and cold the entire week. Lots of nudity going on in or around those hot springs about then.

We passed through the town of Nixon on the Paiute Indian Reservation, last sign of civilization that we would see for the next sixty miles, then on into some of the emptiest desert in the state.

Sarah was quiet, alone with her thoughts. I didn't interrupt. I was still trying to catch up with all of this. I gave her attire a glance or two in the glow of the dash lights to stay awake. Worked, too.

Finally, I said, "Is Dellario your real name?"

"Why? Doesn't it sound real?"

That wasn't an answer. "I don't know how your 'real' name would sound. How'd you come up with Holiday Breeze?"

She laughed softly. "I don't know. I started out using the name Susan Smith, but that sounded boring. So ordinary it could hardly be real. Then I was Ginger, no last name. That lasted a week. But I never felt like a Ginger, so then one day I just thought 'Holiday,' and for some reason it felt right."

"What about Breeze?"

"I don't know where that came from. It's like it fell out of the sky and landed on me."

"And 'Holiday Breeze' sounded real?"

She laughed again. "No. But I liked it. It fit what I was doing, the way I felt when I dressed up and went out."

"Free."

"Uh-huh. And a little bit sexy."

"Ever been married?"

She wrinkled her nose. "No."

She stared at the headlights boring a tunnel through the night. The hills were black against black sky. She held the Audi at seventy, which would put us in Gerlach in a little under an hour. With Nixon behind us, civilization was a gazillion miles away and receding rapidly.

"I had a boyfriend once," she said. "In my sophomore year. It lasted about two weeks."

"Two whole weeks? And one whole boyfriend?"

"How many should I have had?"

"I don't know. I have this image of a line going twice around the block."

We drove without speaking for five minutes. She was more complex than I'd thought. Maybe during these pauses she was doing calculus problems in her head. Finally she said, "So what do you do in that bar all the time? You don't look like a big drinker. I mean, you don't act like it, and I've been around a ton of 'em lately."

"I'll have a few beers. Sometimes more, sometimes less. And lately I've acquired a taste for sarsaparilla. And the bartender gives me the remote for the television, the beer nuts are free, and the place is a ten-minute walk from home so there's no chance of a DUI."

"So, what? Going there is mostly a social thing?"

"Where else can I strike up conversations with hookers? Who, by the way, are fun if you don't take them too seriously."

She laughed. "All right. Touché."

Another ten minutes of not-uncomfortable silence went by, then I said, "When we get there, you probably oughta stay in the car, let me go scout around."

"Yeah? Why's that?"

"That top you've got on. They probably haven't seen anything like that in Gerlach in years."

"Actually, when we get there, I better find us a gas station."

I leaned over. The needle was hovering a sixteenth of an inch above empty.

"This thing gonna make it another forty miles?" I asked.

"Hope so. I should've filled up before we left. Guess I was in too big a hurry after Allie phoned."

"Uh-huh. If we run out, I'll steer, you push."

"Seriously? I had it figured the other way. You'd generate more horsepower."

"Fuckin' engineer."

If the convertible top had been down, her laugh would have carried half a mile into the desert.

* * *

More silence. I had my thoughts, she had hers. I was wondering what Jeri would think about all this and when I should tell her. I didn't want to distract her from the power-lifting competition, which wasn't a self-serving rationalization. I was going to tell her—might not bother with a detailed description of what Sarah was wearing and how much of her it didn't cover—but only when the time was right. Tomorrow in Atlantic City would be low key, elimination stuff, but knowing about Holiday-Sarah might throw Jeri off. It wouldn't take much. If she lost the competition by three lousy pounds she would probably—

"Can I tell you something?" Sarah said.

I swam back to the present. "That's what I'm here for."

She hesitated. "It might be . . . I don't know, sort of awful."

"Awful is my forté, kiddo. If I told you all the things I've done with the IRS, all the mayhem I've caused . . . "

"When we find Allie, or . . . or what's happening with her, I don't think I'll quit. At least not for a while."

"Quit what?"

"You know, going to bars. Doing what I was doing, *am* doing."

"Uh-huh," I said, offering up that deep insight.

"I mean—it's like I've got two lives now. I don't know if I want to give this one up, the fake hooker one. At least not right away. The attention is . . . well, addictive. I know it's a little out there, but I like not being me all the time, the Sarah me. I like dressing up and, you know, feeling sexy."

"Yeah, well, pardon the trailer-park observation, but I don't know how you wouldn't feel sexy twenty-four seven, all year long."

She made a face. "Calculating the moment of inertia of beams and their deflections under loads isn't the least bit erotic."

"Don't I know it. Every time I calculate stuff like that it feels like I'm under a cold shower."

She smiled. "Studying my ass off in a library is one thing, but when I go out and . . . and guys look at me like this, I get a shivery feeling."

"Shivery, huh? You don't get that with beam deflections?"

"Hardly. So here I am, trying to find my sister, but wearing things like this feels good anyway, like I'm in a play. For a while I get to be someone else, someone different."

A sudden thought occurred to me, the kind of epiphany that hits me every other decade. "You're shy."

She stared at me for a moment. "Yes." She looked back at the road, then back at me. "How . . . how . . . ?"

"Sarah is shy, Holiday isn't."

"Omigod, *yes*. You get it. I mean, you really get it."

"Yep. Except right now, I'm not sure who I'm talking to, Sarah or Holiday."

"Hey, I'm *both*. It's not like I'm *schizo* or anything."

"I didn't say you were. But we're talking engineering and hot outfits all in the same breath, so there's a lot of ambiguity floating around this car."

"Well, I'm . . . I'm . . . oh, Jesus. I'm Sarah, but I feel . . . right now with you . . . oh, hell. Never mind."

She went silent. The ride was like traveling inside a coal mine, except with stars. She ran it up to eighty for a while, black jagged mountains off to the right, temperature dropping outside, thrum of tires on asphalt, me unable to think of a single thing to say in this minefield of conversation. Twenty minutes later we passed a small convenience store at a place called Empire. A minute after that we topped a rise, and Gerlach's lights were visible four or five miles away, a little sprawl of lights beneath the dark bulk of Granite Mountain.

CHAPTER FOUR

WE PULLED INTO a Texaco station at the east end of town. Its lights were off, but the sign was illuminated. Sarah stopped beside a row of pumps. No one came out. I got out and checked the pumps. No credit card readers. They looked forty years old and their nozzles were padlocked in place. A sign on the door said the station would open at six a.m.

"That's it for gas in this burg," I told her, getting back in.

"Great."

My sentiments exactly. Maybe I could find someone to open the place up. If not, we were stuck here for the night. I heard Spade or Magnum chuckling in the dark, one of those guys. When it came to women, they were a riot.

Corti's Motel was a hundred yards west of the Texaco station. Beyond that, Corti's Casino was a low cinder block structure next door, lit up in neon. A market up the street was another little neon spark, closed for the night, but the rest of the town was dark except for two or three streetlights. The sidewalks, patches of hardscrabble dirt, had been rolled up and put away till morning.

Pickups and several utility trucks were nosed into slots in front of the motel—a well digger, plumber, Department of Transportation, a power company rig with a bucket lift.

Sarah pulled up in front of the casino and cut the engine. The time was 9:50, Wednesday evening.

"Now what?" she asked.

"Got a picture of your sister?"

She dug a photo out of her purse. It looked like a high school yearbook picture—pretty girl with blond hair, big eyes, pouty lips, generic abstract background of swirly colors. She looked a lot like her sister, almost as beautiful but not quite. Even so, she would turn heads. People would remember her.

"Stay put," I said. I unhitched my shoulder holster, shoved it and the gun under the seat, then got out. Sarah got out on the other side. I stared at her. "What part of 'stay put' wasn't clear?"

"Just stretching my back," she said, stretching her back. Which did amazing things to that filmy top of hers and put the problem of feminine attire in a small town at night in sharp relief.

Jesus.

"Stay put." I went into the casino and waited by the door. When she came in, I took her by the arm and escorted her back to the car. "Stay put must mean something different where you come from."

She gave me an accusing look. "You waited for me in there."

"I get these premonitions."

"Maybe we could look around separately. No one has to know we're together."

"'Stay put' has a pretty much standard colloquial meaning in the United States. It means, stay the hell out of the casino, sugar, and let the PI do what you hired him to do."

"Really? 'Stay the hell out of' and '*sugar*'? 'Stay put' implies all that?"

"You come bouncing in in that top and no one would hear a word I had to say."

"Bouncing?"

"Don't know how else to describe it."

She gave me a sultry look. "Gosh, thanks."

Jesus. She'd metamorphosed into Holiday the minute we hit town. "How about you sit in the car and wait?"

"I could scout around out here, look the place over."

"How about you sit in the car and wait?"

"This place has a terrible echo."

"In the car." I opened the driver's-side door.

She made a face. "You sound like you mean it. The thing is, I might see something useful. I mean, Allie was here, right? At least that's what she said."

"Okay, kiddo, you asked for it. Now I've gotta tell it like it is. Your tits are magnificent and that top isn't covering half of what tops generally cover. It's hunting season so this can be a rough little place, and I don't see how any of that's gonna help us track down your sister right now."

She looked down at herself. "Magnificent? You think so?"

Sonofabitch. "Now isn't the time to get all shivery, *Holiday*."

She wrinkled her nose at me, then shrugged. "Okay. Don't get bent out of shape. Just don't be too long in there, all right?"

"I'll be as long as I need to. Now stay put."

I went back inside and waited by the door for a full minute. The Holiday half of Holiday-Sarah didn't come in, so I finally got to look around. Bar along the back wall, tables and chairs closer to the door, menus stuffed in metal racks on the dining tables, small casino set apart from the bar and restaurant—thirty slot machines, a single blackjack table. Twenty people were inside the building, nineteen of them male, which meant Holiday had better stay the hell outside like I'd told her.

I sat at the bar, put a ten-spot and Allie's picture in front of me, said, "Draft, dark," when the bartender drifted over. Bald guy about my age with a one-inch beard, earrings, tattoos, a scar on his cheek. My scars were better, more recent. It would be a freezing-ass day in hell before I'd wear an earring, pierced or otherwise.

I got the beer—Samuel Adams—he took the ten, set seven back on the bar, shoved the picture back at me with a finger, and said, "Haven't seen her, man." Then, "Holy Christ, that's one hot babe."

Huh? A high school kid and this guy thinks she's *hot*?

Then I saw where he was looking. I turned on the stool in time to see Holiday arrive at the pool table, blond hair still windblown. She picked up a cue stick, two guys ogling her as if they hadn't seen a woman in twenty years.

Not like Holiday, they hadn't.

Aw, shit.

I wandered over and said, "You about ready to head out, sugar plum?"

"I'm a little dry after that drive. I could maybe use a drink."

"Well then, how 'bout we mosey on over to the bar and get you one, then mosey on out of here?"

"Sounds like a plan." She held up a picture of her sister to the two guys, a rough-looking pair in T-shirts, three-day beards, and long hair. After they'd dragged their eyes away from Holiday's chest, they slowly shook their heads as if drugged.

I pulled Holiday away. Forget Sarah. Sarah was gone. In that outfit, she was 99 percent Holiday Breeze even if there was a certain applicable word she didn't like.

"Sonofabitch," I said, once we were outside and the pool guys hadn't come running out to kick my ass and haul the maiden off to a cave in the hills. "Know what we learned in there?"

"What?"

"Nothing. Not a damn thing."

"Those two guys haven't seen Allie. I learned *that*."

"With you dressed like that, they wouldn't have recognized her if they'd spent all last month with her on a beach in Acapulco."

She bit her lower lip and looked away. "Sorry."

"Well, shit." I stared at the empty desert to the south. With no moon it was dead dark, a dry, infinite wasteland. We hadn't gotten anywhere. And we didn't have enough gas to get out of town, which pretty much put the next big problem front and center.

Holiday-Sarah looked down at her feet, then said, hitting the nail on the head, "Looks like we better get a room, huh?"

"*Two* rooms."

"Well, yeah, of course, that's what I meant."

We walked over to the motel, found a wooden sign on a post, lit by a baby flood: FOR ROOMS, INQUIRE IN THE CASINO.

"Stay put," I told her.

"Right."

"I mean it."

"Yeah. I got it, Mort."

"Sonofabitch," I said. "Okay, c'mon. Just . . ."

"Just what?"

"I don't know. Cross your arms over your chest or something."

"What I think you mean—my arms don't really go *across*, they pretty much go under. Which"—she smiled—"sort of lifts."

Sonofabitch.

Back inside at the bar I held Holiday's arm and tucked her into my side, doing my best to hide her from the rest of the room.

The bartender came over, gave her a quick once-over.

"We need a couple of rooms," I said. "At the motel."

"No can do. We're full up."

"Full? You got nothing?"

"Not a thing, man. It's huntin' season."

Perfect. I looked around the room, then back at the guy. "What if I came up with an extra fifty bucks?"

"Don't see how that would put another room on the motel."

"How about a hundred?"

That slowed him down. He closed one eye and stared at the surface of the bar, doing some sort of intricate calculation. "I got a no-show on a reservation," he said at last. "Said they'd be in at nine and it's a little after ten now."

"Uh-huh."

"They could still show up, though. Probably will, too."

"Uh-huh."

"I got a motor home out back."

"Uh-huh." I figured I could keep this up as long as he could.

"So if they show, I could put 'em in that, charge 'em half price, maybe only a third. They'd probably go for that."

He was getting there. Hundred-dollar tax-free bribe made a guy smarter, more flexible. I could've told a relevant IRS joke right then, but decided to keep it to myself. In the punch line, the IRS guy ends up getting a promotion. Damn good joke, but the timing wasn't right.

He looked around the room, then at me, then at Holiday, then back at me, which was a surprise since I wasn't the main attraction. "That hundred. It'd have to be cash, man."

Of course.

I dug out my wallet and came up with sixty-eight dollars. "Got any money?" I asked Holiday.

"In my purse. I left it in the car."

"Go get it."

She went. The barkeep's eyes tracked her all the way to the door. When she went out, he shook himself like a dog. "Man, that there's one mind-blowing girl. If you don't mind my sayin.'"

"Nope."

"*Two* rooms?" He gave me a look. "You wanted *two* rooms? What the hell for?"

"She snores."

"Don't see that as an insurmountable problem, dude."

"Mouth open?"

"Still don't see it."

"And she leaves crumbs in bed."

He grinned. "Okay, yeah. Gotta draw the line somewhere." He held up a fist and we bumped knuckles—pigs of a feather. "Name's Dave," he said. "But if you ever get tired of that snoring—"

Holiday came back. She dug out two twenties and gave them to Dave. He pocketed five twenties then ran my credit card, sixty-two dollars for the room, handed Holiday the key. "Unit nineteen, next-to-last room at the far end."

I walked to the motel. Holiday drove the Audi over, parked in front of the room, got out, and opened the door to nineteen. I took a last look behind me, then followed her in.

Generic seventies room. Cheap print on a wall, peeling walnut veneer desk and chair combo, tiny alcove closet, door in back to the bathroom, small television hung on a wall, heavy drapes, threadbare carpet, forty-watt bulb in a ceiling fixture full of dead bugs.

And one bed, queen-size, with a sag in the middle.

Sonofabitch.

CHAPTER FIVE

She sat on the bed and bounced, all of her.

Wonderful.

I stuck my head in the bathroom, checked out the washbasin, toilet, shower, turned on a tap, got reasonably hot water in about ten seconds, then came back out.

Holiday had kicked off her heels and unbuttoned her top. It hung loose but still covered her, more or less. She pursed her lips at the look I was giving her. "What?"

"What do you think?"

"Hey, I haven't showered all day. This morning at school I took a fluid dynamics test and a structures test, then spent the afternoon looking up civil engineering case law crapola in the library."

"Fluid dynamics. And structures."

"Advanced trusses, if you want to know. So it's been a long day and I feel gritty. I'm going to take a shower, if that's all right with you."

"That's fine. Terrific, actually. But we've got some logistics to figure out here." I got the room key off the table, just in case.

"Yeah, like what?" She ran the zipper down on her jeans and started to work them over her hips. More skin started to show.

"We'll figure it out later." I opened the door and stepped out into the night.

* * *

I could explain all this to Jeri, no problem. She was an adult, a reasonable person, sophisticated. She would understand. No gas in town, we were lucky to get that one room, not my fault it had only one bed. Given all the facts, she wouldn't have a problem with any of this. None at all.

Then again, given the facts of the situation she might shove my head through the nearest available knothole and discuss this with me on the other side. We'd known each other for less than seven weeks, not a long time to end up engaged, not enough time to have learned all the little quirks and expectations of the other, especially a little quirk like Holiday.

I sat at the bar in the casino, trying not to imagine Holiday wet, scrubbing off the day's grit in the shower.

Dave strolled over. "Man, that was quick."

"You think? How 'bout another beer? Same thing."

He ran a tap and slid the glass in front of me. "On the house. First prize. You deserve it."

"You have no idea." I raised the glass to him, then drained half before setting it down.

A big guy in a flannel shirt, blue jeans, and boots came in, took a stool next to mine. About sixty, weathered, full head of gray hair, barrel chest. He had an automatic on his hip, looked like a 1911 .45—a serious gun. He tapped the bar with a finger, signaling for his usual. Dave poured him a whiskey, neat.

You've got to admire a guy who can hold his liquor and fire a weapon of that size. I thought about getting up and putting a dozen people between him and me.

"Oughta show the sheriff here that picture," Dave said.

The guy turned to me. "*Deputy* sheriff. County sheriff's down in Reno." He stuck out a big calloused hand. "Mike Roup, Deppity."

"Mort, PI."

We shook. His hand felt like old leather.

"Mort," he said, giving me a closer look. "Mortimer *Angel*. I'll be a son of a gun. You're the guy found those heads down in Reno a month or two ago."

"Guilty as charged." I like to say that, add a little uncertainty to the conversation.

He laughed, hit his drink, then glanced at Dave. "What picture?"

I showed him Allie's high school photo. He gave it a good long look, fifteen, twenty seconds, then he set it on the bar between us. "How old's the picture? What's her name?"

"Allie. Allison Dellario. Picture might be two years old. About that. You seen her around?"

"Maybe."

"Maybe?"

"Over at the Texaco this evening. Would've been about seven-thirty, maybe eight. Closer to eight, I'd say. Girl in a Mercedes SUV, passenger seat. Blond girl, anyway. Young like that. But it was getting on toward dark, and I was just passing by in the cruiser, comin' in from Empire. I got maybe a one-second look, if that, but it could've been her."

"She was in the passenger seat?"

"Uh-huh. Lady was outside, pumping gas. Older, looked to be in her mid to late thirties. Taller than average, seemed like. Slender. Shoulder-length dark hair. Dark pants, light-colored windbreaker."

"Pretty decent description."

"Don't see many hundred-thousand-dollar SUVs 'round here. It was this year's model, too. I pay attention, keep my eyes open. That's a lot of what I do around here."

"They still in town?"

"Nope. I'd know it if they were. Town here has about as many people as a crowded Burger King. Few more than that right now, though, with all the hunters."

"What color SUV?"

"Dark green. Real nice color. Forest-green but with a kind of metallic sheen to it. Thing was a G550. Big-ass engine. Probably couldn't catch it in my cruiser if we both went flat out. All I've got is two hundred sixty-five horsepower."

"Did you see which way they went when they left?"

"Nope. Hank might've."

"Hank?"

"Guy owns the Texaco. Hank Waldo."

"Speaking of which. I don't suppose there's any chance I could get some gas over there?"

"Tonight?" He laughed. "About now, Hank'll be passed out in his trailer, or gettin' that way. Be surprised if he can stand up."

"Figures. Evening's been like that."

Dave spoke up. "If you got yourself some gas and took off, my faith in humanity would drop to absolute fuckin' zero."

Mike Roup gave Dave a look. "Yeah? Why's that?"

"You oughta see what he's got over in nineteen. Which makes me wonder what the hell you're doing here," he said, staring at me like I was the world's dumbest shit.

"What if she's my sister?" I said.

"Oh, Christ, don't tell me that. Do *not* tell me that. I'd have to go out back and shoot myself."

Corti's was set up like a sports bar, restaurant, and casino, all in one. Four televisions were on, only one with sound. The one over the bar was silent, but I saw a clip of Senator Reinhart getting out of a limo on his way into his Las Vegas campaign headquarters. For a moment I thought he'd turned up, but then a talking head belonging to Rachel Valencia, Channel 4, mouthed words from a teleprompter while the words *STILL MISSING* flashed on a screen behind her. So a presidential candidate and the nation's one honest senator hadn't turned up yet, teeth blazing in a big Jimmy Carter smile. Good deal.

"If you gotta have gas, really *have* to," Deputy Roup said, "I got county gas over at the lockup I'm allowed to sell. It's damned expensive though. I gotta charge eight bucks a gallon."

"Do that and I'll never serve you again," Dave said to Roup.

"Why's that?"

"You still haven't seen what he's got over in nineteen."

"Well, okay, then," Roup said to me. "You're outta luck. I got no gas either."

So Holiday and I weren't stuck here. Fact is, we never were. I could have asked around, got a few guys to let me siphon a few gallons from their trucks for a little cash. We could've made it back to Fernley and stayed at a motel with more than one room. But that felt dumb. We'd made it to Gerlach; it seemed pointless to leave, drive eighty miles south then eighty miles back in the morning even if I had to bribe Dave with that hundred dollars. If we'd done that, I would've missed out on the opportunity to ask around about Allie this evening, which had—possibly—borne fruit. Allie might've been at the Texaco station in a dark green Mercedes SUV earlier this evening. That interrupted phone call hadn't ended in a cry for help or a shriek. It had ended abruptly, with a little chirp of surprise and, "Hey, what—?" as if the phone had been taken away from her, which could have been for any number of reasons. Allie might not be in trouble. But she might be. So here we were, Sarah—or Holiday—and I, in the last room in town. I was going to have to explain all this to Jeri, but I didn't see that as a problem—at least, not a *big* problem. It hadn't been my idea for Holiday-Sarah to pop out of her clothes the minute we got in the room. And I could keep that sort of thing under control. I already had a plan, good one, too. Anyway, leaving wasn't an option. Allie might still show up. If not, come morning I had to talk to Texaco Hank.

"Longer you're here and not in that room over there, stud, the more I'm thinkin' you're twelve ways a moron," Dave said to me, elbows on the bar. "No offense."

"None taken." I stood up. "Gotta go. She's liable to get dressed and come back over here."

"In that outfit she was wearing? Hold on there, pardner. Set a spell. Have another beer, on the house."

I went outside. Voices came through the night, then a woman's distant laugh. An eighteen-wheeler rolled by on the highway, headed north. A dark Mercedes SUV went by, headed south.

I stared at it.

A Mercedes SUV. It might've been dark green. Hard to tell in that light. No way to see how many people were inside.

What were the odds? Did it mean anything? If I chased it down, what then? Honk at it, try to get it to stop? And what would I chase it with? A car about out of gas?

I went back in the casino.

"Man, that was quick," Dave said, grinning. The jerk.

"A Mercedes SUV just went by," I said to Deputy Roup.

He half-turned on the stool and looked at me. "Uh-huh. They do that."

"Any chance you could chase it down?"

"Turns out, it's not illegal to drive through town here. Unless it was speeding or weaving or hit something. See anything like that?"

To lie or not to lie, that was the question. "No," I said.

"Well then." He faced the bar and picked up his drink.

I stared at him for a moment, then left.

* * *

Holiday was in bed when I walked in. She gave me a benign smile and said howdy. She'd settled down. The covers were pulled up high enough that I figured Sarah was back. If so, maybe I could grab a quick shower and scrub off the day.

"So," she said. "What was that about logistics?"

"Never mind. I've got it worked out."

"Really?"

"Yes, indeed."

"Great, tell me how."

She sat up and the covers tumbled down, so that was it for my shower. However, it simplified the logistics. I found a spare blanket on a shelf in the mini-closet, then went to the door. "Sleep tight," I said.

"Hey!"

Man, that girl was lightning on her feet. She had a hand on my wrist before I could get one foot out the door. No top, but at least she was wearing panties.

"What the hell are you doin'?" she said.

"Camping out." I unpeeled her grip and went out, got the door shut, and went to her car. I got in on the passenger side and reclined the seat, arranged the blanket over me, then waited for trouble.

Which took all of twenty-four seconds, then she was out in her panties and her hooker top with one button fixed in the wrong hole, feet bare. She yanked the door open on my side.

"What the *hell*, Mort!"

"Problem?"

"What're you doing?"

"Room's only got one bed."

"And that's a problem because . . . ?"

"I'm engaged, that's—"

"Who said we were gonna like . . . *do* anything? Which, I can tell you, *promise* you, we're not."

Well, she had me there. Voluptuous mostly naked girl in the only bed in the room—who was I to infer anything from that? But in fact no one had said anything about how that was supposed to play out, so I said, gently, "Go to bed, Sarah. Sleep. I'll be fine."

Calling her "Sarah" softened her expression. "Dammit, Mort. You don't have to do this."

"Yes I do."

She stared at me for a moment, then turned and went back to the room, closed the door. I breathed a sigh of relief as I pulled the car door shut. I am a pig, and therefore susceptible.

I shut my eyes, settled in.

Night sounds burbled around me, distant voices, a truck rolled by on the highway. A motel door opened and closed nearby.

Holiday-Sarah opened the driver's-side door and got in fully dressed, blanket in hand.

"Hi," she snapped.

"Hi yourself. Now get out."

"It's my car. I'll stay if I want."

She had me there again. "Okay, then. Night. Sleep tight."

"Night . . . *jerk*."

She settled in with the blanket. I settled in with my eyes wide open. Sonofabitch.

Five minutes later she said, "Mort?"

"What?"

"This is unbelievably stupid."

"When you're right, you're right."

"We've got a *room*. It has an actual, real bed. I promise I won't touch you. I mean it."

Goddamn Audis weren't as roomy or as comfortable as their advertisements made out. Not when you're well over six feet tall. I couldn't stretch my legs out. By morning I wouldn't be able to walk. By morning I was going to be homicidal and I had a gun under the car seat. Everyone in town was going to be at risk. But that room twenty feet away had a shower, which would feel mighty good. The door to the bathroom had a lock. Good solid lock. And the bed was a queen. Big enough for two, no touching. She'd promised.

You listening, Jeri?

I got out. Holiday-Sarah got out. I went to the room. Holiday-Sarah followed. I opened the door, let her go in ahead of me, closed it behind us, sleepwalked into the bathroom and locked the door, good solid lock like I thought, stripped, got in the shower, turned on the water, closed my eyes, let water drum on my neck and shoulders.

So much for logistics. So much for my Big Plan.

Sonofabitch.

* * *

Neon lighting seeped through a crack in the drapes as I came out in jeans and a shirt, no shoes, and crawled into bed.

"Mort?"

"Yeah?"

"You always sleep fully dressed?"

"Only on special occasions—and for the record, I took my shoes off so I'm not fully dressed."

"Well, I'm glad to know this is a special occasion and you're not wearing shoes, but I meant what I said, in case . . . you know . . . you can't sleep in all those clothes."

"Thanks. You're a peach."

"I couldn't do it."

"Uh-huh."

"I couldn't sleep two minutes, dressed up like I was going to the mall. I'd be awake all night."

"Uh-huh."

"Just so you know."

"I had that figured out twenty minutes ago."

"Well, okay then. Just so you know. Night."

"Night."

Five minutes went by.

This entire debacle was all about finding Allie, Holiday's sister. Twenty minutes ago in the bar I might've caught a glimpse of her through Deputy Roup's eyes. It might've been her in that green SUV. Maybe Hank at the Texaco station would—

"Anyway," Holiday broke in. "Here we are."

"Yep. Here we sure as hell are. I thought if you weren't wearing an excess of clothes you could get to sleep without all this ruckus."

"What? This is a ruckus?"

"Feels like it."

"Well, usually I can. Sleep, I mean."

"Give it the old college try. Remember you're a senior now, not a freshman. Night."

"Yeah, night."

Sonofabitch.

Thing is, it's a big world. It could've been anyone in that SUV Roup had seen. But Allie had called a little before eight and said she was in Gerlach, and Roup said he'd seen that Mercedes right about then. But if it *wasn't* Allie, then we were back to square—

"Mort?"

"What?"

"Can I tell you something?"

"Might's well. I'm having a hell of a time gettin' to sleep over here."

"It's kind of personal."

"Due to an unused Ph.D. I got in psychology years ago I'll let you know if I have to bill you for the time, but go ahead."

"I . . . I really like it when you look at me."

A rolling tremor went through me. "Well, I guess that's the way it is with some people." Incredibly lame response, Doc, but to get some sleep I thought I might have to knock her out. Wasn't sure how to do it without incurring an assault charge, bringing the law into it. I'd have to give it some thought.

She sighed. "I just wanted you to know. You know, in case you thought I didn't like you peeking at me or anything."

"Peeking? Me?"

"You know, *seeing* me, maybe feeling guilty. I wouldn't want you to feel like that 'cause, you know, I really don't mind."

"Got it. Night."

"Night." Sigh.

Sonofabitch.

Thoughts about this search for Allie were getting bulldozed off a cliff. I stared at the ceiling, trying to peer through estrogen fog filling the room like tear gas. The ceiling was a thousand pinpoints of light from that textured popcorn shit they spray on. It gave off glints that might've been from little bits of mica mixed in with the crud, something like that. I would have to ask someone, find out—

"Mort?"

"*What?*"

"If I accidentally touch you—'cause it *would* be an accident—I wouldn't want you to think it was intentional. It's just—sometimes I kinda toss in my sleep. Well, not just me. Lots of people do."

"Mind if I ask you something, Sarah?"

"What?"

"How is it you're almost twenty-five? Most college seniors are about twenty-one, maybe twenty-two."

She turned toward me and propped her head up on an elbow. "I was in the Peace Corps for two years. In Peru."

"Peace Corps? I thought that was only for college grads."

"Mostly, but not always. I did it after my sophomore year, after I'd taken most of my math and some engineering courses. And I didn't start college until I was nineteen. I spent the first year out of high school as an aide in a nursing home. It was where my grandma was staying when she broke a hip."

The good girl. Miss Perfect. Studious Sarah, doing the right thing. Sarah, who'd come across Holiday hiding in a closet inside herself and turned her loose at night. A vamp, but not a vam*pire*. At least I hoped so. I would never be able to explain puncture wounds and blood loss to Jeri.

"Peace Corps," I said. "That's good."

"It was, yes. I enjoyed my time there. I met a lot of really nice, friendly people. I spent most of my time helping build a big earthen dam. I even ran a D6 Caterpillar tractor for almost half a year. It was huge, weighed about eighteen tons."

"You did that?"

"Uh-huh. Wore a hard hat and an orange vest and everything. I must've pushed a hundred thousand cubic yards of dirt around."

"Well, hell. I'm impressed."

"Thanks. You seriously gonna sleep in all those clothes?"

"Yup."

"I'm sorry. I feel bad about that."

"Don't."

"Well, I promise I won't touch you or anything. Just in case you get uncomfortable and can't sleep like that."

"Good to know. I'll keep it in mind. Might write it on a Post-it and stick it on my forehead."

"Hey! I mean it."

"Uh-huh. Good night, Sarah."

"Yeah, fine. Good night."

Two minutes later:

"Mort?"

"Yeah?"

"A sword wound? You weren't kidding?"

"A foil, actually. That's a thin sword. In my chest, all the way through and out my back. It was that psycho girl, Winter."

"Jeez. Real bitch, huh?"

"She was, yeah. I ended up killing her."

Silence.

*   *   *

So I got about three hours' half-assed sleep, which put me in a nice surly mood when daylight started to brighten the room. The girl beside me, Sarah or Holiday, not sure which, slept peacefully—of course, since she wasn't twisted up in a bunch of clothes. But I'd made it through the night without irreversible damage, so I was going to be able to look myself in the mirror without having to snarl at a mangy cur staring back at me.

I got up without waking her, put on shoes, then slipped out the door into the new day. The sun was still behind the hills in the east, the sky over there turning a purple-blue color. Every vehicle outside was filmed with dust. A faint smell of coffee was in the air, wafting from the restaurant. It pulled me over through the morning chill and through the door, sat me at a table, and ordered a cup of itself while I tried to wake up, yawning, starting to feel amazed and pleased with myself that I'd slept three whole hours next to Holiday-Sarah who happened to be female and mostly or entirely naked, not sure which. I was a gumshoe with the self-control of a saint. I was a gumshoe like no other.

Sonofabitch.

Surly.

A cup of coffee and my eyes began to focus. I saw a clock. The time was 5:08. I hadn't been up that early in months. Half-hidden in an alcove by the cash register I saw T-shirts hanging on a rack that I hadn't noticed last night. I got up and ambled over, bought a white one with the words "Corti's Casino, Gerlach, Nevada" on the front in blue letters, utterly generic—ten bucks. I marched it over to the motel room, opened the door, tossed it on the bed, then walked back to the casino.

Two more cups of coffee gave me time to glance at the first few pages of a day-old newspaper abandoned on a nearby table. There was more about the fire in Jayson Wexel's house that had killed him—Wexel was Senator Reinhart's chief of staff, which was the only reason he wasn't buried on page eighteen. Nothing gets by those wunderkinds at the *Gazette-Journal*. The fire was either an accident or murder—apparently that was still up in the air. Then Sarah came in. The new T-shirt was tight as a drum across her chest and looked mighty full. No bra, but at least the shirt didn't plunge. She looked about as normal as a girl with her figure can get in a shirt one size too small—a fact I was about to find out. She set yesterday's FedEx package on the table in front of me and sat. "Thanks for the shirt, Mort. It's a size too small. You eaten yet?"

Great. Another of my failings—I can't figure women's sizes in clothing. I set the newspaper aside. "Nope. Just coffee. And, hey, look, you brought in the mail."

"I'm starving." She slid the package an inch closer. "Open it. If it's from your mom, it might be cookies."

"From my mom it'll either be a book or an RPG."

"An RPG?"

"Rocket-propelled grenade. Mom's a corker."

She laughed.

I checked the label on the package. I didn't recognize the return address, which was Abe Handy on Hacksaw Road, Reno.

I pulled out my cell phone and took a few photographs of the shipping label, got close-ups of both addresses.

"What'd you do that for?" Sarah asked.

"What you just observed was a month and a half of PI training poppin' right out of the core of my soul. I can't turn it off." And the fact that the package was sent to me on Ralston Street without a street address, that popped out, too. Whoever sent it didn't have my house number. Interesting. Guess it wasn't mom, so it wouldn't be an RPG, which would've been fun out there in the desert.

Sarah rolled her eyes.

I pulled the tab on the package and zipped it open, lifted the flap, took out something wrapped in bubble wrap. A piece of paper on top read: "Shake the hand of an honest politician."

Right away, I didn't like the looks of that.

I peeled the bubble wrap off, got down to something rolled in a few layers of clear Saran wrap.

Aw shit, no.

CHAPTER SIX

SARAH STARED AT it, eyes widening, then she jumped up with a yelp. "Omigod! What *is* that?"

Heads turned. Still early, but there were half a dozen people in the place and her voice was shrill. She backed away, bumped into a chair occupied by a guy in his fifties in a camo ball cap, camo shirt, boots, hunting knife on his belt.

By then I was on my feet, hoping the thing in plastic wasn't real, wasn't what it looked like. But I knew it was, because I'd been with the IRS long enough to have racked up karmic demerits by the truckload and this was what life had in store for me from now on.

"Sonofawhore," I said, not really aware I'd said it.

The waitress who'd brought my coffee came over, frowned at the thing on the table, then said, "Aagggh," and backed away, face white. A little pinkish slime was visible through the plastic, and a palm, thumb, fingers, fingernails, even a bit of dark hair between the knuckles.

But I've gotten used to this sort of thing—finding body parts, that is—so I recover faster than your basic civilian. I was the first to drag out my phone and dial 911.

About then time got distorted, events tumbled over one another, but it didn't seem long before Deputy Roup came charging through the door with his gun on his hip, holster unsnapped.

I pointed at the thing in Saran wrap. He took a closer look, then stared at me. "What the *hell*, Mortimer?"

"Mort."

"What—who—whose is it?"

"Mine, since it was sent to me."

He stared at me. "I mean, whose hand *was* it?"

I indicated the note on the table. "Might be a clue there. You probably shouldn't touch it though," I added helpfully.

He glared at me, then squinted at the note, then at me. "What's that mean?"

I nodded at the disgusting thing. "My guess—and this's just a guess, mind you, so don't get excited—that's the shakin' part of our missing senator, Harry J. Reinhart." I let that gel for five seconds, then said, "Am I good, or what?"

I don't think Roup cared for the comment, but he'd been a cop for thirty-plus years and he hadn't eaten yet, so he called it in to the county mounties down in Reno, then we sat at an adjoining table and had breakfast. He and I did, anyway, the Hunter's Special—three eggs any style, thick slab of ham, hash browns, buttered toast with jam, enough coffee to float a kayak. Sarah picked at a bowl of fruit with a greenish pallor on her face. Other than her shirt, she didn't look much like the Holiday I'd come to know in the past . . . what? Ten hours? Jesus H. Christ, this gumshoe-dame thing was like riding a rocket sled.

Roup yawned. He caught my look.

"Long damn night," he said. "Fire was reported in the hills up north, west of the highway. Travel trailer went up, eight or ten miles in from the road. Old rig, small, fourteen feet long. I was thinking it belonged to a hunter, but no truck was around, nothing to pull it, and it didn't have plates, so now I don't know. Thing's probably cool enough now to go back, try to find a VIN number." He yawned again.

Hank Waldo came in at 5:53 and had the waitress fill a thermos with coffee. Her hand shook, but she got the job done. Deputy Roup waved Hank over and he took a chair, sixty-six years old, grizzled, oil and dirt on his boots, hair white, nose bulbous, teeth yellow with age and neglect, half a dozen of them missing in front, which made him look like a pumpkin I'd carved when I was ten.

"Remember that Mercedes yesterday?" Roup asked him, hands cupped around his coffee mug. "Green SUV?"

Texaco Hank nodded. "Sure. Third or fourth time it's been by this month."

That got my attention. Made it more likely I'd seen it last night when I left the casino.

"You see a girl inside?" Roup asked. "Passenger side."

At that, Sarah perked up, started listening. *A girl?*

Hank shrugged. "Saw one, yeah."

"Remember her hair color? How old she was? Anything?"

"Don't pay much notice to girls these days, but she looked like jailbait. Thing is, I ain't shit for ages anymore. Edie over there"— he nodded toward the waitress—"she looks like jailbait to me, an' she's thirty-five." He sipped his coffee, then his eyes got sly. "If I went over there and honked one of her hooters, you'd arrest me, wouldn't you?"

"Probably have to, Hank. If she yelled and filed charges. Which I'm thinkin' she would."

"There you go. Jailbait, like I said."

Deputy Roup grinned. "How about the woman with that girl? She would've been the one outside, pumping gas."

Hank looked up at the ceiling, gave that some thought. "Had a city look to 'er, but who else'd drive a car like that?"

"How old was she?"

"Who knows? Coulda been thirty, forty. Tall lady, but prissy lookin', if you know what I mean. Had that look anyways."

"Do you have video surveillance at the station?" I asked.

Hank looked at me, then shook his head. "Nope. Got no use for useless complicated shit. Don't have the time. Never needed nothin' like it, neither."

"Which way'd they go when they left?"

"Down south."

Back toward Fernley, Reno, Las Vegas, Mexico—at about eight p.m., and I might've seen it at about ten thirty, same night, also headed south. Which didn't make sense. Maybe he was mistaken, or maybe there was more than one dark Mercedes SUV in the area. Didn't seem likely, but stuff happens.

"How about those other times you saw it?" I asked.

"North, south. Both ways. Passin' through." He looked up at a clock. "Well, gotta go. Probably got a line of trucks at the station. Usually do, mornings. Nice talkin' to ya." He took off. It was a one-minute walk to the station from the casino. I'd know where to find him if I wanted to talk to him again, which I thought was likely.

"Think that was Allie in the car?" Sarah asked. The pallor had evaporated and color was back in her face. She looked good, starting to draw stares again. We were waiting for Reno police but Corti's was still open for business, only place in town that served food. The hand on the table, presumably the hand of an honest politician, had been covered with a tablecloth. Deputy Roup kept folks away from it.

I shrugged. "It's possible."

"That the girl in the picture you showed me last night?" Roup said. "That high school kid you asked about?"

"Uh-huh. Two years older now."

"Well, then, I'm sorry I didn't stop at the station yesterday, get a better look at her. And that SUV."

Me, too.

Another fifteen minutes crept by.

It was an indication of who's got the money that first on the scene was a helicopter—Channel 2 out of Reno. Second on the scene was another helicopter—Channel 8. Deputy Roup went outside to say "No comment" half a dozen times and keep cameras out of the restaurant, although reporters came in, ostensibly to get coffee. Took them less than five seconds to notice me, the guy who'd located missing persons left and right last July. People who'd ended up dead. They looked at me like ravens eyeing roadkill. Great. Twenty minutes later county cars started pulling up. They had made the run from Reno in just under ninety minutes. Car doors slammed outside. Moments later the casino door swung open. First guy through said, "You!" so I said, "Me!"

Our standard greeting.

Detective Russell Fairchild and his behemoth sidekick, Officer Day, stood smoldering at the entrance. At least Fairchild did; Day looked more like a block of cold concrete with eyes.

Hell of a way to start the day.

"You've really done it this time, Angel," Fairchild said, which is what he always says when he doesn't have a clue but thinks he does. He probably sees lethal injections in his sleep, hates it if the alarm clock goes off before the drugs take effect.

"How about you tell me what I've done," I said. "And this is county, not city, so how's it your jurisdiction?"

A puff of wind left his sails. "It's not. I was invited. When the sheriff heard it was you, he asked if I'd come along."

"And you brought the behemoth," I said, looking behind him. "That was thoughtful."

Officer Day rumbled, deep in his throat. Three hundred thirty pounds—he'd gained a ham hock or two since I'd last seen him.

Less than two months ago I'd been a national sensation. Then it had been Reno PD's problem, but the entire country had followed me like they follow Kardashians, so it was likely that Washoe County Sheriff John Burnley's eyes had bugged out when he heard the name Mortimer Angel mentioned in the same breath as Harry J. Reinhart during an early-morning 911 call.

I had no actual knowledge of that, but I assume his eyes had bugged out because that's what they did when he barged in twenty seconds after Fairchild and caught sight of me—although Sarah was sitting beside me so I might've been wrong.

Burnley was fifty-two years old. A massive gut overhung his belt, so his NRA competition buckle was a trophy—it was said— that had gone to waist. He had brush-cut gray hair, hard eyes, a black automatic on his hip. His uniform shirt was tucked into blue jeans and he had on Nike running shoes, so he'd scrambled out of his house in a rush and wasn't his usual photogenic, uni-formed self, a fact that might bite him in the ass in next year's election.

To forestall a whirlwind of questions, I said, "Over there on the table, Sheriff. It was on my doorstep yesterday evening at about eight o'clock, I picked it up, put it in the backseat of the car, we drove up here to Gerlach, and the package spent the night in the car. We opened it here in the restaurant at about five thirty this morning, and that's absolutely all I know about it."

He didn't look impressed. "We," he said. "You said we. Who's we?"

"I opened the package, Sheriff. *I* did that."

"Uh-huh. Again I ask, 'who's we'?"

"Me," Sarah said. "I got it out of my car and brought it over here this morning."

Burnley stared at her a second longer than I thought necessary. Only one second, which indicated a level of professionalism and control I couldn't begin to touch. "Who're you?" he asked.

"Sarah Dellario."

Burnley looked at the two of us. "You two're what? Father-daughter? Friends? An item?"

So much for forestalling a whirlwind of questions. Sonofabitch. This was going to drag out, and it was going to drag me and Sarah along with it like roadkill under a car. I was going to be a household name again, all across the land of the free. Make that we. *We* were going to be household names, Sarah and I.

But . . . father-daughter?

Shit, that hurt.

A techie of some sort got fingerprints off the hand using a little scanner that sent them off to the FBI via satellite. Man, I could use one of those. More techs got my gun out of Sarah's car, gave it an official sniff test—three of them stuck noses to the barrel and inhaled—determined that it hadn't been fired recently, not that the hand had bullet holes in it.

Sarah and I were separated, put in opposite ends of the room. There we wrote out statements and signed them. Then Burnley and a woman by the name of Carla Estes—forty-something, flat-chested, with a bland, innocuous look belied at times by a suspicious squint—read our statements and together she and Burnley came up with a list of questions that Sarah and I answered, again separately. Fairchild listened in. Fairchild, I imagined, because he had experience dealing with Mort Angel, PI. By far the most interesting question was why Sarah and I had come to Gerlach, of all places, as if Gerlach was akin to a leper colony. This brought up the topic of the search for Allie and Allie's phone call yesterday, which had the benefit of dragging Fairchild deeper into the periphery of this mess since it was RPD's detective squad who had given short shrift to Allie's missing person case.

"Should've asked me to look into it," Fairchild growled at me.

"I didn't ask anyone to look into it," I told him. "Sarah did, and it was over two months ago."

"Not then. You should've contacted me yesterday when you got that call."

"That would've been a grandmaster move on my part. RPD is swift like the eagles."

At that, Burnley laughed, Estes smiled, and Fairchild gave me a look that would have killed a lesser man. Burnley didn't have a dog in that fight, and I gathered there was some healthy competition between RPD and county law enforcement that served them well, kept everyone on their toes.

A digital recorder sat on the table between the four of us, red light glowing. "You and this girl, Sarah, you stayed the night here in Gerlach?" Burnley asked. "At the motel?"

I nodded, then said, "Yes, we did," since the recorder wasn't for shit when it came to nonverbal communication.

"What rooms were you in?" His pencil hovered a quarter inch above a small spiral-bound notebook.

"Nineteen."

Burnley looked up. "Nineteen?"

"That's the one."

Was that a gleam of respect I saw in his eyes? I'd like to think so. On the other hand, Ms. Estes tried without success to hide a moue of disapproval, as if she'd discovered a desiccated roach in her Cheerios right before that first spoonful. Fairchild, of course, being a true detective, wanted more.

"In what capacity were you two there?" he asked, which told me he hadn't gotten his quota of beauty sleep that morning.

I gave that two seconds' thought, said, "About a gallon," and stood up. "We done here?"

Burnley stuck his notebook in a pocket. "Guess so. Unless . . ." He turned to Estes. "You got anything?"

She pursed her lips and was thinking about it when a deputy—not Roup—came over and whispered something in Burnley's ear.

"Well, shit," Burnley said. "This stinkin' job doesn't pay nearly enough." At which point he stared at the recorder then turned it off. "This is not for public consumption," he said. "But finger-prints confirm that the hand in that package does in fact belong to Senator Reinhart. So this day—no, this *month*—is now pure dogshit."

Sarah and I were instructed to say nothing but "no comment" to reporters, which would incite them to no end and make the two of us look guilty as hell about something. It might also make us look like an "item," which would boost my recognition quo-tient around the country. If Reinhart were still alive, I could whip his sorry ass in a presidential primary. His wife—Julia—was a good-looking woman twenty-six years his junior, but in that T-shirt, about to get national exposure, Holiday as the next First Lady would be unbeatable. If, of course, we were an item.

The written statements and the preliminary questioning over with, Sarah and I were allowed to drive back to Reno in the same car, alone. Fairchild might have suggested it. I wouldn't put it past him. Sarah and I had told our stories. Now, if either story changed, they'd nail us to the wall. That might have been his hope. I was making him look bad, finding missing persons right and left.

I drove. Three county cars were ahead of us, six behind, no lights, no sirens. Earlier, when the name Harry Reinhart had come up, they'd scrambled like B-52s in a nuclear alert, but now it was just a casual run back to Reno. I'd gassed up the Audi at the Texaco station. I gave Hank my cell number, told him to call if he saw that Mercedes again, or the girl, or, in fact, any girl that might fit Allie's description. What better person to keep an eye out for a girl than an alcoholic who doesn't much notice "the girls" anymore?

By ten thirty we were on the road, empty desert on both sides, a caravan of white cars front and back, the Audi—still fire-engine red—looking like a ruby in a cheap bracelet.

"Sorry about last night," Sarah said.

"What about it?"

"You know. All the hassle."

I shrugged that off. "No sweat. It made for an interesting night."

"'Interesting.' That's a tepid word."

"How about memorable? That better?"

She smiled. "Really?"

"Hell, yes. I hope never to repeat it."

Silence for two miles. Then: "It was that bad, huh?"

"Well, no. It was . . . different."

She leaned her head back, eyes closed. "Anyway, I'm glad we didn't end up sleeping in the car. That would've sucked."

*   *   *

We weren't done yet. This time the interrogation took place at the Washoe County jail. For the record, their rooms are ventilated better than those at RPD. The one-way mirrors are cleaner, too.

Due to the nature of the victim, the questioning was handled by the FBI, although Sheriff Burnley and Carla Estes were also present.

"Who is Abe Handy?" asked a humorless, no-nonsense agent introduced as Agent Morrison, referring to the return address on the FedEx package. Humorless, I figured, because I had to tell him

Abe undoubtedly referred to Abe Lincoln, and when that didn't register, I said *Honest* Abe? And when he didn't get that, I had to tell him that Reinhart's hand was billed as the hand of an *honest* politician, but that theory and practice might have little in common in this case—this guy was like trying to hold a conversation with a can of paint. And Handy? He wanted to know about that. Well, Agent Morrison, if you'll remember there was a *hand* in that package—sonofabitch. The guy probably had to have every joke in *A Charlie Brown Christmas* spelled out to him.

"How about that address, Hacksaw Road?" he asked.

Even Estes rolled her eyes.

"Think about it," I said. "It'll come to you. Maybe."

But I wasn't about to explain it. If I did, he might think all this tricky insider knowledge was proof of wrongdoing. Agent Morrison made IRS agents look like revelers at a New Year's party.

Then came the questions, a few hundred of them, but Sarah's story and mine hadn't changed, so they cut us loose at four twenty that afternoon. They test-fired my gun then gave it back, reluctantly, since I had a carry permit, and they had nothing to compare the slugs to. Yet. Sarah drove me to my house on Ralston, which was a bust due to eight media vans parked out front—*eight* of them, a new record—and three cop cars and a forensics van. Turns out, you can't find part of a presidential candidate without attracting attention. My neighbors would probably circulate a petition to have me removed by Monday.

"Where to now?" Sarah asked. I slunk down in the Audi as she went past the house, turned left at the corner.

"Dunno."

"How about my place?"

Now *there* was a sterling idea. "No way."

"Why not? I've got a nice apartment just the other side of the university. It's only about a mile away."

I thought about that. Knowing where she lived might be useful. I didn't know why, but being a damn good detective, I decided not to turn down free information.

"Okay," I said.

"Okay, great."

Down University Terrace, across Virginia Street to Ninth, then Evans, around the ring road that circles the campus, then a right onto Highland Avenue, a left onto Beech, and there we were at Sierra Sky Apartments, two-story brick and clapboard, cream with blue trim, nice landscaping, decent parking. A high-end place compared to a lot of apartments in Reno.

"Nice," I said. "Which one's yours?"

"Number twenty-three. On the second floor."

"I'm gonna leave my gun in your car under the seat, so lock up. I'll get it later. Don't get it out and play with it."

"Like I'm gonna play around with a gun."

I got out of the car. She got out, locked up, and headed toward her apartment. I headed for the street.

"Hey!"

I turned. "What?"

"It's this way, Mort."

"Yup. Got that. Now I know. I'll have to see it sometime. Right now's not that time."

She watched me go. I thought she'd come after me, but she didn't. I went past elms and a fence covered with honeysuckle and she was lost to sight.

*　*　*

I was in the Green Room nursing a sarsaparilla when O'Roarke came on duty. He stared at my drink and said, "Hell has froze over."

I was considering a witty comeback, something like, "Screw you," but I'm an adult.

Sort of.

But it wasn't easy with Holiday still attached to my retinas, the way she'd looked in that room last night when the bed cover had tumbled down.

"Okay, time for a Pete's Wicked Ale."

"That's more like it, spitfire," O'Roarke said as he reached for a longneck.

"May even your fleas have fleas."

"Rough day?"

"You might say that."

"Heard something about it on the radio this afternoon. Don't leave without autographing a napkin or one of my butt cheeks."

"Something I hope never to see." I took a swig of Pete's. "I heard somewhere that people still listen to radio. Really old people. Got any great-grandchildren photos?"

He hit the remote, turned on the television over the bar. "Five o'clock news'll be on in a few. Might be more fun today."

Avoiding it wouldn't make it go away. "Turn up the sound," I said. "Let's see the damage." I took a moment to check the picture I'd taken of the FedEx shipping label on my cell phone. I zoomed in and saw that it had been sent from Bend, Oregon.

Then the news came on.

First up was Mortimer Angel and Sarah Dellario, exiting Corti's Casino in Gerlach through a snowstorm of asinine questions. That brought O'Roarke up short. "*That's* Sarah Dellario?"

"Yep."

"Heard the name on the radio. She looks a hell of a lot like your favorite hooker—Holiday."

"Doesn't she, though?"

"And that shirt she's wearing. Man, that's . . . something."

"You oughta see it in 3-D."

Which, then, he did, because Holiday-Sarah chose that moment to wander in and plop down on a stool next to me. In that shirt.

"Thought I might find you here," she said. "I mean, where else would you go?"

"Like I've got no friends in northern Nevada, no life beyond this barstool. Thank you. Anyway, you're really into that shirt, huh? Probably dangerous to try to get it off without a spotter."

She looked down at herself. "Snug little number, isn't it?"

O'Roarke said, "Reminds me of a slingshot I had when I was a kid. Powerful one, too. Kill a rhino with it."

"You're probably remembering the stretch," I said.

Holiday suppressed a smile. "You two're like what, thirteen years old? Anyway, I can't get rid of it. It's special." She looked up at the television. "Oh, jeez. Is that us?"

"Next time you go to class, you'll be asked for your autograph. Or something."

"Well . . . that's sort of a bitch."

"Better believe it. I've been asked to sign a butt cheek."

The news unfolded, talking heads barely able to conceal their delight now that the severed right hand of presidential hopeful Senator Harold J. Reinhart had turned up in a FedEx package early that morning, sent to private investigator Mortimer Angel, the same Mortimer Angel who found the severed heads of blah, blah, blah. There was a nice close-up of me, and an even closer-up of Sarah, braless in her new shirt. Networks were in the business of ratings and revenue. What she was or wasn't wearing wasn't their fault.

"Oh, jeez," she said.

"Yup. Expect movie offers."

Right then my cell phone rang. Played a few bars of *Light My Fire* before I could swipe the screen. It was Jeri, no surprise. "Hi, there," I said.

"Jesus, Mort. I leave you for just one day—what the hell's goin' on?"

"You know. The usual, finding stuff. It's what I do."

"Oh, for Chrissake. I saw it on television. And who was that with you? I mean, *why* was she with you? Sarah somebody."

"Dellario." Holiday-Sarah looked at me, tilted her head. "In fact," I said, "I'm in the Green Room right now and she's right here. We're watching the news. You two should talk." I handed the phone to Holiday. Or Sarah. "It's Jeri," I said. One way or another this was going to get worked out—in the open. No secrets.

Later I would remind myself that I was the one who said they should talk. Me. I did that.

"Uh, hi," Sarah said. "I'm, uh, Sarah."

At that point I had to piece the conversation together. There was a one-sided discussion about her hiring me, private detective that I am, Allie's phone call, the trip to Gerlach, the gas problem, the room problem, the hundred-dollar bribe, more back and forth during which my future was a ping pong ball, so I left. Went out into the casino and up to the mezzanine, got a hot dog with mustard and onions, no relish. I've never gotten sick from a hot dog so I don't worry about what's in them, especially since they're loaded with enough preservatives to kill a rat, and poison has no effect on IRS agents. Got done with that, so I went back to the main floor and found a roulette wheel, put five dollars on red. I won, so I let it ride. Won again, let it ride. Thirteen, black. Let it ride long enough and you'll lose, every time.

Speaking of losing, I went back to the Green Room. Holiday was at a table, comfortably slumped in a chair with one bare foot up on another chair. She and Jeri had been talking for over half an hour. She gave me a smile and a little finger wave when I came in.

"He's back now," she said into the phone, which she kept. "No, he had on pants and a shirt the entire time." Pause. "Well, yeah, he took off his shoes." Pause. "Uh-huh. I think so. I heard him reciting the Boy Scout oath under his breath, sort of like a mantra. Does that count?"

"Gimme that," I snarled. I took control of the phone again. "I didn't recite the fuckin' Boy Scout oath."

"I'm shocked, given what Sarah told me."

"Great. So given whatever the hell she told you, how're you and I doin'?"

"We're doing fine, Mort. She sounds nice. I like her. And, look, we made over ten thousand dollars right before I left, so we can afford to do a little pro bono work."

"Pro bono work?"

"Sarah's sister. Which means you should go back to Gerlach and dig deeper since Allie phoned from there."

"You serious?"

A moment of silence. "Do you remember what you and I do for a living?"

"Sort of," I admitted. I sat at the table. Sarah got up and sat at the bar, ordered a Tequila Sunrise.

"You and Sarah left Gerlach too soon," Jeri said.

"Actually, we were escorted out of town and back to Reno by the FBI and others, including Russell Fairchild. They didn't give us a say in the matter. In fact, they acted kind of stressed."

"Fairchild, huh? How is good ol' Russ, anyway?"

"Still chubby. Still jealous. Still doesn't like me."

"Great. So about Gerlach—there's a lot you didn't ask up there, or get a chance to ask, if Sarah got the story straight, which it sounds like she did. That guy Hank at the Texaco station might've had more information, but probably the sheriff and maybe that bartender, too."

"Deputy sheriff. And the bartender was Dave."

"Yeah, whatever. So you should go back and ask around. Be creative. Try to think like a private investigator."

"Okay. First thing in the morning I'll shoot on up there. Place is a garden spot. I might even buy us some property."

"This evening, Mort. Go now. The trail gets colder the longer you wait. It's eight fifty over here, five fifty over there. You could be in Gerlach by eight o'clock if you hustle, hopefully a little before, since Sarah said Hank buttons up the gas station at eight."

"What else did she tell you? Did she tell you I got three hours' sleep last night and I'm dog-tired right now?"

"She told me a bunch of stuff. And she said your house is under siege by the media. Of course you could stay at my place, which is going to be *our* place, but Sarah's sister has never been to either your place or mine so there won't be much to investigate. You might as well go back to Gerlach since that's where things are happening."

"Sarah told you a bunch of stuff, huh?"

"She did, yes."

"Was it interesting?"

"It had something to do with how she's been dressed. And what she wore to bed last night. It was in the way of full disclosure. She's not hiding anything."

"Don't I know it."

"Don't worry, Mort. It's okay."

"Really?"

"Yes, really."

"It sure feels like we're threading a needle here, Jeri."

"I can see how you'd feel that way. But she's a nice girl, I can tell. I think she and I will end up being pretty good friends. We've got more in common than you'd think. She's kinda *wow*, what I saw of her on TV, but nice."

"Wow, huh? And you aren't worried?"

"Not at all. Should I be?"

"Like you said, not at all. Might not be any rooms available at the motel up there if I go up tonight. It's hunting season."

"Go anyway. Bribe that guy again."

"Dave."

"Whatever. Allie's trail is getting colder by the hour. And take your wig and moustache with you, just in case."

"I hate wearing that stuff, Jeri."

"Take it with you anyway. You're famous again. You never know if you'll need it. Now let me talk to Sarah."

"Really?"

"Yeah, really. Put her on."

I waved Sarah over and handed her phone. She said, "It's me." Then: "You sure?" Then: "Yeah, I could do that." Then: "Yes," and, "Yes," then a little laugh, and, "Okay, bye. Here he is."

She gave me the phone.

"What was *that* all about?" I asked Sarah.

"Nothing. Just girl stuff." She wagged a finger at the phone. "She's still there. Talk."

"I'm back," I said to Jeri, staring at Sarah. "What was *that* all about?"

"Nothing. I was going to tell her something when you took the phone away from her. Anyway, I'm gonna go take a hot soak and do some stretching, then get in bed and read awhile. I've got to be up at seven tomorrow. Let me know if you find out anything in Gerlach, okay?"

"Sure thing, sugar plum."

"Sugar plum?" Her voice had a smile in it. "I'll get you for that when I get back."

"Uh-huh. Looking forward to it."

"Yeah, me, too. Bye, Mort."

"Bye." I ended the call.

Sarah came over, drink in hand, little umbrella stuck in a good-sized orange slice riding sidecar—O'Roarke was giving her the full treatment, no doubt due to her shirt.

"Everything okay?" she asked.

"Just great. Except for that underhanded girl talk and that Boy Scout thing."

"You earned it, big-time. Would've got another merit badge if you hadn't taken your shoes off."

I got up, stashed the phone in a pocket. "See you around, kiddo. Got things to do."

"Where're you going?"

"Home. Hope all the cops and trolls are gone."

"Yeah, good luck with that."

* * *

My going home wasn't a lie, just misdirection. I went over the back fence, then through my side yard, got into the Toyota before ABC, NBC, CNN, in fact any of 'em, saw me. Their vans were all aimed south so I backed out fast and headed north, which caused some predictable confusion and awkward three-point turns.

I made a few slippery lefts and rights that took me north and west, went through quiet neighborhoods at a fairly high speed, then stopped at Jeri's, got the wig, moustache, my toothbrush, toothpaste, forgot to gather up a change of clothes in my haste, then hit I-80 at Keystone, headed east through Reno and Sparks.

The side mirror howls at sixty, but it's quiet at seventy, and you can't hear it at eighty over the distressed whine of the engine, so the run up to Gerlach had a bunch of different vocals.

Got there at five after eight. Lights were out at the Texaco station, so all that hustle was for naught, except sometimes it's good to blow the carbon out of the engine. A purple glow was above the hills to the west as I nosed the Toyota into a slot at the casino, crammed it in between an oil delivery truck on one side and a power company rig on the other.

Dave started a dark draft as soon as I came in the door. He wasn't there that morning when Reinhart made an appearance and put Gerlach on the map so he'd missed all the excitement, had to watch it on TV and get it secondhand from Deputy Roup.

"On the house," he said, pushing the brewski toward me.

"Don't know how you keep this place going, but thanks."

He cast a hopeful look at the door. "She comin' in?"

"Nope."

"Well, hell. Beer's three bucks then." I reached for my wallet, but he waved it off. "Kiddin', dude."

I downed a third of the beer, then said, "Got a room? I'm dead tired. I didn't get much sleep last night."

"Who would? Anyway, this's your lucky day. I got one room left."

"So I don't have to bribe you?"

"Can if you want, but room six is open. Guy got a call from his wife half an hour ago, had to split."

"Good deal. I'll take it."

I signed the register, got the key, took the beer over to the room, and settled in, which amounted to looking the place over to be sure the key worked and the room had a bed, then I took my beer back to the casino.

"That was quick," Dave said. "Didn't find any body parts while you were over there, did you?"

"Not a one. How 'bout a dinner menu?"

I ordered a steak, baked potato, corn on the cob, apple pie. He wrote it up, put the order through a slot in the wall to the kitchen, dinged a bell.

"Got a few questions for you, if you have a moment," I said.

"Gotta keep the booze flowing, but go ahead."

"Last night I asked about a girl, a little older than high school age, and Roup mentioned a green Mercedes SUV."

"Uh-huh. I remember."

"Have you seen an SUV like that around here lately?"

"No. But I'm mostly either in here or at home, which is a shack two blocks off the highway, back of the casino. Fact is, I don't see much of the highway. Not like Mike or Hank."

"I know about them. Know anyone else who might've seen that Mercedes?"

Dave gave that some thought. Still thinking, he went ten feet down the bar and drew a Guinness draft, went another ten feet and whipped up a daiquiri for a rough-looking fifty-something lady in jeans and a camo shirt. "Depends," he said when he got back. "If the lady driving it stopped at Empire, at the minimart over there, someone there might've seen it. Over here, Mike and Hank are the most likely ones to have spotted it, but really, anyone could've. I can't think of anyone else in particular."

Well, the place only had about two hundred people. I could go door to door, blanket the town in a day or two. Which felt like a big waste of time, although I knew what Jeri would say about that. A while back she told me gumshoeing was 99 percent boring and if I wanted excitement then alligator wrestling might suit me. I thought maybe it wouldn't since I don't much cotton to alligators, but I didn't argue the point with her.

"How about the girl?" I asked. "Have you seen her around?"

"Still got her picture?"

I got it out and set it on the bar. Dave gave it a long look in a light under the bar, longer than he had before. He handed it back. "No, but leave your number. I'll call if I see her."

I did that.

"How about the lady she was with?" I asked. "Tall, shoulder-length dark hair? Hank said she was prissy looking."

Dave smiled. "Hell of a description. Don't think you're gonna get anywhere with that, man."

"Yeah. Me either."

My dinner arrived. I took it to an empty table and ate it. Two guys in their thirties were playing pool. Same guys as last night. When I finished eating I got up and showed Allie's picture around the room. The hunters were a bust since they were from out of town. A few locals gave it a look, but shook their heads. I didn't bother with the pool sharks since they'd already seen it.

Outside, the land was dark under a bright canopy of stars. Ten-pound barbells attached themselves to my eyelids. I was about to go crash in my room when Deputy Roup went into the casino, so I went back inside. He was already at the bar. I took a stool next to him.

"Aw, jeez," he said. "If it ain't my favorite private eye."

"Nice to know I'm appreciated."

"You didn't find the rest of our good senator, did you?"

Probably a rhetorical question since I didn't have a "cat that ate the canary" grin. In fact, a fair amount of the news was speculation, official and otherwise, about whether or not Reinhart was still alive. The smart money was on *not*, but a few pundits had pointed out that a person can lose a hand and keep on lying. Those would be pundits on the political right, with whom, this time, I happened to agree.

"Nope," I said. "Just his head."

Roup's head jerked around. "*What?*"

"Kidding." Thing is, people tend to believe me when I say I found a head. Probably shouldn't joke about that.

He shook his head. "Jesus H. Christ, Angel."

"That woman you saw putting gas in that Mercedes SUV over at the Texaco. Would you recognize her if you saw her again?"

"Maybe. Probably would if I saw her in that car."

"Give me a call if you do, huh?" I gave him my cell number.

"Will do," he said. "Goddamn, but you sure do stir things up."

"Not intentionally, Sheriff. I'll be in room six at the motel if you happen to see her." I got off the barstool and headed for the door.

"Angel."

I turned. "Yeah?"

"If you find any more pieces of Reinhart, haul 'em to Reno and find 'em down there, okay?"

"I'll do that. I'll tell Sheriff Burnley you said it was okay."

The door shut off Dave's laughter as I went outside.

CHAPTER SEVEN

MAN, I WAS tired. I'm at least an eight-hour-a-night person. Three hours the previous night didn't hack it. I took a quick shower, brushed my teeth, and fell into bed, out cold in less than a minute.

The knock on the door came at 1:55 in the morning, right in the middle of the best sleep I'd had in a month.

"Wrong room," I yelled.

The knocking continued. Loud, too.

"Sonofabitch," I growled. My eyelids felt grainy. "Go away and die," I shouted. I'm not at my best with grainy eyelids, which is a character fault that doesn't respond to therapy.

The knocking continued.

"Aw, hell." I turned on all twenty watts of a bedside lamp. The towel I'd used to dry off earlier was on a chair, damp, but faster and easier to put on than fumbling into a pair of jockeys, which I couldn't locate, right offhand.

I wrapped the towel around my waist and whipped the door open. "What the fu—?"

It was one of the pool sharks, slim and scruffy, in boots, jeans, a denim vest. Could've used a comb, too, but it wasn't my place to tell him that. "Is this yours, man?" he asked. "Says she is." He had one hand on Holiday's arm, just above the elbow. His buddy was behind them, also scruffy and lean.

Well, hell.

"Yes, she is. Thanks for returning her." I didn't even blink as I said it, I'm that good.

"She's a goddamn hustler, man."

"Well, yeah, sure, I didn't know that," I said, striving for as much ambiguity as I could muster that early in the morning.

"You oughta keep her under better control, Jack."

"*Control!*" Holiday yanked her arm out of his grasp. "You *still* owe me a hundred bucks, Dell."

First-name basis with the sharks. Great. I looked beyond her, at her Audi nosed into a slot fifteen feet away. "Got the keys to your car, honey bun?" I asked her.

"Sure do," she said sweetly, tossing them to me.

I went out in bare feet and a towel—first time for everything—opened the passenger door and got my gun out from under the seat. The things you forget when you're operating on too little sleep.

"Whoa, dude," Dell said when he saw it. He backed up two feet, into his buddy.

"Notice that I'm not aiming this at anyone," I said. "And I'm licensed to carry concealed. Although," I added, trying to be helpful, "I don't have my license on me right now."

"Yeah, I kin see that."

Holiday held out a hand to him, palm up. "Hundred bucks, pay up." She had on another one of those tops that would get her a week in jail in Iowa—faux leather, nice shade of burgundy. I went back to the room and turned, stood in the doorway.

Dell dug in a pocket and pulled out a wad of bills. He folded it once and shoved it into her top.

"Never judge a book by its cover," Holiday said to him as she headed toward me, pulling the money out.

Dell stared at her. "Huh? What's that mean?"

"Never mind." She pushed past me into the room, pulled me out of the doorway, and slammed the door in Dell's face.

"Surprise," she said.

"Hustler, huh?"

"I played a lot of pool in the Peace Corps. There wasn't much to do evenings up there in that village, but they had a pool table under a kind of outdoor canopy tent thing. I got pretty good."

"Dell looked unhappy."

"Dell only thought he was good. Anyway, Dave said you were over here in room six. He's the bartender."

"Yup. We've met. Even bumped knuckles."

"I got two free Tequila Sunrises. Drank most of them so I'm a little woohoo. I went by your house in Reno earlier. Your car was gone. I figured you came back here, so I drove on up."

"I'll have your PI license printed up in the morning."

"Also, Jeri sort of told me she told you to come back here to keep looking for Allie, so that helped a little."

"Okay, forget the license." I shoved my revolver under the bed then gave her a once-over. "Is that a new top?"

She looked down at it, then at me. "Sort of. I've only had it a month. Like it?"

"It looks like it fits okay."

"It's fun. And comfortable. Anyway, here we are. And I've just *got* to take a shower. Last one was last night, in that other room, nineteen."

"Yeah, you'd be pretty ripe by now." I got into bed, pulled the cover up to my chin, then removed the towel and tossed it onto the only chair in the room. Come what may, I wasn't going to spend another night hunkered down in a suit of armor.

She ran a zipper down the front of her top then hesitated before taking it off. "You're acting pretty cool there, Boy Scout."

"I've given up the fight. But I do have one little question for you."

"What's that?"

"What the hell are you doing up here?"

"Looking for Allie. I mean, helping you look for her. Really, I can help. I showed her picture to everyone in the casino tonight."

"So did I."

"I figured. I got a lot of repeats, but some of the people in there hadn't seen her picture yet so maybe they came in after you left. Jeri told me I should come up and help out."

"Did she say how?"

Piqued, she put her hands on her hips. "Which of us is more likely to spot Allie if she's wearing a disguise of some kind, you or me?"

"Who said anything about a disguise?"

"Who says she looks like she does in that picture? We don't know why she's here or what she's doing. Or if she even *was* here."

Good points all. Guess I was still tired. And distracted.

"Jeri sent you?" I said.

"Yeah. She said go—if I wanted to drive this far, that is."

I would have to have a talk with Jeri sometime soon, get this sorted out, but she hadn't sounded the least bit upset by what had happened the other night, which made me think that discussion was going to be pretty interesting.

I turned onto my side. "Hit the shower, kiddo. I'm done."

I heard a zipper go down, heard clothing rustle, footsteps went padding around the room, then I heard teeth being brushed, then the shower came on and the curtain rattled as she pulled it across the bar, and that's the last thing I heard.

By the time she came to bed, I was out cold. For all I know, she broad-jumped in from across the room.

*　*　*

Morning, of course, brought a whole new set of problems. First up was that the chair was six feet from the bed, my towel and all my clothes were on or around it, and my arms wouldn't reach— none of which would have been a problem except that Holiday-Sarah was awake and lying on her side, looking at me.

"Morning," she said.

I yawned. "Same to you."

She smiled. "Very cool. I like that."

I checked the bedside clock: 8:25 a.m. I propped myself up on my elbows. "Up and at 'em, girl. We're burning daylight."

She sat up, legs crossed. The blanket pooled around her waist, which created the next problem, as if I needed another one. It didn't help when she got out of bed and walked over to the chair, rummaged around for a moment, located her panties, stepped into them, and wiggled a little as she pulled them up.

She frowned at me, still in bed. "You said we were burning daylight."

"On second thought, why rush into things?"

"Why not? I thought you wanted to . . . oh." She smiled. "Well, you *know*, Mort . . . "

"How 'bout you get dressed and go next door, order me some coffee, black, no sugar. I'll be along in a minute or two."

"Got a bit of a morning issue there?"

"Coffee. Black."

"For the record, I didn't touch you or anything. And I wouldn't, either. We're okay here."

In nothing but panties she was a stunning sight—like Jeri and Kayla and my ex-wife, Dallas, two months ago—each in their own way. I was impressed by how much my life had changed once I shoved the IRS job and joined the human race. Private investigative work is so underrated.

"Not sure about the dress code this far north," I said. "But I'm pretty sure people around here wear more than that."

She smiled. "Hold your horses. I'm gettin' there." She pulled on her jeans, put on her top, shoes, fluffed her hair, and gave me one last look before opening the door. "Don't be long."

She went outside.

I got up, got dressed, got the hell out of there.

* * *

"Did you sleep with her, Mort?"

"Literally, yes. Figuratively, no."

I was at a table in the restaurant, sitting across from Sarah. She was studying the menu. I had the phone to my ear. It was twenty minutes before noon in Atlantic City.

Six seconds of silence went by while Jeri deciphered what I'd said. Then: "Well, okay, then. But, Mort . . . ?"

"Yeah?"

"I don't own you, you know."

Uh-oh. Here comes a curveball. I can't hit curveballs.

"No one really owns anyone," Jeri said, and she said it with such gentle understanding that I wondered if I was talking to Jeri or a passerby to whom she'd just handed the phone.

No one owns anyone. That sounded like philosophy—not part of my skill set.

"Right," I said.

"I mean it, Mort. I don't own you. I don't want to own you. I will *never* own you. I want to be with you as long as that works. So, if, you know, something were to happen with Sarah, then we'd have to figure out what that means."

"Nothing happened. Nothing that matters is *going* to happen. I've seen a lot of naked women in my time, in case you've already forgotten Kayla. I'm immune."

Holiday-Sarah looked up at me, then back at the menu.

"You are not immune," Jeri said. "Not to that."

"I'm not saying I mind the view. But it's like being in a candy store when you don't need a sugar rush."

Jeri laughed. Actually laughed. I'd known her less than two months, so I didn't know her like I would in another twenty years. Every time I thought I did, she would surprise me. I was trying my damnedest to keep this on the up and up, and she was laughing.

"So you slept with her," she said. "Literally."

"Yup. Snoring and drooling. Like that."

"So what was this? An update?"

"Update. Full disclosure. I didn't want to keep anything from you, you know, in case it was something you'd want to know."

"If the sleeping were to turn figurative, I'd want to know that. Otherwise, I have the feeling that when I get back you'll be ready to rock and roll."

"Christ, yes."

"Good. Me, too. I don't see a problem here."

"Jeri?"

"What?"

"You are some kind of amazing woman, woman."

"Hold that thought. I'll be back in Reno Sunday night at nine thirty, flight number 1168, Southwest."

"I thought you were going to watch your brother compete in the Pan American Judo Championships."

"I was. But you found part of a presidential candidate. I think that takes precedence. And you're famous again. Every time I see a television, there you are. We might want to get a handle on that. And I imagine Sarah's got you going a little, so I might be needed in Reno sooner than I'd thought."

"About that—"

"It's *okay*, Mort. You were snoring and drooling, right? It's not an attractive image."

"I don't know about me since I was asleep, but she sure was." Holiday's eyes flicked up at me, then back at the menu.

"Okay, then," Jeri said. "See what you can turn up in Gerlach about Allie. Try not to find more pieces of Reinhart, and meet me at the airport, day after tomorrow. I'll text you with that time and flight number."

"Nine thirty in the evening, flight 1168, Southwest. Got it."

"Mind like a teal strap. Gotta go. Elimination rounds start in an hour. Love you, Mort." Then she was gone.

"I sure was what?" Holiday asked as I folded the phone and set it on the table.

"Snoring and drooling in your sleep. Unattractively, too."

Her peal of laughter turned heads all over the room.

* * *

At the register I was about to buy Holiday another *Corti's* shirt, next size larger, but she said it wasn't necessary. We went outside and she opened the trunk of her car. She got out a duffel bag, pulled out a shirt, went into the room and changed. While she did that, I found my gun under the bed and stuffed it under the front seat of my Toyota. When Holiday came out she was wearing a yellow short-sleeve T-shirt with a front that read:

The biggest piece of pi is three

"Nerd," I said, after I finally got it, which took long enough that I knew she was going to laugh.

She didn't, though, at least not out loud, but she wrinkled her nose at me. "Actually we nerds prefer the term geek on Fridays. Sets us up for the weekend."

"Geek, then." In fact, neither nerd nor geek captured the essence of the shirt since it was pretty full.

We walked over to the Texaco station. Hank Waldo was disheveled, eyes bloodshot and rheumy. He looked as if he'd had a typical Waldo night. Terrific. I handed him a picture of Allie. "She might've been in that Mercedes SUV you told Deputy Roup about," I said, giving his memory a nudge.

He pulled out a pair of cheater glasses with enough grease on the lenses to lube a Volkswagen—perfect for ID purposes—and gave the photo a five-second look, shrugged, handed the picture back. "Coulda been her. Can't say for sure, though. Anyways, I'll keep an eye out."

"You said you saw that SUV two days ago. A woman was putting gas in it?" This was covering ground he'd already covered, but I thought it might be what Jeri would do since she was a bulldog.

"Yep," Waldo said. "Fairly tall, dark hair, thirty-five, coulda been forty, had a diamond ring on her finger big as an Easter egg."

That was new. Jeri would be proud. "Big diamond, huh? So she was probably rich."

"Didn't need no diamond to see that. That car of hers'd run a hundred twenty thousand bucks, tricked out like it was. And she was dressed rich. She had that look."

"What look?"

He squinted at me. "Rich. You oughta listen harder."

"Any other jewelry?"

He shrugged. "Not that I saw. Just that big-ass rock, must've set some poor sumbitch back forty thousand smackeroos—unless it was that fake zirconia stuff."

Smackeroos. Nice. I filed that away for future use.

"Was she wearing makeup?" Sarah asked.

"Coulda been. How would I know?"

Sarah lifted an eyebrow at me, then turned and looked up at the dark bulk of Granite Mountain to the north.

I said to Waldo, "Yesterday morning in the restaurant you said when they took off the night before, they went south."

"Yep." He pointed with a fingernail full of grit. "That way."

"Later that evening I was outside the casino when a Mercedes SUV came through town from the north, headed south. About three hours *after* the one you saw."

He looked at me through one eye. "One I saw went south. You might've seen a different one."

Maybe so, but the other morning he said he'd seen it going through both north and south in the last week or two, just passing through, so maybe he'd gotten things mixed up. I didn't think pushing him harder on that would get us anything useful. When Jeri came back from the East Coast, she might ask him something that would shake something else loose.

"Well, thanks," I said. "You've been a big help."

"No, I ain't." He turned and disappeared into a service bay.

"Okay, that was fun," Sarah said. "Now what?" She had her hands shoved into the back pockets of her jeans.

"I don't know. Ask around?"

"You don't know? Maybe I missed something. How long have you been a PI?"

"About as long as you've been a hooker."

"Oh, good. Jeri said this was gonna be pro bono, no charge. That's looking like a good thing."

We asked around. My nephew Gregory, for whom I'd worked for three days in July, had told me—warned me—that PI work was boring, that my expectations were unrealistic. A few days later I found his decapitated head on his desk so it turned out he was dead wrong, but that's a different story.

Turns out, he was right.

Sarah and I wore out shoe leather walking up and down the main street—Highway 447—showing Allie's photo around, asking folks if they'd seen her. No one had. Deputy Roup pulled to the side of the road in his cruiser and said hi, read the front of Sarah's shirt, grinned, told us he'd been keeping his eyes open, then took off.

Investigation-wise, however, the morning gave us nothing.

We ate lunch at the restaurant, then I drove us to Empire in my Toyota, five miles away. I hit sixty miles an hour to impress Sarah with the yodeling mirror. She told me gluing a rat to it would work, just let her know if I did because she wanted a YouTube video of me doing it, then we went into the convenience store.

I showed Allie's picture to a couple of clerks. A thin, stoop-shouldered kid with long red hair and freckles, nineteen years old, said, "Yeah, I saw her. She was pretty hot." He took a half-step back at the look I gave him and said, "Uh, you know, kinda."

"When?" Sarah asked. "When was that?" Her look was eager, intense.

"Um, like day before yesterday, I think. Must've been. I was working the evening shift and she came in, got a Diet Coke and like a Cliff Bar or something."

"Sure it was her?" I asked.

"Her hair was darker, dark brown, not like in that picture, but she was really pretty like that. I think it was her."

"Was she with anyone?"

"Some lady. I didn't notice her all that much."

He would've noticed the good-looking girl about his own age, not the ancient broad pushing forty—assuming Roup's and Waldo's descriptions were in the ballpark. Looking back twenty-some years, I couldn't blame the kid.

"Did you see which way they went when they left?"

"South. They went south."

"You sure?"

He shrugged. "I was by the front window when they left." Then he added, diffidently, "I watched 'cause she was really pretty."

"Remember what time it was?"

"We close at ten. It was at least an hour before that. More. Probably between eight fifteen and eight thirty."

Which matched the time Allie had phoned from Gerlach. And now we had another sighting of them going south, which made my sighting of that SUV coming in from the north even more iffy. But then, I knew what I'd seen.

"What's your name, son?" I asked.

"Brian. Brian Jordan."

"If you see her again, Brian, there's a hundred dollars in it for you. Two hundred if you get a license number. Keep your eyes peeled for a green Mercedes SUV."

"Sure thing." He wrote down my cell number.

As Sarah and I went outside, my phone rang. It was Jeri.

"Hi, darling," I said.

A moment of silence. "Darling? Where's Mort? If he's there, put him on."

"Very funny, kiddo. What's up?" I looked around. My Toyota was the only car in front of the store; nothing was moving on the highway. Empty damn place.

"Just thought I'd tell you I made it through the elimination round. I got a total of five hundred ten pounds up on the three lifts, no sweat."

"Bet I could do that with a fork lift," I told her.

"They don't let us use those."

"Then you're probably in violation of a bunch of OSHA regulations. Give me a call if I need to wire bail money."

"I'm gonna go wander around the casinos this afternoon, do the tourist thing, rest up. Final competition is tomorrow. Is Sarah still there with you?"

"Yep."

"You two gonna stay the night in Gerlach again?"

"It's looking that way."

"Not likely to get carried away, are you? I mean, figuratively speaking."

"Not gonna happen, babe."

"Okay, then. I'm going to catch a cab. Call you later, okay?"

"I'll be here."

A couple of mushy "love yous" and we ended the call.

"How is she?" Sarah asked.

"Maybe a little worried. Hard to tell since she didn't sound at all worried." I squeezed into the car.

Sarah got in on the other side. "Next time she calls, I'll talk to her, make certain she knows nothing's going to happen between you and me."

"Think that's a good idea? Having that discussion?"

She looked at me for a moment. "Okay, you're a little bit out there with all of this, so you probably ought to know it went something like this—yesterday in the Green Room you gave me the phone and told me to talk to her. Remember that?"

"Vaguely."

"After a while she wanted to know how we met, and I told her how I'd been dressing up like a hooker to try to find Allie—which, by the way, she said wasn't likely to work—then we kept talking and I ended up telling her I like it when guys look at me in the kind of clothes I've been wearing. She said it sounded like I had a little bit of exhibitionist in me and that she understood."

"She did, huh? She used the word you don't like and said she understood?"

"Uh-huh."

"Was her understanding in an intellectual or personal sense?"

"She didn't say, but I have the impression it was more personal than intellectual, like she really got it, like maybe she would like to vamp out once in a while, have guys check her out. I think she was a little envious, that I was able to go out and do that."

Made sense, sort of. I could see Jeri doing that, or wishing she could but reining the impulse in. She was all business the day we met. She'd given off a pit bull vibe. Holiday might be giving her a vicarious thrill, something she couldn't do herself, at least on anything like a regular, intentional basis. But there were hints. Early August in Myrtle Beach we were caught in a drenching downpour from Tropical Storm Beryl. Jeri's blouse and bra went see-through. Very. She didn't try to hide herself. She told me not to look if it bothered me. I told her it didn't bother me in the least and she said, "So we're all okay here?" Or words to that effect. Casual. No big deal. No further discussion. Given that, I could imagine her in a low-cut dress, guys checking her out, as long as that's all it was. I was going to have to dump that and everything that had happened in the past two days into the magic vat in my skull that ferments information into useful knowledge and maybe learn something. Maybe. Sometimes that doesn't work.

"So then," Sarah said, "I told her about you wearing clothes to bed and reciting the Boy Scout oath—"

"Which I don't remember doing."

"—then you grabbed the phone, which was unforgivably rude, and when I finally got it back she said if I liked not wearing a lot of clothes around you, you would enjoy it and it wouldn't bother her. That was that girl talk you said sounded underhanded—which it sort of was. Earlier, before you came back, I'd told her I like, you know, being looked at, nothing more than that, and I mean *nothing* more. She laughed and said it would get your engine goin' or revved up and it was okay with her as long as it didn't get out of hand."

"She said that? And laughed?"

"Uh-huh."

"My *engine*?"

"That's what she called it."

"I'm gonna have to have a long talk with that woman."

Sarah shrugged. "Whatever. I'm just telling you what she said. And for the record I really like being able to wear whatever I want when I'm around you."

"Or not wear."

"Well, yeah, that's kind of the point. And . . ."

"And? Don't tell me there's more."

"And not having to worry about it getting out of control. She said you're like that, trustworthy as a Buddhist monk, something of a super Boy Scout."

"Aw, shit, no. A Boy Scout maybe, but not a monk."

"Anyway, I like the way things have been the last two days. I wouldn't have told you any of this except you're starting to get a little weird."

"*Me* weird?"

"Uh-huh. I'm okay with it. Turns out Jeri is, too. You're the one who's getting his knickers in a twist."

"Knickers?"

"That's British. It's like getting your panties in a wad, but—"

"—I don't wear panties, kiddo."

"Which I think is a good thing, just so you know. I prefer guys who are guys."

Something still didn't feel right, like there was a piece of this puzzle I still wasn't getting. And I was going to have to quash that monk thing. Where'd Jeri get that? But women are like that—they toy with us because they're more subtle and because they can.

"How long have you known Jeri?" I asked.

"Known her? I've never met her."

Huh. In theory I was a PI, but sometimes theory and practice reside on opposite ends of the universe. Something was going on, something in the background, and I didn't know what it was.

I looked at Sarah and she looked back at me.

"What?" she said.

"There's something you're not telling me."

She pooched her lips out in what looked like indignation. The indignation could've been real, but didn't feel like it. "About what?" she asked.

"You. Jeri."

"Hey, we're television buddies, that's all."

"Television buddies?"

"She saw me on TV yesterday and today—we're all over the place, Mort—and I saw her on TV back when you two killed those two crazy women last month. So she knows what I look like and I know what she looks like, and that's how we know each other."

"Television buddies."

"Yup."

Sonofabitch. I could feel something slippery puttering around in the shadows, but it was pure gossamer. I could've been wrong, since that's my MO when it comes to anything female. But I don't even know myself, much less anyone else on the planet, much less my fiancée who I haven't known two months. How the hell would I know if she'd like to put on one of Holiday's tops—not Sarah's—then go out and make guys sit up and take notice? If so, she damn sure wouldn't be the first.

I went back inside the convenience store and bought a map of Washoe County and a map of the western United States.

"What'd you get?" Sarah asked when I came out and crammed myself in behind the wheel.

I handed her the maps.

"What're these for?"

I fired up the engine. "So we don't get lost. Sometimes when you don't know where the road's going, you get lost."

* * *

I headed back to Gerlach, five miles away. Holiday-Sarah was silent beside me. As we passed the Texaco station, she said, "Was that like a metaphor or a simile or whatever?"

"What?"

"That road thing."

"I don't know. We don't use metaphors in the IRS, kiddo. We use handcuffs and prison time."

She didn't say anything to that. I pulled in at the casino and said, "Let's take your car." I got out.

She hopped out on the other side. "Where're we goin'?"

"North."

I walked over to her car and she trailed along. "North where?"

"Whatever's up there. I don't know, some little towns, I guess. Gimme your keys. I'll drive, you navigate."

She handed me her keys, and I got behind the wheel. She got in as I glanced at the fuel gauge—three-quarters full, good enough. I backed out and drove through town, which took forty seconds, then we went past a few trailers sitting on hardscrabble desert dirt and into the kind of emptiness for which Nevada is world famous.

Maybe this Holiday thing was a test.

But no. Jeri wouldn't do that. Didn't think so anyway.

I don't own you, Mort.

Nor did I own her, didn't want to. She was free to do whatever she wanted. Making demands of someone is like saying you own them—a part of them anyway. Maybe this was exactly what Jeri said it was. Not a test, just the freedom to be who I was—whatever that was, and if something were to happen between Holiday-Sarah and me, Jeri and I would figure out what that meant, just like she'd said. Which wasn't going to be necessary.

"If I'm navigating, where am I navigating to?" Sarah asked, interrupting the nonsense spinning webs in my head.

"What's up north of here?"

A map rustled. "There's Cedarville and Alturas in California. Lakeview in Oregon. Cedarville and Alturas are both kinda far, and there isn't much else up that way unless you go quite a bit farther."

"How far to Alturas?"

She studied the map for a while. "About a hundred miles."

"How far from there to Lakeview?"

"Another forty, give or take. Why?"

"I'm sure I saw a dark Mercedes SUV coming in from the north two nights ago, two or three hours after people said they saw it leaving Gerlach, headed south."

She studied the map. "If it went south from Gerlach, it couldn't have come in from the north later. Not without going back through Gerlach. Not in only two or three hours."

"That's the working theory."

She looked up. "Yeah? You have a theory?"

"Not even a ghost of one."

"Great. Maybe it wasn't the same SUV."

"Which is what Waldo said."

She frowned. "So what're we doing?"

"Burning gas. Looking around. Basic investigative technique."

"Sounds basic all right."

"You have *no* idea."

We drove in silence for a while. The road was almost empty. Every fifteen or twenty minutes a vehicle of some kind would pass by, going in the opposite direction. Finally Sarah said, "I never took a dime from any of those guys, Mort."

"Huh? What guys?"

"All those guys who thought I was a hooker."

"I didn't think you did."

"I never let anyone buy me more than one drink, either. Most of the time I didn't take more than a couple of sips. What I did was, I let them look at me and I asked about Candy."

"Candy?"

"That's what Allie called herself when she was hooking. She told me she never used her real name. She called herself Candy, so that's who I asked about." She was quiet for a minute, then,

"She said she chose that name for a reason. She had this thing she would do. She would tell the guys her name was Candy, then, after a while, she would say, 'Would you like some Candy?' She said it was a way to proposition guys without getting caught. She even kept a few Snickers bars in her purse just in case. If anyone tried to bust her she'd get out a couple of bars and ask what the hell was illegal about offering someone some candy. No one could say she was soliciting, but it got the conversation headed that way."

"Smart."

"In a way. But not really. It was prostitution, selling herself. How smart is that?"

Other than agreeing, I had no answer to that.

"You were something else, though," she said.

"How so?"

"You wouldn't buy me a drink. Gave me that story about your stupid howling mirror. Pretty much chased me away, actually."

"That's the IRS in me. Antisocial stuff gets ingrained. Useful on the job, but it's hard to turn off."

She laughed. "Pissed me off. But later, when I thought about it, it was kind of refreshing. Anyway, it told me you wouldn't know anything about Allie . . . Candy."

"Uh-huh."

"So here we are, headed for Alturas."

"Or farther. I want to see if anyone up this way has seen a Mercedes SUV lately. I think Gerlach's about played out."

Sarah thought about that. "Why would Allie be up this way at all? I mean, what on earth for? This doesn't feel right. It's like we're chasing a really wild goose here."

"Might be. But Allie said she was phoning from Gerlach and no one in Gerlach saw her outside the car. She didn't go into the casino or the motel, so she and the woman were passing through. And they were headed south, which means they came in from the north. So, passing through from where?"

That stopped her.

Finally, she sighed. "Yeah. I can't explain that. Anyway, you're the investigator."

"That's right," I said, even though she was wrong. Jeri was the investigator. I was a half-assed trainee and it was taking a lot of getting used to. I was back to square one in life, as if I'd come right out of high school. With the IRS I knew what I was doing. I was raking in the dough so politicians could pork-barrel it and get re-elected, waste it, maybe send it to Iran so Ayatollahs could build nukes. Here, cruising through the desert, I was just following a thread. Less than a thread. The only part of this PI thing that was still on track was Sarah beside me, filling out her nerd shirt.

"Warm out here," she said. "Indian summer. We could put the top down. I could get some sun."

I pulled to the side of the road, which wasn't necessary since there wasn't anything on the road for miles ahead and behind. We were forty miles north of Gerlach in the middle of the Smoke Creek Desert. We snugged the top into its well, then kept going.

CHAPTER EIGHT

WE PASSED THROUGH Eagleville. At sixty miles an hour it would have taken twenty seconds, but signs suggested I knock it down to twenty-five. Next up was Cedarville, which was bigger. Stops at Chevron and Arco stations didn't produce a single Mercedes SUV sighting.

We rolled into Alturas at two twenty that afternoon. Three minutes later, at the first gas station we came to, I caught a whiff of that Mercedes. A woman in her fifties said she'd seen it about four days ago when a woman stopped for gas in a green Mercedes SUV.

"How old was the woman?"

"Thirties. Coulda been forty I guess. I didn't ask."

Sounded familiar. "Was anyone with her?"

"Like who?" She read the pi joke on Holiday's shirt, shook her head a little, then looked back at me.

"Like anyone."

"I didn't see anyone, but it was night so there coulda been."

"She got gas, huh?"

She smiled. "That's pretty much what they do in this place. I had to close the bowling alley in the service bay."

Sharp. Caustic, too.

"Which way did she go when she left?"

"Up north, hon."

I like it when ladies call me "hon"—gives me a warm, fuzzy feeling, but the north thing didn't give us anything useful since there was a big junction a few miles north. From there, cars could keep going north or head south to Gerlach.

"Anything else?" I asked.

"Yeah. I could use a car like that Mercedes. Not the payments though."

"You and me both."

I left her with my number, told her to call if she saw the SUV again, said it was worth a hundred dollars. If she got the license it was worth two hundred. My standard deal.

Back on the road, we headed north to Lakeview, Oregon.

"Got a decent maybe back there," I said.

"Uh-huh. Be even better if we knew what it meant."

* * *

We got no hits at gas stations in Lakeview. I gave that some thought and decided it made sense. Alturas was less than fifty miles away. There wouldn't be any reason to gas up at both places.

"How about Bend?" I said. "We could go check out the FedEx place where Reinhart's hand was shipped."

"What does that have to do with Allie?"

"Nothing, except it's likely that SUV was somewhere up here, *and* we're already this far north, *and* that package was sent to me. When Jeri gets back, she'll probably want to come up and have a look at the place, maybe bump into a few FBI guys while she's at it. I'd like to beat her to it."

"Bumping into FBI guys?"

"It's fun, trust me."

"Bend isn't all that close, Mort. It's nearly two hundred miles from here."

"One eighty-eight, according to a sign just before we got to Lakeview."

"One eighty-eight rounds up to two hundred."

"Fuckin' engineers."

She smiled. "If we go, we'll probably have to stay the night. It'd be a long drive back to Gerlach if we didn't."

"Uh-huh."

"Either way, we'll have to find a motel."

"Uh-huh."

"Well, okay, then. You're fun to travel with, and it's still a nice day for a drive."

"If you insist, but you should know I haven't had my arm twisted like that in a long time."

She rolled her eyes. "You gonna drive or just talk?"

*　*　*

The road to Bend would've been faster if we hadn't gotten behind one eighteen-wheeler after another, and a few RVs whose owners didn't know the summer tourist season was over. When I retire I'm going to buy a beat-up RV and tour the country at forty-five miles an hour, too. It looks like fun, wallowing along in a gas guzzler. You can see so much more that way, and if you happen to run off the road while rubbernecking, the damage would be minimal—pocket change—unless you're near the Grand Canyon at the time, in which case the damage wouldn't even be your problem.

Twenty minutes out of Lakeview we hit alkali flats. Sarah said, "I'm getting way behind in my classes, so I'm gonna disappear for a while, if that's okay."

"Sure is dark in the trunk, but have at it."

She stared at me. "Disappear *figuratively*, Mort."

"Far be it from me to toss gravel in the gears of science. Just keep down the noise so I can sleep."

"Well, hell. You're no fun. I usually read textbooks aloud while I'm snapping gum."

She hauled out a thick textbook—*Fundamentals of Structural Dynamics*, which looked like a real hoot—and went into heavy-duty college student mode, total concentration, writing in a notebook, the pages of which fluttered in the breeze.

Half an hour into it she said, without looking up, "This math is so sucky. I hate eigenvectors and eigenvalue problems."

"We used those in the IRS. Let me know if you need help."

She laughed, then fell silent again. So here I was, out in the middle of nowhere working two cases—Allie and Reinhart—neither of which was going to earn Jeri and me a dime. Someone had sent me Reinhart's hand. I wanted to know who did it and why. I was on someone's radar, which was more than a little spooky. And, trying to narrow things down, that someone was hidden in at least a quarter of the adult population of the United States, so the winnowing process wasn't going to be easy.

After another hour of hard study, Sarah put the book away and leaned back with her eyes closed, took in the autumn sun with a sigh. She looked like a supermodel and was into math that I would never come close to understanding. If I weren't so good at finding body parts of famous missing people, I would've been intimidated.

We reached the outskirts of Bend at 6:35. I pulled off Highway 97 and we put the Audi's top back up. One of us put on a new shirt in about five seconds, one with an equation on it that said something so cryptic about the number pi that I couldn't decipher it. More intimidation. A quick check with the cell phone told us the FedEx shipping center was on Jamison Street at the northern edge of Bend. We went through the middle of town then circled around a bunch of unfamiliar streets for a few minutes until we found Jamison Street. A sign on the door of the FedEx place told us it had closed at five thirty and would open again at eight a.m. Lights were on in the back of the building, but the front door was closed, office dark. Reinhart's case would have to wait till morning.

"At least we know where it is," Sarah said. "Now what?"

"What d'you think?"

"How 'bout we find a motel?"

"If this place has one."

She slugged my arm. "I've seen six of 'em so far, jerk."

"Six? You counted them?"

She smiled. "Yeah. Good thing I didn't run out of fingers."

"Fingers. That's geeky. See anything you liked?"

"The Slumberland looked good. Quiet. And there was a pizza place nearby."

"Which way?"

"Back south. Off to the right on the main drag, but the rooms look like they're facing a side street so it oughta be quiet."

"Maybe we can get adjoining rooms," I said to see how she'd react to what I thought was the best idea I'd had in a month.

"Coward."

Which answered that. At least she didn't stick out her tongue or call me a monk.

Five minutes later we reached the Slumberland. In the office she muscled me to one side and said to the lady behind the counter, "We need a room," then shot me a lethal "shut up" look. Great. Ten minutes later and eighty-eight dollars poorer, I opened the door to unit twenty-six on the second floor and we went in. Yep, two queen-size beds, like the lady said who'd handed Sarah the keys.

Sarah—or more likely Holiday—stared at the arrangement for a few seconds.

"Which bed do you want?" I asked.

She bounced on one of them then stood up. "Doesn't matter. We'll figure it out later. I'm starving. Let's go get us a pizza."

Right then, my cell phone rang.

* * *

"I lost twenty dollars at the Tropicana, Mort," Jeri said. "At a blackjack table."

"You oughta arm wrestle drunks. It pays better."

"Yeah, right. So, where are you now?"

"Bend. Oregon."

"Bend? What're you doing way up there?"

"About to get a pizza, looks like."

"That's a hell of a long way to go for pizza."

"And, tomorrow, we're going to check out that FedEx place where Reinhart's hand was shipped."

"We? Sarah's with you?"

"Yep."

"Is she there now?"

"Last I checked, but she's fast."

"Great. Can I talk to her?"

"Sure thing. Here she is." I gave Sarah the phone. It seemed as if things went better if I wasn't around to hear half the conversation, so I went outside and stood on the balcony overlooking the parking lot. I thought it would be terrific if a green Mercedes SUV rolled in right then with Allie and a woman in it, but no such luck. The only thing that came in during the six or eight minutes Sarah was talking with Jeri was a Subaru Outback. A guy in his sixties and a woman about the same age got out and went into a room somewhere on the first floor. But it wasn't a bad evening to hang out on a second-floor balcony while the girl I was going to spend the night with chatted with my purported fiancée.

Behind me, the door opened. Sarah gave me the phone. "Jeri wants to talk to you."

"How're you doin', sweetheart?" I said. Sarah went back in the room and shut the door.

"It's late. I'm already in bed. I just thought I'd phone before I conked out."

"Big day tomorrow."

"Uh-huh. I'm ready for it. And . . . Mort?"

"Yeah?"

"I had another talk with Sarah. I know you've got that one room, but she said there's no way anything would happen with you. She just, you know, likes it when you, uh . . . notice her."

"So I've noticed."

"And I know you like to look. I mean, you're a guy. It's what guys do."

"Yup. We're pigs. It's a tremendous defect, like not tightening lug nuts enough or keeping air filters clean."

"No, it's not. Girls look at guys, too. That's what *Thunder Down Under* is all about, in case that got by you. I mean, *I* like to look."

"You do?"

"Oh, for heaven's sake. Yes. And . . ."

"And?"

"And if you *didn't* like looking at women—I mean, Sarah, or girls in general—then I'd think you didn't like looking at me either, and I would hate that."

"I *love* the way you look, Jeri. And I think this one-room thing here in Bend was a lousy idea—not mine, by the way—so as soon as we end this call I'm going to go get another room."

"*No!* I mean, no, don't do that. Please don't."

"I don't want you to worry, Jeri."

"I'm *not* worried. This is getting tangled up, but it shouldn't. It's not that difficult. It's just that I trust you—completely. And I trust Sarah, too. She and I had a good long talk. So I don't want you to get another room because I don't want you to think *I* think it's necessary. It's *not*."

"Jeri—"

"Did she tell you about the bicycle thing in San Francisco? She didn't, did she? I told her I would tell you later, when I get back, but now it looks like I'd better—"

My head spun. "Bicycle thing? What's that?"

"I told her not to say anything, but now I've got to tell you. I was on a case in San Francisco earlier this year when they had this nude bicycle thing going on around the Embarcadero. I was on a sidewalk when hundreds of people came by on bicycles, a lot of them not wearing anything at all. Men and women. Almost all the women were topless. A lot of them were in body paint and nothing else, and some were completely naked, no body paint or anything. Everyone was having a lot of fun, and, well . . . maybe it's weird but I wanted to join in. I wanted to be riding with them."

What to say to that?

"Mort?"

"I'm here. I'm listening."

"When they came by, I suddenly felt like crying. It was so real, all those naked people. So *real*. They could do that and I couldn't. People were on the sidewalk with me, watching. It's called the World Naked Bike Ride. It's an organized thing, sort of official.

Their slogan is, "As Bare As You Dare." It's supposed to be a protest, but I don't think it is, really. It's just people who decided it would be fun to be naked in public for a while, so they have to have a First Amendment reason to do it. There's a bike ride in Los Angeles, too, and Seattle, Houston, Melbourne, Australia—all over. Even London and Madrid. Like seventy cities all over the place, thousands of people. *Hundreds* of thousands of people having fun being free. In Portland last year there were over ten thousand riders. Ten *thousand*, Mort. I want to do it with Sarah in San Francisco. I'm *going* to. I want to be that totally free at least once in my life. Sarah said she'll do it with me, so that's settled—we're going to do it next year. I might wear a *cache-sexe*, but maybe not. I'll have to think about it. I'm pretty sure Sarah won't."

My mind whirled. These were *television* buddies?

"What's a *cache-sexe*?" I asked.

"Look it up. You made me look up *boffing*, although I had the gist. Anyway, I understand Sarah and how she feels. That's why I *really* don't want you to get another room. I'm just doing a lousy job of telling you it's okay, because it *is*."

"So . . . let me see if I've finally got this straight. What you're telling me, in your roundabout, rambling, infuriatingly erratic way, is that it's okay if Sarah's not always entirely dressed around me."

"Oh, jeez, you are *such* a shithead."

"Now that's a term of endearment I understand."

"Well, it is. So anyway, please don't get another room. I would feel awful if you felt like you had to."

"If you insist."

"I do." She was silent for a moment, then, "I'm going to do that bicycle ride, Mort. At least topless, but maybe more, I don't know yet, but I'm going to do it."

"Okay."

"Mean it?"

"I'll watch from the sidelines. I'll take pictures for our old age album. We can laugh at ourselves when we're eighty. Well, at you anyway, although I'm in a group photo with a bunch of IRS agents, so that one's a scream. I'll even help apply body paint to critical areas if that's what you decide to do."

"I'd like all that. Especially the pictures."

"Okay, then. Count me in. When is this supposed to happen?"

"Not for a while. Next March. They meet somewhere around the Ferry Building, down by the bay."

"March? That sounds cold."

"Not in San Francisco. June and July can be cold. Weather is strange there. Mark Twain wrote about it."

"You've already researched this bicycle thing."

"I looked into it in April, before you and I met, then pretty much forgot about it because I didn't think I would be able to go through with it—so it's amazing that you found Sarah, or she found you, whatever. She's perfect for me. I mean, so we can do that bike ride together. And, you know, just *talk* about stuff. Really, Mort, she and I are becoming friends, almost like I've known her for years."

The things I'd never suspected. Each person on the planet is an entire universe of gnarled complexity.

"Mort?"

"Yup."

"You don't think I'm too weird, do you?"

"Not too. Just about right, actually."

"But weird?"

"Everyone's weird, Jeri. Except me, of course. I'm a freakin' pillar of normalcy. But for what it's worth, here's what I think—for every person out there riding a bike in the buff, a thousand other people wish they could but are afraid to pull that trigger."

Softly, she said, "I sure do love you, big guy."

"I love you, too. And the world's gonna go nuts when they see you topless on that bicycle."

She laughed. "Thanks. Hearing you say it makes it sound even more wonderful and fun. Well, I better get to sleep. And, Mort?"

"Yeah?"

"I'm glad I told you. I'm glad you understand."

I didn't know how everything got turned around like that. I was worried *she* wouldn't understand. Women.

"Good night, Jeri. Go get 'em tomorrow."

"I will. Night, Mort. Enjoy, you know . . . the scenery."

I went back inside the room. Sarah looked up from a textbook. "How is she?"

"Naked bicycle riding? Yowzer."

"She told you about that? Why? I thought she was gonna wait until she saw you again."

"She had to because I'm a shithead."

"That sounds right."

"I don't know how you two managed to exchange so much information. I wasn't gone more than half an hour when I left you to talk to her in the bar yesterday."

She chewed on her lower lip.

I said, "Television buddies. There's more to *that* story, isn't there?"

"Little bit. She gave me her cell number. When you left I called her back, and we talked for over two hours, probably closer to three. I feel like I know her pretty well by now."

"So you've progressed to telephone buddies. Next up will be bicycle buddies."

She grinned. "Guess so."

"Naked bike rides. What else came up?"

"Just . . . stuff."

"Sounds like I don't want to know. And what the hell's a *cache-sexe*?"

"Look it up."

"Déjà vu. So how about that pizza, since your communication skills are sucky right now?"

"Finally. I'm starved. Hey, you gonna ride naked, too? You should."

"I'm more a sidelines kinda guy. But I'm a terrific watcher. I'll be the guy with the leer and the camera."

"There'll be a million cameras out there. We'll end up on the Internet, guaranteed. But maybe by March we'll get you loosened up enough to get you on a bike, too."

"Yeah, good luck with that. It would take a platoon of Marines to get me out there naked. They'd have to pedal for me, too."

"She said you're kinda tight. Thinks it's your IRS training, like it gave you a suit-of-armor brain."

"Suit of armor . . . *me*? I don't—"

"Yeah, you do." She grabbed my arm, hauled me toward the door. "Let's go before I pass out. What kind of pizza do you like?"

"Anything with meat and cheese on it without anchovies. What the hell *else* did you two wenches talk about?"

"Wenches. I like that. I'll let her know."

* * *

The place was called Pizazz Pizza of all things, but the pie was first-rate so we left full and happy. Several flat-screen TVs were on in the place. CNN ran a story that showed Reinhart's wife in front of a half-dozen microphones. The sound was turned off so I didn't know what she was saying, but it was probably an appeal of some kind to the psycho who'd hacked off her hubby's hand. She must want the rest of Harry back, hopefully in one piece so they could keep on with that presidential campaign thingamabob that might put her in the White House with him.

Her name was Julia and she was twenty-six years younger than Reinhart. He'd picked himself up a trophy wife. She was a good-looking woman, would've made a Jackie Kennedy kind of First Lady, but that wasn't likely to happen now that it was likely Harry was dead—or at least had lost the ability to shake, which had been his shtick. Actually, it was never likely either of them would have made it to the White House, Reinhart being a dishonest, conniving son of a bitch with hands deep in taxpayers' pockets, but since he lost that one hand at least he wouldn't be grabbing double fistfuls.

Night had come while we were eating. A block down the street we found a Walgreens where I bought a shirt, underwear, and socks, since I'd forgotten all that in Jeri's house—our house—when I'd left Reno, and things were starting to get unfresh.

"How're you fixed for clothes?" I asked Sarah.

"Okay. My shirts and pants are okay, and . . . I've got one more pair of like panties left."

I should have paid more attention to the way she said it, the valley-girl *like*, the nuance, the slight hesitation, but things like that usually go right over my head.

Before we left the store she said, "I've got to study some more. Couple of hours at least. If you're gonna be bored, you ought to buy a book or something, like some crosswords or Sudokus."

"Sudoku? I'd put a bullet through my head first."

"And you've got a gun, which is scary. So buy a novel. I can't study with the TV blaring."

I rummaged the shelves, came up with a John Lescroart novel, *A Plague of Secrets*. I was set. I showed Sarah the title. "Might be something in here about you and Jeri."

"Might, yeah." The way she said it, so matter-of-fact, had me worried all over again.

*   *   *

"Shower first," she said, stripping down to panties as soon as we got in the room.

But Jeri had me trained, so I didn't feel too guilty when I got a good look at her.

Holiday turned at the doorway to the bathroom. For an instant I saw her and Jeri riding bicycles like that, side by side. According to Jeri, even panties were optional. Either way, they would cause a riot.

"We could save water," Holiday said.

"How's that?"

"Showering together, of course."

"Hey, yeah—speaking of things that aren't going to happen."

She looked at me for a moment. "Your loss." She disappeared. Seconds later water started drumming. I sat on a chair and opened my book. I believe it's a sign of maturity that I got to page eight and was actually following the story by the time she came out rubbing her hair with a towel.

"Your turn," she said. "Coward."

I set the novel down. Vapor issued from the bathroom. I looked inside. The mirror was fogged over. I went in and started to shut the door when Holiday stuck her head inside. "You're gonna shower with your clothes on? How interesting. Mind if I watch?"

"If I want to shower fully dressed, I will. And, no, you can't." I pushed her head out and eased the door shut on girlish laughter.

In recent months, showering had become an iffy undertaking. Not long ago—post IRS—I was showering when a gorgeous dance instructor named Kayla popped in with me and things got sudsy and almost got out of hand. Many people—none of them prudes—would say things got out of hand because nothing got out of hand. Now I was ready to repel any and all boarders should it become necessary, which it didn't, so I took a leisurely shower with the bathroom door locked and got clean.

I came out in pants and a shirt. Holiday was at the table in jeans and that T-shirt with the cryptic equation on it, feet bare, nose in a textbook, an industrial-size calculator nearby, notebook, pens, and a nerdish look of concentration on her face. I didn't want to sit at the table and disturb her, so I set up pillows and stretched out on a bed, turned on a bedside light, and went back to my novel.

Two hours later I was on page ninety-one and she hadn't gotten up, hadn't produced a sound other than rustles of turning pages and little sighs of frustration or delight from time to time, all of which deeply impressed me and gave me new insights into this girl.

All that sitting around finally got to me. The drive to Bend had been a long one. I felt stiff. I wanted to get out, move around, walk somewhere, so I got up, put on shoes, and headed for the door.

"Goin' out," I said.

"See you," she said, an automatic response almost unrelated to my leaving.

That was how she would be in a library. Focused, able to shut out distractions. Almost a 4.0 student. A one-in-a-million girl with that brain and that body. A living reminder to the rest of the world that life isn't fair, that luck plays a part, that God throws darts and chuckles at the results.

I walked a mile and a half down the main drag, came back on the other side of the street, and . . . there was a FedEx drop box at a temporary parking spot at the curb, a white steel box with the distinctive FedEx purple and orange lettering on it.

I stopped and stared at it.

Sonofagun.

If I was going to ship a dishonest politician's hand to Mortimer Angel, I would stuff it in a box just like that. I might come walking down the sidewalk, whip the collection box open using gloves, drop the package in, keep on going. Two seconds, max. And I would do it at midnight. When a guy is a presidential candidate, all kinds of FBI scrutiny would rain down on the place from which his senatorial body part was shipped. That scrutiny might not zero in as successfully on a box like this as it would at the shipping facility on Jamison Street.

I checked the box under the streetlight. Pickup was at 7:00 a.m., 1:00 p.m., and 7:00 p.m. I read the instructions. For payment, a FedEx account was needed, or a major credit card number on the shipping label. Good to know.

I'd been gone for over an hour by the time I got back. Sarah looked as if she hadn't moved an inch, except that she was punching numbers into her calculator.

I sat on the other chair at the table and read my novel, best one I'd read all year. Sarah looked at the calculator, wrote down some numbers, then punched a few more buttons. I would never, ever trust a hooker again, no matter how beautiful. The girl might be a nuclear physicist out on the town, letting her hair down. Her IQ might be thirty points higher than mine. I'd thought hookers were fun, if you didn't take them too seriously. Sarah might think johns were fun, if she didn't take them too seriously, which she probably wouldn't find hard to do.

She called it quits a few minutes before midnight. Tossed her pen on the table and stood up, stretched her back and said, "Holy crud, it's late."

"Yup. I haven't seen anyone concentrate like that since Einstein said, 'Well, Martha, it's either MC-squared or MC-cubed and I can't figure out which one. Maybe booze will help.'"

"He never said anything like that." Sarah took off her T-shirt and tossed it in my lap.

"Sure he did. Guy got confused like all the rest of us."

"Are you confused?" She rubbed her breasts for a moment, a job I would've enjoyed, but I am a rock, I am an island, then she went into the bathroom and closed the door.

"I get that way," I called out.

"Shouldn't." Her voice came back muffled. "I thought we had this pretty much settled."

"I'm not confused about this room-sharing thing." I held up the shirt she'd tossed in my lap. "It's this shirt with this god-awful equation on it, the one with pi on it."

$$e^{i\pi}+1=0$$

"E raised to the i pi power plus one equals zero."

I looked at it. "That's the one."

"Euler figured it out. Leonhard Euler, like two hundred fifty years ago. Five of the most famous numbers in all of mathematics, all in one amazing equation."

"E is a number?"

"That's the base of natural logarithms."

"I is a number?"

"Square root of negative one."

"Is that how they talk on the planet you're from?"

She came out in a black thong and set neatly folded jeans on a chair a few feet from me, then got into bed. So that was the "like" panties she'd mentioned earlier.

"Question," I said.

"Shoot."

"Are thongs classified as underwear or accessories, since they apparently cover fewer than three square inches?"

"I don't know. You should Google it." She wiggled a little and set her thong on the night table beside her. "Also, you should turn out the light and get some sleep. It's late."

I'm reasonably good at following instructions if they're simple enough, so I turned out the light, got mostly undressed, climbed into the other bed, fluffed up a pillow, and went right to sleep.

Almost.

"Mort?"

"Yup?"

"When Jeri and I were talking, figuring things out, she said you were in bed three different nights with a really pretty girl, Kayla, showered with her once, and never got laid. Is that true?"

Sonofabitch. "It might be. And thanks for reminding me."

"Were you ever a Boy Scout? You know, the salute, making fire by rubbing sticks together, the oath and everything?"

"No!" I'd been a *Cub* Scout for two years, but so what? And what business was it of hers?

"I just wondered," she said. "Anyway, good night."

And *that's* why it took me an hour to get to sleep.

CHAPTER NINE

WE GOT TO the FedEx shipping center on Jamison Street at nine twenty the next morning. It wasn't a big facility because Bend isn't a big place, but it had half a dozen employees—a girl up front and the rest of the crew out back sorting boxes into bins, loading them into vans backed up to a loading dock, getting ready to head out and deliver presents.

Sarah and I went in. She was in her first pi T-shirt, the yellow one. The girl behind the counter, late twenties, looked first at Sarah, then at me, at which time her face lost most of its color.

"I-I shouldn't talk to you," she said, looking around to see who might be watching us.

"Oh? Who am I?"

"Mortimer Angel. You got that package, the one sent from here with that guy's hand in it. I saw you on TV."

Well, hell. I was going to have to wear that itchy damn wig and moustache after all, like I did in July and August with Jeri. "Mort," I said. "And why can't you talk to me?"

"Not just you. I was told I shouldn't, you know, talk to *anyone* about it."

"Shouldn't, or couldn't?"

"Well, shouldn't." Her eyes shuttled between Sarah and me. "I mean, it was *federal agents* that said it."

"But not the SS? They didn't say 'Sieg Heil' and click boot heels before leaving?" Which, of course, we did in the IRS at the end of every closed Monday morning meeting.

"Huh?"

"You *shouldn't* talk to anyone—but in fact you can, the First Amendment still being what it is, and pieces of Reinhart not being a legitimate national security issue."

Her eyes darted toward the door then back to me. "Look, I go on break at ten. I can see you over across the street at the Dunkin' Donuts for a few minutes, okay? I usually get myself a Colombian in the morning about then. That's coffee. Keeps me awake in here."

I looked out the window. A Dunkin' Donuts was visible a few doors down. "Okay. What's your name?"

"Cathy."

"Okay, Cathy. See you there at ten."

Sarah and I went outside.

"She was scared," Sarah said.

"Feds, IRS—they're about the same, except your basic Fed can only scare you shitless. At the IRS, we laugh at shitless. Really bugs us, though, when people die and cut off our percentage."

We sat in the Audi and kept an eye on the FedEx place.

"Was that true?" Sarah asked. "About Kayla? She was really pretty and willing and you weren't engaged to anyone at the time, not even going with anyone, and you *still* didn't get laid?"

"Don't want to talk about it, kiddo."

"So it's true."

"No comment."

"That's almost sad. Except . . ."

"Except what?" I said, falling for it.

"Except it explains why Jeri trusts you so much. You must have a conscience or something like a big dense block of iron."

"Iron is dense by definition. It's redundant to say so."

"A salient point for sure, but the prosecution still rests."

"We could go get a donut. I'll buy."

"You get one. I'll watch you bloat up."

Which we did, although I didn't bloat up. Much. And at 10:01 Cathy came in. At 9:59 I'd ordered a Colombian to speed things up. I handed it to her as she came in the door.

At a table in back she said, "You're really famous."

"Yup," I said, false modesty not being my style.

"Wow. I never thought . . . I mean, *this's* really cool. But I can't stay very long, so—what did you want to know?" She sipped her coffee and looked at me over the rim of the cup.

"Who shipped the hand?"

"Well, that's what everyone wants to know, obviously."

"Obviously, but do you remember what the person looked like who came in with it?"

"It came from a drop box. No one saw who put it in there."

Exactly what I'd thought last night—but what else would one expect of a gumshoe of my caliber?

"So the Feds drew a blank?" I said.

"Guess so. No one here knows anything at all. It's not like we open packages before we ship them. Everything gets sent through a scanner for weapons and explosives, but that's about it."

"Wouldn't pick up flesh and bone, huh?"

"Nope. *Obviously*, since it didn't."

Second time she'd used that word, putting bullet holes in my gravitas.

"Packages in a drop box are paid by a FedEx account or credit card, is that right?" I asked.

"Uh-huh."

"Which was it?"

"Credit card. Visa. We mark out the number with special ink after we run it and it clears, so it doesn't get sent all over where people can see it."

"Do you know who the card belonged to? Do you get that?"

"Nope. I ran it. To me it was just a number. I bet those agents know, though. They could've backtracked it off the shipping number from our computer system at corporate."

If they got anywhere with that, they would've already swooped down on the guy and it would be all over the news. J. Edgar's boys would be crowing like roosters if they'd caught him, so that name had no doubt sent them straight into a brick wall.

"How many drop boxes are there in this town?"

"Just one. It's on the main street, south of here."

"I saw it. Do you know when the box was unloaded? I mean, when it had that package in it?"

"It was the morning drop, the seven o'clock. We got that off the label—the time we processed it through."

Worst time possible, since the package could have been put in the box at midnight or two in the morning. Just the way I'd do it.

"Anything else?" Cathy asked. "I gotta get back."

I couldn't think of anything more. "Nope. Thanks for talking to us."

"Yeah, just don't tell anyone I said anything."

"Our secret."

She left.

Sarah and I went out to her car. "Now what?" she said. "Can we please start looking for Allie again?"

"One last thing, then we'll head back to Gerlach and get on that."

"What's that?"

"I gotta look at that drop box again. I saw it last night. Mile or so south of our motel."

* * *

The box was still there. Good thing, too, because if it wasn't, tracking it down would've been a bitch.

I stood on the sidewalk wearing the dirty-blond wig, hair half over my ears, no dumbass moustache, and looked around. A bunch of stores were nearby: Ace Hardware, variety, a real estate office, sewing machine sales and service. But at a diagonal across the street, I saw a two-story house with a few missing composition shingles, a gutter in need of repair, three buckled wooden steps leading up to a deep, screened-in porch.

Sarah and I went over. She was trying not to laugh at my wig, and I was trying not to deck her. The porch was in shadow, but close up I could see an elderly man sitting in a glider, staring at the street. An old dog was lying at his feet, asleep.

I went up two steps and rapped on a post holding up the porch roof. The dog twisted its head and looked at me, didn't move otherwise.

"Hep you?" the old guy asked through a screen door. He looked to be in his seventies. He had bushy white eyebrows and needed a shave. His chest was sunken and he had on baggy jeans, a flannel shirt, and bright red suspenders.

"I was wondering about that FedEx drop box over there."

"Lot of folks wonderin' 'bout that box these days."

"Oh?"

"Federal guys. FBI. The hand of that sonofabitchin' liar was sent from there."

"Well, you got his character right."

"No big trick. They's all goddamn liars. Career sons of bitches lookin' out for number one. My name's Fred, in case you want to know who you're speakin' with. You oughta come on in so we kin talk proper-like, 'specially since you ain't alone."

I opened the door and Sarah and I went onto the porch. Fred sized us up, especially Sarah. Old fellow had a good eye. Hope I end up like him.

"Nice to meet you, Fred. I'm Earl. I got a few questions, if you don't mind. Do you see people put packages in that box?"

"Sure do, all day long. What you wanna ask is, did I see who dropped off the package with that liar's hand in it."

"That's the question."

"Answer's no, same thing I told the Feds. How the hell would I know who put it in there? I see twenty, thirty people a day drop stuff off. None of 'em mean a toot or a whistle to me." He leaned forward and looked at Sarah. "You're an almighty pretty girl. What's your name, hon?"

"Sarah."

"Sarah. That's a lovely name. First girl I ever kissed was named Sarah. This here gent with you's one hell of a lucky man, I'll tell you what."

"He's never kissed me. How lucky is that?"

"Well, then he's a blamed fool."

"Don't I know it."

"Earl," Fred said. "You're a blamed fool, ain't cha?"

"Most of the time. So those Feds didn't learn a thing from you?"

"Fact is, they did. I told 'em Reinhart was a lying son of a bitch and got what he deserved, so you betcha they learned a thing or three. They learned that Fred Meyer ain't no fool. Not like them anyways, since they took my fingerprints. Tole 'em I've never in my life touched that box over there, and I didn't kill that lying son of a bitch and ship off his hand, either, but you know Feds."

I didn't know what else to ask. Fred didn't know anything. I was about to turn away when I remembered our search for Allie and the million-dollar question popped out: "I don't suppose you've seen a green Mercedes SUV around here, have you?"

He looked off in the distance for a moment, then said, "Fact is, I have. Huh. *Fact* is, an SUV like that—green, too—stopped at that box a few days back and dropped off a package. Damn funny, you askin' that. You don't see a lot of SUVs like that around here. Worth more than my house here, if 'n I wanted to sell it."

My heart rate went up a few beats per minute. "Did you see who put the package in?"

He thought about that. "A girl. Not old. Pretty, too. I remember 'cause I still like pretty girls. I ain't so old yet that that don't matter to me. I sit out here and every so often a pretty one'll come by."

"Was she driving?"

"Uh-uh. A woman was. Older, but also good-looking, near as I could tell. It was gettin' on toward dusk so the light wasn't so good, but I got new glasses a couple months back so my eyes is fair." He gave Sarah and me a sheepish look. "And, a while back I bought me these at Cabela's." He held up a pair of field glasses. "Good ones, too. Cost five hundred bucks, but worth it. If I see what might be a pretty girl on the street out there, I pick these up and get me a better look."

I showed him a picture of Allie. "Did she look like this?"

He stared at the photo for five seconds. "This one's blond. Girl that put that package in the box had dark hair."

"What if she was wearing a wig?"

"A wig, huh?" He studied the picture a while longer. "The light was starting to go, but, yeah, I'd say fifty-fifty, that's her."

"So, flip a coin?"

"About that. Heads it's her, tails it's someone looks close."

"How long ago did you see them?"

He thought about it for nearly half a minute. "Been four days, maybe five."

"Feds didn't mention them?"

"Can't figure why they'd have a reason to. Damn strange, you askin'." He gave Sarah a questioning look.

"He's like that," she said. "It's exhausting."

He stared at her shirt. "Biggest piece of pi is three." He chortled. "That's a good one. Oughta get me a shirt like that, piss off my brother."

Sarah and I walked back to her car.

A pretty girl that might have been Allie, and a good-looking woman in a green Mercedes SUV. About the right number of days ago, they'd put a package in that drop box. Jesus H. Christ. I'd made a connection so unreal it was like being in the Twilight Zone. Next person over the horizon would be Rod Serling.

* * *

"That's just . . . impossible," Sarah said as I parked the Audi at the Slumberland, a final pit stop before we headed back to Gerlach. "Allie couldn't be mixed up in that mess."

I didn't know what to tell her. Allie had phoned from Gerlach. A green SUV was seen in Gerlach about that time with a girl who might have been Allie inside and a woman driving. A girl in a green SUV had dropped off a package in the same box Reinhart's hand had been put in, with a woman driving. The whole thing might be nothing but coincidence and coincidences happen, but I had the eerie feeling it was all tied together somehow. I also had the feeling that the FBI wasn't anywhere near it.

I could've been wrong on all counts since that's part of my MO, but it was still eerie as hell.

Up in the room I looked around. I didn't see anything we'd left behind. Sarah had extra clothing and school things in her duffel bag. She came out of the bathroom in jeans and her pi shirt. "I'm ready," she said. Her tone was distracted. The possibility that her sister was somehow tied up with the Reinhart thing had her brain spinning.

By ten forty we were out of Bend and on the highway, headed south through low scrubby hills covered with pine.

"What do you think?" she asked.

"Dunno. Anything's possible."

"Allie can't be involved with Reinhart," she said in a voice that lacked conviction.

"She was hooking."

"I know."

"And she was working casinos where there's money and a different clientele than you'd find on Lakeside or Fourth Street, so there's a possibility there."

"I know."

I didn't know what else to say. Sarah got out a textbook and said, "I can't think about that right now. I'm going to study."

Which she did, all the way to Gerlach—God bless those nerd genes. She got in there and seriously wrestled with eigenstuff, which was more than I could've done even if I had the slightest idea what that stuff was. I've always found structural dynamics boring.

* * *

We arrived in Gerlach that afternoon at three twenty. I parked the Audi beside my Toyota and we sat there in silence for a moment.

"Got any reason to stay the night?" Sarah asked.

"Not that I can see."

"Guess I'll go back to Reno then. I need to keep studying, and I probably ought to give it a rest for a while—I mean, the way I've been around you. Although," she added, "it's been a blast."

"Uh-huh," said the master of repartee.

"Seriously, Mort. Allie couldn't be involved."

"Even so, I wouldn't run any of it past anyone, like the police or the FBI. Especially the FBI."

She gave me a look. "Like I was going to."

Not sure why I told her that. It just came out. Putting the FBI on that trail might turn a whistle-stop carnival into a full-blown circus, with Sarah and me in the big tent, center ring. It might end up in the news. No telling how that would affect Allie, wherever she was, whatever was happening with her. It's not like Sarah and I were withholding evidence in a murder investigation—for two reasons. One, that green SUV might be nothing at all, and two, no one knew if Reinhart was dead or alive. The lying sonofabitch might've shipped his own hand, he's that fucking dishonest.

Sarah and I got out. She came around the car and got behind the wheel, then looked up at me. "See you back in Reno?"

"Yup. Especially now that you and Jeri have progressed to the telephone buddy stage."

"Not just because of Jeri. And not only because of Allie, either. I'll see you, too, I hope. You're a good guy, Mort. You're still going to try to find Allie, aren't you?"

"Sure am."

"I'll be around. I want to help, if I can." She hesitated. "Would a tiny little good-bye kiss be out of the question?"

"Probably not."

I leaned in and got a lip press, a soft, warm peck that didn't linger and didn't have any discernable heat. Friends. Nice.

She backed the Audi out and sped away.

I watched her go, then went into the casino, sat at the bar, and ordered a sarsaparilla. Sweet and bitter, sort of medicinal, a hint of vanilla, hint of wintergreen. Dave wouldn't be in for another two hours. The bartender on duty was a hefty gal in her midthirties in a Corti's T-shirt, nice face, dark brown hair held back in a ponytail, smell of cigarettes around her whenever she got close.

"If you're driving," she said, pushing the sarsaparilla toward me, "I'll have to cut you off at three of these."

Smart-ass. Jeez, I hate smart-asses.

"Not to worry," I smart-assed back. "Three of these and I'll either be on the floor or swingin' naked from the chandelier."

She put her elbows on the bar and leaned closer. "I'm Cheryl. No one ever got fried on sas'prilla. But if you'll do that chandelier thing, the next two'll be on the house."

"I'll give it some thought."

"You do that. Give me a little lead time if the urge strikes. My cell phone takes decent video. You could go viral."

* * *

I was at the bar working on a second sarsaparilla when my cell phone rang. It was Jeri. She was the new national champion female powerlifter in her weight class.

She was almost giddy with happiness. "I did it! Omigod, Mort, I really did it! I mean, I thought maybe I could but I didn't really know 'cause there's this girl, Carla Neilson, who is really good, looks like a cement block, but I beat her by six pounds."

"Wow! Super, Jeri! That's great, terrific!"

She bounced all over the phone call for a few more minutes then settled down. "Where are you? Is Sarah there?"

"I'm in Gerlach. Sarah went back to Reno."

"Oh. Well . . . why did she . . . ?"

"College, study. And she said something about giving it a rest."

"Giving what . . . oh."

"Yeah. That's a bucket that can get pretty full."

"You got, like, an eyeful, huh?"

"Plenty. So, you still getting back tomorrow? Southwest 1168 at nine thirty?"

"Yes. Oh, jeez, I can't wait to see you. I'm still so high. First place was fifteen thousand dollars, and I got a big gold-plated belt buckle and a first-place ring and everything."

"I can't wait to see them. And you. Jeri?"

"Yeah?"

"How's your engine?"

That stopped her for a few seconds, then: "It's runnin' hot."

"Mine, too. Any chance of getting an earlier flight?"

"I don't know. Want me to check?"

"Yes. If you can, do it. Spend some of that prize money. It'll be worth it."

"Okay. I'll let you know. And, Mort?"

"Yup?"

"I love you."

"Love you, too. Get that engine back here, huh? I'm about to throw a rod."

"A rod, huh? That sounds serious. I'll try."

"Try hard." I ended the call. Bartender Cheryl shoved another sarsaparilla at me and pointed at a deer-antler chandelier six feet above my head. "Got your trapeze ready," she said. "I'll hang onto your clothes."

"Gotta give you a rain check on that. And I'll take this sarsaparilla to go."

"Well, shit." She pouted. "Ain't that just my luck."

* * *

I arrived back in Reno at five forty-five. The day was still warm, sun a few hours above the Sierras. Jeri had called as I was near Fernley. She'd managed to get a red-eye flight out of Atlantic City that night at 9:15 Eastern. She was about to board the plane. With the change in time zones she would land in Reno at 12:35 a.m.

"Perfect time of night, kiddo," I said.

"You'll be still up?"

"I'm up now."

"Well . . . keep it that way."

We left it like that. Maybe this Holiday thing was working out. Maybe Jeri knew what the hell she was doing.

If I didn't throw a rod in the process.

* * *

Coming out of the security barrier, Jeri slammed into me. Man, that felt good. And the kiss, and the supple, strong woman-stuff in my arms.

Really strong. During a hug she picked me up, all two hundred thirty pounds, which for her wasn't hard but still felt weird. When she put me down I picked her up just to show off a little.

"Wow, Mort. You been workin' out?" she said with her feet a foot off the ground, her face two inches from mine.

"Shows, does it?"

"Let's go home and find out how strong you really are."

"Your place or mine?"

She made a face. "Mine. Yours is probably infested."

Media and cops. Back in July, early August, my house was a media-infested nest, which is what it was again, or had been the last time I saw it. When I finally caught up with the person who sent me that package, there was going to be one more homicide in Nevada.

Never say things like that, by the way. Something out there in the dark hears every word.

In fact, there was never any doubt that we would end up at her place, second floor, in a king-size bed less than a month old. We'd bought it in anticipation of a lifetime of good hard use together. It had a memory-foam mattress that can be something of a trampoline, which memory-foam isn't supposed to do. That took place after a water-saving shower during which we got reacquainted with what it means to get wet, slippery, and naked, not in that order.

When pulse rates eased below eighty and I managed to get her left nipple out of my mouth, I said, "Say there, you're a pretty hot little number."

Her legs were wrapped around my waist. "Put that back in your mouth and do what you were doing. That felt really good."

"Actually, I have a better idea."

"Yeah?"

"It's a little aerobic. If you're exhausted from your flight, you'll have to okay it."

"Why don't you just show me? If I don't like it, we'll put that nipple back where it was."

"Well, okay, then, here, check this out, sugar plum."

Her eyes widened. "Omigod, yes, that's a *much* better idea."

I am a god.

CHAPTER TEN

Starvation drove us out of bed at ten forty-five that morning. Blood-sugar levels were reaching critical lows. Jeri and I still had a few interesting ideas worth trying out, but those would have to wait to be implemented in a manner worthy of their inventiveness.

I got out of bed hunched over, feeling like I'd been run over by a Mack truck. She weighs only a hundred thirty pounds to my two thirty, so my being a god might've been a slight exaggeration.

Breakfast was a five-egg omelet for me, a three-egg omelet for her, both of them loaded with three kinds of cheese and—sautéed in coconut oil—red and orange sliced peppers, diced ham, mushrooms, spinach, and pine nuts.

We sat at her dining table with a view of grass, trumpet vines, lavender, and a good-sized maple tree in her backyard. On the table was a championship belt buckle and a first-prize check for fifteen thousand dollars, of which Uncle Sam would want roughly four thousand for having been such a big help with her training. If she forgot, the IRS would make sure the transfer of funds took place in a timely fashion because the IRS is such a helpful organization, pretty much like your favorite aunt.

I held her hand and said, "I can see you naked on a bike in the streets of San Fran," which was a terrific opening line, designed to get me back upstairs within the hour.

She smiled, looked me in the eye. "Pretty weird, huh?"

"Sure, but I can still see you on that bike, having the time of your life. You and Holiday."

"You mean Sarah?"

"Nope. Holiday. That's her name when she's feeling her oats."

Jeri looked down at her orange juice then back up. "So what's my name when I'm like that?"

"I don't know. I've never seen you like that. I mean, in public, which is where the difference lies."

She looked out the window. "I'll think about it. If you come up with something fun, let me know."

"Will do. So, now that we've got two critical hungers out of the way—"

"For now."

"For now, yes, though I might have to run you back upstairs as soon as this food settles—just, you know, to top things off. But there's something I think you should know about Reinhart and Sarah's sister, Allie."

She stared at me. "The way you said Reinhart *and* Allie . . ."

Sharp.

"There might be a connection."

She tilted her head, waiting for more. So I laid it out, the phone call from Allie when Holiday and I were in the Green Room, the Mercedes SUV at Gerlach with a young girl in the passenger seat and a thirty-something woman driving, the package shipped from Bend, old Fred Meyer checking out girls with binoculars and the SUV stopping at the drop box, a young, pretty girl that looked a lot like Allie getting out, putting a package in the same box Reinhart's hand was left in, an older woman driving that SUV.

"Jesus, Mort."

"Yeah. I oughta wear a cape."

"Not that. What I mean is, what a pile of coincidences."

"It's a pile, all right."

"The girl got out, put the package in that box, so it's not like she was being held prisoner or anything." Jeri stood up. "C'mon."

"Where to?"

"Computer."

I guessed our new bed was going to be put on hold for a few. Jeri had that PI look, the kind of focus I'd seen on Sarah's face when she was studying and everything else was put on a back burner.

Jeri turned on her computer.

"What're you lookin' for, honey bun?" I asked, trying to show interest since I'm a PI in training as well as a love object.

The *honey bun* thing didn't faze her, didn't slow her down, so this was serious. "A green Mercedes SUV?" she said. "That deputy said it wasn't a year old. A G550, right? He would know. There can't be a lot of those around."

She got into the DMV database, typed in the information, and sat there staring at the screen.

"How long does this usually take?" I asked.

"Depends."

Which meant it was one of those experience things. This was what that ten thousand hours of training was supposed to hone to a razor edge. I sat on a hard wooden chair and stared at the screen with her, honing that razor.

A list appeared on the computer monitor. Jeri hit keys and the list reordered itself. "Registered owners," she said, peering at it. She read off several names: "Eikelberger, Harris, Newcomb, Odermann, Quist, Roberts, Shaw, Szupello, Williams. Did you run across any of those names in Gerlach or Bend with Holiday? Any of them look familiar?"

"Nope."

"Me either." She sat there looking at the screen, lips pursed.

"Dead end?"

"You kiddin'? We're just getting started."

Well, hell, I didn't have a thousand hours of training yet. This was going to take a while. My education, that is.

Jeri concentrated on the screen. "Whatcha doing?" I asked.

"Looking at addresses."

She read them off. "Any of them mean anything to you?"

"Nope." It was Nevada DMV, so the list was from all over the state. Over half were from Las Vegas, which figured.

Jeri pursed her lips. "Okay. Now, we have to dig deeper. Maybe none of these are *that* SUV, but we don't know. If it was from out of state, especially California, then we're probably screwed. Okay, next up are legal owners, lien holders, which, since that Mercedes was almost new, might mostly be banks, credit unions, Mercedes corporation financing."

Which they were, with a few exceptions. But none of that felt like it was getting us any closer to who was driving that SUV.

Jeri leaned back, frowning.

"Now what?" I asked.

"*Now* . . . I guess I've got to pull out the big gun."

"*Now* you're talkin'."

She smiled at me. "You don't have any idea what the big gun is, do you?"

I looked down at myself. "Hell, yes. What do you think we were—?"

"Oh, jeez. Holiday really wound you up, didn't she?"

"Not so you'd notice. Well, maybe a little."

"Not just maybe. I'll have to meet her in person. We can do something about your gun later, but right now, the big gun is Ma Clary."

"Ma Clary?"

"Maude, but you'll end up calling her Ma like everyone else. If you don't, she'll have your kidneys for breakfast."

"You don't sound like you're kidding."

"I'm not. You'll see."

* * *

It was Sunday, so Maude Clary was in a housecoat when we got there. She had a beer in one hand, cigarette in the other. She lived in a three-story house on Arlington, south of California Avenue, half a mile from downtown Reno. The third floor was all dormer windows so the rooms up there would have mostly sloped ceilings. Two other women about the same age lived with her. One was a widowed sister, Agnes Villars, the other a tenured political science professor at the university, Colleen Pesarik.

Ma was a fireplug—five four, a hundred eighty-five pounds, with substantial low-slung breasts, a forty-two-inch waist, and a demeanor that suggested where Jeri had gotten hers—that pit bull attitude I'd experienced the day Jeri and I first met. Temperament like that is often transferred via a kind of osmosis. Maude was sixty-one, thirty-two years older than Jeri. She was Jeri's mentor while Jeri was working on her PI license. Funny it had never occurred to me to ask Jeri who'd trained her. Guess we were having too much fun in that new bed after I'd convalesced. In fact, considering that naked bike ride thing that was in the works, Jeri and I still had quite a bit of that gettin'-to-know-you stuff to talk about.

Ma was the Big Gun. In the first minute I had her pegged as a .44 Magnum. Even a licensed PI needs professional help every once in a while. Ma was a PI with an office downtown, as I found out later—*Clary Investigations*. She'd been in the business thirty-five years and had contacts and sources in the community like the roots of a banyan tree. She'd done favors, made friends, and evidently had the goods on a few folks in the city's and county's law enforcement agencies and the DA's office, not to mention down at the state legislature in Carson City. Later I discovered she had a few useful friends whose livelihoods weren't strictly legal.

Ma looked me over. "Couldn't see how tall he was on TV," she said to Jeri. "From down here, he's a big'n."

"I'm even shorter. You should see him from here."

"I'd *like* to see him from down there," Ma said, "but you two're engaged."

"Hey, there's another person in this room," I said.

"Who happens to be the topic of conversation, doll," Ma said. "Get used to it." She took a pull on her beer, and it was only a few minutes past noon.

Pit bull.

Bare feet flapping in mules, Ma led us into a sitting room. It had a six-thousand-dollar chandelier and wickedly ornate cream and burgundy velveteen wallpaper, which, against all odds and logic, wasn't hideous. The house was huge, five bedrooms, four baths, but it was home to three women, so I thought it had to be huge to avoid trouble. Suppositions like that are going to hang me up at the Pearly Gates, I just know it.

Inside and out, the house was a jewel. An aura of money hung in the air, oozing out of the walls. Not millions, but it was clear that these old gals weren't hurting.

Ma plopped down on a couch with a flowery design, looked at me, and patted the place next to her. "Right here, darlin'. Sit."

Darlin' sat. Jeri smiled and took an overstuffed chair, facing Ma and me across a glass-topped coffee table held up by porcelain cherubs. Okay, that bordered on hideous.

Ma patted my knee with a pudgy hand that resembled a ham. She looked at Jeri. "Okay, hon, what's up? Been a while since I've seen you. Not since the hospital." She turned to me. "And you, big guy. Person'd never know you took a sword in the chest. You look pretty fit."

"He is," Jeri said. All she'd had was a mild concussion, so her stay in the hospital back in August wasn't as long as mine. Mine had involved bedpans and unmentionable procedures.

"Yeah?" Ma said, distracted from her initial question.

"Very."

"Well, that sounds good, since you two're gettin' hitched."

"Real good," I said, injecting myself into the flow, which got me another pat on the knee.

"So," Ma said to Jeri. "What's goin' on? You got somethin' needs special handling?"

"I think so. We're hitting a dead end on a vehicle. All we've got is a description: green Mercedes SUV, new. A G550. Owners and addresses aren't anything we recognize."

"At least it isn't a goddamn white Chevy sedan two to five years old. Then you'd be down shit creek."

"Isn't that *up* shit creek?" I asked, stepping in it.

Ma looked at me. "Up shit creek, you could float back. Down shit creek without a paddle, you're hosed. Never understood that 'up shit creek' crapola."

Pit bull.

"So what you're wantin' is deep background on the owners," Ma said, facing Jeri again. "See if anything useful turns up."

"Uh-huh."

Ma looked up at me. "It's not strictly kosher, digging around like that without a court order, which we'd never get."

"Yup. Got that."

"Not strictly kosher—*meaning*, it's frickin' illegal, boyo."

"Yup. Makin' my Boy Scout ears flame red."

Ma guffawed, then turned to Jeri. "It'd help if I had an idea what names *would've* rung a bell with you, if it ain't the owners."

Jeri nodded at me. "Mort? You're up."

I looked at Ma. The top of her head came to about my chin. "Names that'd ring a bell, huh? I've got a good one for you."

"Yeah? Shoot."

"Harold J. Reinhart."

Silence like we were swaddled in London fog for ten seconds. Then, "Well, hell, that's a good one all right."

She fished in a pocket, came up with a pack of Camels and a Zippo. She lit up as neatly as a Marine, blew a cloud of smoke toward the ceiling.

Camels. Holiday's brand when she was fake smoking in a bar. Ma wasn't faking, though. Her voice had a little gritty rasp to it.

"Dicey," she said. "Reinhart. Could set off alarm bells if I went diving in that pool without a raincoat on."

An impressive mix of metaphors for sure.

"It's one of the names you might run across," Jeri said. "There are others. People around Reinhart." She got a sheet of paper out of her purse and handed it to Ma—names she'd pulled off the DMV site. Registered owners of the kind of SUV we were after.

Ma looked it over for half a minute. "These are names you got that you never heard of before, that right?"

Jeri nodded. "So what we need are names associated with these that we might recognize."

"Associated." Ma stared at the paper. "People around Reinhart. Relatives, business partners, political backers, maybe spouses and maiden names of those people, favorite singers, like that?"

"Probably not favorite singers," I said.

"Settle down, hon." She patted my knee again.

"I only say things like that because I like it when you pat my knee, Ma."

Ma brayed laughter, hard enough to make her cough. "Don't do that, darlin'. I'm not as tough as I look."

Right. She was a two-dollar steak in a Hell's Angel roadhouse.

"Glad you two're having fun," Jeri said. She blew me a kiss from six feet away.

Ma closed her eyes and thought for a while. "Okay, so I come up with names associated with registered owners of these SUVs. We're lookin' for a connection to Reinhart—either Reinhart himself or someone around him who's associated with someone around one of these SUV owners, that about right?"

"That's it," Jeri said. "Mort?"

"If I could figure out what she said, yeah."

Ma looked off into space for a while. "Not gonna be easy," she said at last. "We'll need background from both sides—Reinhart's and SUV owners. Have to look deep, too. Reinhart's wife, children, campaign manager, publicity agent, possible running mates, which I don't think have been put out there yet. Not sure who'd want to run with that meathead anyway." She looked at me. "Who else, boyo?"

"Pat my knee, Ma."

She did.

"You two're a laugh a minute," Jeri said, but she couldn't help smiling.

"Jayson Wexel," I said. "Harry's so-called chief of staff, who—imagine this—was either an accidental death not long ago, or a not-so-accidental murder. Found in his house, which had burned to the ground."

"Talk about a big goddamn bell clangin' away," Ma said. "I'd put him on a list right up there with Reinhart himself."

"Right," I said. "There's a lot going on. Whoever chopped off Reinhart's hand didn't like him much, so we need to look into his enemies, too. Whose toes did he step on on the way up? Wexel's been with him a long time so he might've been involved in that toe-stepping thing. Who is Reinhart running against? And he's got a trophy wife, so there's probably a non-trophy wife out there who might be nursing a grudge. A guy like Reinhart probably has a crooked lawyer lying around, too, maybe a few girlfriends lurking in the wings."

"Christ, all that'll make a long freakin' list," Ma said. "Not easy to get at, either. Especially secret girlfriends."

"What about the lawyers of all those people?" Jeri asked.

"Lawyers?"

"Privileged conversations allow them to conceal unethical behavior. You might want to look into the lawyers of people close to Reinhart, political insiders, close friends—"

"Je-sus," Ma said. "What you want is a phone book. Bet you don't know any of those people, which means I'll have to round up their names. That'll be a job and a half in itself. One other thing..."

"What's that?"

Ma patted my knee. "Reinhart's hand was sent to *you*, darlin'."

I looked at Jeri. Jeri looked at me. Silence for half a minute. Then Jeri said, "Mort was nationally famous not long ago."

"Still am," I offered humbly.

"What I *mean*, Mort, is you were well known when that hand was shipped. Because of what we did this summer."

Interesting that we were talking about shipping Reinhart's hand around like it was something from Hickory Farms. We never did anything like that in the IRS.

"Guess you'll have to look into people close to me, too," I said to Ma. "Like Jeri over there. She looks pretty tough. You should find out if she owns a chainsaw."

Jeri hit me in the face with a pillow then said, "Mort and I will handle the Reinhart-Wexel side of things—public records stuff, try to identify people close to them, as many as we can."

Ma nodded. "I'll have to dig way down in that list when you're done." She took a drag and blew a plume of blue smoke skyward. "I'll work on these"—she held up the sheet of SUV owners Jeri had given her. "Who knows? We might get lucky and get an early hit on the two lists."

I patted Ma's knee. "That's the spirit, kiddo."

She laughed, coughed, then leaned toward an ash tray on the coffee table and stubbed out her cigarette. "Piece a cake," she said. "Whole thing shouldn't take more'n two months."

"Two months—?"

"Kiddin', greenhorn. Take it easy." She patted my knee one last time then gave it a squeeze.

* * *

"Greenhorn?" I whispered to Jeri as we were going down the steps to the front yard. Early afternoon sunshine filtered through elms that were starting to think about shucking their leaves.

"Don't take it personally. To her, *I'm* still a greenhorn. She's really good, Mort. I mean, *really* good. There's no way we could do this without her."

"She didn't teach you her best tricks? The quasi-legal stuff?"

"Nope. She said it would just get me into trouble. Said it was best if I kept things on the up and up for the first ten or fifteen years. Told me if I discovered my own tricks, I'd have a better idea how to cover my tracks."

"Smart lady."

"You have no idea. Seeing her like that, in a housecoat with a beer in one hand, you'd never know, never even guess. Her going rate is a hundred fifty bucks an hour."

I stopped. "Christ, Jeri. We'll be broke in four days."

She grabbed my arm, kept me going. "Maudie owes me for other stuff. Something I did for her two years ago when I was still training with her. This's free, no charge. If I'd brought up her fee she would've given me the evil eye, turned me into a pillar of salt."

Other stuff. I wondered what it might have been, but Jeri said she didn't want to talk about it. Ma could tell me if she wanted to. When we got back to Jeri's we got right on that list-making. Well, there was a half-hour delay that ended with us in the shower—and a phone call just to make the day complete.

"Whew," Jeri said at one point, right before the shower. "I need to meet this Holiday person in person. See how she did that to you."

"Uh-huh," I said. Maybe not a good idea, but I keep thoughts like that to myself.

"Without even touching you," Jeri added.

"Uh-huh."

Jeri snuggled up against me. "How about tonight, Mort?"

"How about tonight what?"

"Meeting Sarah. Or Holiday, whatever. If she has time and wants to, that is."

"Television buddies, telephone buddies, bicycle buddies," I said as a delaying tactic. Which worked for all of forty-five seconds.

"Huh?"

I gave her the history of that progression. She laughed and kissed me on the forehead. "Bicycle buddies. I like that. You should call her. Maybe we can see her tonight."

"Turns out, I don't have her number."

"Turns out, I do."

"So you could call her."

"Do I sense a little reluctance there?"

"Not at all, sweetheart. I was thinking of spending a week or so in Uruguay. Now's a good time for me."

She gave that some thought. "I've only seen her on TV—after you found Reinhart's hand. How is she really—in real life?"

"Pneumatic comes to mind."

She looked at me with one eye. "That's not a description I've heard before. How's it work?"

"I'm going to let you think about it."

After the shower when she was looking at herself naked in the mirror, she turned and looked at me. "As in, pumped-up kinda full?"

I touched my finger to my nose.

Jeri laughed. "Now I've *really* got to meet this girl."

* * *

Which she did.

But first there was a lot of easy-to-find public record stuff to look up: Reinhart's Wikipedia biography, press releases, news items. We got thirty-two names in half an hour. Then a lengthy grind on the computer during which I learned more than I wanted to know about databases, Google searches, and a few programs Jeri subscribed to that required an investigator's license, not available to the general public. Before she started on those secondary sources, she handed me her cell phone, after she'd already proactively tapped the screen to call Holiday-Sarah.

"Hello?" Sarah said.

"It's me, kiddo," I said, giving Jeri the eye. She smiled sweetly at me then held her ear an inch from mine to listen in.

"Everyone calls me kiddo," Sarah said. "So who's 'me'?"

"Nice try. You studying?"

"Like a fiend. My brain's getting full and I'm starting to see double. What's goin' on?"

"Want to meet Jeri?"

"Sure! When? Where?"

Eager. I still didn't know everything they'd talked about during that three-hour phone call a few days ago.

Jeri took the phone from me. "Mort's favorite bar, Sarah. That okay?" I kept my ear near the phone in case I needed to grab it and throw it against a wall.

"Jeri! Wow, what a coincidence. I was just talking to Mort."

Jeri laughed. "I don't know what happened. He was right here. Next thing, he was gone."

"He was like that in Gerlach, too. I'd, like, take off a shirt or something and he'd disappear."

Terrific. This was going just swell.

Jeri nudged my ribs with an elbow. "We were going to go to the Green Room tonight, Sarah. Would you like to meet us there? Say, eight o'clock? Not too late?"

"Sure, perfect. I'll be there. My first class tomorrow isn't until ten in the morning."

"Could you dress up?" Jeri said. "You know, like you do."

"Uh, are you sure?"

"Yes. I'll try to find something kinda like that so we won't look too different. Well, I probably won't be as pneumatic as you but I'll do what I can."

Jesus H. Christ.

"Pneumatic? That sounds like something Mort might say."

Sonofabitch.

Jeri slid an arm around my waist, pulled me closer. "He did. He's very impressionable."

"Um. That's good, I guess."

"It has been, yeah. Since I got back."

Sarah laughed. "Good. I'm glad. I'll see you at eight."

"Uh-huh. See you." Jeri ended the call.

"Remember who set this up," I said. "Don't blame me for how things turn out."

"Yeah? Why's that?"

"Two gorgeous women, only one of me. What do you think?"

*   *   *

I'm never right about that and I don't know why. I think it's because women are strange. In July, when Jeri met my ex, Dallas, I expected fireworks, carnage, cannon fire booming across the room. What I got was two hot broads discussing running shoes, 10K runs, exchanging recipes, and chuckling about the only guy in the room.

So there was Holiday, already at the bar with a Tequila Sunrise in front of her, wearing silver high heels and a red dress so short and open in front that I felt my eyes bug out. My life flashed in front of my eyes when she slid off a barstool and came toward us, first time Jeri had ever laid eyes on her. Holiday had gone all out. Her dress plunged so low I could see a sapphire stud glittering in her navel.

Then they hugged.

Didn't expect that.

Je-sus, that was one cushioned, rubber-bumper hug—like they were best friends who hadn't seen each other for five years. I saw O'Roarke's face go slack at the sight.

Jeri had gone to Victoria's Secret that afternoon and left me in charge of the computer. She came back with a bag I wasn't allowed to peek in. When we drove to the Golden Goose in her Porsche, she had a crocheted wrap over her shoulders and across her chest. Night chill, she said. She took it off as we entered the Green Room and suddenly she was in a black dress showing enough cleavage to cause a riot of her own. I'd never before seen her like that in public. Ten seconds later the two of them were hugging.

I wanted in on that.

Didn't happen.

In fact, I was left out for thirty long seconds, an afterthought to the evening's festivities. But slowly I understood it, which is how I understand things. I was the centerpiece. I was their connection. As such, I should have been important, but I was an afterthought.

Eventually they got around to me. Jeri held my arm, looked at Holiday, and said, "Omigod, Mort. I didn't realize how strong you were. I mean, how strong you had to be."

Yep, me plenty strong.

"I mean," Jeri said. "Just look at her."

Holiday piped up, "He's a rock. Like Gibraltar."

"He must've been. You, uh, weren't always dressed up even . . . even *that* much, were you?"

Don't answer, don't answer, don't—

Holiday took Jeri's hand and said, "Let's go talk." She started to lead Jeri away, then tossed me a look. "You should get a drink. We'll be back after a while," and Jeri said, "I could use a white wine, Mort."

Oh, yeah. This was goin' just great.

But Mike Hammer never had it this good. Oh sure, a stray dame or two crossed his path, but compared to me Mikey was a piker, an amateur. And Spade? Sammy was a nobody, not a blip on a radar screen.

As directed, I delivered the wine then took a stool at the bar. O'Roarke sidled over with a grin on his mug so wide it must've hurt.

"How's it goin', spitfire?"

"You can't tell?"

"Nope. I don't know if you're a hog in shit or about to get your nuts handed to you. So . . . sarsaparilla or a Pete's?"

"Pete's. And a shot of bourbon. The good stuff."

He shoved a shot glass and a bottle of Wicked Ale toward me then put his elbows on the bar. "You're somethin' else with pieces, pal. Amazing, really."

"Pieces?" I glanced at the girls, chatting animatedly at a table thirty feet away. "Don't let those two hear you say that."

"Pieces of *people*, dude. Heads and hands. You're on TV all the time. Wish I was that good at something."

"Oh. Those kind of pieces. It's a gift."

He looked at Holiday and Jeri. "There's your woman with a thousand-dollar-a-night hooker. Explain that, buckaroo."

"She's a college student, not a hooker. An engineering major, so that thing about gluing a rat to the mirror was based on real science. She's only been playing the part of a hooker. Other than those bits of information, I can't explain a damn thing."

"They sure are dressed . . . up."

I leaned closer, lowered my voice. "You've been bartending a long time, Patrick, my boy."

"By no stretch am I your boy, but go ahead."

"By now you're about thirty percent psychologist, right?"

"Closer to forty. I've been asked to be a guest lecturer up at the university."

"What do you know about exhibitionism?"

He smiled. "Know it when I see it, man, and I see my share. In here it's 99.9 percent women. That's all I know, but I gotta say, it sure don't bother me none."

CHAPTER ELEVEN

Jeri and Holiday talked for an hour and a half. An hour and a *half*, while I got barstool rash. I didn't ask Jeri what they discussed. Some things are better left unknown. But when we got home that evening the lovemaking was slow and meaningful and deeply satisfying.

The next morning, however, I tried to nudge a little information loose. Broaching the subject obliquely, I said, "So, what did you two broads talk about last night for five freakin' hours?"

Jeri laughed. "It wasn't even two hours. And it was just broad stuff."

"That's the same as girl stuff, right? Only riper?"

"And, you know, the bicycle ride next year."

"Yeah, well, I expected that. Half marathons and bike rides are important. You have to know things, like tire inflation pressures and what to wear—*or not*."

"Uh-huh."

"And what color body paint to use and what to paint it on?"

She laughed again. "That, too."

"I'm pretty good with a brush. Point me at a pair of tits and I can really go to town."

"I'll bet. She wants to get you on a bike, too. Naked."

"That'll be the day."

That was all I got. They were a sly, slippery, underhanded, and sneaky duo—an entire thesaurus of slick stuff.

And friends, which bordered on eerie.

But that day, Monday, was different—the computer work was a laugh riot, assembling a list of names at a snail's pace, everyone we could find who had been in Reinhart's or Wexel's orbit. We tracked down people who knew their spouses, kids, kids' spouses—rounded up maiden names, business partners, lawyers, personal physicians, dentists, masseuses. Actually, no masseuses, but that would've been a real coup.

Later that afternoon we trudged over to Clary Investigations and passed through a cloud of Camel smoke getting close to Ma's desk. She was squinting at a computer screen with a hands-free headset on, listening to someone. She held up a finger, making sure we didn't tip off whoever it was that someone else was in the room.

"I need it by five o'clock, Andy." Pause. "Hell, yes, *today*. I'm going like a bat outta hell here. Which means you're going like a bat, too, if you get my drift." Pause. "That's right, snowflake. Clock's tickin' so get on it."

She clicked off, then turned to us. "Andrew Bartlett Hecht. Son of a bitch thinks he can play me, he's got another think comin'. I got that ol' boy's number. What's up, guys?"

Jeri handed her the list we'd been working on. "Here's what we've got so far, Ma. People close to Reinhart and Wexel."

Ma looked it over. "This'll keep me busy."

"Sorry about that."

Ma gave her a severe look. "Don't be. If it hadn't been for you, I'd . . . well, I don't know where I'd be. Not here, that's for sure. One hand washes the other."

She'd been working the other side of things, tracking down people connected to owners of the SUVs. She gave Jeri a list of the names of people she'd found so far. Jeri and I looked it over. I'd never heard of any of them. Neither had Jeri. I gazed around Ma's office. She had windows that looked out onto Liberty Street, and a sideboard with what looked like a bullet hole in it. Very cool.

"What we'll do," Ma said, "is alphabetize both lists, make it easier to spot anyone who pops up on both. Don't see anyone yet, but the lists are still fairly short. Keep trying. I'll probably end up with two hundred names in a few days, then I'll switch over to your Reinhart-Wexel list and we'll hit it from that direction."

Jeri and I left.

"Now what?" I asked when we were outside.

She shrugged. "We got the easy stuff. Now we dig harder."

Back to her place. More computer work. She only had that one computer so I watched and learned. Then she sat me down and gave me instructions. After two hours my eyes started to cross. I got coffee and used it to wash down a caffeine tablet, blinked a few times, then gave it another hour. This was a hell of a lot less exciting than an IRS field audit. At least there I'd had a concealed weapon under my coat for when greedy disgruntled people wanted to keep what they'd worked hard to get. Only thing I was likely to shoot now was the computer.

* * *

So that was how Monday went—and Tuesday, Wednesday, all the way to Sunday afternoon at one fifty-five when Maude phoned and told us she finally got a hit. Good thing, because I was fed up to here with computer work. I'd been traveling or at Jeri's ever since Reinhart's hand had turned up, hadn't been inside my house since I'd gotten my gun for Holiday, which I hadn't needed except to back off Dell and his buddy. Friday I'd driven by and the media ghouls had cleared out. It's hard to stake out a place for a week and sit on your hands while the world moves on. My bed had a forlorn look, wondering when I'd be back. The house looked sad, too. I gave a moment's thought about selling it, but with single-pane windows and roof shingles fifty years old, it had become a family heirloom. It would've been like selling the family dog just because it farted too often and had a little mange.

Jeri and I trooped over to Ma's office. She'd been working the Reinhart-Wexel side of things for the past three days. She looked drained when we went in, but exultant, too, now that a name had finally floated to the surface.

Sort of a name, sort of floated, as we soon learned.

"Martin Harris," she said. "He's on the list of registered SUV owners—a former executive director of the Nevada chapter of the Cystic Fibrosis Foundation. The chapter's current secretary is one Inez Brooks, wife of Nolan Brooks, Reinhart's campaign finance officer. Martin and Inez's tenures at the Foundation overlap by four years, so it's certain they'll know each other."

"Sounds thin, Ma," Jeri said.

"It *is* thin. It's tissue paper, but right now it's what we've got. If I keep digging, odds are something else'll come up. Connections between people are rich beyond imagining. You ever heard of 'six degrees of separation'?"

"No. What's that?" Jeri asked.

"Except for the Unabomber, everyone on the planet is connected to every other person by no more than six separations. A friend of a friend of a friend—like that. So it's likely I'm going to find more connections if I keep at it a while longer, dig deeper."

"Except for the Unabomber," I said.

"That's right. Teddy's not even connected to himself."

Jeri smiled. "So where is this guy, Martin Harris?"

"Tonopah. He retired there two years ago."

Jeri closed her eyes and thought for a moment. "Tonopah. Not a big place, but it's bigger than Gerlach."

"Yep," I said, not yet connecting two whole dots.

"Keep at it, Ma, and thanks," Jeri said. She led me out the door and onto Liberty Street, a block west of the municipal courthouse.

She hauled out her cell phone.

"Who're you calling?" I asked.

She held up a finger. Into the phone she said, "How would you like to go to Tonopah?" She looked up at me. "With Mort."

Uh-oh.

"That's right. We might finally have a lead. Uh-huh. Nope. Uh-huh. Okay, then, great. He'll be over in about an hour." She ended the call.

"He will, will he?" I said.

"He will, or should. And you'll never in a million years guess who that was."

"Whoopi Goldberg again? Man, you two."

"Oh, so close. Take another shot at it?"

"My favorite hooker?"

"Got it in only two tries. You'll be a flatfoot yet."

"And we're headed to Tonopah. Won't get there until nearly dark. Sure you want me back in that girl grinder again?"

"She's not fun to be with?"

"Fun, yeah. The view's something else, but I don't—"

"Are you tempted to go beyond viewing, Mort?"

"Well, let's see . . . it's hard to dredge up some of the really boring stuff that happened up in Oregon . . . okay, you said *tempted*, didn't you? No, can't say that I am."

She wasn't amused. She put her hands on her hips with pique in her stance. "We've already had this discussion. One more time and I'd like this to be the end of it, although knowing you . . . Anyway, I *trust* you. And I trust her—"

"Jeri—"

"Just listen, Mort. I trust her for reasons in her past that she told me in confidence and that I have no right to tell you. But she had an interesting childhood that might explain things—a little anyway. Not traumatic or horrible, but . . . interesting. She can tell you about it if she wants to, that's up to her. Thing is, you don't *need* to know, and that's all I'm gonna say about that."

"She's pretty free about what she wears around me. Or doesn't wear."

"I know. It might have something to do with that thing in her past. I don't see it as a problem. I'm not threatened by it. It doesn't hurt us and it gives her something . . . well, something she doesn't get otherwise. It took a while to convince her I was okay with it, but I finally got through." She looked into my eyes. "When you came back from Bend, did you feel as if she'd taken part of you away from me? Like there was less of you for me than there was before?"

"No. Not at all."

"There you go. Isn't that what's important? She wants to help find Allie—which she can. If her sister is in Tonopah, Sarah would be more likely to recognize her than you. I'm going to stay here and keep working on our lists. You two go check out this guy, Martin Harris, see if there's anything there."

"It felt awfully thin. Like you told Ma."

"It might very well be nothing, but you never know. And if this Martin guy goes out, like to a bar or someplace, even a post office, Sarah—Holiday—might be useful. There's no telling what she could find out that you couldn't."

* * *

Hell, yes. Holiday could wring information out of a washrag, if that washrag were male.

We took the Toyota. She wanted to take her Audi, but I told her it was possible we'd end up on a stakeout. Tonopah isn't a big place. That hot-red Audi would stand out like a flamingo in a bird bath.

"Here we are again," she said as we headed toward Fernley on the interstate. She was wearing a T-shirt with *Pi are not square, Pi are round, cornbread are square* printed across the front. Another pi shirt. Engineers were hilarity incarnate. Who would've guessed? The shirt was easy to read, too, stretched as tight as it was.

"Yeah, here we are," I said. "Which means I'd give a month's pay to know what you and Jeri talked about the other night in the Green Room."

She laughed. "Be worth it, too."

"How 'bout I bribe you? One month's pay. Cash."

"Not a chance."

"Underhanded, Machiavellian broads."

"Uh-oh. You figured us out. That's trouble."

"I don't have diddly-squat figured out."

She gave me a look. "Jeri and I agreed that . . ." Her words slid off into silence. She looked out the side window.

"What did you two agree? Keep talkin', college girl."

"Anyway," she said, apparently losing track of what she'd been about to say. "Your stupid mirror's whistling. It's really annoying. Either pick up the pace, or slow down. Something."

I picked it up to seventy. Tonopah was two hundred forty miles from Reno. Might as well get there, see if we could get a handle on Martin Harris. It was, after all, Sunday, the day retired folk typically cut loose and really paint the town, right after church and a nap.

* * *

We arrived at seven fifteen with the sun half an hour above the western hills. We traveled up a miles-long incline coming in from the north. The town sprawled over the hillside, over 6,000 feet above sea level—no surprise that the day was starting to turn chilly.

We'd ridden in silence ever since passing through Fallon, sixty miles east of Reno. Sarah was in full-blown study mode with a textbook open on her lap, chuckling at all the fun stuff in there. Or maybe chuckling was only my imagination. Snarling might have made essentially the same sound.

On the way south I interrupted her only once.

"Holiday?"

"Mmmm?" Still nose-deep in her textbook.

"What is this with you and Jeri? And me?"

"God, I hate eigenvectors. I mean, calculus is easy. This crud is something else." She pulled her nose out of the book and gave me a perplexed look. "Huh? What'd you say?"

"Nothing."

She went back to her textbook. I looked at her and thought I caught a little smile. Not entirely sure about that, though.

* * *

"Almost there," I told her.

Sarah put her papers and book aside. We were a mile north of the town limit, slowing to forty-five.

"Lovely," she said as we passed by weedy lots and run-down buildings. Everything looked sunbaked, frost-heaved, weathered, old. The place had been losing population slowly but steadily the past two decades. Median income was down, the median age of its residents was up. It had become a retirement mecca, "mecca" being a relative term. It was a place for people who'd had their fill with the crime, traffic, noise, foul air, and chaos of the cities. Add drive-by shootings to that list. Given all that, the mecca thing was working for many of Tonopah's residents. A quick getaway from a crime spree here would take three to five hours at high speed. Might as well drive straight to the county jail, save everyone a lot of time and aggravation.

We passed McGinty's Diner and a fifties motel, the Stargazer. A Texaco station was next door. Farther on we passed a gaudy place called the Clown Motel.

"Now *there's* a fun-lookin' place," Holiday said.

"Ain't it, though."

"Where're we staying?"

"Mizpah Hotel and Casino. Jeri made reservations."

"Reservations? Plural?"

I sighed. "She might've said *a* reservation."

"Jeez, Mort. You almost stopped my heart there." She gave me a Cheshire cat's grin.

I pulled around to the rear of the Mizpah, a five-story edifice of reinforced concrete and brick built in 1907, now registered as one of the Historic Hotels of America.

Recent events had made my face one of the more memorable ones in the country, so I put on a blond wig that felt dumb and a big blond moustache that felt even dumber, then dumb and dumber and Holiday went in the rear entrance of the Mizpah and down a short, wide hallway of blood-red fleur-de-lis wallpaper into a good-sized lobby with more blood-red wallpaper, mahogany trim, and balusters. I looked around, felt history oozing out of the walls. My mother was younger than this place. A dozen or so people were sitting in chairs, chatting in groups, standing around. The last few minutes of sunlight came through cut-glass windows and put a glow on the red carpet, potted plants, burnished wood, crystal.

Holiday ducked into the Wyatt Earp Bar, gave it a look, came back out. "Promising," she said. I didn't ask.

We went to the hotel desk and I rang a bell. Seconds later a girl in her twenties showed up. Short dark brown hair, a gap-toothed smile, a little stud in her nose that might have been put there with a blowgun. I was thinking a recent trip to the Amazon hadn't gone as well as the brochures made out.

"Help you?" she asked.

"Got a reservation for Angel?"

She checked her computer. "Don't see one." She looked up at me, frowned, and said, "You, uh, you look sort of like—"

Hell. "Yeah, I look kinda like some troublemaker in the news. Causes me no end of grief, lemme tell you."

"But your name . . . Angel . . ."

"Angel's my first name. It's never suited me. I've gotta get it changed." I pointed at her computer. "Try DiFrazzia."

She gave me a doubtful look, then went back to the computer, chewing on her lower lip. "Uh . . . nope. Nothing like that."

"Try Dellario," Holiday said.

The girl's face lit up. "Ah, yes, here it is."

Sonofabitch. Dellario? I was going to have to have a talk with Jeri. She'd already forgotten my name, and we were about to get married. What's up with that?

We got a King Room, cleverly named because it held a single king-sized bed. Holiday had wanted the "Lady in Red" suite, but it was taken. It was said to be haunted by the ghost of a lady in red, a prostitute named Rose who'd been murdered by a volatile gambler who found her in bed with a client. The world in 1914 had its share of geniuses, too, since the guy appears not to have known or cared what Rose did for a living until it was thrust in his face. Of course, the guy might have been preoccupied with text messages on his cell phone and not always been aware of what Rose was up to. Sad to say, I think I could shoot that theory by a bunch of today's teenagers and get a lot of bland looks.

Holiday bounced on the bed, all of her, which is what she does, then we gave the place a quick once-over, used the bathroom, then hiked down three flights to the lobby. At a gift shop I bought her a pastel purple sweatshirt with "Mizpah Hotel" across the front above a rendering of the hotel with a setting sun in the background.

"Really?" she said. "You want me to cover up?"

"I know it doesn't have a blessed thing to say about pi, but hang onto it anyway."

"At least it's a nice color. Nice picture on the front, too."

"Glad you like it. Let's go see what Martin's up to."

We went outside. Sarah shivered in the dusk, put the sweatshirt on twenty feet out the door. "Okay," she said. "Good call."

I had Martin Harris' address, but the streets were a tangled mess of spaghetti looping through the hills. I bought a local map at a Chevron station. Harris had a place on Goldfield Road, half a mile out of town, east of the highway.

We went a quarter mile uphill, turned left onto Goldfield, went past a few trailers sitting on dead, patchy yards, then around a low knob of rock fifty feet high. A few houses came into view, one of them the Harris place—single-story clapboard in a fenced-in yard. A shed was in back, three stunted pines out front, a three-car detached garage with its doors down, a four-wheel ATV with fat tires at the east side of the garage. The front windows of the house had a view of fifteen or twenty miles of brown rock and scrub sage in the valley to the north.

Martin Harris might take exception to people watching his house from a parked car, but knocking on the door and asking about Reinhart's hand wasn't an ingenious option either. I drove slowly past the place while Sarah and I took it in, didn't see an SUV of any description, then kept on going.

I turned around at a wide spot in the road a quarter mile away and came back.

"This isn't working," Sarah said as we passed the place again.

"No shit, Shirley."

"We don't know what's inside that garage, Mort."

"At least we found the place," Great Gumshoe replied.

"Good goin'. Be nice if we knew what this guy looked like, huh?"

"Yup."

"You've got that moustache on, and that nasty wig."

"Nasty?"

"Actually, it suits you. But the point is, you could go knock on the door and ask something, like does he know the . . . the . . . well, pick a name, like the Dellarios. Which of course he won't, but least that way you could get a look at him."

"Or you could go ask."

She shook her head. "Nope. I might have to talk to him in a bar or a Laundromat or something. He might talk to me, but not if I've already knocked on his door. Especially if he's hiding something."

Well, shit. She was already a greater gumshoe than I was. I was going to have to rethink this career move.

"Let's go back to town," she said.

I thought about that, then did as she suggested. I dropped her off at a Scolari's supermarket on U.S. 95 and Air Force Road.

"Be cool," she said.

Advice from an expert. I waved, headed down 95 then east on Goldfield, pulled into Martin's driveway, got out and went to the front door, rang a bell. Behind me, the last rays of the sun were giving some high cirrocumulus a faint pinkish cast.

A woman answered. Late sixties, gray-haired, heavy, pleasant face, in jeans and a work shirt with the sleeves rolled halfway to her elbows. "Yes?" she said. "Can I help you?"

Expecting Martin to answer, I thought fast, which took a while. "I'm looking for the Dellario place, ma'am. Thought it was here on Goldfield Road, but it's been a while—nine years—and I don't have the house number, so . . . I can't find it."

"Dellario? I'm sorry, but I've never heard of them."

"Him, unless he got remarried. Guy I knew in college. I, well, I guess it's a long shot, but maybe your husband might know him."

"Marty's out right now. I sent him off to buy milk. He'll be back soon, if he doesn't get to talkin' with anyone, which is what he does."

No information. Perfect. A glance behind her told me the house was well kept, with decent furniture, good carpet. A Mercedes SUV might be a stretch, but maybe not. The mortgage on this place would be half of what it would be in Reno.

"I'll stop by later if I can't find Bill," I said. "Bill Dellario. I'd really like to see him, or find out what happened to him."

I wasn't sure how that pile of lies was going down, but her face didn't change expression. She looked like a nice person. And she didn't fit the description of the thirty-something woman who'd been driving Allie around—if it was Allie. But she could have a daughter about the right age and the DMV said the Harrises owned a green Mercedes SUV, so the situation was still fluid.

"You could come in and wait," Martin's wife said. "I've got a pot of coffee on."

"Thank you kindly, ma'am. But there's a few things I ought to do in town. I'll stop by later if I haven't tracked Bill down."

"I'll let Marty know. Well, I guess that'd be sort of hard since I didn't get your name." She smiled at me.

"Earl," I said. "Earl Johnson." Damn good thing that popped out. I could see myself hopping around, face red, cheeks puffed out, looking like a real winner as I tried to come up with a name.

"Earl, I'm Janet. My husband is Martin—Marty."

I said good-bye and left, drove back to the supermarket. Holiday was outside, talking with an elderly man in the parking lot. They were standing beside a green Mercedes SUV. The old guy had his door open but he wasn't going anywhere. I pulled up three spaces away. As I watched, Holiday took off her sweatshirt, shook out her hair, pushed her chest out another inch as she took several seconds to turn her sweatshirt inside out, then put it back on. Inside out? But she'd gotten the bulky thing off and had the old guy's full attention. I sat in the car watching them talk, then got out and circled far enough around the Mercedes to catch Holiday's eye, then went into the Scolari's.

She came in five minutes later.

"How'd it go out there?" I asked.

"It's not them. I mean, that's not the SUV people have been seeing up around Gerlach."

"How'd you get that?"

"Marty and I are buddies. I asked him how he likes his car and we got to talking."

"Uh-huh. Marty liked your chest, too."

"What he could see of it when I thought to turn my sweatshirt inside out. I didn't want him to leave right away. Anyway, he was rear-ended down in Vegas a week and a half ago and his car's been in the shop since then. He got it back two days ago."

"That's convenient. Wonder if we can verify that."

"I got the name of the body shop. He said they did a 'real fine' job so I asked him for the name in case I ever need one."

"I'll have your gumshoe license printed up in the morning."

She beamed at me, then took me by the arm and led me out to the Toyota. "Okay, now I want a shower. Then dinner."

"A shower, huh?"

"That's right." She gave me a look. "You up for that?"

A shower? *With* Holiday? Nope.

"Nope," I said, just to avoid confusion later.

She made a face at me.

* * *

We drove back to the Mizpah and went up to our room. She started removing clothes, sweatshirt and T-shirt first. "A shower, Mort? That's all, I promise." She looked down at herself. "Except . . . you could help me wash these."

"Looks like a big job, but no, I'm good."

She made another face then pulled off her jeans, folded them, set them carefully on a chair. She strolled to the bathroom in panties, then turned and stood in the doorway.

"Last chance."

"Go ahead. I'll read." I'd already got my Lescroart book out of a duffel bag. I held it up, showed it to her.

"Spoilsport. Jeri okayed it, by the way."

"Okayed what?"

"Us, showering. You know, if it happened to happen."

I stared at her. "She did?"

"Uh-huh. A shower, no serious touching. But, yeah."

"*Serious* touching? What the hell's that mean?"

"She didn't spell it out exactly. But I think it meant the sort of thing that might tend to escalate—which I promise it wouldn't."

"Sounds like something that could've used more clarification. But the point's moot anyway. Y'all have yourself a nice scrub."

"Your loss."

"Go."

She went. I believe it's a sign of ongoing maturity that I read another ten pages of Lescroart's *A Plague of Secrets* while Holiday got wet and naked and I could have been in there, and possibly some sort of limited touching had been okayed by my dippy fiancée with whom I was going to have to have another in-depth talk even though she'd spouted some nonsense about hoping our last talk would be the end of it.

Don't think so, Jeri.

Holiday came out *au naturel*, doing something impromptu with a towel that might've been an inept attempt to dry off. I think that's what she was doing, but it had the flavor of something done decades ago onstage with ostrich feathers.

"Your turn," she said. "Unless you want to watch while I dry my hair."

I set the book down. She looked terrific—slender hips, three-quarter Brazilian trim, great legs, flat stomach. Jeri trusted me. She had encouraged me to give Holiday this, but after half a minute my retinas started to overheat so I got up and headed for the bathroom.

"Gonna shower in your clothes again?" she asked.

"Yep."

"You could undress out here, not get your clothes damp in that fog in there."

"Maybe next time."

Hands on hips, she stared at me. "Have you never been naked in the presence of a woman before? I mean, really."

I went into the bathroom.

She stuck her head in. "Hey, fair is fair."

"Life isn't fair, kiddo."

I shut the door and locked it. From the other side I heard a muffled voice say, "For the record, I've seen erections before."

Great.

CHAPTER TWELVE

DINNER WAS DOWNSTAIRS in an ornate dining room of expensive wallpaper, walnut and mahogany, plush carpet and chandeliers, with the kind of prices that tend to make my eyes bulge. But we were told it was already paid for. The final bill, whatever it might be, was covered by a credit card. That would be Jeri's. This was a business expense incurred during an investigation, so the IRS was getting gouged roughly 25 percent. With the wine, that would run thirty-eight dollars, so I figured the president wasn't going to make it to Martha's Vineyard next year.

Holiday wore a blue silk dress with a modest amount of cleavage showing. She looked terrific. On the other hand, I looked ridiculous in the blond wig and moustache—which made the Lambrusco Red, lobster tails, steak, baked potato, and the crème brûlée a chore, and made Holiday smile.

A glance up the street after dinner told us there was no point in walking around, especially with the temperature in the low forties and dropping, so we hit the Wyatt Earp bar and spent a couple of hours running the tab up another forty-two bucks. Holiday turned heads and I got looks that said "what the hell is a girl like that doing with a dipshit-lookin' loser like you."

Holiday switched to Long Island iced teas, which promised to be interesting. Halfway through her second one, she said, "I told Jeri about my . . . my past."

"Uh-huh."

"Which is why she's okay with us being together like this. One reason, anyway."

"Uh-huh."

"You sure do 'uh-huh' a lot."

"Only when I don't have any idea how to respond."

"You've never asked me much about my past."

"I know you were in the Peace Corps. And you're a pretty good pool player and a hell of a serious student."

She made a face. "There's more. I mean, I've been kind of . . . you know, free around you. I feel like I owe you an explanation."

"Whenever you're ready."

"I'll think about it. Anyway, I wouldn't tell you here. Maybe later, upstairs."

"Well, then, how 'bout another Long Island, kiddo?"

"Oh, sure. Get me drunk, get me loose. You're a bad person, Mort. Really."

"Everyone says so, so it must be true."

"It is. Okay, I'll have one more of these little puppies."

* * *

She drank less than half so she wasn't slurring her words much and she didn't stagger up the stairs to the fourth floor, but I had an arm around her waist to make sure she made it safely.

I am trained and therefore skilled in the art of taking clothes off a woman who's had too much to drink. Turns out it wasn't necessary with Holiday, but she did have me unzip her dress and hold her arm while she stepped out of it. She ambled off to the bathroom in panties, and I heard teeth being brushed. She came out, no longer overdressed, and piled into bed. "Your turn."

I went in, came out minutes later in underwear, which earned me another, "Spoilsport."

I got into bed, kept the offending article of clothing on, and turned out the light. She moved a little closer in the dark and found my left hand, held it in both of hers.

We lay there for five minutes without speaking, connected by hands, then she said, "When I was young, my father was killed in a motorcycle accident. Some guy ran a red light and Dad was hit by a car doing over forty miles an hour. He died instantly. He was twenty-seven, three years older than I am now—practically a kid, now that twenty-seven doesn't seem very old anymore."

I murmured something about being sorry, but she didn't respond to that. Holding my hand was all she wanted or needed. She gave it a little squeeze from time to time as she talked. This, then, was what Jeri knew, what she had heard. Maybe all of this with Holiday was about to make some sort of sense.

"I wasn't quite five years old when he was killed. Allie hadn't even turned one. Suddenly my mother was alone with two kids. She was only twenty-six. I can't imagine being twenty-six with two kids that young, husband gone like that.

"But she was incredibly beautiful and still young. Half a year later she married a nice enough guy—Gerald. Her name is Barbara, by the way, but everyone calls her Barb. Gerald was twelve years older than her, not a lot, really. It's not like he got himself a trophy wife after dumping the first. He'd never been married, but he fell for my mom. Hard. They're still married, in case you're wondering.

"He was in imports. Didn't export anything. But he'd go off to Singapore to buy stuff, negotiate prices. And Bangkok, Hong Kong, Taiwan, the Philippines. Not so much to Japan. He was fairly rich then—not nearly as rich as he is now—but he was building up the business so he traveled a lot and he took his beautiful new wife with him every time, especially the first six or eight years."

The room wasn't entirely dark. Light filtered in through filmy curtains across a window facing the main street. Headlights sent moving shadows across the ceiling. Holiday turned on her side and faced me. I could see the shine of her eyes. She held my hand a little tighter. A warm breast touched my left arm, which was distracting and nice because of my pig gene.

"They couldn't take me and Allie with them on those buying trips. They would go off for two weeks at a time, sometimes as long as a month. When they did, I stayed with my aunt Alice, who was . . . odd. Nice, but different compared to the rest of the world. She's my mother's sister, nine years older than my mom. Alice had, well, *has*, two kids of her own, which I've got to tell you about, but first you have to know that Aunt Alice, was—still is—a professor at the University of San Francisco. She teaches multiculturalism classes, among other things. She was a child all through the middle sixties and early seventies when hippies were big in San Francisco—all that flower children, free love, love-in stuff. She was too young to have gotten into it, but San Francisco is still a liberal city and there's an aura of the hippie era hanging around today, especially around the Haight.

"Anyway, Auntie Alice proved she was into multiculturalism in a big way. She had two kids, two boys by different fathers, two different races or at least two different cultures. The first was Ravi—after Ravi Shankar, of course—and the second was Dylan, after Bob Dylan, but she would never call a son of hers Bob or Robert, of all things, so she went with Dylan's last name.

"Ravi's father was Middle Eastern—Pakistani. He and Aunt Alice never married. They were together for maybe half a year.

After she got pregnant, he took off, which I think suited her just fine. By the way, she's fifty-five now and has never been married, and *that* suits her, too. Then came a Mexican guy, an illegal, who knocked her up and took off. Actually, I don't know if either of them really *took off* or if she chased them away, but neither one was around long enough to have been like a father to the kids."

I said, "Ravi was older than Dylan, right? I'm trying to keep things straight."

"Uh-huh. Ravi is two months older than me. Dylan is two years younger. When my mom started traveling with Gerald, my sister, Allie, wasn't two years old. Alice wouldn't take two children, certainly not a kid eighteen months old. She said three children was plenty, more than enough, so when Mom and Gerald were gone, Allie stayed with Mom's brother, Brett, and his wife, Gina. They had a girl—Misty—a month older than Allie, so that worked out.

"I was five when I first started staying at Alice's. So was Ravi, and Dylan was three. Innocent ages. And . . ."

Holiday got up on an elbow and pressed her lips on mine, then hovered over me. Her face was a shadow, eyes reflecting pinpoints of light. "Things are going to get a little bit strange now. Not bad, but kind of strange."

"Okay."

She kissed me again, no heat, but a kiss all the same, then she settled back down like before, my left hand in both of hers, with that wonderful firm breast against my arm. I took it to be part of that non-serious touching Jeri had mentioned, so I did my best not to let it bother me.

"Come bath time, Aunt Alice would toss all three of us in the tub together. At those ages, five and three, a lot of mothers do that to save time, get everyone clean at once. Back then that's what we did, laughing, rubber duckies, plastic boats, lots of bubbles. I was at Alice's four or five times a year, two to four weeks at a time. The boys became like brothers.

"Next year I was six and the boys were four and six, still not a problem, all of us piled into the tub together.

"Next year, Alice moved into a new place. It didn't have a tub, so she hustled us into a shower. By then, Ravi and I were seven. Sometimes Alice would get in there with us. She was really free like that. None of us thought it was strange. It's just how it was. It was one of those good-sized showers, so it wasn't really crowded, even with four of us in there. I guess we sort of bumped around, but that was part of the fun. It was even more fun when Alice showered with us. That happened half a dozen times that year. I still remember all of us laughing.

"I think it was the next year, when I was eight, that I started to notice the difference between the boys and myself. What I mean is, to *care* about the difference and . . . well, to like it. I thought it was cool even though I didn't yet understand what the difference meant.

"But the thing is, to jump this story forward a little, I showered with Ravi and Dylan until my eleventh birthday—every time it was time for our nightly shower at Aunt Alice's, there we were."

"Eleven, huh? Wow."

"Yeah, I guess. But shower time was more like a party. It was fun, not really a wow. It was . . . normal, what we'd done for years. We'd grown up with it. Maybe it was a little weird that Aunt Alice didn't think anything about it, but that's just how she was. If there was a wow part, it was how much I got to like it, especially when Ravi and I were ten, going on eleven.

"Mom and Gerald were away when I turned eleven. We had a birthday party for me, and that night after the party Alice came into my room and sat on the bed and told me she thought I was getting a little old to be showering with the boys. I told her I didn't mind, that it was fun, but she said it was time. She even gave me my own loofa as a kind of growing-up gift, and that was that. We were done."

Holiday squeezed my hand. "So. What do you think?"

"Ravi probably has a lot of terrific memories."

She laughed. "Yeah, maybe."

"And . . ."

"And what?"

"And, I have a nice firm breast against my arm that's getting a lot of attention."

"Well, good. I was hoping. Anything else?"

"I don't know. That was quite a story, reasonably interesting—notice that I didn't fall asleep—and I guess it might be part of why you like doing what you do, but I'm not sure it explains why Jeri thinks you're safe for me to be around, other than trusting me—which, of course, only makes sense because I'm an IRS monk."

She was quiet for a moment, then, "The first time I had sex, I mean the very first, one-and-only time I've *ever* had sex, it wasn't that great—borderline awful, in fact—I got pregnant. First time, and *boom*. I was sixteen. I was terrified. I didn't tell my parents. I ran to Aunt Alice and she paid for an abortion. And that was it for sex. Done. Now, I don't miss it. It's hard to miss something you've never really had. It's like it threw a switch in my head, like I'm no longer wired for it. I like being undressed around guys like I was with Ravi, but that's all, and it's almost impossible to arrange since guys want to do a lot more than look. And, of course, no one likes a tease. It's not that I'm *trying* to tease—I mean, that's not why I do it. Not at all. It's just . . . the way I am. It makes me feel alive." She turned more toward me. "So—what do you think? Pretty messed up, huh?"

"Because you feel alive wearing sexy clothes, or not wearing anything? Hell no. A lot of women love it when guys look at them, even if they drool. The guys, that is. It's even more understandable given your past at Alice's. So how's little Ravi doing these days? And Dylan? Those two must've been warped for life, showering with you like that. I might've, too, although I would've risked it."

"Well, you missed your big chance earlier this evening."

"Right. And now I feel bad about that. So, about Ravi? Was he institutionalized?"

She laughed. "Little Ravi is six foot one and married. His wife is really pretty. He's a lieutenant JG in the Navy. He graduated from Annapolis. I saw him last year and he just grinned at me. Normal as a guy gets. He has a son two years old."

"So Dylan must be the one who took the hit."

"Dylan is a pre-med student at U.C. Davis. He has a 4.0 GPA and a steady girlfriend. He stopped showering with me when he was eight, going on nine. He and Ravi are fine. I'm the one who maybe got pushed a little out of shape by what we did. I don't even know if it was showering with the boys that did it. Being with them like that was fun and interesting but it didn't really amount to much. It was never a big deal, even that last year. I mean, I was only ten when we quit so it's not like I had boobs or anything. Then Allie went missing and I started looking for her in bars, and, I don't know—maybe that early stuff came back and sort of slammed into me. But right now it's all I've got so I don't want to give it up, at least not yet. It's the only thing that gets me, you know . . . wound up."

"Yeah, about that . . ."

"Don't worry, Mort. I take care of it."

"Uh—"

"If it gets to be too much, I take care of it, that's all."

"How much of this did you tell Jeri?"

"All of it. And she said she understands . . . me."

She still had my hand in both of hers. We lay like that for a few minutes, not saying anything. Her hands were gently kneading mine, maintaining contact. Finally she said, "So, Mort—when you look at me or watch me or whatever—"

"I know."

"Maybe not. What I was about to say . . . I'd hate to think I'm teasing you, but Jeri said not to worry. That . . . you know . . ."

"Let me guess—that she would take care of me."

"Uh-huh. She laughed when she said it, but I think she meant it."

"Don't worry, kiddo, she did. And then some."

"Good. I'm glad. Last thing I'd want is to come between you two. If I did, that would be the end of it for me."

Another minute of silence, then I said, "Gettin' kinda late. You ready to sleep?"

"Probably a good idea." She turned loose of my hand, gave me a quick hug that had a little breast in it—but she couldn't help it and I didn't blame her for it—then she moved away. "Night, Mort."

"Night."

Two minutes later:

"Mort?"

"Yup."

"Um, I'm not quite sure how to say this."

"Just out with it. That's best."

"Well, okay. It's just—Jeri really did okay that shower thing. If it happened."

"Uh-huh."

"And, you know, if we did, a little boob rub in there would be nice, and I promise it wouldn't lead to anything more. If it wouldn't be too much for you."

* * *

And *that's* why I lost another sonofabitchin' hour of sleep then dreamed I was in a supermarket buying cantaloupes.

CHAPTER THIRTEEN

JERI PHONED AT six thirty the next morning, Monday, when Holiday and I were still asleep. She apologized for the early call, but Ma had come up with another lead, one that looked promising. Jeri wanted to wait until I got back to Reno so she and I could pursue it together, so—an early wake-up call to get us up and moving.

Holiday and I piled out of bed. Well, she did. I sat on the edge of the bed and watched while she dressed—which, walking around and sorting through various clothing options, took her a while—not a bad thing to wake up to in the morning. Almost as good as coffee. Caffeinated.

"Rushed it," I said. "Three minutes, forty-five seconds."

"Rushed what?"

"Gathering clothes, putting them on."

She smiled, fastening the last button on a fresh shirt. "Well . . . I was sort of embarrassed. Which was strange, but kind of nice, too. I mean, it had a little more zing to it than before, probably because of our talking last night."

"Zing is good, now turn your back."

She laughed.

We ate breakfast in the hotel café, and passed the city limit on the way north at seven fifty a.m. after verifying that Martin Harris had indeed had his car repaired at Desert Eagle Body Shop in Vegas during the time he said it was there. This was investigation at a snail's pace. His Mercedes SUV wasn't the one we were trying to find. One down, eight to go. Jeri had told me investigations lead to dead ends more often than not, so get used to it.

Ma had come up with another hot lead. I hoped it was hotter than the one we'd just followed. I put the Toyota up to seventy-five and hustled us back to Reno. In the desert, with sage-covered playas sloping upward into dry barren hills, I saw a tear roll down Sarah's cheek.

"Hey," I said.

She gave me a wan smile and wiped her eyes. "It's nothing."

"That doesn't look like nothing."

"I'm just being silly. Do you have Kleenex in here?"

I got a small package of tissues out of the glove box, handed it to her.

She took one, dabbed her eyes, and sniffed. "It's been so good for me lately. I mean, it's been so intense, not like in the bars. But it can't last, since you've got Jeri. Then it'll be back to . . . well, to sort of nothing much."

"There are a lot of guys out there, Sarah."

Her voice took on a bluesy note. "Sure. Boy Scout types who like to look but don't need more than that. Lots of 'em out there."

Damn. That Boy Scout thing again.

"You're like one in a million, Mort. In case you didn't know."

Well . . . yeah.

"So," she went on, "I guess I'm crying about what I've lost. Or will lose in a while—soon, most likely. I know it's dumb, but if this ends, which I guess it'll have to, then what? I know I'll live, but life will be so empty and gray. I guess I'm just spoiled."

"There's got to be someone out there who would fall all over himself to look at you and breathe heavy while doing it."

She smiled. "You didn't do any heavy breathing. Last night *or* this morning."

"Yeah, I did. I just know how to hide it."

"Great. Now I need a personals ad: Heavy breather wanted, must have Boy Scout personality."

"Never know what you'd get with that."

She let out a pained laugh. "I wouldn't get you. Thing is, I don't think this stupid fake hooker thing will work anymore. It's nothing like what you and I have been doing the past few days."

I shrugged. "Guess not."

"After being with you, it wouldn't. Now . . . I don't know. I don't suppose Jeri would loan you out from time to time? Like once a week. Let me wind you up pretty good, then she can take you over the edge?"

"Over the edge, huh?"

She looked at me. "Well, *yeah*. Seems like you'd need that."

Made me smile. "Once a week, huh? Wouldn't hurt to ask." Her, not me. Me it might hurt. Me it might put in the hospital. Then again, maybe not. Jeri was full of surprises these days.

"Yeah, right. I'll just—'Hey, Jeri, send Mort over so he can watch me . . . I don't know, take a long shower or water my plants, whatever.' I'm sure that'd go over big."

"She told me she understands you. There's that."

"What? You think she wouldn't mind?" Holiday's voice held a hopeful note, as if she thought there might be a chance.

I didn't know how to answer that so I didn't try.

"What about you, Mort? Would you? You know, *if*?"

Those were some rip-roarin' questions. Nothing like that ever came up when I was working for the IRS. Would I like to watch a gorgeous girl take a shower? Me? You kiddin'? I'd *so* hate that. I would rather walk on hot coals. What would I do if Holiday asked Jeri and Jeri said, sure, you can have him on Tuesdays?

"I'm gonna have to take the fifth on that, kiddo."

Another strained laugh. "Sorry. I know I'm not being fair. I just feel kind of broken right now. I'll get over it. But . . . damn, I think this is gonna be hard."

* * *

I dropped Holiday off at her place in Reno then went over to Jeri's. I found myself involved in an epic lip lock four seconds after I got in the door. When we came up for air, Jeri said, "We've got another lead on the Reinhart thing, and how'd it go with Sarah?"

"Interesting, as usual. And I got that story you said was up to her to tell me. Showering with the boys."

"Pretty wild, huh?"

"A little, maybe. I've heard worse. How about we go take a walk? I've been sitting for over two hundred miles."

It was a nice day, shadows dappling the sidewalks, birds in the trees, not much traffic, temperature in the seventies. We did the river walk—headed west toward Keystone Avenue then through Idlewild Park with the Truckee River to our right, ducks floating in a pond to our left, and I told Jeri what happened in Tonopah, including how long it took Sarah to get dressed that morning. And about her tears in the car on the way back, and her comment about maybe getting yours truly on loan from time to time.

"Almost four minutes to get dressed? Wow. I could get mostly decent in a minute fifteen."

"Give 'er a break. She was still half asleep."

Jeri smiled. "And she gets to wind you up on Tuesdays, then I get to take you over the edge?"

"Over the edge was her idea, Tuesdays was mine. I didn't tell her that, though. She didn't seem in the mood for humor right then."

Jeri took a deep breath, blew it out. "We should turn around, go back." She took my arm, got us headed east at a fair clip.

"Things are that bad, huh?"

"No. I just want to get you into bed and make sure nothing got broken. Sounds like you might've been wound up pretty tight."

"I'm okay, but I appreciate your concern."

"You don't sound rational. We should walk faster."

Which we did.

Jeri looked up at me. "She cried? Really?"

"A few tears. She's been having a pretty good time lately, but knows it isn't going to last."

"I think Tuesdays would be okay. I don't normally have a lot on my plate on Tuesdays."

I stopped dead. "Don't tell her that. She might not get it."

"You're not on a leash, Mort. Neither am I, in case you didn't know. C'mon." She got me walking again.

"So, *off* leash," I said. "That include you and other guys?"

She made a face. "No, and that's not even *close* to the point. The point is, if I decide I want to, it'll be my decision, *mine*, not yours, not ours, but mine alone. It *has* to be. Then I would tell you about it and we would decide what it meant. So you've seen a lot of Sarah lately, literally, and now we need to decide what that means in terms of us."

"I'm right here, Jeri. I'm not going anywhere."

"So am I. And now I want to get you into bed, so I think we've already decided how it's gonna go. I really like Sarah. I understand her. Strange as it sounds, I'm glad she's been enjoying herself. And it was safe, no one got hurt, you and I are still fine, so . . . let's walk faster, okay?"

* * *

I still didn't know what to make of all that, but I didn't have a lot of time to think about it because up in our bedroom Jeri put me over the edge, twice, and yesterday and this morning slipped into a fog bank, then oblivion.

When I awoke, it was to a big bowl of chicken soup, Jeri's idea of a joke. "Might need it after your Boy Scout heroism with Sarah. Chicken soup fixes all kinds of things."

"Ha, ha. I'm going to have to do something to purge that Boy Scout image, and I don't think it'll be pretty." I sat up higher in bed. The bedside clock showed 2:15. A glance out a window and I decided it was afternoon, probably still Monday, although Tuesday wasn't out of the question.

"Knowing you I'm sure it'll be really ugly. Now . . . that thing about loaning you out has me wondering—should I or shouldn't I?"

I stared at her.

She laughed in my face. "Eat your soup."

"You didn't answer the question."

"You didn't ask one."

"That should-I-or-shouldn't-I question that *you* asked."

She gave me a quick kiss. "Shut up and eat."

"So we're good? This soup is what it appears to be? It hasn't been seasoned with garlic, thyme, arsenic, any of those special ingredients?"

"*Hey!* We're great, in case you don't remember the past couple of hours."

"Seems like there was something going on. It's hard to put my finger on exactly what, but . . . something."

She took the soup out of my hands, put it on a night table, then reached under the covers, grabbed, and said, "That bring back any of it, bucko?"

"Oof. Yeah, it does. Gimme that fuckin' soup."

* * *

"Odermann," Ma said. We were in her downtown office, a musty room that smelled of floor wax, cigarette smoke, and a side dish of *eau de bathroom* drifting up a communal hallway. Ma was sitting at her computer, looking up at Jeri and me. "I was digging around Jayson Wexel, Reinhart's chief of staff, guy that died in that fire, and got a hit on that list of owners of Mercedes SUVs."

"Came up with a registered sex offender or someone with a serious criminal background, right?" I said. I try to be helpful, act as if computer searches are the highlight of my day. And I was still a little loopy from some recent activity.

"Close," Ma said, not batting an eye. "I got a hit when I looked into Wexel's personal lawyer, Leland—"

"Ah, the lawyer did it. Who woulda guessed?"

Jeri elbowed me in the ribs, so that lovey-dovey thing with the soup was now in the past.

"—Leland R. Bye," Ma went on, giving me the eye, "Wexel's lawyer, has a brother-in-law, Bob Odermann, living in Sparks. Got Bob via Mary Odermann, Leland Bye's sister. Bob wouldn't be on my radar except your list has a Mercedes registered to a Mary Bye Odermann who, it turns out, died two years ago, which makes me think someone was being too smart for their own good. I'm thinking Bob has the Mercedes, not Mary. If the car was registered in Bob's name I wouldn't be all over this like wool on a sheep, but registering the car in the name of a dead woman sorta raised a flag."

"Sorta?" Mr. Swifty said before I could stop him.

Ma laughed. "Irony ain't your thing, is it?"

Well, shit. These two women were gonna make sure I didn't make my next Mensa meeting. Time to shut up and listen, especially since this was entirely for my benefit. Jeri already knew the story.

Ma said, "You probably oughta know what those two drive, in case you gotta follow 'em. According to DMV records, Leland Bye owns a 2017 blue Lexus SUV, and Bob Odermann has an old Honda Civic, 2004, red. Unless, of course, he's using Mary's Mercedes."

"So," Jeri said to me, "we go nose around Odermann, see if we can get a line on that SUV since it's in his deceased wife's name."

"We, to be clear, meaning you, me, and Ma, right?" I asked.

"Close. You, me, and Sarah, if she has time. Ma's gonna keep working on the lists. Odermann might not pan out."

"Great. I was hoping you and Sarah would get together and talk over that Tuesday loan program, get the kinks ironed out."

This time my ribs were backhanded, kinda hard, too. But then Jeri patted my cheek and said in a matter-of-fact tone, "We'll see."

Sonofabitch. If only I could figure women out. They toy with me and I don't think that's right.

"Tuesday loan?" Ma asked. "Kinks?"

"Tell you later," Jeri said. She took me by the arm and led me out of the office.

"You wouldn't run that nonsense past Ma, would you? She's brutal. I'd never hear the end of it."

"Who said it was nonsense? Anyway, I was gonna loan you out to Ma, not Sarah. Well, maybe both of them, but Ma's got dibs. Now come on."

* * *

It was Monday, late enough that Sarah's classes were over. She was eager to go with us. Jeri drove us over to her apartment without asking for directions, so they'd done a passel of talking, getting to know each other—and I like the word *passel*, don't feel as if I get to use it often enough.

"Hi, Jer," Sarah said. *Jer*. Then to me, a subdued, "Hi."

"We talked," Jeri said to her. "Everything's fine."

Sarah smiled and Jeri hugged her. Said something in her ear I didn't hear, and Sarah's smile got wider. She gave me a happy face.

Women. Can't live with 'em.

"So what's up?" Sarah asked.

Jeri said, "We might have a lead on Allie. And Reinhart, if he's in the mix, which looks likely. It might not be anything, but it looks better than the one in Tonopah."

Sarah's face fell. "God, I wish Allie would call again. Or text, Facebook me. *Something*. I hate this not knowing."

We piled into Sarah's Audi—we'd taken Jeri's Porsche to Sarah's apartment—with me in back where the leg room can be measured in meters, not inches, so my turning sideways in the seat was just theatrics. Jeri told her about Bob Odermann and the SUV registered to Bob's dead wife as we drove to the address in Sparks that Ma had come up with. In fact, Ma had supplied us with four addresses, the home and business addresses of both Odermann and Wexel's lawyer, Leland Bye.

"His wife has been dead for two years but the new car was in her name?" Sarah asked. "That's gotta mean something, doesn't it?"

"Uh-huh," Jeri said. "It could mean Bob's really unobservant."

Damn, I wish I'd thought of that.

But then the talk turned to such amiable chatter about health food and where the best organic produce could be found in Reno that it was as if Oregon and Tonopah had never happened, or was such a non-issue that none of it warranted discussion—or that there was a hulking pile of ears in the backseat that didn't need to hear any of what they might really want to talk about.

Well, they were wrong. The ears craved information.

Anyway, we arrived safely in a residential neighborhood in Sparks and cruised slowly past a nondescript one-story house that was well maintained but . . . nondescript. Like hiding an egg in an egg carton, it blended in with the rest of the houses on the street to the point that it hardly existed: light blue vinyl siding, off-white trim, aluminum-frame windows, asphalt roofing shingles, front door with a small glass insert at eye level, fourteen hundred square feet, all on what looked like a sixth of an acre with a forty-foot poplar tree in the backyard, leaves just starting to turn color. Net worth, no more than a hundred sixty-five thousand. It didn't exactly shout, "My dead wife can afford a new Mercedes SUV." But then, how many dead wives in the neighborhood could?

The time was three thirty-five p.m. No car in the driveway. The door was rolled down on a two-car attached garage. No sign of life.

"Now what?" Sarah asked.

"Let's go see where the guy works," Jeri said. She gave Sarah the address of a print shop on Kietzke Lane.

The shop was small but it looked clean and was in a fairly decent location. I didn't think it would support a Mercedes SUV, but that was only an impression. Bob might've paid off the mortgage and could now afford a car worth two-thirds as much as his house. Not a great financial move by any stretch, but his kids might be grown, wife gone, insurance policy kicked in a hundred grand, and he might be feeling upwardly mobile again.

The Fine Printing Company—a great name that probably took a lot of thought by a passel of big brains—shared a parking lot with a Jiffy Lube next door. It was impossible to tell which cars belonged to the owners or customers of which businesses, but none of them was a Mercedes anything—SUV or otherwise. The only green car on the lot was an aging Saturn SL2.

"Now what?" Sarah asked again. We were parked on the street, almost in front of the place.

"What do you think, Mort?" Jeri asked, looking not at me but at the print shop.

Ah, finally bringing the backseat into the loop. "Looking for a little professional advice, are we?"

She turned and stared at me. "I was under the impression that someone in this car is training to be a gumshoe, so I thought I'd give that person a chance to shine like a freakin' beacon."

"Was that irony? I have trouble with irony. Although that rhyme at the end was totally awesome, dude."

"Mort—"

"How about I go in and order up ten thousand fliers? See if good ol' Bob is in there."

"How about you go in and ask what ten thousand fliers would *cost*, maybe save us a couple thousand dollars?"

"That'd work, too."

"Got your wig and moustache?"

"Yup."

"Then go get 'em, hotshot. We'll wait."

Man, that was a lot of irony. I put on my disguise, such as it was, and went into the shop. Two guys were there, both in their fifties, so I had a fifty-fifty shot of picking out our suspect—if you get both ways that worked out. If I wanted to really screw this up, I could ask which one of them was Bob.

Or not.

"Hey," I said. "Which one of you's Bob?" I had to half-shout over a printer that was chucking out paper by the ream.

A mostly bald guy in overalls looked up. "That's me. Who wants to know?"

"I do. Name's Steve. Earl said you do good work here."

"Earl who?"

"Earl Johnson."

"Don't know an Earl Johnson, but we do good work here so it don't matter. What can I do you for?"

"I need ten thousand fliers. I'm looking for a cost estimate."

He stared at me. "*Ten* thousand?"

Well, shit. That would weigh about a hundred pounds. I caught the disbelief, read his body language, and did a gumshoe shuffle that would've made Jeri proud. I would describe it to her later, see if it got me more chicken soup, or maybe something better. "Christ, did I say ten? I meant a thousand. *Ten* thousand and I could stuff nine thousand of 'em in my walls for insulation."

He snorted a laugh. "Okay, a thou. CMYK? Black and white? Can't give an estimate if I don't know what you're after."

"CMYK?"

"Four-color printing."

Well, shit. I didn't know crap about printing. But I am a trained professional, so I said, "I don't know crap about printing, Bob. Do you have something like a brochure or a chart? Maybe I can pick out what I'm looking for."

"Uh-huh. Right here." He tapped a finger on a well-worn price sheet with little sample images on it, taped to the countertop.

I stared at it, tried to check out the shop while I was at it, and finally decided a thousand CMYK fliers for two hundred ten bucks was just the ticket. Inspired, I said, "Fliers are for a Mercedes SUV I've gotta unload. Damn thing's not even a year old, too."

He stared at me for a moment, eyes locked with mine. "Huh," he said, then sort of shook himself and said, "I'd put an ad in the paper, but that's just me." He gave me a curious look. "A thousand fliers to sell a car like that? Man, that don't sound right."

I tried to look dumb and innocent. I think I got the first of those right. "Two ten, huh? Maybe we don't need a thousand. I'll talk it over with the wife and get back to you on that."

"Got to keep that ball and chain happy, uh-huh."

"Don't we all?" Thought I'd see if he would mention he'd been cut loose. But he didn't, and I didn't want to have to come up with any specifics about my Mercedes, such as engine size or how many wheels it had, so instead of a manly knuckle bump, I rapped Bob's countertop twice and got the hell out.

I headed down the street so he wouldn't see that I was in a car with two potential ball-and-chains in it, neither of whom had come in with me. Sarah pulled to the curb a block away and I got in.

"What'd you find out?" Jeri asked.

"A thousand full-color fliers'll cost us two hundred ten bucks, honey bun."

Sarah laughed. And it was a damn good thing I was in the backseat, out of reach of people with short arms.

CHAPTER FOURTEEN

"WHAT TIME IS IT?" Jeri asked after I'd given them the rundown on Bob, not that there was much to run down.

I checked my watch. "Four fifteen."

"Let's see if Leland Bye, Esquire, is at his office." She gave Sarah an address on California Avenue, several blocks west of the federal courthouse in Reno.

Sarah parked kitty-corner across the street from a two-story glass-and-steel office building that had a sign out front for five lawyers and two CPAs. Jeri stared at the building, evidently thinking like an investigator. I stared at Jeri, thinking like a guy who might like to toss her into bed later that evening and rough her up.

Jeri won that round, but I wasn't giving up hope.

"Okay, looks like I'm up," she said. "You two wait here."

She got out and walked over to the building. I got in front with Sarah and watched Jeri disappear inside.

"How're you doing?" I asked.

"Okay, good. Better now. She . . . when we hugged, what she said was, 'Good for you.' Which I guess means she's fine with—with what you and I have been doing."

"And I got chicken soup, so we both made out like bandits. Oh, and I brought up that lend-lease thing you mentioned. We're on for Tuesday evenings."

"What lend—oh, Mort, you didn't! I wasn't serious. You know that, don't you? I mean, I wasn't . . . really . . ."

Truth lies in the hesitations. Hope springs eternal. Sarah took my hand and kissed my palm. "One in a million," she said. "But don't bring it up again, okay? It was just kind of a joke. Really. I mean, if *she* says anything . . ." She fell silent.

"Yup."

Jeri came back out. She stopped at the car and looked in at me, in her seat, maybe deciding if she could haul me out and dead-lift me before packing me in back, so I beat her to it and packed myself.

"He's there," Jeri said, getting in. "And there's a small parking lot at the side of the building. I didn't see a green SUV of any kind there, but I saw a dark blue Lexus SUV, so I think we could follow him easily enough if he leaves."

"What's he look like?"

"Attractive white-haired guy, slender, looks like a runner. Hair is pure white, like snow, so he's either prematurely white or has it dyed, since Ma says he's only fifty-one."

"Did he look guilty?" I asked.

"Well, of course he looked guilty. He's a lawyer."

"What I think I meant was, is this getting us anywhere?"

"Right now we're scouting the territory, Mort. Now I know which office in there is his and I know what he looks like. You've had a look at Odermann. We might try following Bye if he leaves, see where he goes. Or we could go check out his residence right now, fill in that gap."

Which we did, more or less unsuccessfully.

Leland Bye lived in southwest Reno in a gated community, which probably had something to do with Shakespeare's line: "The first thing we do, let's kill all the lawyers." Jeri pursed her lips as she contemplated what to do about the guard and the gate, then she shrugged and said, "We better not push our luck.

We've got Bye and Odermann in our sights, but we don't want them to know it."

"I'm sort of confused," Sarah said. "Who is this lawyer? How does he fit into all this again?"

"He's Wexel's lawyer," Jeri said. "We're giving Wexel a close look because he was Reinhart's chief of staff, and he died recently. Suspiciously, too. Mary Odermann is—was—Bye's sister. She died two years ago, but a green Mercedes SUV was registered in her name in May, using Bob Odermann's home address."

"So we ought to keep an eye on this Bob guy, right? I mean, if he's got the SUV."

Jeri thought about it for a moment. "You and Mort found three people who said a woman in her thirties was driving that SUV. I'm pretty sure it wasn't Mary, and I'm almost as sure it wasn't Bob in drag. Although these days that's not something you can count on."

Another round of silence settled over us.

"Might be Mary's sister, if she's got one," Sarah said.

"Or," Jeri said. "Bob's girlfriend, a close neighbor, the wife of a friend. Or Leland Bye's wife or a girlfriend, one of his secretaries, or maybe his daughter if she looks a little old for her age."

"Well, shit," I said. "Aren't you a pip, raining on this parade?"

More silence.

"I wonder if Bob Odermann even knows there's a Mercedes SUV registered to his wife," Sarah said uncertainly.

"I think he does," I said. "When I mentioned that I wanted the fliers to sell a Mercedes SUV, he stared at me for a moment like I'd sprouted wings. Took him a few seconds to shake it off."

"So he's probably involved somehow," Jeri said. "Now what we need is something like that with Bye. See if a similar comment gets a rise out of him."

"Back to his office?" Sarah asked.

"Maybe we oughta hold off on that, think about this for a while. We might get Ma's advice while we're at it. She's probably at home by now. We could go over there, talk to her."

"Or," I said. "We could sit around a table in the Green Room where they've got beer and beer nuts."

Jeri turned and looked at me. "Beer has nuts? I didn't know."

"Well, aren't you a pistol, sweetheart?"

Jeri smiled, then shrugged. "Ma would probably go for that. I'll find out." She pulled out her cell phone.

* * *

We held a powwow in the Green Room. O'Roarke was just coming on duty so I gave him two free-drink coupons—I still had about twenty left from the fistful he'd given me in the hospital—and we sat around a table, Jeri and Sarah with Cokes—free, no coupons needed—Ma and I with Wicked Ales straight from bottles like real men. Sarah was in a modest T-shirt and jeans, Jeri in a yellow blouse and white pants, so things had settled down, at least for now.

"I've been all over that SUV, trying to get at the financial end of it," Ma said. "Not gettin' anywhere, though, but Bob's last 1040 had his gross income at only fifty-four grand."

I perked up when I heard *1040*. It's hard to turn that shit off. Ma put a hand on my knee and said, "Take it easy, boyo." To everyone—including me—she said, "Mary Odermann owns that Mercedes outright, so maybe you *can* take it with you in spite of what everyone says. Anyway, if she owns it, then so does Bob. How that happened, I don't know. I don't see a lending institution of any sort giving him—or her, God rest her—a loan for a hundred-twenty-thousand-dollar car. *And*, I'll bet she doesn't drive much."

"What if he didn't buy it?" Jeri asked. "What if he doesn't have it and never did? It looks like he knows about it, but . . . what if?"

Ma cocked her head at Jeri. "My, what interesting thoughts."

Jeri took a sip of her Coke. "I think Leland Bye is in this thing up to his waist, if not to his neck. Maybe he put up the money."

"Got us a conspiracy by the tail, huh?" Ma said.

"Could be. In what, exactly, I don't know, but we've got two women, Allie and this other one, driving around doing stuff it looks like they don't want anyone knowing about. Like shipping the hand of a presidential candidate to Mort, which I have to say I don't like one fucking bit." She gave me a look.

"Same here," I said. "It's been a real drag."

"Jesus," Jeri said. She turned to Ma again. "I get scared when he gets serious, so right now I'm good, but you should try to dig a little deeper around Leland Bye. Try to find out who's got the car now, how it was paid for."

"Leland I can do, but that car ain't easy, hon. Especially who's got it now. If it hasn't been reported stolen, anyone can drive it. If they don't get pulled over or get in an accident, there's not gonna be any record of who's been behind the wheel lately."

"Exactly my point. Something's going on that someone doesn't want anyone looking into, not with a vehicle registered to a dead woman. I don't know how Mort getting that hand fits with any of this, but if it weren't for that SUV popping up all over the place up north and this FedEx thing, we wouldn't have the slightest idea there might be any connection between Allie and Reinhart."

She looked at Sarah. "You and Mort made that giant leap up in Bend with that guy, Fred Something. I'll bet the FBI isn't on the same planet as us right now, investigation-wise."

"Maybe we ought to turn it over to them," I said.

Ma stared at me as if I'd lost my mind. "Bite your *tongue*, doll. We cut this tree down, we get the lumber. I'm talking *Good Morning America, The Today Show, Dateline, Hannity*—"

"Hold it down a little, Ma," Jeri said, looking around. The bar had another three or four people in it by then.

Ma patted my knee. "Got a little carried away there, but you get the idea. This could be retirement, Caribbean beaches, Fiji, lovely brown men in tiny bathing suits bringin' me mai tais in a cabana." Her eyes danced. "Anyway, I'll keep digging. We gotta find that SUV. That's key. We find that and we're golden."

But we weren't *golden* yet. Things were squishy, which felt like a long way from golden. On the bright side, Ma was probably right about us being miles ahead of the Feds. I oughta know. I used to be one. The size of any bureaucracy is inversely proportional to its effective IQ. Put twenty FBI guys in one room and the collective IQ wouldn't be sufficient to open a can of Spam. A task that size would require weeks of high-level meetings, an organization chart, an environmental impact statement, and a look at applicable OSHA regs. Same thing in the White House and Congress, which keeps me awake nights, considering how little Spam figures in the bigger scheme of things, like an imploding affordable health care system.

Ma took off, thinking Caribbean beaches. That left me, Jeri, and Sarah—and, surprise, they wanted to talk alone again. So I sat at the bar and tried to chat up O'Roarke about low-fat recipes and color coordinating our clothing, but he wasn't interested.

Sonofabitch.

So I used another Wicked Ale to help nudge my thoughts about this Reinhart-Allie-Odermann-Bye mess. I gave that up after about thirty seconds. We didn't have enough information. Did

Odermann have the SUV, or didn't he? Did Bye have anything to do with any of this, or was his dead sister a dead end, leaving Bye out of it? Was Bob a criminal mastermind? And Jayson Wexel, forty-nine, chief of staff to the High Priest of Prevarication, cremated in his house. Was that an accident or murder? I hadn't heard the official result of that yet. And Reinhart's hand. Was the good senator dead or alive? What about Mortimer Angel? What was *he* in all of this?

"Do you think I might've killed Reinhart and shipped his hand to myself in a fugue state?" I asked O'Roarke as I ran a bead of moisture around the bar top with the tip of a finger.

"I wouldn't put it past you."

I turned on the barstool. Jeri and Sarah had their heads eight inches apart, talking quietly. Maybe some sort of lending program was in the works. Maybe they were comparing notes.

"Think I'm paranoid?" I asked O'Roarke.

"Hell, no. People really *are* out to get you, spitfire." He nodded at Jeri and Sarah. "Those two especially."

Well, shit. Enough of this. I went back and sat with the girls. "What's up?" I asked, always a great opening line.

"Jesus Christ, Mort. She asked if you wanted to shower with her and you turned her down? You didn't tell me *that* part."

"I didn't want to brag. When you're done chatting you'll find me at one of the roulette wheels."

I got up and left.

* * *

The three of us ate dinner at the Peppermill buffet, one of the top three buffets in Reno. They allowed me to choose the venue—probably a consolation prize. I chose the Peppermill because the parking was easy and I could have roast beef and other fine cuisine, and they could have salads with chickpeas and beets and other stuff that wasn't meant to support life—though looking at those two gorgeous broads, I might've been wrong about that.

When we left the casino, the sunset was a band of golden fire above the Sierras. A discussion ensued, resulting in Sarah driving us back to her apartment so Jeri and I could retrieve Jeri's Porsche and Sarah could entertain herself with a textbook and a report that was due on Wednesday, day after next.

"Where to?" I asked Jeri when we were alone, headed south on Valley Road.

"You didn't shower with her? Wow."

"We could talk about something else. That salad you had at the Peppermill looked mighty tasty. Beets and sprouts, yum."

"Seriously, Mort? You wasted water?"

"Yup, nope. I mean, I showered later, so I guess yup."

"Jesus." She shook her head, then reached over and rubbed my neck, gave it a little massage. "You're something else."

I didn't say anything. She was right, of course, but I decided to let my natural humility shine through.

"How about we swing by Odermann's place?" Jeri said.

"You're driving, kiddo."

She smiled, hit I-80 and headed east, got off at Vista, looped through an aging subdivision, and pulled to the curb across from Bob's house. A glow behind curtains suggested someone was home.

We sat there for a while, then Jeri turned off the engine.

"Stakeout?" I asked.

She shrugged.

"Be a lot faster if I go kick in the front door, ask him about that SUV," I said.

"You should do that, see how it turns out. The essence of PI work is experience."

Okay, she had me there.

We settled in and began to talk in earnest. An hour passed, then another. Somewhere during the third hour I was finally convinced that all the antics with Sarah—Holiday—was not an issue with Jeri. If there was an issue, it was undetectable, a sneeze in a hurricane. Something about Holiday had gotten under Jeri's skin, something about shared loneliness, frustration, desire, fear, repression—a real potpourri of emotions, too tangled for me to sort out. But Jeri kept at it—what else are stakeouts for?—speaking quietly, doing her best to explain it to me, and, I thought, to herself. I think she knew what she felt, but hadn't known why—not entirely. Talking it out seemed to help. Finally she blew out a gust of air and said, "Anyway, Mort, I understand all of this. I get it."

"Not sure I do. Yet. I mean, your acceptance of it."

Her voice remained serious. "Maybe you will and maybe you won't. This thing about not owning you. It feels . . . deep."

"I'm not a deep guy."

"You're deeper than you think. Anyway, Bob's lights have been out for over an hour and stakeouts are ten percent boredom and ninety percent having to pee, so let's get the hell out of here."

Which we did.

CHAPTER FIFTEEN

MA SAID, "I found another connection with those lists, but I don't like it. I like the Odermann thing."

"What'd you find?" Jeri asked.

Tuesday morning in Ma's office, with bagels. Mine could've used a breakfast steak and a fried egg on it, but no such luck.

"Okay, try to follow this," Ma said. "Reinhart's wife—her name is Julia—has a married brother living in Alaska. The brother's wife has a sister named Lana who married a George Szupello and they live in Vegas. In case you've forgotten, Szupello is on the list of those SUV owners. If the name hadn't been so far out there, I never woulda found it. Szupello of all things."

"Jesus H. Christ, that's thin," I said. I didn't know how the hell she'd found it. Jeri had said Ma was good, but maybe she was too good, coming up with stuff like that.

"It's a drop of spit in Tahoe," Ma said. "Lake Tahoe has enough water in it to cover all of California something like a foot deep."

"I didn't know that," I said. "Nice stat."

"You two," Jeri growled. "Can we keep it on track?"

Ma grinned. "Anyway, there it is, but I wouldn't follow up on that on a bet. At least not yet."

"We'll keep after Bye and Odermann," Jeri said. "I like it that the SUV was registered to a dead woman."

"I sort of like Julia," I said. "We oughta stake her out."

Jeri turned to me. "Why? She pretty?"

"What I saw of her on TV, she ain't bad." In fact, she was or is a fairly typical trophy wife, given what I know about trophy wives, which is to say they're younger and prettier than the wife who helped make the guy successful, and they're interested enough in an older man's wallet to grit their teeth and put up with the sex thing. And, having come up with that great analysis, I said it aloud.

"Okay, you're not a complete idiot," Jeri said.

"I glow under your praise, darlin', but I like Julia for another reason. If Reinhart is dead, who benefits?"

"The entire country," Jeri said. "How's that help us?"

"*Cui bono*," Ma muttered.

We both stared at her. I was about to burp her when she said, "In case you're Latin-challenged, that's Latin for 'who benefits.'"

"Man, I gotta remember that," I said.

Jeri said, "Can't see that she benefits. Odds are she isn't gonna be First Lady now. Or even the wife of a powerful politician, even if he is a low-life grub worm. Let's get outta here. We'll go check out Odermann or Bye, Ma."

"Yeah, bye," Ma said.

"Bye, bye, Ma," I said.

Jeri spun me around and shoved me toward the door. "I don't know if you're gonna make it as a PI, Mort."

"Why's that?"

"This is serious fucking business and you're a goddamn flake and a half."

Ma's bray of laughter followed us out the door.

* * *

Jeri drove us straight to Sarah's place where we switched cars again. Holiday and I sat up front in the Audi while Jeri took the backseat. I knew it was Holiday because cleavage was abundant.

I had the impression Tonopah had worn off and someone's hormones were starting to flare up again.

We parked on California Avenue across the street from a place called the Dancing Hippo, which hardly seemed like a good name for a place that caters to an anorexic crowd in high heels. I'd been in there one time, with Jeri, and almost starved to death on one of their sandwiches before I made it out the door. Eighty feet away, Leland Bye and four other attorneys were making two or three hundred dollars an hour while we sat in the car and watched the place and made something like, oh, zero dollars per hour. But the view was terrific so I didn't complain. Every so often I looked up at the office building, just to be sure no one had moved it, which, if they had, would have made me look like a damn fool.

We had a license plate and VIN on Mary's SUV, but no SUV. During our travels around town we'd picked up a brochure from the local Mercedes dealer and had pictures of a Mercedes G550 so we could tell one of those from any of a hundred other SUVs. If it showed up, we'd be all over it.

Yawn.

At twelve fifteen, Jeri said, "We could go over to the Dancing Hippo and get something to eat."

"No we couldn't," I said.

"Why not?"

"They don't have anything in there to eat, that's why."

"Tofu."

"Just what I said. Negative calories. It takes more calories to break that stuff down than you get when it finally turns to pond scum and shoots on through."

"Je-sus, what a fuckin' image," Jeri said.

"Phone Ma. See if she's got anything on Julia."

"Julia?" Holiday asked.

"Reinhart's wife," Jeri said. "Mort's got a bug up his butt."

"Really? There's a doctor's office across Virginia Street, over on Ryland."

I shook my head sadly. "I distinctly remember someone telling me I wasn't cut out for this PI thing since I was a flake and a half, and here I am with two flakes. So how about that Julia thing, huh?"

Jeri shrugged, got Ma on the phone, put her on speaker, and told her to look into Julia.

"Been there, done that," Ma said.

"No hits?"

"Nothing much. Other than it don't look like she's in line to be First Lady anymore, what with a husband who probably can't tie his own shoes—if he's still alive, that is, which I wouldn't put a lot of money on."

"How about the basics, Ma?" I said. "Age, address, that sort of thing."

"Hold on, I got that somewhere around here." Papers shuffled, then: "Okay, she's thirty-six, blond, five foot nine, hundred thirty-two pounds—bitch—no children, been married to Harry for eleven years. They got hitched six months after he got rid of some baggage by the name of Rhonda Reinhart, née Fenner, of Bryn Mawr—la-de-fuckin'-da—the same year their youngest kid, Kyle, graduated from Ha'vid—more la-de-da—with a Ph.D. in economics. I think you'd be better off looking into this Rhonda lady since she's the one who got dumped, except she's remarried, lives in Baton Rouge, and her name is Rhonda Alsford now. So, back to Julia . . ." She read off an address in the hills of southwest Reno where a starter home would run newlyweds in the seven-hundred-thousand-dollar range. A look at a city map and, lo!—same gated community where Bye lived. I liked that, except that particular *community* sprawled over the hills like fungus and involved hundreds of homes, maybe a thousand, some of which were nearly two miles from the guard shack. Big place. I also liked Rhonda, who had been tossed aside like a used Kleenex—revenge being a dish best served cold according to all the experts.

"Think you could get us in there, Ma?" I asked. "The place is gated."

"Is one and one two?"

"Wait, I'll ask." I looked over at Holiday. "You're the engineer. Is it?"

"In binary, one-one is three, so I don't know."

"Binary, huh? We could've used that in the IRS to keep people off balance. So, Ma, it's looking like we're kinda stalemated on that math problem—"

"Je-sus Christ," Jeri said. She took the phone off speaker and from what Holiday and I got from the one-sided conversation that ensued was that one and one were in fact two, and given roughly ten minutes' notice, Ma could get us through any gated community in Reno or Sparks.

"I'll let you know," Jeri said. She hung up, then gave me a slit-eyed look. "Reinhart's wife, Mort? What the hell for? We've got this Odermann-Bye thing cooking."

"Call it gumshoe intuition."

"Right. I'll do that. In the meantime, I'm gonna go over to the Dancing Hippo and get something to eat. You with me, Sarah?"

"Absolutely."

"Just don't get tofu," I called out as they crossed the street.

* * *

When they got back, I was finishing off a slice of pizza.

"Where the *hell* did you get that?" Jeri asked as she and Holiday got back in the Audi.

"Dominos. They deliver."

"You had it delivered?"

"Uh-huh. Medium-size meat-lover's special. I told 'em to hold the tofu."

"Some guy came by, delivered pizza? No physical address, just a car parked at the curb?"

"It was a girl, actually. Cute, too. But yeah, I gave her a five-dollar tip and she only had to drive half a mile so this was her lucky day."

"They delivered to a car? Seriously? Economy must really suck right now."

"Does, yeah. Anyway, since I'm getting bed sores on my butt, I came up with an idea."

"Do I want to hear it?"

"Probably not, but I want to go back to Gerlach and watch the highway. I can sit outside that motel and see everything that comes by. Only place that SUV has been seen is up north. I phoned, got a reservation. They said they'll hold the room for an hour, till I phone back."

"I don't know, Mort. Maybe. It's not the worst idea you've come up with. Want to take Sarah with you?"

"Well, no. I was thinking I'd catch a little alone time." I looked at Holiday. "That okay?"

She bit her lower lip. "Sure. Fine."

Didn't sound fine, which probably meant I'd just disappointed someone. "I thought you had a report due tomorrow?"

"It's finished. I know someone who could turn it in for me. But if you don't want me along, that's fine."

Jeri tracked this exchange, didn't say anything. I was on my own. When I first thought about being a PI, I'd thought about dark alleys and bullets whizzing past my ears. This was worse.

"A little down time won't hurt any of us," I said. "So, yeah, I'll go up there, ask around, keep an eye out, be back tomorrow. That okay, honey bun?" I said to Jeri.

"If you want. We're kinda spinning our wheels here." She gave me a questioning look and flicked her eyes toward Holiday, but I gave her a little head shake that said no. I got a minute eyebrow lift in return that said it might be nice if I reconsidered. But she'd said she didn't own me, so I was taking her at her word. I was free to do what I wanted.

I got out of the car then bent down and looked in. My Toyota was parked at Jeri's place. "I'll walk. It's less than a mile. I'll be in Gerlach by four, four thirty. I might even see that SUV on the drive up, you never know."

"Call me," Jeri said.

"If you find out anything about Allie," Holiday said, "let me know right away. I'm really worried."

"Will do. See you two later." I gave them both one last look then took off, west on California, north on Arlington, walking fast to work off the pizza, eager to get on the road, be alone for a while. I hadn't known I needed it, but the idea of heading out on my own felt good. I wanted some quiet time to think without having to talk. It's not that easy to do around an estrogen mist. Thinking, that is.

* * *

I called Corti's Motel from Jeri's place, told 'em I'd keep that reservation, then I got on the freeway, headed east.

North of Nixon the road was devoid of traffic. I scattered a few crows picking at roadkill on the way up, got to Empire at four p.m., reached the Texaco station in Gerlach seven minutes later.

I pulled in and filled the tank, gave Hank Waldo forty bucks and got change.

"You see that Mercedes SUV again, Hank?" I asked.

"Nope." He spat on the ground.

Good enough. Sometimes gumshoe work is quick and easy. I parked in front of the motel and walked over to the casino. Cheryl was tending bar and handling motel registration. She was still hefty, still pretty, still mid-thirties, still smelling of cigarettes.

"Sarsaparilla?" she said as I sat at the bar.

"What a memory. I'll take the sarsaparilla, and you're holding a room for me."

She got the 'rilla first, pointed out the chandelier in case I'd forgotten, then pushed a motel registration form toward me. "Got you in fourteen," she said. "I'll be over later, about ten."

My jaw dropped.

"Kidding," she said. "I'm married. To Dave, who you might've met. The other bartender? He'll be in in a couple of hours."

"Yep. We've bumped knuckles."

"Then you two've bumped more than he an' I have this week."

Jesus. I would have to quit talking to women.

I walked over to the motel with a room key and my drink, went inside, hauled a chair outside and sat, tilted back against the wall, and started to watch the highway.

CHAPTER SIXTEEN

HUNGER DROVE ME over to the restaurant at eight forty-five. The sun had been down for an hour and the night was quiet.

No green SUV. In fact, maybe one vehicle had gone by every ten or fifteen minutes, so it wasn't like a Macy's Parade. I hadn't gotten anywhere, but I'd made an effort, I had been diligent, hadn't fallen asleep, and all of that felt good.

Dave was at the bar when I went in. Cheryl was there, too, so I was careful since there was a grenade in the room and I didn't know if anyone had pulled the pin.

Evidently not. Dave sent a dark draft my way, and I ordered up a medium-rare sirloin with a baked potato and a salad. I ate at the bar where I could keep an eye on the TV and keep the beer current and cold.

"Where's the little lady?" Dave asked, wiping a glass.

"Reno."

"Long way from here."

"About nine minutes in that rocket car Andy Green drove in the Black Rock up here in '97. Seven hundred sixty-three miles an hour."

"Fast, yeah, but that thing doesn't corner worth a shit."

"Good point."

"Still looking for that girl? What's her name?"

"Allie. And, yes."

"No one like that's been in here lately."

"Not sure I'd expect her to. She might've been in a Mercedes SUV, here in Gerlach and around." I didn't want to give away that Bend sighting. "I've been watching the highway from outside my motel room."

"Yeah? I'd rather watch granite decompose."

"Gettin' that way myself," I said as I downed the last bite of steak and pushed my plate away.

Another clip of Reinhart was on the TV. When a presidential candidate's shaking hand turns up without the candidate, it makes for a real fine story, one with legs. Reinhart was still missing so it was looking like he was out of the race, although if he showed up he could count on the sympathy vote. I got another glimpse of Julia Reinhart, dodging cameras, dodging questions. Jayson Wexel got a solid thirty-second mention. The FBI was calling his death a murder now, and yellow-journalistic speculation sells beer and cars. Reinhart and Wexel had probably stabbed five hundred people in the back over the years, so the FBI ought to be hip-deep in suspects by now. I wondered if it was smart for Jeri, Ma, me, and now Sarah, to keep that green SUV away from them. Ma might have a point about it being our tree to cut down, but that slippery Mercedes was getting to be damned annoying.

Cheryl shoved a sarsaparilla in front of me and nodded at the chandelier.

"Rain check," I said. "Pulled a muscle in my shoulder."

"Well, shit."

I got another draft and headed off to my room. I took a shower and dried while watching the television, then sat in bed for an hour reading my Lescroart novel, found out Lescroart is pronounced *Les-kwah*, then hit the lights and passed out.

* * *

The next morning I was halfway through a stack of pancakes with sausages and scrambled eggs when Deputy Roup came in, sat at my table, and ordered up another Hunter's Special.

"Back again?" he said.

"Yep. Real nice place you got here, Deputy."

"You've been a hell of a boon to the local economy, Angel."

"Always glad to help out."

"City council's thinkin' of hiring you to stick around and find more body parts. Turn folks here into millionaires."

"This place is a city, huh?"

"We might be shy a few people, but we can call it any doggone thing we want. Still looking for that SUV?"

"Uh-huh."

"Don't know if this'll help, but a white Mercedes G550 went through here four or five days ago."

I paused with a load of pancake on my fork. "White?"

"Unless my eyes're goin'."

"Which direction?"

"South. Toward Reno."

"Right on through? Didn't stop for gas?"

"I asked Hank. He would've seen it if it had."

"Did you see who was driving?"

"A woman. Not old, not young. In her thirties, I'd say. Brown hair, shoulder-length or longer, dark glasses. That's about it. All I'm getting are two-second looks. I still don't see myself pulling folks over without some sort of a reason."

White, not green.

"Same year as the green, huh?" I said.

"Uh-huh. We don't get a lot of 550s through here, but now you got me looking."

Another Mercedes SUV. It came from somewhere up north. I checked my watch. 8:40 a.m. Bend was a long way off, over three hundred miles, but if I pushed it I could be up there by one thirty. I could have phoned around, tried to find a car painter or body shop in Alturas or Bend that had recently painted a green SUV white, which might be a stretch, but I thought it was worth looking into. A lot better than watching granite decompose. I gave Jeri a call, told her about the white SUV, told her what I wanted to do.

"Wait a few minutes, Mort. Stay there. I'll call you right back."

"What's up?"

"Just wait." Then she was gone.

I got myself another cup of coffee and stared at the TV above the bar. Terrorists had blown up more stuff in France. Animals. I don't think they're politically motivated at all. That's just an excuse. They're delinquents—ninth-century bad boys who get off humping camels and blowing stuff up. If they finally got what they say they want, they'd still hump camels, blow stuff up, and use Allah as an excuse. Low-life barbarians, but dangerous with twentieth-century technology.

My cell phone rang just as Ma Clary came in the door. I stared at her thinking *sonofabitch*, then said into the phone, "Hey, guess what, Jeri, Ma just walked in."

"Really? Now *there's* a coincidence for you."

"Tell me about it."

Ma pulled out a chair and sat at the table, gave Deputy Roup a smile. "Tell you about what?" she asked me.

"Nothin', Ma. I am a leaf in the wind."

Ma turned away from me. "Deppity Roup. How're you doin', doll?"

"Jest fine, Ma. How 'bout yourself?"

"What's going on?" Jeri said in my ear.

"Not sure. It might be old home week. You sent Ma up?"

"She wanted to get out. She thought she'd help you ask around Gerlach, but now it looks like you two oughta go up to Bend, check around, see about that white SUV. She'll be really good at that."

Ma ordered a beer from a waitress about nineteen years old then lit up a cigarette, blew smoke skyward.

"Gotta go, Jer," I said. "Ma's on fire here." Ma looked at me, then cackled.

"Talk to you later," Jeri said. "Learn from her, Mort. She's a hell of an investigator. Bye."

"Bye."

"What was that about old home week?" Ma asked. "If it's what I think it was, you're in big trouble, boyo."

"No comment."

Ma turned to Roup and pointed a finger at his plate. "What've you got there, Mike?"

"Hunter's Special."

"Looks good. I'll have me one of those." She turned and called halfway across the room. "Hunter's Special with that beer, hon."

"Want to make it to go?" I said, ears ringing.

Ma stared at me. "Why would I want to do that?"

"'Cause we're headed to Bend in about five minutes."

She continued her stare. "Not without my Special, we're not." She called out again, "Put a rush on that food, hon. And make it to go." Then she turned to Roup. "So, doll, what's the story? You don't call, you don't write—"

"Got myself hitched, Ma. Two years ago."

"Well, shit. That puts a damper on things. Guess that means you an' me aren't gettin' together till you get divorced again, that about right?"

"Lookin' like it, yeah."

Ma turned to me. "So, boyo, what's this nonsense about you and me goin' all the way to Bend, huh?"

* * *

The brown Caddy Eldorado floated over the highway as if on a cushion of air, which was a combination of good shocks and soft springs, circa 1963. It also made travel iffy at more than fifty miles an hour so the scenery wasn't exactly whipping by.

I drove. Ma ate.

"Goddamn Mike," she said. "Gettin' himself hitched like that. He sure knows how to take the fun out of things."

"Yep. Goddamn Mike."

She stared at me, then laughed, took another bite of ham. "Think that SUV might've been painted white, huh?"

"I think we better try to find out."

"Good instincts. And it's good you made contacts in Gerlach, got eyes on the street like that."

"I appreciate that, Ma. Thanks."

We drove in silence for a while. Ma finished her breakfast, stuffed the remains in a plastic bag, put it on the floor behind her seat. She looked out the window at the desert. The day was overcast with a hint of fall in the air. That wouldn't last. It was late September. We had a month or so of Indian Summer coming up, but the weather was starting to bounce around.

A car passed us doing seventy-five or eighty. Made us look like we were parked in the middle of the road. Nice.

"I'm glad Jeri finally found someone," Ma said. "Been a while. Too long. She needed someone. She told you what happened when she was twenty-one, didn't she?"

"You mean Beau?" Beau was a guy who'd gotten Jeri pregnant, took off as soon as she told him, which had soured her worldview for the next six or seven years. She'd miscarried at two months, which had been a mixed blessing.

"Yeah, Beau. That little shitbird—may he roast in Hades."

"She told me."

"Now there's a guy who needed cutting off at the knees, except it turns out he did her a favor, splitting like that. No telling what her life would be like if she'd married him. He was good-looking and charming and turned out to be a sleazebag anyway. There are times when a person is better off alone. A lot better." She looked at me. "But you. You're just what she needs."

I didn't know what to say to that, mostly because I didn't know where Holiday fit into what Jeri wanted or needed.

Ma said, "Jeri saved my butt two years ago. She tell you?"

"No details. Just that whatever it was, you wouldn't charge her for your time on this thing with Reinhart and Allie."

"Damn straight I won't." She leaned the passenger seat back a few notches. "Been a long time since I rode over here in this seat. It's more comfortable than I remembered. If I fall asleep, wake me up when we get to Bend."

"I'll do that. I saw an air horn in the trunk."

"Touch it and you're a dead duck." She closed her eyes and leaned her head back. "Guy came into the office eighteen years ago. Name was Isaac Biggs. He wanted me to find his ex-wife, said he wanted to reconcile with her. Ex-wives, ex-husbands, those are always red-flag deals. You get a lot of lies, people saying they want one thing when they really want another. Biggs was a red flag as soon as he walked in the door. A walking, talking red flag, twenty-eight, scruffy, trouble on the hoof. I listened to him, didn't take him on as a client so confidentiality wasn't an issue. But I had his ex-wife's name and some other stuff, so I found her myself after he left, told the police in Salt Lake they better keep an eye on her for a while. Which they did, farmed it out. Biggs went and hired another PI who found the ex-wife. Biggs showed up one day later, actually got off a shot with a gun from outside the house, missed the girl by six feet. He was drunk, dumb as a post, got hit with a bean-bag round by a pretty good rent-a-cop and was sent up for attempted murder."

"Sounds like a fun guy."

"A real sweetheart. He had sixteen years to figure out how he got caught, why some guy was right there at the ex-wife's place waiting for him, finally figured it was me that ratted him out, and he showed up at my office when he got out of prison. Jeri and I were there trying to locate some lady's son who'd taken off with a bunch of her jewelry and her car. Biggs came storming through the building, which was his big mistake, but that scumbag was and always will be as dumb as a pound and a half of chickenshit. Jeri isn't one to wait around and see what's what before she acts. She got beside the door—Lord, that girl is quick on her feet!—and when Biggs came through she saw the gun and broke his leg with one kick. Broke his knee, actually. Kicked it from the side and shattered it. She put him down so fast he didn't get to use the gun, but his finger jerked on the trigger and he put a hole in that sideboard you might've seen, which reminds me every day that that bullet was meant for me. I probably ought to mention that she didn't stop with the knee. She's an alley cat. She picked him up like a sack of grain and hauled him across the office, slammed his head through a window, didn't send him on through though, then she hauled him back inside and broke his nose, jaw, bunch of teeth. When the police came, they had to take him out on a gurney. He's in the Nevada state prison in Carson doing twenty-five without parole. One thing I owe Jeri for is the pleasure of watching her kick Biggs' ass so hard he's probably still bouncing. That and my life, so, yeah, no charge for anything she needs, ever. If not for her, I wouldn't be here."

"Remind me never to piss her off, Ma."

"Not sure you need reminding. You saw what she did to that psycho Victoria, didn'tcha?"

"Yep." In fact, that was a memory I still treasured. Victoria had come through a door thinking murder, and Jeri kicked her under the chin so hard it ripped her esophagus loose internally, broke her neck, and shattered her jaw. I remember seeing a piece of tongue fly across the room. Victoria was dead before she hit the floor.

"She is some kinda bobcat, that girl," Ma said. "Told me about this thing with Holiday that has you tied up in knots."

Aw, jeez.

"I've been around the block a time or two, in case you hadn't guessed," Ma said.

"Really? All the way around at least twice?"

"That's right, boyo. So here's a little something you might not know. A lot of us gals don't want to be jail keepers."

"Jail keepers?"

"Wardens, prison guards. Take some poor schmuck and tell him what he can and can't see and think, can and can't enjoy. If I was with some guy, I wouldn't want to tell him he couldn't at least look at women—half-clothed, naked, whatever—just like I wouldn't want him to tell me I couldn't look at naked men, if that's what I wanted to do. I've been to *Thunder Down Under* at the Grand Sierra Resort—with Jeri, in case you didn't know. The last thing I need is some uptight warden micromanaging my life, telling me what I can and can't do like that. So here you got maybe eighty million adult women in the country, and I'd guess eighty or ninety percent of 'em are wardens, mind police, whether or not they know it or care to admit it. But that leaves ten or twenty percent who aren't, and Jeri is one of those. Umpteen million women out there are smart enough to know you can't reach into a guy's head and throw that eunuch switch. Guys are what they are. We gals are, too, but that's a secret we don't let out. Get a warden who thinks she can change what turns a guy's head, she's an idiot, fooling herself. She thinks by guilt tripping and snarling loud and long if he so much as glances at another woman that she's changed him, but all she's done is driven him underground and made him realize he's married to a jail keeper and he'd better keep his head down. All jail keepers get is surface behavior and resentment. That includes mind wardens who are male, too, so it works both ways."

"This is a hell of a discussion, Ma."

"Let me know if I'm boring you."

"I'll do that."

"Anyway, Jeri's worried that you don't get it, so I'm putting in my two cents, that's all."

"Lately I've felt like I'm on loan."

She stared at me. "You're somethin' else. I can see why Jeri's worried about you. She isn't loaning you to Sarah. Not sharing you, either—not in any usual sense of the word. If you want another two cents on top of the two I just gave you, here's a concept: Jeri is sort of gifting you—to each other."

"Gifting."

"Both you and Sarah, in case you don't get it. Letting you do what you want. That's a gift. Think about it, boyo. That's all I got for you. Except Jeri isn't a jail keeper and she isn't worried about you two, so unless you and Sarah are in deeper than you're telling, you oughta just settle down and enjoy the ride. And if you want another penny—if I looked half as good as that girl I'd dress up and turn a few male heads, lemme tell you. Life never gave me that, but if it had, I would've been all over it in a heartbeat."

"Now I've got a whole nickel, Ma."

"Yeah? Spend it wisely. Now if you don't mind I'm gonna catch a little shut-eye."

Which she did. Two minutes later she was fast asleep, leaving me alone with my thoughts, working on jail keepers and gifting.

* * *

I woke Ma up a few miles outside of Alturas. We cruised the main street from one end to the other and back, found a guy who did minor body work on cars along with brake jobs and tune-ups, but he'd never painted a car in his life.

So, back on the road.

A quick look around Lakeview, Oregon, gave us a body shop that would paint a car, but they'd never painted a Mercedes SUV.

So, on to Bend.

Ma drifted in and out of light dozes. I had to stop at a roadside gas station and get a Red Bull to keep going. A hundred miles from Bend Ma was awake so I said, "Gifting."

Ma smiled. "Keep chewin' on it. Probably best if you try not to think like a guy."

"No sweat. I'll do that."

A hundred miles. It took two hours and we didn't get to Bend until four twenty in the afternoon. Twenty miles out, Ma pulled out her cell phone and found three body shops, no car painters.

We hit Bud's Body Shop first. Bud and two others hadn't seen a Mercedes SUV, green or otherwise, so we drove over to Lou's Auto Body on SE Railroad Street. And hit pay dirt. Lou was a one-legged guy in a wheelchair who no longer did body work, but his son and two employees did.

Lou was sixty-five years old, with spindly arms and a pot gut, white whiskers. He'd gotten on Medicare two months ago, and was elated to have dumped a health care plan that had been cost- ing him an arm and a leg. He pointed to the missing leg, told us he'd given it as last year's premium. Nice.

"Nine hundred fifty dollars a month with a ten-thousand- dollar deductible. Sonofabitchin' ACA was about to bankrupt my ass," he said. "Affordable Fucking Care Act, my limp dick. Washington's full of imbeciles. So what kin I do for you?"

"Lookin' for a Mercedes SUV," Ma said. "Green, didn't look like it needed painting, but it might've been brought in and painted white anyway."

"Yep. Did that. Pretty weird deal, lemme tell you."

Ma and I looked at each other. Ma was smiling. I might, later, but I was still too surprised to smile. I was a hell of a fine gumshoe. Remarkable, really. If I'd had feathers, I would've preened, turned my head all the way around, and pecked mites off my back. This was great. We'd been looking for a green SUV, but the son of a bitch had turned white.

"Lady said she didn't care for green," Lou said. "So why'd you buy a green one, I asked her? She told me she'd bought it off some guy for peanuts so between that and a new paint job she'd still come out ahead. Me, I'd have kept the green. Car wasn't a year old, paint was in perfect shape, but she wanted it white, so, hell, I'll take her money. Charged her twenty-four hundred bucks. She paid it without battin' an eye."

"Do you have the charge slip?" Ma asked.

"Nope. She paid cash."

"Cash. That seem right to you?"

He shrugged. "I've been in this business forty years. I've seen cash before."

"Was anyone with her?"

"Like who?"

"Like anyone."

"Didn't see anyone. She came in alone."

"When was that?"

Lou couldn't remember. He wheeled himself into his office and thumbed through a pile of receipts, pulled one out. "Brought it in just last Thursday." He shook his head. "What's today? Wednesday? Wasn't all that long ago. My damn mind's going. Can't remember much of anything these days."

"How about the VIN number?"

"Got that," he said. "Change the color of a car, law says I gotta take down the VIN number, report it to the DMV."

"Uh-huh. Knew that. What state were the plates?"

"Nevada. Don't know why she didn't get it painted in Reno, Sparks, Carson. I asked, but she said she was visiting her sister up here and she'd be around a couple of days, so why not here? Me, I don't look a gift horse in the mouth, so I took her money."

"Who'd you report the VIN to?"

"Nevada DMV, of course." He gave Ma the VIN and she typed it into her cell phone.

Ma turned to me. "Hell. If I'd thought about a color change I might've picked up on this in Reno. I'll have to remember this." To Lou she said, "This place got Wi-Fi?"

"Yep. So's I can roll around, stay connected."

"Mind if I get in?"

"Nope. The password is 'BABS by Lou.'"

"BABS?"

"Bad Ass Body Shop. Don't tell anyone 'round here or they'll start cloggin' up my Internet."

"Don't you worry, doll." She hustled out to the Eldorado, came back with a laptop, and got online with Nevada DMV using her investigator's access. "Ah-hah," she said. "VIN for that SUV is registered to Mary Odermann, but now it's got the color as white, not green, so they changed it. Hell. I shoulda been checking that every couple of days for all those cars."

"Live and learn, Ma," I said.

She gave me a dim smile. "Yep. I missed that one." She turned to Lou. "What'd this woman look like?"

He thought about that for a moment. "Let's see . . . seems I remember dark hair, kinda long, dark glasses, even here in the shop, and she had on some kinda hat with a big brim."

"How tall?"

"From down here in this chair, hard to tell. Five seven to maybe five ten. Fairly tall side of average."

"How old did she look?"

"Somewhere in her thirties. Doubt if she'd hit forty yet."

"Thin, fat?"

"Thinnish. Not heavy. Good figure, what I could see of it."

"Round face or thin? Moles, anything like that?"

"Don't really know from round or thin faces. And I didn't see anything like a mole anywhere. Probably wouldn't anyway. I don't generally take note of that kind of thing. If she was missing an arm or leg, I'd've seen that, probably bought her a drink."

"Fingernail polish?"

He tilted his head. "Yeah. Saw that when she counted out a bunch of bills, paying for the work. Sorta red, with some kinda design on the nails like they do nowadays."

"How long was the car in for painting?"

"Day and a bit. She came in right about noon. We were eating lunch. We got right on it, had it painted by five, had it drying under heat lamps all night. She picked it up that next afternoon, Friday."

"So she spent the night here in Bend."

"Must've, yeah. Probably at her sister's."

"Got an address for the sister?"

"She didn't give one."

"Phone number?"

"Didn't leave that either. She said she'd be back and that was that. Acted in a hurry. Kinda tight-ass."

"Did anyone here in the shop drive her anywhere?"

"Nope. She said she'd phone her sister, have her come pick her up."

"Did you see that happen?"

"Not me. Might ask one of the boys, though. I don't get around so good, so I didn't go look outside when she left."

Ma turned to me. "Did I miss anything?"

"How were her teeth?" I asked Lou.

Ma laughed. "Jeri said you were hopeless. C'mon." She pulled me toward the three-bay garage.

"Any of you guys see that lady whose Mercedes you painted white last Thursday?" she asked in a loud voice.

All of them came over. All of them had seen her. They were a grease-stained lot, grease in their hair, paint on their clothes. Two of them could've used haircuts so they didn't look so much like girls from the back, but that wasn't my business or my problem.

"Any of you see where she went?" Ma said. "What car picked her up?"

"No car," said a tall, skinny guy with paint-speckled glasses. "At least not right out front. She headed down the street on foot, that way." He pointed.

"Then what?" Ma asked.

The guy shrugged. "Then nothin'. She was gone, so we got to work on her car. Rush job."

"Was anyone with her? Waiting outside or anything?"

He shrugged. "Didn't see anyone."

"What was she wearing?"

"A dress, kinda summery. Day was warm enough."

"What color dress?"

"Blue. Bluish. Had stuff printed on it, like flowers."

"How'd her legs look?"

All three looked at each other. "Good, right?" the skinny guy asked the others. "Yeah, real good," a chubby guy said.

"How about her chest, guys?"

The skinny one grinned. "That was pretty nice, too."

"There, see?" Ma said to me.

"See what?"

"No eunuch switch, so I don't look for one."

She thanked the three guys and we left. Ma headed down the street in the direction the one guy had pointed. I kept up with her. "No eunuch switch," I said.

"One guy in a hundred actually has one. Guys with names like Percy Milquetoast, Roger Gelding, things like that. Doesn't get my old heart racing, lemme tell you. One problem with *Thunder Down Under* is half those guys are into guys, not girls. I wish they'd make them wear something like a purple sweatband so I'd know which was which. Go to something like that, all you can do is hope the one that really gets you in a lather is a *guy* guy, not just well-muscled eye candy dreaming about Brad."

When we reached the corner, Ma shaded her eyes, looked west toward the main drag. "I don't think there's a sister up here. Let's go get the Caddy and check some nearby motels, see if we can find out where she stayed."

CHAPTER SEVENTEEN

WE HIT THE main street, SE Third, and looked both ways. A few blocks south was the Cascade Lodge. An Econo Lodge and a Motel 6 were up north, two blocks away.

"Might be harder to figure out where she stayed than which body shop she used," Ma said. "Body shop with three guys versus a motel with umpteen employees and foot traffic in and out. But she dropped the car off around noon last Thursday, and it's Wednesday now, middle of the week, so the same people might be manning the desks. We've got a decent shot at this. So look around, boyo. She's on foot. Which way would she go?"

I looked both ways again. Fairly busy street. The Econo and Motel 6 were on the far side of the street, but closer. The Cascade was a block farther away, but on this side of the street. Traffic lights would make it easy to cross over. But she was in a Mercedes, and the Cascade was a step up from the Econo and the Six.

"Left," I said. "Cascade Lodge."

Ma smiled. "You show promise. Let's go."

I drove south, pulled into the registration parking area, and we went in. A girl was at the desk, late twenties, pretty, Hispanic, halo of glossy black hair around her head and shoulders, big eyes, full lips, wearing a pale blue polo shirt with the Cascade logo on it.

"Help you?" she asked in a slight Spanish accent.

Ma nudged my hip, low enough that the counter hid it. She walked a few feet away and checked out brochures for local outdoor activities—hiking, river rafting, local rodeo, horseback riding.

"Hi there, sweetheart," I said, hoping I'd hit the right note. "I'm trying to track down a woman who might've checked in here about a week ago."

"You look juss like that guy." Her accent picked up a notch, put a little extra *ooo* on look, turned it into "luke." I liked that.

"What g—oh, yeah, him. I've been getting that." Sonofabitch. I'd forgotten my wig, moustache.

"Him on the TV. He good lookin', juss like you." She gave me a smile with some heat in it. A tag on her chest said *Sophie*.

Okay, this was working out, now that we'd gotten over the shy, awkward, getting-to-know-you part. "Thanks. Maybe we could get a drink later, Sophie."

"I get off at ten."

In my face. That old PI black magic was still alive and well, ghosts of Spade and Hammer in the corners, hooting and catcalling, slapping each other on the back.

"Great," I said. "Where's a good place we could meet?"

"There's a lounge down the street. The Evergreen." She leaned closer, lowered her voice. "It would juss be, you know, for a drink."

"Absolutely. But, uh, I'm looking for a woman who was here, or might have been, a week ago. Alone, in her thirties, maybe in a sort of blue print dress, a few inches taller than you, dark hair."

"You know this woman?"

"No. I'm trying to find out who she is."

"You a cop?"

"Nope. I'm a PI. Private eye."

"Yeah?" She smiled. "I like that." She looked around. "I saw a woman like this, but, you know, I could like lose my job if . . . you know."

"Uh-huh," I said. The Evergreen was definitely in my future. Having gotten the gist of things, Ma had moved farther away. In fact, as I watched, she went out the double glass doors and stood outside, looking around.

Sophie stared at her. "That your mother?"

"Nope. She's a PI, too. We're working together." And it was a good thing she was outside or, due to sudden death syndrome, this conversation with Sophie might be over right now.

Or maybe not. Maybe Ma would laugh it off. She was actually about the right age to be my mom. She didn't appear to have a huge ego when it came to her age or her looks. But I could be wrong, and if I had to guess, I'd say I was since being wrong is more or less my MO. Anyway, back to Sophie, who was looking at me with what I thought was a shy but interested smile. Probably wrong again.

"So," I said. "See you at the Evergreen? A little after ten?"

"Okay. Uh, what your name?" Name came out "nem." Nice.

"Steve," I said. Steve sounded like a safe name, unlike Bubba or Spike, or even Jack—ever since that awkward Ripper business in London a while back. I wasn't going to learn anything about the SUV lady until after ten, and I didn't want to scare Sophie off.

Little did I know.

* * *

"Got me a hot date, Ma," I said.

"Attaboy."

"Evergreen tonight at ten. Bar down the street. I think maybe Sophie saw the woman we're looking for, but I can't be sure. She might just want a nightcap."

"Sophie, huh? Cute little thing, too."

"Yup."

"Good work. Except I don't expect a lot outta her unless you can get a charge slip or a license plate number, which I don't think is gonna happen tonight at the Evergreen unless she's got one hell of a memory. Anyway, right now we could use us a place to stay."

I looked back at the desk through the glass doors. Sophie was watching us. She smiled at me. "We're at a place now, Ma. It looks like the kind of place that might have rooms."

"Uh-huh. It also has a hot Latin number at the desk who would check us in—so she'd know what room you're in and she'd have access to a room key."

"All very true and interesting, but what's your point?"

"Figger it out."

"I am trusted, Ma. Around naked women, too. Ask Jeri. I am a rock, I am a freakin' islan—"

She grabbed my arm and hustled me toward the Caddy. We got in and Ma said, "Motel 6, boyo. We'll get a couple of rooms then check out this Evergreen place. Then we'll find us a place to eat. So are you gonna drive this thing or do I gotta push?"

"Go ahead. I want to see how fast you can get 'er going. Ten miles an hour and I'll buy you dinner, including appetizer."

"Drive."

We ended up in rooms fourteen and fifteen at Motel 6, fifty-two bucks each, two queen beds in the rooms, Wi-Fi, comfortable but generic, with mints on the pillows. A knock on the door roused me from my enchantment with the accommodations.

"Didn't order room service," I called out.

A bark of laughter came from outside. "Let's get goin', boyo."

I opened the door, then looked back inside. "Look, Ma. Mints on the pillows. We landed in paradise."

She pulled me out the door. "Evergreen," she said. "Let's see what kinda place it is."

Every bit as generic as Motel 6, the Evergreen Lounge was a dim dive a couple blocks south of the Cascade. Radioactive green lighting under the bar reflected off rows of bottles along the wall below mirror tiles marbled with gold streaks. Dark red Naugahyde booths along one wall, a few tables in the middle, eight stools at a twenty-foot bar, soft jazz, no jukebox, dark blue indirect lighting, restrooms in back. Not one surprise in the place.

Ma and I sat at the bar and downed beers, ate pretzels and beer nuts. We were the only customers, so the place wasn't exactly doing a land office business. The bartender was a woman about my age with a tattoo of a railroad spike imbedded high on her left breast, a devil with a pitchfork on her right shoulder, and boredom flattening the look in her eyes.

At Lou's Body Shop Ma had put the VIN number of the SUV into her phone. She pulled it out and stared at the number as if it would tell her something.

"Mary Odermann," she said after a while. "Green SUV painted white. Means it's likely we're on the right track, even if Mary is pushing daisies. I think it puts us on Leland Bye, big-time— Mary's brother and a lawyer to boot. Right now I don't see Bob Odermann anywhere near that SUV."

"I thought he looked startled when I mentioned that I wanted to sell one just like it."

"Uh-huh. There's that. Still don't see him near it. Mary's not driving it. Don't think Bob is, either. But if we don't get anywhere with Leland, we'll pin a tail on Bob for a while."

We finished our beers. I wondered if one more would look un-professional when Ma said, "Go check out the men's room, doll."

"Doll. I like that, Ma."

"Men's room?"

"Don't have to go, but thanks for takin' care of me."

She gave me an exasperated look. "See if there's a back way out, like a window."

"Oh, right. Good to know in case of fire. I'm on it."

She rolled her eyes.

The bathroom had a window a dwarf could go through. I went back to the bar. "Small window," I told her. "I could maybe cut off my head, toss it out."

"Sounds like a good idea."

Back outside, I checked my watch: 6:10 p.m.

"Let's eat," Ma said. "Drive around. First place we come to that looks like it might have a half-decent steak, let's go in."

Which was Buck's Chuckwagon. Posters of New York steaks and curly fries in the windows pulled us in.

I had mushroom sirloin tips and a cold-water lobster tail from the North Atlantic. Ma got a steak on cilantro lime rice. Steaks and beer—I told her she was my kind of woman. She patted her stomach and said, "I've given up the fight, doll. I'm no one's kind of woman anymore. Screw both Jennifers and the Kardashians, *and* a shitload of others who've set impossible standards."

Which put a little damper on the evening. Read between the lines, Ma wouldn't mind being somebody's type. I could only guess at the sort of low-level undertow of depression that formed the day-to-day of her life—wanting what she no longer expected to have.

Like Holiday—the thought crept into my head. Holiday needed what damn few men would be able to give her.

Then there was "gifting"—Ma's word, and a concept I was having trouble assimilating into my worldview. Gifting was—what, exactly, if not loaning or sharing? No doubt something subtle, which put it well out of my reach.

"You about done there?" Ma asked.

I stared at my plate. Yep, clean. "Guess so, unless we want to order up another round of steaks."

She tossed three twenties on the table. "Let's go."

"Hey, I can get it."

"Don't know why, since it's paid for already. What you *can* do is drive me to a grocery store where I can get some cigarettes and a six-pack, pick up a book. I'll be damned if I'll watch television, all that mind-sucking 'reality' horseshit, not even as real as hobbits."

My thoughts exactly.

At a Safeway she bought John Sandford's latest Virgil Flowers novel, a six-pack of Coors, and a carton of Camels, all of which ended up costing more than our steaks. But I was quick on the draw this time, so I paid.

"You ain't paying for my smokes, boyo," she said. "I buy my own cancer."

"Too late, Ma. And you'll live to be a hundred."

She looked away. "Last thing I want is to live to see a hundred."

I didn't say anything. There was that depression again. Maybe it was a nighttime thing, a shadow that falls over the soul when the day is done. A line of burnt orange showed above the hills and a few stars were out in the east. No moon. It would be a dark night.

We went to our rooms at Motel 6. She unlocked her door, then looked at me. "Be careful with that chickadee, Mort." She was in the room, door closed, before I could respond.

"Yeah," I said to the night. "I'll . . . do that."

Next on my bucket list, I'm gonna replace Leno.

* * *

The chickadee came in at ten fifteen wearing shiny red calf-length boots, a black leather miniskirt and a black leather halter top, bare midriff showing, fresh lipstick, liner, and eye shadow, shiny black hair four inches below her shoulders, a red flower in her hair.

Whoa.

She had perfect brown skin. She was a bit stocky, but it all looked solid and ready. Her hips were wide, arms strong, legs good all the way up into that short skirt. Her breasts cantilevered out from good shoulders, full, erumpent, majestic. That Cascade Lodge shirt had hid more than I'd suspected. I guessed her waist at thirty inches, which isn't slender but isn't bad, either. Tucked beneath that impressive chest, her waist looked almost small.

She sauntered up and kissed my cheek. "Hi, Steve."

Steve, right. Gotta remember that. I'd blanked on my name at the sight of her. She was looking like a handful, and all I wanted was to find out about the lady in the SUV. Tonight looked like it was going to be one of those personal sacrifices we gumshoes make when the going gets rough.

"Evening, Sophie. Uh . . . nice outfit."

She managed to push her tits out another improbable half inch without tipping over. Lipstick made her mouth look ripe, somehow reminding me of strawberries and cream. "Glad you like it. I change at where I work, come right over, see you. So, what you drinkin'?"

"Moose drool."

She made a face. "Drool from the moose?"

I smiled. "Good stuff. What can I get you?"

The same bartender was still on duty. Sophie said to her, "I like a pink lady, not so much gin please, and double grenadine." Then to me she said, "We go sit in the booth, okay?"

"Perfect." I got off the stool and looked at the booths, none of which were occupied. "Let's take the one over there with my two buddies, Hammer and Spade."

She stopped dead. "No one there, Steve."

"Sometimes I hallucinate. But don't worry, it's fun."

She frowned. "What is this 'lucinate?"

"Never mind." I headed toward a booth, but she took my hand and led me to the farthest booth from the door. I got her seated then sat across the table from her where I could keep an eye on the front door, a safety measure that's right there in the PI manual.

She frowned again. "Why you sittin' over there?"

"So I can see you better."

A glow appeared in her eyes, then faded. "You should sit next to me. You can see everythin' okay."

"I'm good."

"Okay, I sit over there." Which she did. Bumping me with a sturdy hip, she shoved me farther into the booth.

The bartender came over, set the pink lady in front of Sophie, then went back behind the bar. One old guy was at the far end of the bar, drinking shots. Two women in their forties were at a table twenty feet away, heads together, talking earnestly in low tones. Just those three people.

Sophie put a hand on my thigh, which gave me choices. I could remove it and reduce the odds of having a meaningful discussion about the SUV lady, or I could leave it where it was and maybe give the chickadee the wrong impression.

I left it there. It was warm and a bit high, so I thought I'd better get the ball rolling before this gumshoe-girl thing kicked itself into a higher gear.

"That lady I mentioned earlier," I said. "Did you see her? She might have been in a blue dress."

The hand on my thigh crept an inch higher. "We have to talk 'bout her now?"

"Yes, now. She might have come into your motel and gotten a room last week, Wednesday or Thursday."

Sophie pouted. "She not your wife, girlfriend?"

"Nope."

"Why she so important?"

"I think maybe she's a bad woman, Sophie. I'm trying to find out."

"What kind of bad woman? What she do?" Her hand started making little circles an inch or so from my crotch.

I cleared my throat. "I don't know. Mail fraud, maybe."

The circles slowed for a moment, then started up again. "What frawed mean?"

"Shipping biohazardous material. It's a federal offense."

The circles stopped again. "Fed-e-*ral*?" she said in a Spanish accent with a hint of wariness.

"I'm interested in how she looked, any marks on her face like moles, scars, color of her eyes, thin face, big nose, things like that."

"I din't see no scars, like yours, which is very . . . sexy. I theenk maybe her eyes is blue, like her dress."

"How about her hair color?"

"Is dark, except I theenk maybe she was wearing a, you know . . ." She patted her hair. The accent was picking up speed.

"A wig."

"Yes, a weeg."

"Was anyone with her?"

"Like who?"

"A girl. Younger than you. Pretty."

"No. She was all alone."

"How did she pay for the room?"

"Juss money. She gave me a beeg bill, a hunnerd dollar."

Cash. Sounded like our gal. And, I hated to admit it, but Ma was right, this wasn't getting us anywhere. In fact, so far I'd say it was nothing, other than that hand now gently kneading my crotch—which was light-years away from getting us anywhere near the lady in the SUV.

"You didn't get a license plate number, did you?"

"She was . . . no car. She say it was being feexed. Steve?"

"Yeah?"

"I show you sometheeng, okay?"

"Sure, what?"

"This." She popped a couple of snaps on her halter and placed my hand on a warm, firm, luxurious, Spanish-speaking breast— the left one, if I wasn't mistaken—and held it there.

Choices: One, cough and pretend you don't notice. Two, jump up and yell something. Three, squeeze. Four, fake a heart attack.

Three won, because it was a round, very supple boob the size of a large cantaloupe and I'm a peeg. Oh—and cantaloupe is great with a scoop of vanilla ice cream in it. Just sayin'.

She smiled. "Is nice, yes?"

"Very nice." And Jeri would hear every detail about this, too— except for the hard nub of nipple against my palm, which seemed irrelevant and more than she really needed to know.

"Sophie?"

"Yes?"

"I need to know about this woman. Anything you can tell me. Anything more." I started to pull my hand away, but she gripped it in both hands and pressed it harder against her.

"I'm theenking," she said.

Far be it from me to break the concentration of a witness, so I waited. She started moving my hand around on her breast. We were facing the room with a view down the length of the bar. We could see everyone in the room, two flat-screen TVs over the bar, the front door. No one was paying any attention to us.

"Steve?"

"What?"

"I have not had a man for *two weeks*."

"Two whole weeks? And you're still alive? How is that?"

She smiled. "You make the joke, yes?"

"You could go into shock at any moment. If you do, we'll need to elevate your feet."

She stared into the room. Her hands stopped moving my hand on her breast, which meant I had to do all the work. Which I did.

"Like that," she said. She pointed at one of the two televisions. "The woman in the blue dress, she looked juss like that."

I leaned toward Sophie for a better look. On the television, a lady in a beige suit was in front of a bouquet of microphones. The sound was turned off, so I couldn't hear her words, but, just like me, Julia Reinhart had gone well beyond her allotted fifteen minutes of fame.

Julia.

Which meant Ma was wrong about Sophie not being useful.

Man, was she gonna be pissed.

CHAPTER EIGHTEEN

BUT IT WAS late and she was probably asleep by now, so telling her about my latest success as a gumshoe would have to wait until morning. Meanwhile, I had a breast filling my right hand and then some, success of a somewhat different kind, directly related to my new career—it never once happened when I was terrorizing citizens with the IRS—and I had to find a way to extricate it since Sophie still had a death-grip on my hand, holding it in place.

"We should leave," I said.

"My place only four blocks away," she purred.

"I gotta hit the men's room," said the dwarf.

"You hurry, Steve. I am so hot—like you wouldn' believe."

"I'm on it."

That bathroom window wasn't looking any bigger than it had earlier. I hoped the Jaws of Life wouldn't be needed. I remember a guy on TV who crawled through an unstrung tennis racket. I say it was unstrung to avoid confusion whenever I tell this. He stuck an arm and shoulder through, then his head, dislocated the other shoulder, took half a dozen deep breaths and let it all out because he couldn't squeeze through the racket with a lungful of air, couldn't take a breath with that thing around his chest either, so the entire operation looked like an interesting form of suicide, but right now I was glad I'd taken notes.

I put one arm through, then my head, didn't bother with that dislocate the shoulder part, wormed my chest through sideways, let out some air, felt the frame at my front, back, sides, and popped out, hung upside down for a moment, then dropped to the ground trying for a tuck and a cool-looking somersault, which didn't work out, then lay on the ground and said hi to Sophie who was eight feet away at the end of the alley staring at me.

"You are a shithead," she said.

"Yes I am."

"For all night, I only coss fifty dollar."

"Only fifty smackeroos? A bargain at half the price."

She turned on her heel and left. I got in the Caddy and took off. Later when I told all this to Ma, she about busted a gut.

*   *   *

"Julia," she said in the morning at an IHOP over French toast. "Makes sense, sort of—a lot, actually—but what the *hell*, Mort."

"My words exactly."

"We gotta phone Jeri, let her know."

"Nope."

Ma stared at me. "Nope?"

"You know Jeri. She might go out and tackle this dame on her own. But we don't know what's going on. Reinhart's hand chopped off, shipped to me, Wexel dead, burned to a crisp. If Julia Reinhart is involved, we've got to check her out as a team."

"Dame?"

"*And*," I went on, "if Sophie was just blowing smoke to keep my hand on her tit, then checking out Julia might not be dangerous or productive. Either way, it can wait, so we don't call Jeri."

"You had your hands on the chickadee's tits?"

"One hand, the right—so only one tit, the left. And you're picking up on the most insignificant details here, Ma."

"Tits are insignificant? I can see why Jeri trusts you. Raises a few other questions though." She looked at me with one eye.

Jesus H. Christ. Women.

* * *

"Gifting," I said, breaking a twenty-minute silence. The word was giving me fits.

"Uh-huh. Speaking of insignificant details."

We were thirty miles south of Bend, roaring south at fifty miles an hour. Every hour that passed, we went fifty whole miles, by God. I was thinking *Chariots of Fire*.

"Doesn't feel insignificant to me," I said.

She shrugged. "If I had some hot guy gifted to me, even if all I could do is look, you wouldn't hear me complaining about it, boyo. Been a long goddamn time since I've seen a guy buck naked." She gave me a challenging look. "Think I'm too old to care?"

"Not even close, Ma. But this thing with Jeri and Holiday has me spinning in circles."

"Christ, I haven't heard a guy whine so much in forever."

"You're no help."

"Can't say I didn't try. It's like gettin' through a brick wall."

So I shut up.

* * *

To Reno from Bend via Gerlach was some four hundred fifty miles. We left Bend at nine twenty, keeping an eye out for a white Mercedes SUV. With a stop in Lakeview for lunch, a quick bite in Gerlach, we pulled into Reno at eight forty-five p.m., full dark, nine hours on the road, so there was another day shot. Ma phoned Jeri from Gerlach, gave her an update on our progress as we neared Fernley, then called again as we reached the eastern edge of Sparks.

I parked the Caddy at Ma's place. Jeri was already there in her Porsche, waiting for us.

"Learn anything useful?" Jeri asked.

"You tell her," Ma said to me. "I'm beat. Anyway, you're the one that got the chickadee hot an' talking. Be sure to tell her about that window thing, too. If you don't, I will."

"Chickadee?" Jeri asked. "Hot? Window thing?"

"Thanks, Ma," I said. "I owe you one."

Ma waved and went into the house. I smiled at Jeri. "I am a gumshoe like no other."

"I believe that. What'd you do this time?"

"I'm hungry. How about we go home, get something to eat, and I'll tell you about it?"

"How about we go to the Golden Goose where Sarah's waiting for us? You can choose the restaurant, how's that?"

"Is that Sarah or Holiday?"

"She didn't say. We'll see how she's dressed."

* * *

We stopped by Jeri's place first. I took a five-minute shower to freshen up. Jeri took a five-minute shower at the same time, which, as luck would have it, made it easier to get my back scrubbed. Then there was another ten-minute delay caused by the shower delay, then another quick freshen-up splash in the shower, then we got dressed. Jeri wore tight pants that hugged her butt nicely, and a tight top that hugged the rest of her. Damn, she looked good.

When we walked into the Green Room, Jeri and I looked at each other and said, "Holiday," at the same time.

She was sitting at the bar with a guy in his thirties, showing two inches of tight tanned tummy in a shimmery two-piece outfit. The lower part was a skirt that ended above mid-thigh; the top revealed as much as it concealed. She slid off the stool when she saw us, and she and Jeri hugged again. Buddies.

"Mort found something," Jeri said.

"Yeah? What?"

"We should hit a restaurant first," I said.

Holiday said good-bye to Ryan, no last name, thanked him for the drink, then we left. Ryan, NLN, watched us go out the door. He gave me a look that said I was a selfish son of a bitch, for which I didn't blame him, but some of us are gumshoes, and some of us aren't.

We settled for a light meal in a coffee shop. Over a burger and fries I told them about Bend, the body shop, the white paint job on the green SUV, then the Evergreen and Sophie and someone's hand on what prudes and malcontents might say was an oversized boob. Then the boob in the bathroom, escaping through the window, and Sophie in the alley calling me a shithead, a moment I will hold dear in my heart until the day I die.

"Jesus, Mort," Jeri said. "But Ma said you found something up there and it wasn't some girl's breasts, so what was it?"

"Oh, that, yeah. Slipped my mind. Just that there's a good chance the SUV we've been looking for is being driven by Julia Reinhart."

Jeri and Holiday stared at me. I checked my forehead, worried that I'd grown a third eye, which would've put a damper on the evening.

I had the burger headed toward my mouth when Jeri grabbed my arm and set it down for me—slammed my arm down would be more accurate. Christ, she was strong.

"You *twerp*. You went on about some girl's tits and waited all this time to tell me—us—that little informational gem?"

"Twerp?"

She was beautiful, and her face was a study in exasperation. "That's like shithead, only I can say it a lot louder in public."

"Well, I had to get in an informational mood, dear heart."

"The shower forty minutes ago didn't put you in the mood?"

"That mood was entirely different. It wasn't informational *and* nutritional, like this one." I held up a French fry. "It's important not to confuse the two."

Holiday hid a smile. Jeri sat back and stared at me. Finally, she said, "Okay, twerp, tell us about Julia Reinhart."

"There isn't much to tell. She was on TV in the bar and Sophie said the lady who stayed at the motel looked just like her."

Jeri didn't like that. "That doesn't mean it was Julia. It could have been someone who looked sort of like her, that's all."

"Entirely possible. But then, you start looking at the big picture and Julia makes sense. A lot more than some random woman who happens to resemble her."

"Which still doesn't make it Julia."

"What about Allie?" Holiday asked. She was picking at a bagel in front of her, pinching off sparrow-sized bits.

"That I don't know. Sophie said she didn't see a girl with the woman."

"Things are still squirrelly," Jeri said. "I don't mean you didn't do good or get us somewhere, but there's still a lot we don't know."

"True. But one thing we've got is the VIN number on that SUV that went from green to white. It's the same as the VIN registered to Mary Odermann, so we've nailed that down."

"Meaning what?" Holiday asked.

"Meaning," Jeri said, waving one of my fries around, "we've got to track down Julia, see if she's driving a white Mercedes SUV, then check its VIN number, see if it's the one registered to Mary Odermann, and if all that checks out, *then* we've pretty much got her. Then maybe we can find out about Allie."

"Who no one has seen in a week and a half," Holiday said. "If it *was* her."

Jeri put a hand on her arm. "We're gettin' there. This has been a pretty weird deal. I mean, with Reinhart's hand being sent to Mort and Reinhart's chief of staff being murdered. As far as we know, the FBI isn't even in the game right now. And I don't think we want them in, at least not yet." She stole another of my fries, chewed on it thoughtfully, then said, "We know where Julia lives. We have an address. Ma says she can get us into that gated community. What say we give that a try tomorrow?"

"I'm in," Holiday said. "My last class is at noon. I can be ready to go at one or a little after."

I nodded. "I was gonna go bowling, but I'll blow it off."

"One o'clock it is, then," Jeri said, then swiped my last fry and dipped it in catsup, smiled at me as she ate it. "Now I want to hear more about that Sophie deal. Sounds like you had fun up there."

"Okay, then. Let *me* tell *you* about cantaloupes."

"Oh, no."

"Oh, yes. They're round and about *this* big and they taste real good with vanilla ice cream."

"You *didn't*. Please tell me you didn't."

* * *

Sarah wasn't going to be ready until after one p.m., so Jeri and I slept in. By eleven we were at Ma's office, and by eleven fifteen she had us a pass through the gate into the exclusive neighborhood where Julia and Harry Reinhart lived, not that we expected Harry to show up. Ma knew about fifteen people who lived there, one of whom was a private investment counselor by the name of Nathan Milbarger. Milbarger seemed eager to please. He phoned the gate and told them he had a party of four coming in between one thirty and two, and one of those people would be Maude Clary.

We went in Ma's Caddy. Ma drove. We picked up Sarah at her apartment at one twenty and roared off in the Chariot of Fire, south on 395. Sarah was in sandals, black jeans, and a white UNR sweatshirt with the Wolf logo on it, looking very much the pretty college coed.

We were waved through the gate by a guy in his midtwenties as soon as the name Milbarger floated out the driver's-side window. Up and around we went through a maze of streets, none of which went in a straight line for more than a hundred feet. We never did see Milbarger's house, but a map and some backtracking got us to a three-million-dollar mansion with a million-dollar view of Reno and Sparks spread out below in the valley and a pretentious fountain in a front courtyard—a half-naked maiden pouring water out of a jug into the water at her feet. So this was where Nevada's lying senator lurked when he wasn't lurking in his Washington D.C. townhouse, chuckling about his latest taxpayer rip-off. Nice. Wish I could pull strings and have money come in under the table—as long as I didn't end up in Hades in molten lava, which might be where Harry was even as we sat in the car and thought about what to do next.

"Two cars are registered in Julia's name," Ma said. "A Lexus IS 350 Sport in her name alone, and she and Harry have an Audi Q7 SUV in both their names."

"How about Harry alone?" I asked.

Ma checked her cell phone. "Lexus IS 350 Sport. They got his and hers. His is black, hers is red."

None of which was in sight now. The house was on a dead-end street with a wide turnaround at the end, so traffic was nonexistent. Doors on the four-car garage were down. We were in a brown 1963 Cadillac Eldorado idling at the curb, a car Hispanic kids in a gang might drive—which was a very politically incorrect observation, but accurate, as politically incorrect observations often are. I wondered how long we could stay there before a politically incorrect police car or two pulled up behind us. Another multimillion-dollar house was across the street, so I gave us ten minutes, fifteen tops.

"Time to roll," I said.

"Right-o," Ma said. She swung the car around at the end of the street, then stopped. The street ended at a sidewalk and a low rail fence. Beyond that, a hillside of dry sagebrush went on for miles, nothing but empty scrub and rocks. No big fence, no barbed wire, no razor concertina wire to keep undesirables out.

"What do you think, Jeri?" Ma asked.

"Doable," Jeri said. "Might be worth the risk."

"Better if there was a moon out."

"City lights ought to be enough."

"Huh?" I said, obviously out of an important loop. Then I said, "Well, yeah. City lights oughta be plenty."

Jeri laughed. "Plenty for what, Mort?"

"Uh . . . pinochle?"

Ma guffawed, then put the Caddy in drive, and pulled away. "For a little nighttime recon, doll," she said.

"Yup," I replied. "That or pinochle, either one. There's a place on Virginia Street that sells cards that glow in the dark."

"But are they pinochle decks?"

"Well . . . shit."

The day was still young, however, so we decided on a Denny's Restaurant for a late lunch and strategy session. We took a booth. I sat across from Jeri and Ma, next to the fresh-faced coed.

"Okay," Ma said, once we'd ordered and had drinks in front of us. "Two things. We can try to track down Julia and follow her, see where she goes, what she's doing, or we can try to find that SUV." She kept her voice low to keep the conversation private.

"The car might be at her house," I offered. "Two birds with one stone."

"Hence tonight's recon, boyo, if it becomes necessary."

"Why wouldn't it? Not that I'm into skulking since the last time I did that it almost got me and Jeri killed."

"If we found that Mercedes somewhere *else* we wouldn't have to get into that garage, which is iffy, that's why. So if we go after that SUV to check its VIN, what's another way we might find it?"

We thought about that in silence for a while.

Finally, Jeri said, "It's registered to Mary Odermann, who no longer exists. Bob Odermann does, however, and Mort got a little bite when he mentioned a Mercedes SUV to Bobby. But we've also got Leland Bye, Mary's brother, who happens to be a lawyer, and you can't trust a lawyer farther than you can lob a politician."

So we thought about *that* for a while.

Finally, I said, "I wonder if the fish and chips I ordered was the right choice."

I got a few hisses from that, so I said, "And I wonder what Bob would do if someone went back to that print shop and asked him point blank about his wife's SUV."

We gave that some thought.

Then Sarah said, "I could do that. He's never seen me. I don't have to tell him my name. But what would be the point, exactly?"

"Shake things up," Jeri said. "It's not the worst idea out there. If Odermann is involved somehow and if he's trying to keep a low profile, he might do something, make a mistake. If Sarah went in and shook Bob's tree, it might rattle him enough to make him go somewhere, do something. If so, we could follow him, see where that takes us."

"Except it's hard to imagine a print shop guy being involved in the assassination or death of a presidential candidate," Ma said, so we thought about that for a while. Then she said, "But then there's Bye. We could do the same thing there. One of us goes in, says something about an SUV registered to his dead sister, then walks out, see if anything falls out of that tree."

We were thinking about that when the food arrived, so we dug in and thought about Bye and Odermann while we filled up. And I wouldn't be having fish n' chips at Denny's again but that's another story, nothing to do with mystery SUVs or lawyers.

"Okay," Ma said. "Suppose we shake a tree and Julia gets a phone call and takes off, or worse, ditches the SUV. Shaking a tree could end up hurting us. We'd better have eyes on her at the time we rattle either Odermann or Bye."

"Gettin' complicated," I said.

"How about this?" Sarah said. "I'm walking in the hills and I get thirsty, so I hop over that little fence we saw and ring the doorbell at Reinhart's house. If no one answers, then . . . well, then I don't know. But if Julia is there I can ask for a glass of water then leave, phone it in. I could watch the house from the hillside right as someone asks Bye or Odermann about that SUV. If Julia leaves, I could see which car she's in. Someone could wait along the road outside that guard gate and follow her if she takes off."

"Spreads us a little thin," Ma said, "but it's doable. It'd take you a while to hike up to the house. It'd take me a month. Oughta have some binoculars with you, too, just in case."

More silence. Jeri got out her cell phone and got into Google Maps, figured out the closest overland approach to Reinhart's house, which turned out to be 2.6 miles, a quarter mile or so up Court Shoe Lane in southwest Reno, then a hike southwest through sagebrush into the hills.

"So," Jeri said. "Who do we shake, Bye or Odermann? And if we're gonna do it today, we gotta get going. It'll take Sarah a while to get into position."

"Most likely snake in the grass is Leland Bye," I said.

"Weakest link might be Odermann," Ma said.

"Or," Sarah suggested, "one person could hit them both, five or ten minutes apart."

"I like that," Jeri said. "I'll do the shaking. But if something does fall out of a tree, we might not know which tree did the trick."

"Unless," Ma said, "you hit Bye first, then wait half an hour before hitting Odermann. If something shakes loose, it'll probably happen pretty quick, won't take half an hour."

Sarah stood up. "If we're gonna do this, I've got to get going. Court Shoe Lane. I'll find it, but I need a ride back to my place, and I'll need some binoculars."

"When you're ready, I'll shake Bye and Odermann," Jeri said.

"I'll wait outside the gate and follow Julia if she bolts," I said, sliding out of the booth.

"Hit Bye first," Ma said to Jeri. "I'll watch his place, follow him if he leaves. Once you talk to Odermann, hang around and keep an eye on him. Everyone know what to do? Everyone's cell phones charged up? Everyone got everyone's number?"

We all nodded, I tossed money on the table, and we headed for Ma's Eldorado. She made a quick trip to Jeri's, dropped all of us off. Sarah got Jeri's binoculars, then the two of them headed off to Sarah's apartment in the Porsche. I tossed two wigs and a moustache in the Toyota and took off. Nothing was going to happen for a while, not until Sarah got in position, so I parked down the street from Bye's office building and watched the entrance. His ride was a dark blue late-model Lexus SUV. I spotted it in a side lot, so odds were he was in. Maybe I'd get lucky and he would go somewhere, like to Julia's.

Twenty minutes later, Ma parked down the street the other way and reported that Sarah was out of her car, hiking into the hills. I waited a few minutes longer, then headed for the road—Parkway, actually—that wound up into the hills toward the gated community.

CHAPTER NINETEEN

I WAITED.

Sarah hiked.

Jeri parked down the street from Bye's office. She had Ma's Caddy in sight.

This thing we were winding up was beginning to store energy.

At four thirty-five, Sarah told Ma she was in position. She didn't see any sign of life at the house. She was about to ring the bell, see if anyone answered. Ma reported all that to Jeri and me.

I waited.

Ten minutes later, Sarah reported back. Julia was home and Sarah had gotten a glass of water. Julia was cold, brusque, not happy to see her. She'd gotten Sarah out of the house as soon as possible. Sarah was headed back into the hills to keep an eye on the place, see if anything happened when Jeri started shaking trees.

I waited.

Jeri hit Leland Bye's place first, which, according to Jeri, went something like this:

Jeri (in front of Bye's desk having blown by a secretary who'd failed to tackle her): There's a Mercedes SUV registered in Mary Odermann's name, Mr. Bye. Your sister Mary, just to be clear.

Bye (startled): Who the hell are you?

Jeri: But Mary is dead, has been for two years, so . . . what's up with that?

Bye (settling back in his chair with a jittery, calculating look): I don't have any idea what you're talking about. How'd you get in here, anyway?

Jeri: Just thought you ought to know someone is using your deceased sister's name. You might want to let the DMV know, see if they're interested. (Exit stage left)

Jeri reported the contact to Sarah, told her to watch the house. She said Bye had looked squirrelly.

Four minutes later, Julia Reinhart took off in the red Lexus IS Sport. Sarah reported hearing a chirp of tires as she left. She said she was going to jog downhill, that she'd be back at her car in less than thirty minutes in case she could still be useful.

Ma phoned me. "Bye left his office, Mort. I'm following in my car. Jeri is on him in hers. Son of a bitch is driving kinda fast. Keep an eye out for Julia. Sarah says Julia is headed your way in that red Lexus. Oughta be past the guard gate in two or three minutes."

"On it," I told Ma. I started the Toyota—an invisible car, but it was going to have to compete with a Lexus. Maybe I should've shaken the trees while Jeri watched the gate. Too late now.

But we had two people on the move. I didn't know about Ma in her Chariot, but I doubted that Bye could lose Jeri. Thing is, she was in a hot Porsche, and Bye might be checking his rearview mirror more than usual. I would give a bundle to know if he and Julia were on phones to each other right then. If so, I'd pay double to listen in.

Ma hooked all four of us up in a conference call, which would wear batteries down faster but looked necessary with everything that was going on.

Julia went down the forty-five-mile-an-hour Parkway at sixty. Side mirror howling, I stayed two hundred yards back hoping she would get the ticket, not me. We crossed South Virginia Street and got on 395, headed north. She picked it up to seventy. I stayed on her tail, a quarter mile back. I had a Bluetooth in my ear for hands-free driving. Safety first.

Looks like we'd stirred up a hornet's nest. Bye and Julia were acting guilty, all right. Of something, and it was obviously related to Mary Odermann's SUV, which, adding another layer of sneakiness, had been painted white. I still wanted to see Julia in or around that SUV just to be sure, but for the moment all of us were having a grand old time.

In fact, we didn't have any proof that Mary Odermann's SUV was the one that had been spotted in Gerlach, or that the young girl Deputy Roup had seen in the SUV was Allie, but this was all we had, and it was looking better all the time.

Ma's voice buzzed in my ear. "Bye has slowed down. Maybe tryin' not to get pulled over. We're going north on Arlington, crossing Second Street now."

I told everyone that Julia was still rolling north on 395, so it looked like she and Bye were about to get together.

Leland Bye ended up in the parking garage of the Golden Goose Casino, which I thought was perfect. Odds were that he and Julia were going to meet there, in a room or a restaurant. Jeri had gone past Bye in the garage and parked nearby on the third level. She was on him, following in a shoulder-length big blond wig and black-frame glasses, bright red lipstick, wearing a red cardigan. Bye hurried along a skyway above Sierra Street and into the Goose. In his office Jeri had been in a white shirt, black pants, dark glasses, no lipstick. She trotted to catch up and was ten yards back when he went through a wide lobby toward a bank of elevators. She'd put on a double strand of fake pearls and had a Macy's bag in one hand that held a ball cap and a bulky blue sweatshirt.

I was still on Julia. No surprises at the Spaghetti Bowl—a big sloppy interchange where US 395 did a square dance with I-80. Its planning and construction had proceeded in fits and starts over a thirty-five-year period, finally ending up as the ugliest rat's nest of roadwork in the Western Hemisphere. Julia looped around the mess and went west on I-80, still headed toward the Goose.

This was like watching the pieces of a puzzle float across a table and assemble themselves into a picture that was trying to make sense, except this picture was still a muddy abstraction, like a late Picasso reflected in a funhouse mirror.

Sarah made it back to her Audi about the time Julia parked her car on level four of the Golden Goose's garage. By then, Jeri and Bye were in the revolving restaurant at the top of the Goose on the thirty-seventh floor, the Golden View, which made one revolution every forty-eight minutes. Bye was watching the entrance and Jeri was watching Bye, forty feet away. Ma said she and Bye had done business together in the past and he'd recognize her in a heartbeat, disguise or no. Jeri was trying to keep a low profile, glancing at Bye every so often over the top of a menu. Our conference call was still up and running. Jeri told Sarah to hustle over to her apartment and ditch the UNR sweatshirt, put on a fairly hot outfit, then get on up to the Golden View. Julia had seen her not long ago, so if she could do something with her hair in a hurry, that would be great.

About then, Julia came in, also in sunglasses and a wig, this one reddish brown and feathered. Disguises all around. She'd been on television a lot lately; it figured she didn't want to be recognized. She sat kitty-corner from Bye and immediately their heads were together. Two minutes later, I arrived. I sat opposite Jeri with my back to Bye and Julia, shielding Jeri from their sight. Jeri reported that Julia had a hand in Bye's, which was interesting.

So far so good, but we still had no idea what any of this meant, other than Bye and Julia were close, and Mary's SUV was somehow involved.

Jeri and I ordered drinks. Bye and Julia ordered drinks, but also ordered something from the menu. It looked as if they were going to be there awhile. Both of them were shooting wary glances around the room. The place wasn't yet a quarter full. It was still early for the dinner crowd. The sun was getting low. In another hour the panorama below would improve remarkably.

Thirty minutes later, Sarah showed up in a slinky black dress and a bouffant black wig. Cleavage and big librarian's glasses gave her an even sexier look than usual. Having kicked the boulder that started this avalanche, Jeri departed, keeping her face averted from Bye. Sarah—now Holiday—took her place, watching Bye and Julia over my right shoulder. Julia was sitting sideways to Sarah. If she recognized the girl from the hills, that would be the ball game. Holiday took a moment to put on black lipstick, further altering her appearance, giving her a Gothic Transylvania-librarian look. Jeri and Ma stayed below on the second floor, waiting for me or Holiday to report in if Bye or Julia left. Ma and Jeri's cell phone batteries were getting low so Ma ended the conference call, which ended the faint sound of casino conversation in my ear.

There wasn't anything all four of us needed to say anyway. All we could do now was wait and see what happened. I stuck my cell phone in a pocket and removed the Bluetooth earpiece. A waiter came over and hovered over Holiday. She asked for an iced tea and I ordered a Dortmunder Lager, which arrived in a pilsner glass. I also ordered us a plate of stuffed mushrooms.

"How are you holding up?" I asked her.

"Great. This is pretty exciting." She lifted her head an inch and popped a glance over my shoulder at Bye and Julia.

"Glad you like it. We world-class PIs try not to lead tedious lives. Works, too, when we're not staring at a computer eighteen hours a day or plowing through decades-old microfiche."

Holiday smiled, sipped her iced tea, studied the ice in her glass for a moment, then looked up at me. "Has Jeri said anything more about . . . about Tuesdays?"

"No, but things have been busy lately. And Ma and I were out of town for two days up in Bend, so there's that."

"Uh-huh. Speaking of which—that girl up there, Sophie, wasn't boring was she? It didn't put you to sleep, feeling her up like that?"

"She had to slap me awake twice. Does that count?"

Our stuffed mushrooms arrived. I took one. Holiday gazed out the window, then looked down at her hands. "An interesting word came up a while ago when Ma and Jeri and I were talking and you weren't around."

"Oh? What word was that?"

"I just wonder if you heard it. Gift? Or gifting?"

"Ah, yes. One of those, or any of their common derivatives. Ma brought it up on the drive to Bend."

Holiday smiled a little. "What do you think? I mean, is that possible? I . . . I wouldn't even know how to bring it up again, you know, with Jeri."

"Me either."

"And then, after you two are married, that would be the end of it, wouldn't it? So it's almost like, why start?"

"I'm not the best person to ask. You and Jeri might have that discussion. Probably with me out of the room."

"But if we did—I mean, I know it's strange, but if she and I worked something out—then would you . . . would you *want* to?"

I remembered hearing that the restaurant was eighty-four feet in diameter, so we were rocketing along at 1.1 inches per second, counterclockwise. At the moment we were headed due east. I looked out the window toward Mount Rose.

"Mort?"

"I'm a guy, Holiday."

"Could you say it in plain English, please?"

"I don't have a eunuch switch."

"English?"

I met her eyes. "Yes. You're very beautiful. It's not the kind of thing I would get tired of quickly. Might take me fifty years."

"I'm glad. Although . . . maybe that makes it even harder." She reached across the table and took my hand, squeezed it, then let go.

"Speaking of which, you shed a few tears coming back from Tonopah."

"Sometimes I still feel like crying." She made a little gesture at her dress. "Wearing something like this doesn't feel the way it used to. It's not as good as it was before. It doesn't compare to the way it was with you in Tonopah or up in Oregon."

"I'm sorry."

She sighed. "Me, too. Tonopah was wonderful. Now I'm just sort of . . . blah. But that 'gifting' thing is stuck in my head and I can't get it out." She gazed out at the city, then back at me. "It's driving me crazy, like I don't know right or wrong anymore, like my world has been turned upside down."

"There's got to be someone out there for you, someone who can give you what you want."

"Right. Someone like you. Lots of them around. I see them on street corners all the time. They wear signs."

She split a mushroom with a fork and speared half, put it in her mouth, chewed slowly. Her eyes had a shine to them that picked up lights in the room.

Finally, she said, "You're something else. You don't know how different you are, do you?"

Hell, yes. I find heads and people send me hands. An entire nation awaits my next move. But I didn't tell her that because I'm a sensitive chap and I could tell it didn't fit the mood.

"Makes me want to fucking cry," she said.

CHAPTER TWENTY

IT WAS FULL dark and we'd made nearly three revolutions by the time Bye and Julia pushed their chairs back. They gave the room a guarded look as they stood up to leave. Holiday and I hadn't said anything about gifting for over an hour, but it was still in her eyes—even after the Dungeness crab cakes I ordered because Bye and Julia were taking their sweet time over dinner.

I fumbled my cell phone out and speed-dialed Jeri. "Houston, I think we have liftoff."

"About time. Let me know when they get on the elevator."

"Roger, Houston. Expect a text."

Holiday smiled. "She puts up with a lot, doesn't she?"

"She's a sweet kid that way. Unlike my mother who abandoned me when I was six."

"She didn't."

"No, but she wanted to. She would intentionally lose me in big department stores. After age six, Christmas was all downhill."

Holiday rolled her eyes. Then Bye and Julia walked past us so Holiday and I put our heads closer together to hide our faces. She kissed me until they were far enough away, which was an excellent PI move and very nice.

"More, please," she said when I backed away.

"Can't. Houston awaits."

When the elevator door closed on the lawyer and the erstwhile senator's wife and would-be First Lady, I texted Jeri with the news. Holiday and I got up. I dropped sixty dollars on the table, then we went over and hit the down button.

Jeri and Ma weren't there when we got to the mezzanine. My phone rang. The screen showed a picture of Jeri.

"Yeah? Who's this?" I said.

"Your fiancée and she's damn tired of waiting around so don't start. I'm in my car. Leland and Julia are in a lip-lock beside his car, might need chiropractic help to separate, so I don't know how long it'll be before I get to tail anyone."

"Hang in there, kiddo."

"Actually, they're giving me an idea of what you and I might do later. That six-minute thing yesterday has worn off entirely."

"I'll have you know that was a ten-minute thing. You'd think the afterglow would last longer."

Holiday lifted an eyebrow at me.

"Okay, both of them are getting in Bye's car," Jeri said. "Gotta go, Mort. Stay tuned."

* * *

Jeri followed them out of the parking garage and Ma followed Jeri. That parade stayed together all the way out I-80 to the town of Fernley with Ma and Jeri trading places to reduce the chances that the lovebirds would know they were being followed. At one point, Ma had to push her Caddy up to seventy-five, a death-defying feat. Holiday and I piled into her Audi. She drove. She'd parked her car next to my Toyota in the garage, so I got my gun from under the seat before we headed out. We were only three or four minutes behind Ma and Jeri by the time we reached Sparks on I-80, but it took us most of the way to Fernley to catch up. Finally, Ma's Eldorado came into view, at which point we passed her, then Jeri, and took over the lead in the chase.

We were back on a conference call, three-way, with me, Ma, and Jeri talking to each other. Jeri suggested that Holiday and I pass Bye's SUV before it reached the first Fernley exit. A second exit off the interstate would take us into the east end of town if Bye got off at Fernley, which seemed likely. With the Audi ahead of him, the parade following him wouldn't be so obvious. Holiday could get off I-80 two miles away and come back, or hit Highway 50 and keep going, if Bye and Julia were going all the way to Fallon.

Not a bad plan. Holiday gunned it and we shot past Bye and girlfriend Julia at eighty miles an hour, a mile before they reached the first Fernley exit. Less than a minute later, Jeri reported that Bye had indeed exited at Fernley, so Holiday raced up to the next exit and got off, went south about three-quarters of a mile to Highway 50 and headed back west on the main street through town.

Jeri dropped back. Ma took over the lead. Bye went through town, passing Holiday and me in the Audi in the opposite direction. The Lexus turned south and went through an older neighborhood that thinned out into widely spaced ranch houses, dark under elms and willows. The road had no streetlights. A sign at the turnoff onto the road read: *No Through Street.*

"They're gonna spot me if I keep this up," Ma said.

"Drop back and turn off," Jeri said. "Use a blinker. Let them see you turn. I'll take him."

By then Holiday and I were a quarter mile behind Jeri and catching up fast. It wasn't a through street so we were going to run out of pavement after a while.

"Fun," Holiday said.

"Damn near a riot," I replied. "Just remember Wexel is dead and Reinhart's hand was FedExed from Oregon."

Far ahead, I saw the brake lights of Bye's Lexus come on, then he turned left off the road. Headlights revealed the skeletal arms of a few dead trees, a broken-down pole fence, a ragged line of waist-high weeds. A hundred yards off the road, a dark single-story house was nestled in a grove of willows.

Jeri drove past the place, kept going.

"Slow down," I told Holiday. "Go by at twenty-five."

I squinted at an address on an old mailbox, but couldn't read it. The post was one of those welded chain-link jobs that look like a cobra. Bye's Lexus had stopped beside the house, lights on, aimed at an old single-car garage. As I watched, the lights went out.

"Keep going," I told Holiday.

A quarter mile down the road we passed Jeri's Porsche parked with its lights off. Jeri was outside, waiting for us. We went by and Holiday cut the lights before making a U-turn and coming up behind the Porsche.

Jeri walked over. Holiday powered down her window.

Jeri leaned in. "I'm gonna go check the mailbox for an address. And I want to see if lights come on inside or if I can hear anything in the house. Mort, you coming?"

"Try to keep me away." I opened the door.

"Be careful," Holiday said as I got out.

"No need. Got my pit bull and my gun."

Jeri and I walked up the road toward the house. In my ear, Ma said, "What's going on, guys?"

"Checking the house, Ma," Jeri said. "I'm gonna get this thing out of my ear. I need to listen to the night. Leave yours in, Mort."

Lights came on in the mystery house, twin yellow rectangles in the night. Somewhere in the distance, a dog barked.

We reached the mailbox. Jeri turned on a tiny flashlight on her key ring, shielding its glow from the house with a hand.

"Number 4062," she said. "Remember that. And we're on Old Aspen Road, in case you didn't know."

I didn't, of course. I hadn't taken note of the street sign when we came in, so I still had stuff to learn. "Does that mean there's a New Aspen Road around here somewhere?"

"Not necessarily. Think about it."

Man, I hate smart-asses.

We watched the house for several minutes. Lights were on in a room facing the street. The place was silent. I shivered in the dark. Soon it would be October; nights were starting to get chilly.

"I'm goddamn starving," Jeri said.

"You didn't get anything at the Goose?"

"How could I? Ma and I didn't know when those two would up and leave. How about you and Holiday?"

"You don't want to know."

"Humor me. I can enjoy food vicariously."

"We'll see about that. She and I had stuffed mushrooms and Dungeness crab cakes."

"I was wrong, you were right. Take it back."

"No take-backs, honey bun."

"You two have a nice talk? You were up there for two and a half hours."

"Yep. The conversation roamed wild and free."

"I'll bet." She looked toward the house. "It's pretty dark out here. How about we walk up this driveway a ways?"

"Got my gun with me, sugar."

"Well, try not to use it. Anyway, was that a yes?"

"A little way, maybe. Not sure what you think we're gonna see, and there's a chance we'll get caught, so . . . how about we don't."

"Do you always think like that? Out loud and circular?"

"You should've heard me in the IRS. I could panic a husband and wife like nothing you ever saw."

She sighed. "Actually, I think you might be right. I can't see us getting close enough to peek in windows. I wish I knew what they were saying and doing in there."

"You're the one who saw them kissing."

"Uh-huh."

"So there's a grotesque saying about a beast with two backs that might apply right about now."

"Heard that one. I've never liked it either." She was quiet for a moment. "Jeez, I'm goddamn starving, Mort."

"Another saying I've heard recently."

Two minutes later, the lights in the house went out. We waited, but no one came out to the Lexus. The night stayed quiet.

"Maybe we oughta come back later," Jeri said. "It's not like we're going to knock on the door and say we're out of gas and can we use their phone to call triple-A."

"You gotta admit, this is an interesting juncture in the evening. Wife of lying presidential hopeful in what looks like a tryst with a lying, cuckolding lawyer."

"Adjectives, Mort."

"Just sayin'."

"Okay, let's go. I'm about to eat my own arm. I won't make it back to Reno without food, so where's a good place to eat around here?"

* * *

The four of us ended up at Pancho and Evita's, a Mexican food place worth coming back to every month or so. Stuffed mushrooms only go so far, and Dungeness crab cakes are tasty but even more smackeroos per calorie. I had the three-enchilada plate and, since either Holiday or Jeri was going to drive me back to Reno, I had two Corona beers, straight from chilled bottles. Everyone else had this or that Mexican dish, so it was like a fiesta in there, about what I'd expected when we first drove up.

* * *

Ma and Holiday took off, so Jeri and I found Old Aspen Road and tooled on down in her Porsche at twenty-five, found the cobra mailbox. Lights were off in the house, but a sliver of crescent moon glinted off Leland's Lexus, which hadn't moved.

"Methinks a beast stirs in the night," I said.

"Gives me a half-decent idea," Jeri responded. She put a hand on the back of my neck and rubbed for a moment, then put the Porsche in gear and drove us back to Reno.

* * *

Jeri's half-decent idea turned out to be fully indecent and took an hour and a half to implement in its entirety. And that was after the enchiladas had worn off enough that we could move in a reasonably athletic and flexible manner. The upshot was that we staggered out of bed at eleven forty-five the next morning and my eyes wouldn't focus. I stood there blinking for half a minute, trying to get them going.

"Wow," Jeri said.

"Synoptic, on target, and you managed to slip a little hussy note in there. Impressive."

"And I'm starving again."

"Me, too," I said. "I could use a stack of homemade waffles."

"Thing is, putting those little square indentations in pancakes is so goddamn time-consuming."

"Waffles R Not Us?"

"You got that right."

It took me three tries to figure out how to hold Jockey shorts to get my legs through the proper holes. Jeri watched for a while, then offered to help. "Just about got it whupped, kiddo," I said. "Only got one more permutation left to try, but thanks anyway."

"That's a big, impressive word."

"Being educated, I excel in wig birds. I mean, big words."

"You need coffee."

"Coffee would help. And which one of us stole my pants?"

Turns out, one of us had only misplaced his pants in the heat of a rapid undressing. That got sorted out and we arrived fully dressed at Ma's office after we'd teamed up to make toast and omelets, put stuff in the dishwasher, retrieved my Toyota from the parking garage at the Golden Goose and parked it back at Jeri's place.

Jeri had given Ma the address of the mysterious house the night before. Ma had come up with the name of the person who paid taxes on the place, which wasn't the same as the owner. The actual owner was First Interstate Bank since the place was purchased less than a year ago with ten thousand down. But Leland, it turned out, who didn't own 10 percent of the property, paid a hundred percent of the taxes, so FIB was making out like a bandit, as banks do.

"Owned by Leland Bye, Esquire," I said. "What a surprise."

"Uh-huh," Ma said. "Could've knocked me over with a feather when I found out."

"Guy's had it less than a year, huh?" Jeri said.

"Nine months. Got it last December. Paid a hundred thirty-two five for it. Twelve hundred sixty square feet on a four-point-three-acre lot. Two bedrooms, one and a half baths, built in 1957."

"As the wife of a presidential candidate, you'd think the Secret Service would know where Julia went and what she did on a fairly regular basis," I said. "That's if Harry has Secret Service protection at this point—which, someone chopping off his primary shaker like that, would be a hell of a black eye for the Service—and so soon after that Columbian hooker thing, too."

Ma stared at me. "I don't think he was under their wing yet. But if he was, would they consider something like Julia's cheating to be their business? What I mean is, would they tell Harry or just keep an eye on her?"

Jeri said, "If I had to guess, I'd say the latter. Not sure they've quite gone Gestapo yet."

"IRS is Gestapo, hon," I told her. "We've got a lock on that. No one muscles in."

Instead of cracking one of my ribs, she kissed me, so I must have done good that morning. "Such a facile little mind," she said.

"I've just been damned with the faintest of praise."

"Yup."

"You two should get a room," Ma said.

I looked at Jeri. "We could do that."

She shook her head. "Nope. I'm saving myself for my wedding night."

Ma cackled. "You two."

I said, "Okay, here's a thought. An out-of-the-way love nest is purchased. Two fairly good-looking people, both with a lot to lose, meet up when the urge strikes, as urges do. At that point no Secret Service is involved, everything is cool. Then a lying senator upsets the apple cart by suddenly deciding he's qualified to be the leader of the free world. Julia finds herself in the spotlight. Now the media wants to check this babe out, look into her past, root through her underwear drawer, dig up enough dirt on her and Harry to fill Hell's Canyon. Suddenly Harry's cheating trophy wife is thrust onto the world stage. I wonder how that played."

Ma screwed up her face. "Not so good, I'd say." She knocked a cigarette out of a pack and lit up.

I checked my watch: 3:45 p.m. "How about we go cruise by the love nest, doll?" I said to Jeri.

"Doll, huh? You looking to get laid again, hotshot?"

"Pretty soon, yeah."

"Je-sus, you two," Ma said. "Get outta here."

* * *

All was quiet at the nest. We rolled by at four thirty-five and scoped the place out. The Lexus was gone. No other cars were in sight. In daylight we could see how remote the house was. The nearest house was back up the road, a quarter mile away. Farther along, nearly half a mile away, a two-story house sat at the end of the lane. It looked as if Leland and Julia had valued their privacy. We hung a U-turn and came back. Jeri stopped near the cobra-chain mailbox, and we watched the place for a while.

After a while, I said, "Drive in, walk in, or keep watching since this is so much fun?" I settled my gun more comfortably in its holster.

She chewed on her lower lip. "How about we give it an hour, maybe two, see if anything moves. If not, then I say we drive in, see what's what."

"You're the boss."

We sat there with the engine ticking as it cooled. A breeze walked a few dead leaves across the road.

Minutes passed. Silence settled in and grew heavy.

Finally, I said, "A word has come up recently. It came up last night at the restaurant. It's giving me fits, thinking about it. Even trying to think about how to think about it is giving me fits."

Jeri smiled. "Sounds like you. What word is that?"

"Gifting."

She stared out the window. We were a mile from Fernley's main street. Nothing was moving. After a while she said, "It's kind of a big word, Mort. I believe Ma came up with it, at least in the context currently afoot."

"I thought . . . as long as we're sitting here on an empty road, an intellectual conversation might keep us from drifting off into irreversible comas."

"Intellectual, huh?"

"Don't know what else to call it, even if it's not."

She blew out a breath. "Two weeks ago, nothing like that was in my head. Gifting, I mean." She didn't say anything for another minute. Then, "I really like her, Mort."

"I know. I do, too."

"She's . . . different, but so am I. She'd like to have something the world isn't prepared to give her."

"Know that, too."

"It's about experiencing sexual feelings, not actual sex."

"Yup."

"When that gets bottled up, it can hurt. A lot."

"Yup again."

"But . . . it's not up to you to fix it. It's not your problem."

"Uh-huh."

"But, you could, on occasion. Almost like you were watching television."

"Television, huh?"

"I guess it would be pretty live TV, but yes."

"Live, all right. Thing is, that feels complicated."

She closed her eyes and scratched her forehead with a finger. "It could be, yes, if we let it. I think it puts you on the spot. I think you're feeling damned if you do, damned if you don't."

"Nailed it."

"So you're between a proverbial rock and a hard place, except that depends on how all of us think about it. I mean, how each of us views the situation."

"Uh-huh."

"So . . . what if it's all right with me?"

"That's pretty much where I get stuck. Still."

"Because you think I'd be jealous. That if I agree to it, it would only be because I'm being nice. That in truth I'd hate it."

"Nailed it again."

She turned to me. "Jealousy is a kind of sickness, Mort. It declares ownership. It turns people into property. It denies their right to be who they are. I'm not that way. I don't have the jealousy gene. The tighter you hold on to someone, the less of them you get. If you're happy, I'm happy, and if you and I are happy together, then what's the problem? Anyway, this thing with Sarah isn't just my decision. I mean, if we're talking about decisions it would be up to you, too. You'd have to want to do it. Which brings up another big problem. For you, I think."

"What's that?"

"How do you say yes, you'd like to give her what she wants if you think I'd hate it? How do we even have that conversation?"

I sighed. Couldn't do anything else.

"So it's up to *me*," Jeri said. "I'm the one who has to make it okay, and it's like I don't have the words to do that." She hesitated. "Except . . . I want to try something, and I need for you to trust me. I mean, trust me completely. I'm going to ask you one question, just one, and I want a *completely* honest answer and I don't want you to try to figure out what I want that answer to be. Will you trust me? Please?"

"Okay, yes. Ask away."

"Seeing Sarah—Holiday—not fully dressed. Would you like to keep doing that for a while?"

"Yes."

She sagged, and I knew I'd blown it. Her shoulders slumped. She took a deep breath. "Oh, thank God," she said. "We got through it. No one died." She pulled my head down and gave me a kiss. It lasted awhile and got sloppy. When we came up for air, she said, "Then *do* it. It doesn't hurt us. It doesn't. It *really* doesn't. I'm not a jealous person, and that's me being honest, too."

I shivered.

Jeri held one of my hands in both of hers. "I don't know why I like her so much. I just do. I've had, quote-unquote, best friends before, but nothing like her and not for a long time. It's like I can tell Sarah anything. Maybe it's because I was a lot like her for so long. Seven years, after Beau. That was a dark place. You got me out of it. Now Sarah's in a place that feels pretty much the same—and, if you're willing, maybe you can help her to get out of it, too."

"I'm not sure about that. I don't think she's trying to leave that place. She's trying to . . . to stay there, enjoy being there."

"People change."

"Uh-huh."

"And even if she didn't, she would still enjoy it and you'd have fun."

"Yep. Can't deny it. You got me there."

"I don't 'have' you, Mort. I'm not trying to put you on the spot. I'm just saying—she would like it and you would like it and that's all right. I mean, if you *didn't* like it, that would be pretty weird."

"Well, no one's ever accused me of being weird before. I am the freakin' epitome of normal. I am on the highest tiptop part of a bell-shaped curve of pristine twenty-four-carat male normalcy."

She laughed, a nice musical sound in the car. "There. That's the Mort I know and love. Sarah likes to show herself, that's all. It makes her feel alive. She can't really do it in a bar, but she can with you. Then I get to fix you, which I have to say is a blast."

"Ah, an ulterior motive eases out of the fog. The world begins to make sense."

"Well, good. You figured it out."

I took a deep breath. "You really want this, Jeri?"

"For Sarah, yes. For you, too."

"Okay, then. I'm not going to hold you to it. If things change and you want it to stop, tell me. Just because that train is rolling doesn't mean it can't be brought to a halt."

"Got it. Thank you." She smiled. "So . . . when?"

"When what?"

"When do you want to . . . fire her up again? It's been a while since you two were in Tonopah."

"How 'bout a week and a half from Friday after next?"

"Je-sus, Mort—"

"Tonight? Tomorrow night? What've we got coming up? Last thing I want is to miss poker night with the boys."

"Tomorrow night would be good. If that's okay, I'll let her know, let her start getting that pump primed."

"That's not a pump that needs priming, Jeri."

"Maybe not, but trust me—she'll be dancing on air." She got her cell phone out, tapped the screen, got on with Holiday.

Dancing on air. That was *nothing* like my time in the IRS, so maybe I was making progress. I don't remember dancing on air or making anyone else dance on air the entire time I was unloading people's bank accounts, garnishing wages, threatening to take their homes, sell their children. Dancing on air wasn't the image that came to mind in the morning when I laced up my jackboots to go out and rake in Uncle Sammy's hard-earned dough. Uncle's boys, of which I used to be one, had a lot in common with old-time muscle wielding baseball bats who raked in protection money to protect store owners from . . . from old-time muscle with bats who raked in the protection money. Gimme money or I'll break your legs. That sounded familiar, except breaking legs was replaced with garnishing wages.

But how had I arrived at *this* place? I tried to follow the path that led from Holiday telling me to stuff my mirror in the bar two weeks ago to this point, this discussion with Jeri in her Porsche as we kept an eye on Leland and Julia's love nest. I couldn't do it. The path had too many twists and turns. But I did get something out of a few minutes' thought while Jeri was on the phone with Holiday. What I got from this entire female tsunami rolling over me was—women are a hell of a lot more complicated than men.

Well, I'd already known that, so the truth was I hadn't learned anything at all. The knowledge just got driven deeper into what I jokingly refer to as my brain.

* * *

"Okay," Jeri said. "That really made her day. Let's go look the place over."

"Expecting to find what, exactly?"

"Won't know until we find it. But a white Mercedes SUV in that garage out back with the VIN number we're looking for would be a real winner."

She started the Porsche and pulled into the driveway. The time was 6:20 p.m., the sky gray with clouds, a breeze making tree limbs sway, dislodging early fall leaves. I watched the house as we drew near. Nothing moved. Curtains were pulled across the windows. The love nest was empty. Even so, I loosened the .357 in its holster.

Jeri pulled up in front of a detached garage—a wide single-car structure circa 1957 with a flat-panel door, slightly warped, that would swing up and inward on twanging hinges—I knew the type.

We got out. I glanced at the house. Still no movement. From this angle I could see a door in the side of the garage and a single dirt-grimed window. Jeri and I went to the door. It was locked, but just like it says in the PI manual, that old lock yielded to the dumb-ass credit card trick, first time I'd ever tried it. Before we went in, I went behind the garage. Junk was piled against the back wall, and what might have been a good-sized woodpile was beneath a blue tarp. Another house stood three hundred yards away across an empty field of dry weeds, half-hidden by scraggly lilac bushes.

I went back to the door, shook my head at Jeri. We went in . . . and there was a white Mercedes SUV.

Sometimes life gives you a break.

"Got it," Jeri breathed. "This is why we never saw it around town. She kept it out here."

The car had been driven in with its hood almost touching the back wall. The sides of the place were taken up by shelves with junk on them: old coffee cans of screws and nails, shelf brackets, piston rings, rusty tools, moldering magazines. I pulled my gun and looked the place over while Jeri checked the VIN with her little flashlight. First she shined the light into the cargo hold of the SUV. "Back seats are down. There's a bundle of rags or something in there."

"VIN number," I replied. Light in the garage was dim, coming through two windows clouded by dirt that had been building up since Eisenhower was president.

She shined the light through the windshield on the driver's side, then grunted. "This's it," and maybe her words were the reason I didn't hear the footsteps behind me, but it might have been that the garage floor was old soft dirt, almost like powder.

"Don't move." Julia's automatic made a nasty ratcheting noise as she chambered a round. "You with the flashlight, get over here."

I looked at her, framed in the doorway. The gun in her hand looked like a cannon, muzzle aimed at my chest. I felt my breathing stop dead. Her eyes bored into mine.

"Well, if it isn't Mortimer Angel," she said quietly.

"Mort."

"Drop the gun . . . Mort. *Now.*"

It plopped into dirt near the garage wall.

Julia glanced at Jeri as Jeri rounded the back of the SUV. "That's far enough, girl. Unless you want this big old boy to die right where he's standing."

Jeri stopped moving. She looked at me, then back at Julia. She was twelve feet from Julia, on the far side of the SUV. I was six feet from Julia. For a moment, all three of us stayed like that.

Why was it always me who kept Jeri from going after the one with the weapon? Why was I the chosen patsy? In Jonnie Sjorgen's old mansion in August it was that psycho girl, Winter, with a deadly foil buried half an inch deep in my back, who kept Jeri at bay.

"This gun's got a four-pound trigger pull," Julia said. "I've got three on it already, so don't anybody twitch or anything." She was more than a little nervous. Her voice was shaky, which wasn't good. One little spastic jerk on that trigger and I'd be gone.

She had on jeans and a long-sleeve shirt, running shoes, no jewelry except for a diamond ring on her left hand the size of an aspirin . . . or an Easter egg.

"Take it easy," I said.

"You take it easy." She looked around, eyes wild, but beneath that surface uncertainty was a murderous look. Right then I should have jerked sideways, dropped to the ground, tried to take out one of her knees, given Jeri a chance to drop her with one good kick. But I didn't do any of that. I just stood there with the bore of what looked like a .45 locked on my chest. In fact, it was a 10mm Glock, which was the next best thing.

Julia licked her lips, trying to figure out what to do next. Given another minute I might've tried something, but she looked at Jeri and said, "Turn around, girl. Get on the ground, lie down, facedown." Her gun stayed on me.

Jeri hesitated, gave me a look.

"Do it now, girl, *right* now, or he's *dead*."

Lot of shrill emphasis there. Jeri did as she was told. To me, Julia said, "Now you. Turn around. Sit. Legs out in front of you, hands behind your neck and lace your fingers."

She'd watched a lot of television. Thing is, it worked. I sat with my back to her, put my legs out, laced my fingers, heard something move behind me, a rustle of something, then the world went black.

CHAPTER TWENTY-ONE

I WOKE TO darkness, movement, a rumbling sound, the hum of an engine. My head felt as if it were hanging on by a thread of bone and gristle. I could count my heartbeat by a throb pulsing through my skull behind my right ear. I might have another concussion. Sonofabitching concussions were going to be the death of me yet.

My eyes were open but I couldn't see anything. I wondered if I was blind. A minute later, a pale sweep of headlights slid across the roof of the car, and I breathed a sigh of relief.

"Mort?" Jeri whispered.

Maybe it was Jeri. It might have been a hallucination, or a breath of wind under an eave.

"Mort?"

I decided to answer. "Yeah?"

"Thank God, oh thank God. I didn't know how hard she hit you."

Plenty hard, honey bun.

"Mort? You still there?" Her voice sounded like it was inches from my ear. "Don't go back to sleep."

"Yeah, nope." I tried to sit up, couldn't. I tried to make sense of the world I was in, couldn't do that either.

"Stay with me, Mort. Please."

"I'll . . . try. How long've I been out? Where are we?"

"Hour and a half. We're in the back of that Mercedes SUV. That thing I saw earlier is in here with us, too."

None of what she'd said could be good.

"Where'd she come from?" I asked. "There weren't any cars at the house. No one was there."

"She was. Leland's Lexus was behind the garage under a tarp. And, I don't know, maybe they were keeping the SUV hidden in the garage after she used it so much."

"Where're we goin'? Where's she taking us?"

"I don't know. She didn't say. We've been on the road for at least half an hour."

I tried to move my hands. Couldn't. They were tied behind me. My ankles were bound, too. "I'm tied up."

"Me, too."

"How the hell did she get me in here?" I asked. "She didn't look that strong."

"She made me help. I did most of the work. She had a gun on you the whole time."

"So you finally got some use out of your powerlifting."

"Jesus, Mort—"

Julia's voice floated back to us. "Shut up, back there."

"Make me," Jeri said. Her voice was loud in my ear.

The car jerked a little on the road, then Julia laughed. "Fuck you, girl. Go ahead and talk. Say good-bye to each other."

Man, I hated that bitch.

"Where're we goin'?" Jeri called out.

"You'll find out soon enough."

"Can you sit up?" Jeri whispered to me.

I tried. Couldn't. "No. My head hurts like hell. I think I've got another concussion."

"Shit," she breathed.

"Maybe not too bad," I said hopefully.

"See if you can roll over, away from me. I'll try to untie your hands. I can't get to my knots, but my fingers are free. We won't be able to talk but we should try to keep her talking."

It hurt, but I bent my legs and levered myself onto my right side. Jeri faced away from me, and I felt her fingers scrabbling at my wrists, exploring the knot.

"Where's Allie?" Jeri called out.

"Allie?" Julia said. "That whore child who started all this? I called her Candy, since that's what she called herself."

"Candy, Allie. Where is she?"

"About fifty feet down, that's where. You'll find out."

My blood felt icy.

"Fifty feet's a long way," Jeri said. "Probably took you a long time to dig something that deep. When'd you start, around 1998?"

"You want details, girl? You want to hear a story?"

"Why not? It's really boring back here."

Julia laughed again. "Ballsy little bitch, aren't you? Well, maybe you deserve to know. How 'bout you, Mort? You up for a story while I drive you two off the edge of the world?"

"If it'll keep you awake. Fall asleep at the wheel and it'd ruin my whole day." I hate it when I lie like that, so I said, "Actually, if you hit a tree, I hope your air bag doesn't inflate."

More laughter. She was in control. But the laugh had a nervous undertone to it, so this wasn't her everyday self. She was operating outside her comfort zone, like most people when they decide to solve life's little problems with murder. She was in this thing up to her neck and everything had to go just right from here on out or her life was over. Which made her dangerous as hell, but there was nothing Jeri or I could do about that. Yet.

Jeri's fingers plucked at a strand of what felt like quarter-inch sisal rope around my wrists, the kind of coarse blond stuff used to make a cat's scratching post.

"Since Candy started this mess, let's start with her, shall we?" Julia said. "My Harry had a fondness for young pussy, but what guy doesn't?"

Had, I thought. That answers that, not that I thought Harry was still kicking around somewhere, still lying, shaking with his left.

"Including Leland," Jeri said. "Which, against all logic would be you, Julia, considering your room-temperature warmth. Did you shed your skin several times a year, growing up?"

Silence from up front. Then, "I could pull over. Give that man of yours another whack on the head—harder. I've still got that hunk of wood I used in the garage. Just let me know, girl."

Jeri remained silent.

"Thought so," Julia said. "So . . . darling Candy. Jayson Wexel was Harry's go-to guy when it came to rounding up girls. He'd been Harry's right-hand man for nearly twenty years. Not many people knew Jay by sight, not like Harry. Jay had been supplying Harry for years. Harry was too scared and too well known to pick up girls on his own, so Jay became the middle man. He was good at it, not that picking up hookers requires great skill, but Candy was his crowning glory. She was a lovely thing, a hooker, true, but she wasn't blown out and scabby like most of them get in no time at all. According to Jay, Harry was quite taken with her. She was twenty years old. A smart girl, but also stupid and greedy. She got seven hundred dollars for each of Harry's visits, which would only run an hour or two, five minutes of which was the banging part since that's all he was good for, but when he announced his candidacy she saw a million dollars. A million, like that was a magic number, like that would set her up for life. So right out of the blue she told him she wanted a million or she'd go to the newspapers, TV, maybe the police, she didn't really know, but whoever she told, it would sink his bid for the presidency before it got an inch off the ground. She made a video during their last meeting, so it wasn't going to be a 'he said, she said' deal. She showed him the video, even gave him a flash drive with the two of them on it to keep him terrified. She had him cold and she knew it.

"Harry freaked out. He told Jayson, his chief of staff. Then Jay told me, since we'd been seeing each other for a while. He wasn't a bad lover for a guy closing in on fifty. He kept in shape, ran half marathons. We managed to keep our arrangement from Harry for the two years he and I were together."

"Jayson," Jeri said. "Who is dead. Murdered. Found burned to a crisp in his own house."

"Yes, that was unfortunate but necessary," Julia said. "But that would be getting ahead of things, so how about I come back to it?

"So—Candy and her blackmail scheme. We couldn't undo it, not after she'd made that video. We couldn't talk her out of it. Jay and I had to think fast to keep it under control. It wasn't going to play itself out quickly, not with the kind of money involved, and Candy was a loose cannon, maybe with a loose mouth, so we had to do something about her. Years ago, Jay had been to an abandoned mine in the desert north of Gerlach. He was something of a rock hound, had a pretty good collection. We needed an out-of-the-way place and didn't have time to find anything better. Jay went back, scouted the place, decided it was as good as any we were likely to find, so he checked ads in the paper and came up with a nice little travel trailer for cash, towed it out there, set it up.

"I talked to Candy, told her who I was—Jayson introduced us since he was the one who'd picked her up in a bar—and I convinced her she was on the right track with this blackmail thing, that Harry and I were finished and I wanted in on the money, too, but for it to work it needed our help, that she needed people on the inside to keep Harry calm, keep him rounding up the money without doing something that would blow up his bid for the presidency, which would mean no one would get a dime, including Candy.

"Jayson wasn't a fool, either. When Harry said he was going to announce his candidacy, Jay knew it wasn't going to happen. Harry wasn't going to quit with the girls. He was eventually going to get caught. Like Clinton, he couldn't keep it in his pants. I could just see him in front of a bunch of microphones telling the world 'I did not have sex with that woman'. Last thing I wanted was for anyone to think I should do some sort of wretched Hillary apology—which I wouldn't have. Before doing that, I would have set Harry on fire. I mean literally. Gasoline and a match.

"But none of that was going to happen. Harry wasn't going to be president unless a miracle of some kind happened. I knew it, but he didn't. He was a self-deceiving, self-aggrandizing fool who often believed his own lies. In their desire for power, politicians can be some of the dumbest halfwits in the country."

Jeri was still working on the knots around my wrists. I thought I felt them loosen a little. My shoulders were burning with the effort of holding my wrists up to where she could reach them.

"But back up," Julia said. "One way or another I was going to leave Harry. I had to. I mean, First Lady? Seriously? What if that miracle did occur? Who the *hell* with even half a brain would want to be First Lady? Who would want to get stuck under that miserable fucking microscope? Not that Harry was headed that way. A liar and a skirt-chaser? He was a caricature of a man who just happened to be good at fooling voters—not that that's a formidable skill these days. My skin crawled whenever he touched me, so it's not as if I disapproved of his adultery. He was a jowly, out-of-shape, larcenous old man with a pot gut that looked as if he had a thirty-pound ham in his shirt.

"I had to leave, get out. Due to a ridiculous prenup I'd had to sign, I was going to get next to nothing—two hundred fifty thousand dollars. But if Harry died, I would get what Harry had managed to steal from taxpayers and turn into millions more with his shady land deals and insider trading. In spite of that, I wasn't thinking about bumping him off, not until Candy found out who she was balling and decided to turn it into what she thought was real money. The hookers he'd been with didn't know who he was, just some rich old guy with a hard-on the size of his index finger. The few who found out were happy to keep quiet for an extra thousand or two. Stupid, but maybe not. At least they're still alive.

"Anyway, Jayson wanted out, too, and he wanted out with more than a severance check and a damp handshake. Harry didn't see Candy after she demanded the million. Jay acted as the go-between, and he told Harry the darling little hooker had figured out what the presidency was worth and had upped her demand to five million, in cash. We did that to keep Harry scrambling, keep him off balance. Of course, Harry couldn't come up with that much in cash, so Jay told Harry that he had explained the real world to Candy, that it couldn't be cash, bills, but it could be in a brokerage account in her name, but even that would take time—liquidating that much in real estate and other holdings couldn't be done overnight. Jay told her some of that. He spun her silly little head around, telling her about the difference between a cash account and a margin loan account in a brokerage house. He told her he'd already set up a cash account for her and money was coming in. He faked papers showing that she was getting rich. I pacified her by bringing a little actual cash to the trailer every few weeks, three or four thousand dollars at a time, just to keep her happy. And fresh food, water, beer, whatever. And I talked to her since she got lonely. I became her friend. We were in this thing together. I kept her there and kept her happy because Jay and I didn't know if we would need her at some point to keep the scheme going. She had a generator so she had power. She had lights, a microwave, a little refrigerator. She could watch DVDs. I went up at least twice a week to be with her, bring her gasoline and supplies, let her know Harry was coming up with her million dollars and all she had to do was be patient, give it time.

"And, of course, he was, not that Candy was ever going to see it. It had to be kept quiet, so Harry stayed out of it. He let Jay handle things. Jay got his attorney on it, Leland Bye, who hired another attorney to manage the sales, and a broker who set up the account to receive funds as they became available. I knew Leland. About a year ago, Jay put me in touch with him to try to break my prenup."

"And to stick his tongue down your throat from time to time," Jeri said. "At that house in Fernley. And maybe to stick other things in other places."

"My *goodness*, aren't you a crass little bitch?" Julia said. "Once everything was over, Leland and I were going to be married."

"A fairy-tale ending for sure."

"If I were you, I'd watch my tongue, girl."

The road rumble went on and on. I wondered where we were, where we were going. I asked Julia.

"To the trailer. We're about thirty miles from Gerlach. It'll take us another hour and a half to get to where we're going. But are you enjoying the story? Are the pieces coming together?"

"It's psychotic but interesting. Of course you're going to have to tell the whole thing again after the FBI rounds you up."

"Not going to happen."

"We found you. They'll find you."

That slowed her down. She thought about that for a mile or two, then said, "How *did* you get onto me, anyway?"

"We put two and two together and came up with four. The FBI can put two and two together and come up with five or six, but they'll eventually whittle it back to four and put you away."

Julia laughed. "Two and two. I don't think so. But you *will* tell me, Mr. Angel, I promise you that. Anyway, to continue, the money kept coming in, but eventually it slowed. The attorney Leland hired did what he could with Harry's assets, even short-selling some of it, but couldn't break much more loose. Sales of some holdings would take too long, at least a year. By then we'd accumulated close to four million in the cash account, so it was time to end it, which meant getting rid of Harry . . . for all kinds of reasons. To inherit, I needed him dead. Jay needed him dead because Harry knew about Candy, the blackmail, Leland, the money. Harry could have blown everything up, unraveled the whole thing—if he found the courage. Not likely, but it was possible. And we were due to get Secret Service protection in a few weeks. Harry was doing well enough in certain polls to warrant it. If we ended up with a pack of agents keeping an eye on us, I figured we'd be screwed.

"Jay knew about Leland and me. He and I ended our fling about the time I met Leland. Jay also knew about the Fernley place. I told him to take Harry there, tell Harry Candy was there, that she wanted to talk to him, make some sort of a deal. Jay knew this was it, end of the line. He dropped Harry off, didn't come inside. I was in the house, alone. I told Jay I would let him know when Harry was gone. Harry had a duffel bag with a hundred thousand dollars in it he was going to give to Candy. It was supposed to appease her, keep her quiet, buy Harry a little more time. As instructed, he came in the house without knocking, and I crushed his skull with a length of iron pipe. I'd practiced on a tree outside, hitting it at about the right height. One hit as he came through the door and Harry was gone. Not just out, but gone from this earth.

"And, God, was I happy. I stood over him for five minutes, weeping for joy. For a while I couldn't see through my tears.

"But then Jay was the problem. The brokerage account was in my name alone. I had nearly four million dollars and Jay was going to want half. If he didn't get it, I knew he would blow the whistle on both of us and damn the consequences. We'd been close once, but as far as I was concerned, he couldn't be trusted."

Still working on my hands, Jeri snorted. "Speaking of people who can't be trusted."

Julia chose to ignore that. "I went to his house. I had my Glock and the pipe and I went in with a key I had from the time we were together. He was drinking. He was about half drunk when I pointed the gun at his head and told him to turn around. I didn't want to shoot him because of the noise. Goddamn Glock is loud, but I would have shot him if I had to. He was stupid and turned around, so I hit him with the pipe—not too hard, just enough to put him down. He was out, not dead, but he was after I wrapped a plastic bag over his head and kept it there for an hour while I did other things."

Suddenly the rope was off my wrists, but my hands didn't come free. Which made no sense. Then Jeri shifted and whispered in my ear, "Bitch put one of those plastic ties around our wrists, too.

I can't do anything with that. I'm going to turn around and try to free your legs."

I felt her move, push against me, felt her weight move along my body, knees in my back, then the pressures changed and she was working on the rope around my ankles.

Julia said, "When I was young, a teenager, my dad had a fire going in the fireplace. The logs were round, set in the fireplace in a dangerous way, as we found out. Once the bottom logs burned down, the top log rolled out, right into the middle of the room, sparks and embers flying. I remember screaming when it came out, this flaming thing rolling out into the room. My dad jumped up and kicked it, got it back onto the hearth. It's still a very sharp memory. Interesting how the past works, though. It gives you ideas. I know fire people, like marshals, can go through a place and determine how a fire was set. They can find traces of gasoline or whatnot, and then they know. So I started a fire in Jay's fireplace and got the logs burning. I took the bag off his head and dragged him up into a recliner, put some booze in a glass nearby like he'd been drinking, which he had, then waited. I had to wait a long time, until the logs looked about right, then I used a poker to pull the top log off and roll it out into the room. It sat on the rug, burning. After a while the room started filling with smoke and a smoke alarm went off so I got out of there. It was dark. I'd parked up the street. I got in my car and left. Jay was dead. All I could do was hope everything looked right. Later, though, they said it was murder so I guess it didn't fly."

"No smoke in his lungs," I said.

"Huh?"

"He was dead when the fire started. They wouldn't find any smoke in his lungs. You have no idea what you're doing."

She didn't say anything for a minute, then went on as if she hadn't heard a word I'd said. "Anyway, I went back to Fernley and got Harry into the back of this car, where you are now—and in case you didn't know, that bundle beside you is Leland. With Harry gone, Jayson Wexel dead, Candy dead, Leland was getting flaky. I'll tell you about Candy in a moment. Last night, Leland and I had a good time at the Fernley house, one last time, but I couldn't let him keep worrying about everything and possibly blowing it."

"Black widow," Jeri said.

For a moment I thought Julia would take offense to that, but she kept driving. I felt my skin crawl, lying there next to Leland.

"I took Harry up to the trailer. There's an old mining tunnel in the side of the mountain not far from where Jay put the trailer, and there's a shaft in the tunnel off to one side that goes down fifty feet and ends in a pile of rubble. It used to be boarded up, but the boards have rotted out. Candy was still at the trailer. I told her the money was ready and all we needed to do was get rid of Harry. She and I dropped him down the shaft, after she'd cut off his hand with a rusty saw she found in the tunnel. I was in favor of cutting off his head so everyone would know he was really dead. I needed him dead so I could inherit right away. But Candy had heard Harry's slogan and thought she'd turn it into a joke. She remembered you, Mr. Angel—Mortimer. It wasn't that long ago that you found those heads, the mayor's and the DA's. It was her idea to send Harry's hand to you with his stupid slogan on a note. At first I didn't like it, then it occurred to me that it was such a weird, random thing it would get investigators running in circles, chasing ghosts. I wouldn't have thought to do that. I didn't really want to cut off Harry's head and send it anywhere, so Candy's idea worked out. She and I packaged Harry's hand, drove to Bend, and left it in a FedEx pickup box."

"How'd you get my address?" I asked.

"I didn't get all of it. Only your name and Ralston Street, but obviously that was enough. You're famous, Mortimer. I was sure it would get to you, and of course it did."

Man, I didn't like her calling me Mortimer. If she gave me a chance, I would drop her down that mineshaft on top of Harry.

We rode in silence for a while. She'd told us most of it, but not all. Jeri was still working on my ankles and I wanted to keep Julia distracted.

"Why put this car in Mary Odermann's name?" I asked.

"Why not? I didn't want it in my name, and Leland didn't want it in his. He knew his sister's date of birth, social security number, everything else he needed. He handled it. He gave Mary's husband, Robert, five thousand dollars to not say anything, just let the car be in his wife's name, that he, Leland, would pay the registration every year. keep up the insurance, whatever was needed to keep it legal. He told Robert he wanted to keep an affair quiet that could mess up his life if it got out. Maybe Robert was a romantic, because he went along with it—either that or the five thousand dollars did the trick." Julia laughed. "Anyway, that was months before Candy entered the picture. Leland bought the car so he and I could see each other. We couldn't afford to have my car running out to that house in Fernley. Harry and I had vanity plates. My car was SENATR2, which was much too visible."

"Leland bought you a hundred-thousand-dollar car," Jeri said to keep her talking. "What a guy."

"Wasn't he, though? This turned out to be really useful when I was hauling stuff out to Candy."

"Why'd you have this love-mobile painted white?" I asked.

She was silent for five seconds. "It *is* white. What do you mean 'have it painted'?"

Truth is in the hesitations. "About a week ago it was green."

She was quiet for a long time, thinking. Then the car slowed as we went through Gerlach. I hoped Deputy Roup was on the ball, watching the highway, that he would pull her over and bust her ass, at least stop her and question her, but no such luck. The car picked up speed as we went out the other end of town, back into empty desert. I didn't know how far the trailer was from Gerlach, but I didn't think we had much time left. Jeri was still working on the rope around my ankles.

"You've found out some stuff," Julia said. "Interesting."

"The FBI will think it's interesting, too."

"I don't think so," she said. "I think you and Nancy Drew back there got lucky. You called the little whore Allie a while ago, so you know her name. So you know her, which means you're connected to her somehow and you stumbled across me. She phoned her sister when I was pumping gas in Gerlach. That must have been it. I don't think Harry's hand had a thing to do with you finding me."

"Wrong," I said. "You were seen dropping that package into a drop box in Bend."

She was quiet a while longer. "I still don't see it," she said. "I still think you got lucky . . . if you want to call your situation right now *lucky*."

Ha, ha. Really—I wanted to kill her. Somewhere to the north I hoped to find a mineshaft with her name on it.

Then my legs came free. Julia hadn't put plastic ties around our ankles, which was a mistake. If I could get Jeri's legs free, she could kick Julia to death, just like she'd almost kicked Victoria's head off her shoulders back in August. Jeri's head was toward the front of the car now, and mine was toward the rear. I felt her legs move until her feet were at my hands, then they stopped. I began to work on her knots, exploring, trying to figure out how the knot was tied, where the ends were.

"Still doesn't explain why you had this thing painted white," Jeri said.

"Which was at Lou's Auto Body in Bend," I added, hoping she would make a mistake if she got rattled. "Lou was the guy in the wheelchair, in case you didn't know."

Again Julia was quiet for a while. Then she said, "I'd been through Gerlach in a green car at least twenty times in the past few months. Then Candy phoned her sister, which was stupid. I didn't like that. I thought a change of color would be a good idea."

"That's all? A good idea?"

"What else? It *was* a good idea. I was doing everything I could to stay off anyone's radar."

"Real good," I said. "Here's how good it was: the VIN number of a car is reported to the DMV if its color is changed. The FBI will be all over that. But speaking of a change of color, you'll look good in an orange jumpsuit."

More silence.

Finally, she said, "This thing is registered to Mary Odermann, Leland's sister. Leland is about to disappear off the face of the earth. So how does this car come back to me?"

I didn't have a ready comeback to that. I was having trouble with my head, listening to her and working on Jeri's knots—which felt like I was trying to untie a rock.

"I don't see how any of this can get back to me," Julia said. "I spent all afternoon wiping down the Fernley house. I was finishing up when I saw you two out there on the street, watching the place. I'm so glad you decided to check the garage. Gave me a scare, but it gave me the chance to clean up that loose end, too. I didn't know you or anyone was onto me."

"The FBI won't be far behind," I said.

"Don't think so, Mortimer."

Bitch.

"When did you murder Allie . . . Candy?" Jeri asked.

"Murder. That's such an ugly word."

"I'm sure what you did to her was much nicer."

Julia laughed. "Not long after she phoned her sister, we stopped at a convenience store in Empire. She was hungry. I didn't want to stop but I had to keep her happy, not worried. We got back on the road, headed toward Reno. Candy was giddy with joy, about to get her million dollars. She was hugging the duffel bag with the money I'd given her at the trailer and the hundred thousand Harry brought to the Fernley house—over a hundred thirty thousand altogether—"

"Which you've got now."

"No, genius. I threw it out a window. Of *course* I've got it. It was night, dark. I could see at least ten miles in either direction. So I stopped the car suddenly, acted sort of shocked and got out, went to the back of the car, told her to get out too, and the dumb creature got out, came around back, and I shot her in the chest. One bullet and she was down."

I shuddered. She'd said it like she said she'd bought herself a Diet Coke and a package of Fig Newtons, no big deal.

Then the car slowed and we turned off the highway. Inertia told me we'd turned left, which was west. Now we were bouncing over ruts, which made it harder to keep my fingers working on Jeri's knots.

"I got her into a plastic garbage bag and wrestled her into the back where you are now," Julia said. "I went back, through Gerlach, back to the trailer, dragged her into the tunnel, dropped her down the shaft on top of Harry."

"Then you burned the trailer right down to its wheels," I said, remembering what Roup had said two weeks ago.

Another few seconds of silence. "Where'd you get that?"

"I come across things. The FBI will, too. Look at all the things I've learned. They might be following us right now with their lights off, about to bust you. I have the feeling you're headed for a lethal injection."

We bumped along another mile or two in silence.

"After you disposed of Allie, you came back through Gerlach," I said. "I saw you go by. You kept going, didn't stop for gas." I tried to remember what time that was. "It was about ten thirty at night."

Julia muttered a curse, kept driving. "If you think I'm going to stop now, you're out of your mind."

Well, shit. A person could at least hope.

The road got steeper and began to wind around more. We were going up into the hills. I worked harder on Jeri's ropes. My fingers were already raw, but it was worth it because suddenly the knot got looser and I was unravelling it, and then Jeri's feet were free. She scooted down to where I could start working on her hands, but if she had a plastic tie around her wrists that might not be as useful as having her feet free. Her feet were deadly weapons.

Five minutes later, I had gotten nowhere with the knots, and the car felt like it topped a rise to a level spot. It slowed, then stopped.

"Everyone out," Julia said in a singsong voice. She opened her door. A light came on over my head. I was on my back, looking up. After all that darkness it was like staring into the sun.

The rear hatch of the SUV popped open and swung up. I could see Julia from about mid-thigh on up as she stood back a little way with the Glock in her hand. "You untied her feet, Mortimer. Good work. You, girl, sit up. Do it *now*."

Jeri sat up. Her face was three feet from mine when Julia pulled the trigger. The bullet hit Jeri in the face and blew out the back of her head.

No—!

CHAPTER TWENTY-TWO

I HAD A snapshot of blood and brains and bits of bone hitting the back of the front seats, then everything went black because suddenly Jeri was gone and all sense of reality was blown into whirling bits that had nothing to do with this world. For a few seconds I was out among the stars, in the infinite nothingness of space where there was no Earth, no SUV, no Julia, no sound, no sensation, nothing . . . then the world roared back and I was lying on my back but I couldn't think because Jeri was gone and my life was over and it was too sudden too swift too impossible she couldn't be gone forever and this was a dream except it wasn't and Julia was hauling Jeri out by her feet and my love slid by me and plopped on the ground which was the first thing I heard since that gun had gone off and ended my life.

Then hatred exploded through me and I had to kill her, had to get my feet under me, get outside and stomp Julia into the dust and keep stomping until she was bloody flesh and broken bones mashed into the dirt and that wouldn't bring Jeri back but I had to—

I pulled my knees violently into my chest and threw my head back as Julia was dragging Leland out of the cargo bay, wrapped in a blanket. The momentum rolled me out of the SUV in a somersault that landed me on my feet, then flopped me into the dirt on my back. I tried to kick Julia's right knee, missed by inches, then she was backpedaling with that gun in her hand and I saw the muzzle come up at me. I rolled to one side as the gun went off. I don't know how close the bullet came but I kept rolling and got my knees under me, then my feet, leaped to one side as the Glock blew another bullet by me, then I was running around the far side of the SUV, putting it between me and her. I ran across a kind of clearing, zigzagging left and right with gunshots behind me and bullets flying, but it's almost impossible to hit someone with a handgun under those conditions if you're not an expert. I kept running, wondering if she'd get lucky, then I was eighty feet from the car, a hundred, sprinting through darkness under the stars with a pale yellow sliver of moon hanging low in the west.

Seconds later, more bullets came toward me, but she was firing blind now from two hundred feet, then three hundred, no hope of hitting me. My feet got tangled in a tough hunk of sage, and I went down, tucked my face into a shoulder as I hit the ground, hands still bound behind my back. I stayed down until the bullets stopped, then looked toward the SUV, saw a tiny light where it stood in the clearing where Allie's trailer was a pile of cold ash and scorched metal, then I got up and jogged farther into the empty desert where Julia couldn't see me, couldn't follow, didn't have a hope of finding me where she might be able to erase the pure, white-hot hatred for her I carried out there in my heart.

Jeri was gone.

Forever.

She would never be back.

I slowed to a jog and tears filled my eyes. I couldn't see a thing except blobs of dark on black. Suddenly my throat closed up and I couldn't breathe. I fell to my knees and choked on my tears.

My love was gone.

I collapsed, folded up with my arms behind me, and sobbed.

God, Jeri—no.

No, no, no, no.

I stayed like that for a long time, unable to stand, unable to see. Finally I heard the sound of an engine. I staggered to my feet, partly hunched over. Headlights swung around in the night. Taillights put a red glow on clumps of sagebrush, then the SUV bounced away into darkness.

I vowed then that Julia would die. I would hunt her down and kill her.

Not the police. *I* would do it.

Me.

If I didn't, I wasn't worth anything on this miserable earth.

CHAPTER TWENTY-THREE

I MADE MY way back to where Jeri had been murdered. She and Leland were gone, mostly likely dumped down that vertical shaft Julia had mentioned. Forty yards away I could see the black maw of a tunnel in the hillside.

Jeri would be in there.

I could hardly breathe, thinking about that.

The last dregs of moonlight revealed the remains of the trailer Julia had torched two weeks ago. I explored it, located the sharp edge of a piece of sheet metal, and went to work on the plastic tie holding my wrists together. It took ten minutes, but the tie finally popped apart and my hands came free.

I couldn't go into the tunnel—I couldn't *not* go in the tunnel. I walked over without thinking, went in thirty feet, and saw nothing. It was pitch black. Stumble around and I could fall into that shaft . . .

. . . and be with Jeri forever.

Then Julia would win, which couldn't happen. I turned around and came back out, quivering with pain and fury. Hatred for Julia was a molten indescribable thing inside me. I had to kill her. *Had* to.

* * *

I walked out. The moon went behind the hills and the land was dark, illuminated by starlight—barely enough to see the trail out, a rutted track between miles of rolling sage. I checked my pockets. I still had my wallet but no cell phone.

As I walked, I thought about Jeri and Julia, Jeri and Julia, love and hate, love and hate. But now Jeri was pain that tried to bring me down, make me give up, so I concentrated on Julia. I had to get to her. She knew I was still alive. What would she do? Where would she go? How could I track her down?

The night grew cool. I shivered as I walked, stumbling in the dark. I remembered Deputy Roup saying the trailer fire had been eight or ten miles in from the highway.

A long way to go in this black, horrific night.

Julia.

I saw a knife enter her belly, slide up slowly, watched her guts spill onto the floor at her feet, saw her staring down in horror and disbelief at her own bloody intestines. I saw her die slowly, then slip away into Hell. I wasn't the person I was yesterday or even an hour ago. Now I was a monster.

I walked.

An hour passed. Two. Three.

Julia.

She would have to run because I was alive. She would have to go soon. A cold, icy fury settled deep inside and seethed within me, allowing me to start thinking clearly again.

How would she run? Where to? She had the cash she'd used to pacify Allie. Could she put it into an account that would allow her to use a credit card? Could she use it to get prepaid cards? How would she get to that brokerage account, and when?

Thoughts of Jeri returned. I couldn't leave her down in that pit. I had to get her, or someone did. And Ma had to be told.

Ma.

If anyone could track Julia, Ma could.

I topped a rise and saw a lone pair of headlights slowly moving through the blackness, heard the distant throb of an engine.

The highway.

The headlights slid by, almost without sound, headed north out of Gerlach. Now gone. They'd been about two miles away.

I kept walking, shivering, loathing Julia. I envisioned another fantastic death for her, listened to her screams as she died.

Which made me sick and didn't help.

I said Ma's phone number aloud. We'd memorized each other's numbers while tracking Julia and Leland. I still knew Ma's but I needed a phone.

Jeri's number was . . . she would never answer again. I would never again hear her voice. Tears filled my eyes as I stumbled along in the darkness.

I had to phone Ma, I had to get to Reno, Ma had to try to track Julia. Julia would leave a trail. Jeri's brother, Ron DiFrazzia, had to be told. And Sarah, what about Sarah?

I didn't know. Jeri had liked her, even loved her like a sister. Sarah would have to be told, but not right away.

Ma first.

Call the police? Tell Deputy Roup when I got to Gerlach? Tell Russell Fairchild? Phone the FBI? How could I get to Julia if she was caught by the FBI or Reno police?

Couldn't. That would end it. In fact, Julia might skate on all the charges, if charges were even brought against her. Did anything tie her incontrovertibly to the murders other than what she'd told Jeri and me? If so, I didn't see it. Jeri was gone, so it was my word against Julia's. Where was the proof that would put Julia away, absolutely, without question?

There wasn't any.

None of us could tell the police, not Ma, not me, not Sarah. Ma would know what to tell Ron DiFrazzia, if anything. Maybe he had to be kept out of it. Whatever happened, I was going to end Julia's life. *I* would.

A faint gleam appeared ahead. Oil on blacktop. I'd reached the highway. Nothing had come along since I'd seen that one vehicle, forty minutes ago. I reached the blacktop and turned right, south toward Gerlach, and started walking. After a hundred yards or so I passed a vertical marker. I put my face six inches from it and slowly made out a number in the dark, forty-four. Mile marker forty-four. I put that in my head and kept walking.

An hour passed. I went by mile marker forty-seven.

Another half hour went by, then I heard an engine behind me, a big diesel from the sound of it. Then headlights appeared, red and yellow lights outlining the cab of an eighteen-wheeler.

I stood at the side of the road as it drew near and stuck out my thumb. It felt stupid. Who out here wouldn't need a ride? But I stuck my thumb out anyway. I squinted into a blinding crescendo of light. Air brakes came on before it passed me. The rig slowed, came to a stop fifty yards beyond me, lights illuminating the blacktop and sage in muddy color. I jogged to catch up. The passenger door popped open. I stepped up, opened the door all the way, looked in. A guy in his fifties with a three-day growth of gray stubble stared at me in the cab's yellow light.

"Hell of a place to hitchhike," he said.

"You got that right." I rubbed my forehead above my left eyebrow, concealing much of my face until the cab's light went out.

"Didn't see a car. Broke down somewhere off the highway?"

"Uh-huh. About seven miles up in the hills. East." I told him east instead of west to keep this to myself. Julia was in my head. I was a gun, aimed at Julia. I didn't want anyone else near her.

"Name's Barry," the guy said.

"Steve," I told him. "Thanks for stopping."

He got the rig going again. "No problem. Damn sure wouldn't leave a guy walking out here at night."

"Thanks again. How far is it to Gerlach?"

"'Bout eighteen miles. I'm stopping there. That suit you?"

"Uh-huh. Got a cell phone I can use?"

He got one off a ledge in the console. He hit an icon and handed it to me. It was still attached to a charger cable. I put in Ma's number, heard it ringing.

"Yeah what?" Ma's voice was sleepy, abrupt.

"It's me, Ma."

"Mort?"

"Uh-huh. I'm up in Gerlach. At least I'll be there soon. I need you to come up and get me." I felt my heart breaking all over again. Suddenly I could barely force the words out without sobbing.

"Gerlach? Whatcha doin' up there?"

"Come get me, Ma. Now."

"What's . . . can you talk?"

"No."

"Okay, I'll be up there soon as I can. You gonna be in that casino place?"

"Only place open twenty-four hours. I'll be there."

"Need me to bring anything?"

I thought about that.

"Mort?"

"Can't think of anything. I just need you."

"I'm on my way."

I ended the call, handed the phone back to Barry after deleting Ma's number from the outgoing list.

"Your mother, huh?" he said.

"Yup."

"I call my mom at one thirty in the morning, she'd have me fried and half-eaten before the sun got up."

"Yeah."

At the flat response Barry looked over at me. "You okay?"

"I've been better. But I'll live."

* * *

Barry pulled into a packed-dirt parking lot behind the Texaco station and left the rig running. If I was going to get Julia, I couldn't be seen by any of the locals in Gerlach. Barry wasn't a local guy, but I couldn't go inside the casino. I wasn't up here tonight. I'd played no part in anything that had taken place at that abandoned mine. If I was here in Gerlach, the story would unravel and drag Julia into it. The FBI and the police would be involved, and I would never be able to get to her.

I thanked Barry. He walked to the casino and I stayed outside, waiting for Ma to show up. The night was chilly. I walked between the Texaco station and the casino, keeping in the shadows, trying to stay warm.

By the time Ma arrived in her Eldorado at three twenty, I was cold, shivering. I figured she'd left two minutes after I'd called her and driven faster than fifty—not a good idea in that car. She must've had an idea that something bad had happened. Just how bad, she had no idea.

I flagged her down between the Texaco station and the motel. I got in on the passenger side and broke down entirely. I sobbed. I howled. My heart tore loose inside my chest. I died in that car all over again.

"Omigod, Mort. Oh, no. What, *what*—?"

"Drive," I said. "Reno." The words didn't sound human. They were something that bubbled up from the depths of the ocean, liquid sounds that tore out of my throat as if I'd choked them up.

Ma drove. She headed back south, back to Reno, and I just let the tears and the pain flow. We were well past Empire when I came up for air, still barely able to breathe.

"Jeri?" Ma asked. "Where's Jeri?"

"She's dead."

Ma had feared it. What else could do this to me? Yet she had to pull to the side of the road and turn off the engine. She bawled. We performed a duet of pain the likes of which I'd never imagined two people had ever done before.

It was twenty minutes before she could drive again. We got going, doing no better than forty miles an hour. I tried to get my voice to work as I told her the last of it, Julia taking us into the hills, opening the rear hatch of that SUV, shooting Jeri without warning in the first three seconds, just pure outrageous murder. I didn't tell her what had hit the seats, a red mist of what had been Jeri a hundredth of a second before—the stuff that had been Jeri, that had made her who she was, suddenly blown into eternity by the most evil bitch in the history of the world.

Ma couldn't talk. She drove with tears in her eyes, swallowing often, sometimes letting out a faint mewling sound. I gave her a little more of it, when I could talk.

Finally, on I-80, ten miles west of Fernley, I said, "I want her, Ma. I've got to kill Julia. So we can't go to the police. No one can know I was anywhere around Gerlach tonight."

She nodded. "I figured. Don't worry, we'll get her. You and me, boyo. I'm in. That bitch is already dead."

"Jeri can't stay in that mineshaft, so . . . so how . . . ?"

"I know what to do," Ma said. "You said the turnoff's at mile marker forty-four?"

"Yes."

"I'll handle it."

"I'm so sick I want to die, Ma."

"I know."

"Not until I get Julia, though."

She turned to me. It was still dead dark outside. "I've got this, Mort. I know what to do. This is pure hell, but I know what to do. Have you got clothes at Jeri's place?"

"Yes."

"Okay, then. We'll start there."

* * *

She drove around back to a detached garage at Jeri's house, didn't pull the car inside. We got out and she told me to go to the back door and strip before I went inside.

"Strip, Ma?"

"Right down to bare skin. Your clothing will have dirt on it that could be used to prove you were at that trailer. If you're shy, leave your underwear on until you get inside then toss it out the door. Go take a shower. Scrub everything—especially your hair, fingernails, and get between your toes. Do a damn good job of it, lots of soap. Then get dressed."

I did as I was told.

I came downstairs in jogging shoes, blue jeans, a sweatshirt. Ma was pacing, thinking. She looked up when I came into the room. "Gotta get Jeri out of that hole," she said.

"I wasn't going to . . . to leave her there."

"You can't get her. No way. If you did, you'd get tripped up by a hundred legal issues. It'd be impossible to get her a proper burial unless you brought Julia into it, or tried to. That would be a mess like you wouldn't believe. Julia wouldn't be charged and they might put it on you. Only way to get Jeri out of there, is to report this. I'll do it anonymously. Five minutes after they bring bodies up, fingerprints will be transmitted to the FBI. Ten minutes after that, this place is going to be crawling with cops, so we can't stay here. Let's get that shower upstairs completely dry, then clear out."

I dried the shower with a towel. Ma packed it into a big plastic bag along with the clothes I'd worn while escaping from Julia. One last look around and no one could tell we'd been there in the past twelve hours, which was all that mattered.

Ma backed the Caddy out and headed east on Second Street.

"Where to?" I asked.

"You want to get Julia, right?"

"I have to." Deep inside, in a place that would never fade or be forgotten, I was an unspeakable hell pit of fury. Julia had to die. I knew it was wrong. I knew the thought made me an evil person, a killer, a monster, but I couldn't rid myself of it until I rid the earth of Julia. Then, maybe, I could be human again—if I could live with the knowledge. And if I couldn't, then so be it, but Julia had to die.

"We're not in too deep yet," Ma said. "You can still let the cops do their thing."

I shook my head. "I can't think of anything that proves Julia was up there tonight or did the things she told us she did. Nothing implicates her. The Fernley house, that SUV we've been tracking, the trailer—none of it was in her name. Nothing is conclusive. If we went to the cops, she would end up untouchable. Right now she's running. She's vulnerable."

"That's the way I see it, too."

"So where are we going? What're we going to do?"

"This's gonna be hard, Mort. Real hard. But you've got to go to Sarah's place."

"Ma—"

"You need an alibi for the time Jeri was up there when . . . when she was killed." Her voice caught as she said it and her eyes got bright again. Finally, she said, "It hasn't been long. They'll pin down time of death for her pretty close. As soon as they find Jeri, they're gonna want to talk to you. You can't have been up there, so you need an airtight alibi, unbreakable. If they put you up there, then Julia's gonna walk and you're in the middle of a year-long legal and media circus. You have to have been somewhere else, and Sarah's your best shot. If she'll do it."

"Is that fair? Bringing her into this mess?"

"She's already in it. Not what we're planning for Julia, not yet, but she has to be told. So about gettin' involved, we'll have to let her decide. Now let's get over there."

We arrived at the Sierra Sky Apartments at 6:10. The sunrise was an orange glow above the eastern mountains when we climbed outside stairs to the second floor and paused at the door to number twenty-three.

"You sure about this?" I asked Ma.

"No. But it isn't very damn often that I'm sure about anything, so let's do this, see how it goes."

I rang the bell.

Waited.

Rang again.

A light came on inside, then an outside light. Seconds later, the door opened and Sarah was there in a robe, staring at us.

"Oh, no," she said. "What . . . ?"

"We need to come in," Ma said quietly.

Sarah looked terrified as Ma went past her. I put an arm around Sarah's shoulders, got her away from the door, then closed it behind us. Ma took one of Sarah's hands. "Jeri . . . It's Jeri," she said. "She . . . she . . ." Then Ma started to bawl all over again.

Sarah let out a little cry and started to fall. I took part of her weight, then suddenly had to take all of it when she passed out.

I picked her up and carried her into a bedroom I'd never seen before. A queen-sized bed was rumpled, covers thrown back. I set Sarah down and pulled the covers over her.

She only stayed out for a minute, then her eyes popped open. She tried to sit up. "Jeri . . . Jeri, she's not . . . oh, please, no—"

Ma sat beside her. "She's . . . gone. Allie is, too."

Tears almost splashed out of Sarah's eyes. Her lips quivered and she started to wail. Ma did her best to keep her from making too much noise. She held her—didn't say a word, just held her, which was all anyone could do. I stood there like an ox, feeling useless, which of course I was.

It took twenty minutes before we could talk to Sarah and start to get things under control.

"I . . . I have to go to the bathroom," she said. She got up, went through a door, closed it. Ma went over and opened it, went inside. They came out a few minutes later, Sarah still in her robe, eyes red, still snuffling, and Ma guided her back to bed. Ma took Sarah's robe as she got under the covers again. I stood there and watched all of this, still feeling perfectly male and useless.

"You two are gonna have to trust me right now," Ma said. She looked at me and said, "Get into bed and hold her, Mort."

"Ma—"

"I don't have time for a big discussion. I know what I'm doing. Take off your jeans and that sweatshirt and get in. I want to see two people with arms around each other in twenty seconds or I'm gonna kick some big tall PI ass all over this room, and I mean it."

So I stripped down to underwear and got in bed with Sarah and held her. As soon as her arms were around me, she was crying again and I was, too. It barely registered that she was naked, something of a first for me.

Ma gave us a moment, then said, "Okay, I've got things to do. It'll take me a while, at least two hours, probably more like three. When I get back, I'll let myself in, and if I don't see you two right where you are now, there's gonna be hell to pay. You two need each other. You need someone to hold on to. I've got another reason for you to stay together, but no time to get into it. When I get back we'll talk turkey, but right now this is what you need, so stay *put*."

She left.

* * *

What I learned is that holding another human being is a way of sharing life. Ma left us like that to make us know we weren't alone in the world, that our lives still meant something because we could give and receive comfort with another human being. It wasn't sex. It had nothing to do with sex. It was human contact—skin on skin—and it kept us from slipping away. I think if Ma could have been in there with us, she would have, but Ma was tougher than we were. And, like she said, she had things to do. I wasn't tough. I didn't know how near I was to death, but suddenly I felt that Sarah was keeping me from sliding over an edge into a place from which I would never return, never be able to reach Julia. And maybe I kept Sarah from sliding over that same dark edge. This was a nightmare that wouldn't end. There was no end to it because Jeri was dead and that was impossible.

So we held each other and cried and shared the only contact that made sense right then, someone warm, breathing in your arms, keeping you going, and Ma, the toughest person I've ever met, did what needed to be done.

She left the house and drove all the way to Fernley, to the house on Old Aspen Road, approached the place with a .38 police special in case Julia was there. She checked the house, then went into the garage and found my gun where I'd dropped it in the dirt. The gun was a loose cannon, no pun intended. Its serial number would put me in the thick of all this. The police would connect Bye with the house since it was in his name and he was in that mineshaft with Jeri and the others. They would go out to the Fernley house, look around. I didn't know what they would find, but at least Ma had removed my gun. Julia had probably gotten Jeri and me out of there as quickly as possible yesterday evening and hadn't gone back. Leland's Lexus was still there, under that blue tarp. No telling where the Mercedes SUV would eventually end up. Last thing I would ever do is ask Detective Fairchild about it.

Ma also wanted to check inside Jeri's Porsche to make sure it didn't have anything in it that would point to me being in Fernley with Jeri, watching Bye's house. The Porsche was where she and I had left it, and it had to stay there. It was part of the story the police would start to put together. Ma gave the place a last look then drove back to Reno. In a Walmart she purchased a cheap cell phone and the least amount of minutes possible. She paid with cash, drove several miles to south Reno, phoned the Washoe County Sheriff's office, and told them they would find some bodies west of mile marker forty-four north of Gerlach about nine miles off the highway at an abandoned mine, down a mineshaft, and one of the bodies might be that of Senator Reinhart. A mile away she stuck the phone under a tire of the Caddy and crushed it, got out, gathered up the pieces, and dropped them into a trash barrel outside a 7-Eleven a few more miles away. In a dumpster at a random apartment complex she tossed the clothes I'd worn up north, and the towel I'd used to dry Jeri's shower. When she returned to the Sierra Sky Apartments it was full light outside. She had a Walmart scarf over her head, using it to partly conceal her face.

Sarah and I were asleep in each other's arms when Ma came in. While she was gone we had cried, talked quietly, and I'd kissed Sarah's salty tears, but I'd been awake for nearly twenty-four hours, walked over thirteen miles, and losing Jeri had all but killed me, so I finally passed out. Not long after, Sarah had followed me into sleep.

"Wake up, you two," Ma said softly.

Sarah stirred, then shook me a little. My eyes opened. They felt grainy from all the crying—the salt of dried tears.

"You can get up and get dressed or stay where you are, but we have to talk," Ma said.

I looked a question at Sarah.

"Stay," she said.

"We're good, Ma," I told her. "What's up?"

Ma drew up a chair and sat. Sarah and I propped up on pillows with the covers pulled up high, then listened.

"I phoned it in, then crushed the cell phone," Ma said. "They'll probably be up there in an hour or two. If they go by helicopter they could be there sooner. It'll take a while to get Jeri out, but once they do it won't take them long to ID her, probably a matter of minutes, then things'll get popping—for you, Mort. They'll find Reinhart's remains so the media circus is gonna start up again as well. But right now, Sarah, you have a big decision to make. Huge, actually."

Ma laid it out. If we put the police onto Julia, there was a good chance she would escape. The SUV, the Fernley house, the trailer—nothing was in her name. By now she'd probably abandoned the Mercedes after wiping it down thoroughly, or she might've set it on fire since that was her way of getting rid of things, although she hadn't burned down the Fernley house. There might not be enough evidence to put her at the mine in the hills, and even less to convict her of murder.

"Mort and I are going to track Julia down and . . . get rid of her," Ma said. "She has no idea who I am or how good I am, but she's as good as found. It couldn't be any more illegal, Sarah, but it's going to happen. Julia murdered Reinhart, your sister, Leland Bye, Jayson Wexel, Jeri. I'm sorry about your sister and, well, I really can't think about Jeri, not right now. That's just too much, too horrible. I've got too much to do. But if we're going to get Julia, Mort has to have an alibi for the time Jeri was up at that mine, and it's gotta be *tight*. Police will have a good idea of time of death for her, and a lot of people know she and Mort were together, so they're gonna be all over Mort, and soon.

"So the question is, can you provide that alibi? Right now you haven't done anything illegal, but if you tell the police Mort spent the entire night with you here, that could land you in prison."

"I'll do it."

"That's a real fast answer," Ma said. "Now I want you to *think* about it. If they bust your story, you're done for."

Sarah stared at her, then at me. "We know she killed Jeri. Did she kill Allie, too?"

I held her hand under the covers. "Yes. Last night, Julia told us she shot Allie on the highway less than an hour after you got that call from her in the bar."

Sarah closed her eyes and took a deep breath, opened her eyes again. "I'm in."

Ma leaned closer. "You'd better be goddamn sure about that because this isn't a kid's game, Sarah. This is your *life*. Mort's, too."

"I'm sure."

Ma looked at her awhile longer. Then she nodded. "Okay, then. Odds are the police or the FBI will be all over this apartment, and that could happen in a matter of hours. Well, maybe a little longer since it'd take them a while to find a connection between you two. In fact, they might not make that connection independently, but once they get hold of Mort, and he says he was here with you, they'll be all over you and this place like ants at a picnic."

"You don't have to do this," I said to Sarah.

She squeezed my hand. "Yes, I do."

Words were one thing, the hand squeeze was more intimate, more certain.

"If they can't bust Mort's alibi, then you're safe, Sarah," Ma said. "Everything depends on that. So if you're still in, here's what's got to be done. The two of you have just one story to tell, and it has to be the same story, but not using the same words, so listen to me and get this straight. You two spent last night right here, the entire night. By now there's probably a little of Mort's hair in the bed. It'd be better if Mort wasn't wearing anything, but—whatever. You might do something about that. The bed's got to look right in case they get a warrant and grab the sheets. I don't know how likely that is, but there's no point taking a chance. After I leave, the two of you should shower—*together*, in case you're not tracking this a hundred percent. This apartment has a story to tell. Mort needs to put his fingerprints in the usual places and then some—kitchen, bathroom, bedroom. You two got that?

"Now back up. You two ate dinner here last night. You didn't go out. Figure out what you ate and who cooked, who cleaned up. The remains of a meal have to be in the garbage—cans, wrappers, dishes in the dishwasher, the whole nine yards. Same for breakfast this morning. I saw some DVDs in the other room, so you watched a movie last night. Two movies might be better since that would use up more time. Decide which ones you watched—things you've both seen. You didn't do a lot of talking because you could be asked what you talked about, and that's complicated. More complicated than you can possibly imagine. You didn't talk about anything important. It's hard to remember what since it was so trivial. Mostly you made out a lot, but you didn't have sex, if anyone asks, because they could even check that, although it'd take a hell of a warrant to get you in for a test like that, Sarah. I don't see a judge signing off on that, but with the Feds these days you never know. Either way, you don't offer that information. If they ask, you tell them. If they don't, you don't say anything."

Ma looked at Sarah. "Where were you yesterday, before you and Mort hooked up?"

"My last class was at one. I left the campus around two."

"Anyone see you after that?"

"No. I came back here and did a bunch of studying."

"Okay, that's good. So when did Mort come over?"

Sarah looked at me. "Four o'clock? Something like that?"

"That works," I said. "Jeri and I got to Fernley around four thirty. No one would've seen me in Reno after four."

"Your car's at Jeri's place," Ma said to me. "So how'd you get over here?"

I looked at Sarah. "Did you pick me up at Jeri's?"

Sarah looked at Ma. "Did I? Does that work?"

"It does. The fact that no one saw it happen isn't proof that it didn't. They'd get nowhere trying to prove a negative. So, Sarah, what's your story here, in a nutshell?"

She thought for a moment. "I picked up Mort sometime around four yesterday afternoon at Jeri's. We came back here. We've been together here ever since. We spent the night together. We made out, watched a movie, didn't have sex, and didn't go out anywhere."

"Good. Talk over what you did yesterday after Mort got here. Dirty up some dishes. When I leave, have breakfast. If the police question you about things, paraphrase it so you don't use the same words. Don't be too certain about the times you did things. Plus or minus half an hour is good enough.

"And, Mort, you need to account for your time from the time you got up yesterday until Sarah picked you up. You're not making up an alibi since nothing happened at Fernley or at the mine during that time, you're just accounting for time."

"I slept in. Jeri was gone when I got up so I went out walking, alone. I did the River Walk, came home and made a sandwich. Sarah and I had previously arranged to meet at four at Jeri's. She thought she would be through studying by then."

"Really?" Ma gave me a skeptical look that would make a cop proud. "When did you two make that arrangement?"

Sarah looked at me. "When we were up in that restaurant the evening before, right? We were there nearly three hours. I'm pretty sure the waiter would remember us if he's asked."

"That's right."

"Good enough," Ma said. "Now explain why the hell you two would meet at Jeri's, of all places. Why would you throw your affair in her face like that?"

"It's not an affair," I said. "I was gifted to Sarah, she was gifted to me, and Jeri was doing the gifting. Jeri and Sarah are the sort of friends you don't see every day."

Ma smiled. "If anyone doesn't believe it, send 'em to me, I'll spin their heads around. And I'm glad we're getting some mileage out of that word.

"Okay, you two were questioned up in Gerlach two weeks ago when you found Reinhart's hand. Then Jeri and Reinhart and all the rest of them are found up there, murdered. Count on being asked about that. A lot. But you don't know one single blessed thing about it. Two weeks ago Allie's phone call took you up there to find her. You showed her picture around and a few people thought they might have seen her, but you never found her. End of story.

"Once I leave here, I won't be back since I don't know nothin' about this place. We've been in the Green Room at the Goose from time to time, so let's meet there tomorrow night at ten. Until then, you two stay together, all the time. Keep an eye out when you come to the Goose—don't let anyone follow you. I'll get there around nine thirty. When you get there, don't sit with me, don't notice me. Keep away. If anyone wanders in who looks remotely suspicious, I'll get up and leave. You two stay awhile, have a drink. If that happens, we'll try again the next night, same time. After a while, if it looks okay, I'll come over and sit with you, so get a table out of the way, toward the back."

She looked around the room. "In case you haven't noticed, I haven't touched anything in here that'll take a print. When I came back I opened the front door using gloves. I was never here. I don't know where you live, Sarah. But we know each other pretty well. I know all about this 'gifting' thing, and it doesn't bother me one bit since I'm not a tight-assed old broad.

Anyone wants to gift me a good-lookin' guy, I'm ready. That'll shut down any questions they might ask me about that. My car is parked a quarter mile down the street, not in the parking lot here. And I hid my face with this scarf when I came back this morning." She looked around the room one more time, then at us. "What else? Did I forget anything? I'm tired. I'm starting to feel mushy in the head."

I tried to think, too. It was hard, complicated, but the alibi was the ball game. It had to fly. Then something did occur to me. "What about that conference call we made the other day? All four of us were talking at one point. If we're asked, what was that about?"

Ma considered that. "Okay, Allie was still missing. We've been trying to find her. I'm a PI and so is Jeri. Jeri asked me for help. And of course Sarah was in on it. We were talking about that, what to try next. Didn't get much of anywhere with it, but we talked it over."

"Why didn't we get together to talk about it?" I asked. "Why do it over the phone?"

"We didn't because we didn't. There wasn't any *why* about it. It's not like all of us decided one way or another. I did that. I phoned all of you, set it up as a conference call since that was convenient at the time, that's all. If anyone doesn't like it, too bad."

Ma thought for a moment. "Police won't know who killed those people. In fact, if they don't pin it on Julia they'll never know. But Jeri is in that mineshaft, which puts Mort front and center, maybe me, too, a little anyway, because I trained her, so the rest of the story is that none of us knew Jeri was doing anything regarding Reinhart's hand. Mort got the package with the guy's hand in it, which was weird, and that's all we know about that. That's *all*.

Don't give the police any maybes or suppositions, like maybe Jeri was looking into the Reinhart thing on her own, even if it seems obvious. Let the police come up with their suppositions and maybes. The less you two say, the better.

"You don't know Allie and Reinhart were found in a mineshaft. You don't know anything about a mineshaft. It's likely the police or FBI will put it together that Reinhart was seeing her. It won't take 'em long to find out she was hooking. You knew it, so you can tell them if they ask, but that's where it ends. None of us knows a thing about her being with Reinhart. Nothing at all.

"As of now, don't phone anyone. In particular, don't phone me. Phone calls leave records. Don't act suspicious, but be aware that it's possible you'll be watched or followed.

"If the police question you, you don't know where Jeri is. You don't know she was found north of Gerlach. The only place you've ever seen Julia or Wexel is on TV, and you've never heard of Leland Bye. Even if the police give you a bit of information, don't repeat it and don't use it, act as if it pretty much went in one ear and out the other. At first you don't know anyone was killed. You don't know bodies were found. If they tell you bodies were found, you don't know *where* they were found, you don't know *who* was killed, you don't know *anything* about any of this. You . . . just . . . don't . . . know. And in fact, we *don't* know. We don't know if Julia put Jeri and Bye into that shaft last night. She could've hauled them away. Maybe Reinhart and Allie are down there, but we really don't know that either since Julia could've been lying, so again, *you don't know.*

"I've got to leave. You two should shower—together—make breakfast, get something to eat. Stay here awhile, then, best thing I can think is both of you go to Mort's house. Go there to pick up more of Mort's clothes since he doesn't have any here. It's possible the police will be there. If so, that's when the game will really begin, so be prepared—but at some point, Mort, you've got to make an appearance so it might as well be at a time and place that makes it easy for the police. Remember that you're not in hiding. Not at all. Don't sneak around. Don't look around as if you've got anything to hide. Let all the information come to you. Don't put anything out there yourself. Walk around happy, holding hands, smiling. Talk. Laugh. Don't look like—well, like you do now. You don't know Jeri is gone. Do all your crying now and get it over with."

She took one last look at us, then at me. "Don't shave, Mort. I'm thinking you might need that briar patch in a while."

Then she put on the scarf and left.

The room was quiet. Sarah rolled back into my arms and held me. "This's gonna be hard," she said.

"I know."

She looked up at my face. "I don't mean this alibi thing. I can handle that. I mean Jeri being gone. Allie, too, but mostly Jeri. God, Mort, I'm so sorry."

I didn't trust my voice, so I just held her. She laid her cheek on my chest. "I'm okay with this. Giving you an alibi." She thumbed the elastic on my shorts. "You should take this off, like Ma said. It'll be more like what we're supposed to be doing here."

So I did. It still had nothing to do with sex. I held her for a while. Holding her felt good, as if we were keeping each other from drifting away into a very dark place. I even fell asleep for a few minutes. Besides, if you're going to go out and kill someone, it's a good idea to rest up.

Finally, we got out of bed, showered together, got dressed, and did all the things Ma told us to do. Later, we went to my house on Ralston Street where the police finally caught up with us.

CHAPTER TWENTY-FOUR

THE STORM CAME and went. It was a lot like Ma had said it would be. I ended up in a stuffy interrogation room with Fairchild and Officer Day and several others. Their eyes were hard and alert as I told them how I'd spent the past twenty or twenty-four hours—with Sarah Dellario, age twenty-four and gorgeous.

"Gifting," Fairchild said. A gleam of respect appeared in his eyes. I wasn't in the mood, but the gleam didn't last long so I didn't end up in the county jail on an assault charge.

Sarah verified my story—which was actually an alibi, but no one called it that—and I verified hers. We didn't embellish a thing. Ma was good, she'd prepared us perfectly. They verified that gifting thing with her and it didn't come up again, which might've been due to jealousy since they were essentially a herd of pigs.

Then the FBI had at us because of Reinhart's involvement, but Fairchild's interrogation had been good practice. We kept it simple. We didn't know anything. A couple of them found it remarkable that young, beautiful Sarah would have anything to do with a crusty old relic like me. Sarah lit up at their suggestion that a girl like her couldn't find me attractive. After they cut us loose, she told me she bit off a few heads, anger that lent much authenticity to her words.

With Jeri dead, I was a suspect, which is the way it works. It's often the husband or boyfriend, although the boyfriend rarely

has occasion to murder a presidential candidate and several others while doing away with the girlfriend. Reinhart's and Wexel's
deaths were a shroud of mist over everything.

With Allie dead, Sarah was a suspect, which is also the way it
works, although Reinhart was a good-sized wrench in that theory
as well. I was beginning to like him better for all the muddy water
he was churning up. If I'd still had his hand I might have shaken
it. The FBI went through Sarah's apartment with combs and shop
vacs as Ma thought they might, but Ma's details held up.

I stayed with Sarah that night and we comforted each other.
She tried to study but had to give it up. We didn't eat a lot. We
watched a movie that barely made it as far as our retinas. By nine
p.m. we were back in bed, still close, clinging to each other, and I
finally went to sleep, so tired that I didn't even dream.

* * *

At ten p.m. the following evening we walked into the Green
Room. Ma was there, alone at a table, working on a glass of wine
with the glow of a cell phone on her face. She glanced up when we
came in, then went back to her phone.

As directed, Sarah and I sat in back, thirty feet from her. I
went to the bar. It was O'Roarke's night off. The barkeep was
a woman, Ella Glover, twenty-eight, dark hair, good-looking,
maybe fifteen pounds overweight, which is nothing in this day
and age. She smiled, said hi. She'd been working there for eight
months. I brought back a Tequila Sunrise for Sarah, a Wicked Ale
for myself. We sat where we could keep an eye on the entrance
and talked quietly.

Twenty minutes later, Ma came over and sat at our table.

"I think we're okay," she said. "If anyone comes in and gives us a second look, let's meet tomorrow at the Fireside Lounge in the Peppermill, ten p.m., same as tonight."

Then Ma dropped the bomb: Mary Odermann had boarded a flight late that afternoon in Vegas, headed for Orly Airport in France with a change of flights in Denver. For a woman who'd died two years ago, Mary really got around.

"Already gone," I said, thinking that Mercedes SUV was going to end up in a Vegas chop shop.

"But not forgotten."

"So now I've got to go to France," I said. "Or wherever she goes once she gets there."

"You and me both, bucko," Ma said.

"And me," Sarah put in.

Ma looked at her. "Not sure about you, hon. I appreciate the thought, but it's gonna be a pretty rough trip. In and out, fast as we can get it done."

"I loved Jeri, too. I can help. Not with . . . with whatever you're going to do, but finding her, maybe following her if we have to."

Ma looked at her, finally nodded. "It'll take some doin'. First thing, none of us can go under our own names, so we'll need fake IDs, passports, credit cards, the whole nine yards, and that'll take time and money. I know a guy, which'll help. We can cut the time down, but that'll mean the money will go up. A lot."

"Whatever it takes," I said.

"You and I can go as mother and son," Ma said without batting an eye. "I still don't think Sarah should go. I want you to think it over. Seriously think it over. Both of you. What we're talkin' about here is murder, even if I don't see it that way, down in my bones."

"Not murder," I said. "Justice."

"You're not gonna get the authorities to back you on that. We do this quietly and do it right, or we end up in prison for a very long time. And you"—she looked at me—"are a special problem."

"My forte, Ma."

She smiled, not something she'd done lately. "Half the people in the country know your face. You'll need a damn good disguise and it'll have to be on your passport, driver's license, everything."

"Whatever it takes," I said again.

Ma shrugged. "Money. That's what it'll take. Maybe more than you can afford. And," she said, reaching into a big purse, "we'll need these." She hauled out three inexpensive cell phones.

She handed one to me, one to Sarah. "Burners. Anonymous, can't be traced to you or to anyone. All they are is a number, not a name, and I paid for 'em with cash, three different Walmarts. This is how we'll contact each other while we're doing this thing."

She handed out prepaid phone cards, good for three months. We scratched off silver coatings, input numbers, and got our phones up and running. We traded numbers and put them into our contact lists, without names. I was "A," Ma was "B," Sarah was "C." Sneaky, but that wasn't the end of it.

"If your phone rings," Ma said, "answer it with 'hi,' nothing else. Wait until one of us identifies himself before saying anything more than that. That way if any of us loses a phone or has it stolen or confiscated, none of us gets caught."

"Spooky," Sarah said.

"Yep," Ma said. "As of now, we're off the grid. We're goin' black, people. And you—" she looked at me. "You're gonna need that beard like I said, so don't shave."

* * *

Six days after Jeri was pulled out of the mineshaft, she was cremated. That was not a good day for me. It wasn't a good day for
any of us. Jeri's mother was at the service, and her brother Ron
and his wife, Brittany. And Ma, Sarah, me, and two dozen others. I got up and said a few words in a broken voice, and Ma said
something, and then Ron.

When it was over, Ron and I got together with Ma and figured
out what to do with Jeri's house. Ron wanted me to have it—if I
wanted it. He said I had made Jeri happier in the two months we
were together than he'd ever seen her. He didn't want to profit
from her death. He had cosigned on the loan when she bought
the place. All he wanted was for the new mortgage to be in my
name alone.

Ma got her lawyer on it, a wiry, gray-haired old guy by the name
of Haldan Matz. I gave him power of attorney to sell the house
on Ralston Street and purchase Jeri's house, work out the financing, appraisal, and the title stuff, hire a realtor for the Ralston
house, set up automatic payments on Jeri's place. I didn't have the
heart or the time to do it. For thirty-five hundred dollars, Haldan
and his staff handled all that mind-numbing detail. All I did was
take everything I wanted out of the Ralston house and pile it
into a U-Haul, stash it in storage. There wasn't a lot of stuff, but
I kept the couch with the odor of mom's bulldog, Brutus, forever
embedded in its fibers. It was the world's most uncomfortable
couch, but it had history. I thought maybe I'd ship it to Mom in
Hawaii, get back at her for naming me Mortimer and sending
me all those anti-IRS books. The Ralston house also had history,
but its time had come. In its place I would have something closer

to Jeri, a house with a real office and a home gym where, in July, she'd tossed me around like a sack of rice—how could I let that go to someone who wouldn't appreciate it like I would? It also had a real kitchen and an almost-new king-size bed, not used nearly enough.

We didn't tell Ron we knew who'd murdered Jeri. If we had, he would've wanted in on what was going to happen to Julia and I didn't want him to put his life on the line like that. I didn't want Sarah's life on that line either, but she refused to back down. She'd lost both Jeri and Allie. Allie had been cremated a day after Jeri. Ma, Sarah, and I had driven down to Aunt Alice's house in San Francisco for the memorial service. Aunt Alice in a peasant blouse and an ankle-length tie-dyed broomstick skirt was everything Sarah had described when we were in Tonopah. She and I got along like old friends. And I met Dylan and his girlfriend of two years, Karen, and Sarah's parents, Barb and Gerald, back from Hong Kong and Taiwan where they'd been on another buying trip. Ravi couldn't make it. He was off playing Navy, but his two kids and his wife, Debbie, were there. We had a lot of wine and good eats, but I can't say it was a happy occasion.

* * *

Ma's guy, Ernie Saladin, aka "Doc," short for "Documents," came through. The "paper" was superb, better than first-rate. We had passports, MasterCards and Visas, driver's licenses, Costco cards, AAA, social security cards, a few others. I even had a Best Buy card with credit for purchases on it. Our passports had been stamped in several places and had a slightly worn look. It took ten days and cost thirty-six thousand dollars and took some underhanded money shuffling to keep it from the IRS, but I knew how to keep the IRS in the dark since I knew what did and didn't work.

Doc was based in Santa Fe, New Mexico. Ma had overnighted a thumb drive to him with high-resolution photos of us. I was older. My hair was almost white, cut in a modified flat top, a style that had gone out of style decades ago, but I was an old codger and it suited me. I had the start of a beard. I had deep wrinkles at the corners of my eyes, bags under my eyes, glasses with heavy black frames and an actual prescription in case anyone looked through them. The glasses gave my eyes fits, but Ma said nonprescription eyeglasses are a dead giveaway. I only had to wear them for photos and going through customs, things like that, so a short-lived eye-watering blurry world was worth it. I had a nonprescription second pair stashed in my carry-on bag. And I had a big mole below my left eye to one side that pulled a person's eyes off the centerline of my face, keeping their eyes off my nose and lips. I wore a three-piece Salvation Army suit and a truly ugly tie, things I'd never worn while working for Uncle's Gestapo—well, an ugly tie was standard with the IRS so there's that. I wasn't Ma's son, either. I was her husband, sixty-two years old. We were Mr. and Mrs. Stephen T. Brewer. T for Thomas. Ma was Martha, but I called her Marti.

And through it all, Ma tracked Mary Odermann's credit card into Paris and into restaurants and museums and bars and clothing stores. And, most especially, into Hotel L. Empire, and a few days later, into Boutique Hotel Konfidentiel on Rue de l'Arbre where it looked as if she'd settled in.

And then, seventeen days after Jeri was killed, we were ready to go.

* * *

"Marti" and I flew out together as husbands and wives often do. We flew out of San Francisco. Sarah drove to Las Vegas and was on a flight that left a day later. Sarah was Ashley Gilley. All of us were going to Paris for pleasure, not business. What that pleasure was, I didn't specify and neither did Ma, but it wasn't sightseeing.

The flights were long but uneventful. The food was marginal, as airline food has become. Customs in France was no problem. The officials weren't even rude, which was a surprise. Steve and Marti sailed on through, caught a shuttle into Paris proper, and settled in at Boutique Hotel Konfidentiel. Ashley arrived a day later and got a room not far away at a hotel called France Louvre on Rue de Rivoli.

We met at noon in the lobby of the Konfidentiel the day after Sarah arrived and made plans. Ma was still able to track "Mary's" credit card, so we knew Julia was still around. Asking the hotel staff for her room number didn't seem like a splendid idea given what we were there to do, so we began the process of stalking.

Ma and I hung around the lobby of the Konfidentiel. I was an old guy who read newspapers, mostly *The Connexion*, which was in English. In French, I might've held the damn thing upside down. I also thumbed through magazines. Ma moved around some, into the hotel's restaurants and the gift shop, keeping a sharp eye out. Julia, of course, wasn't going to look at all like the wife of a murdered presidential candidate so we had to give women a close look without appearing to do so.

Sarah had been to Julia's house in Reno, asking for water, so she wore a curly black hairpiece that spilled halfway down her back, dark glasses, bright red lipstick, sandals, a long black skirt, an ivory shirt, and a lightweight navy blue jacket. She circulated more widely, outside the hotel and into nearby shops and restaurants that Julia had frequented. She didn't stray far, but she covered some likely ground.

It took only two days.

At three thirty of the second day, Ma watched as Julia came off an elevator—a lift—strolled through the lobby and out the door without a word to anyone. She was a blond with bouffant hair under a wide-brim hat, sunglasses, a tight-lipped, standoffish look that didn't invite conversation.

Ma got on the phone. Sarah answered with "hi," and Ma said, "Yellow dress, cream sweater, big hat, front door." At the door she looked out and said, "West on Rue Saint Honoré," and Sarah said, "Got it." Julia didn't make it sixty yards from the hotel before Sarah was on her tail.

Ma's job was to ride the elevator up with Julia once she made it back to the hotel. She settled into a chair in the lobby beside me to wait. She didn't fidget, tap her foot, anything; like a spider waiting for meat, she just waited. I felt more like a black mamba, wanting to strike, to sink in poison-filled fangs.

Sarah followed Julia from fifty to a hundred yards back. They went west on Rue Saint Honoré to Rue du Louvre, then to Rue de Rivoli, south to the Louvre. Julia didn't go into the museum. She kept on to the Seine, then along the Quai du Louvre, turned north again on Rue du Pont Neuf where she sat at a tiny outside table and took her time with an espresso as people passed by on the sidewalk. Then she wandered north on Pont Neuf, pausing to examine colorful clothing in shop windows, entered a few of them, came out of one with a bag that held a newly purchased something, and finally reached Rue Saint Honoré again where she turned a corner onto Rue de l'Arbre and headed back to the Konfidentiel.

Sarah phoned it in.

I saw Julia come in. I wanted to kill her then and there, but that wasn't the plan. My fingers tingled as the woman who'd murdered Jeri crossed the lobby, paused for half a minute at the main desk,

then continued on to the elevators where Ma was standing, looking at a row of illuminated numbers that indicated on which floor
the elevator cage was at the moment.

Julia hit a button for a different elevator. When the door
opened, Ma got on with her. Ma was old, harmless, overweight,
an old woman in a hairdo that had gone out of style twenty years
ago. Ma didn't say anything to her. She let Julia hit a button for a
floor—fifth floor—and Ma smiled, then stood at the back of the
cage and watched the numbers change.

When the door opened, Ma followed Julia out then
stumbled slightly and dropped her purse. She bent over stiffly
and picked it up, then slowly ambled down the hallway behind
Julia. Julia opened the door to room 508, and just like that, we
had her.

* * *

There wasn't any point in delaying. We knew right where Julia
was, and we didn't want to become fixtures in the place. We had a
job to do and we were either going to do it or we weren't.

I was ready, I knew what to do, but cold sweat formed under
my armpits all the same. Now it felt different. Now it was real.
This might be justice, but it was also murder. I was not a murderer,
at least not yet. Suddenly I wondered if I could do this.

Then I saw Jeri again in the back of that SUV, heard the blast of
Julia's Glock, saw the impossible spray of Jeri's brains on the back
of that front seat, and I was ready again, feeling the sick fury deep
in my chest, gripping my heart.

My phone chirped. I answered. Ma said, "Five," and hung up. I
got on an elevator and took it to the fifth floor. Ma was waiting by

the elevator when I came out. We walked down the hallway and she pointed wordlessly to room 508.

"You okay?" she asked.

I pressed my teeth together hard to keep them from chattering. "Yes," I hissed.

"Close your eyes," Ma said. "Visualize those first few seconds one more time." Lord, she was tough. We'd talked it over, discussed how to do it. If I didn't do it, Ma probably would. At least she would try. I gave it a moment, eyes closed, then nodded to her.

Ma gave me a small towel from her purse. I wrapped it around my fist to make a kind of boxing glove. I stood to one side of the door, out of sight of the peephole.

Ma knocked softly. "Mademoiselle?"

A kind of grunt came from within.

"Mademoiselle Odermann?" She spoke English with a heavy French accent. "I have a bill from a shop on Rue Saint Honoré. They say the charge slip was not properly signed."

That had to work. If it didn't, we might never get a chance like this again.

But it did. The door clicked, opened an inch, and I hit it with the meat of my shoulder, not too hard, not hard enough to make a lot of noise, but it knocked Julia a few feet into the room. I went in fast, no thought now, just working on what I'd visualized a hundred times in the past two weeks. Before she could cry out I hit her in the solar plexus, a kind of uppercut that paralyzed her breathing, not too hard, but hard enough. Her eyes widened and her mouth opened like a fish, but she couldn't make a sound. She spun away, tried to run, and I grabbed her from behind, pinned her arms at her sides, lifted her off her feet and carried her into the room.

Ma shut the door behind us, then went past me and stripped the duvet off the bed, spread it out on the floor.

Julia writhed in my arms, but she still couldn't breathe. A hit like I'd given her would make her feel like she was drowning. She wouldn't be able to get air for nearly a full minute.

I stretched her out on the floor on the edge of the cover, then held her arms at her sides as I rolled her into the duvet with her head out, swaddling her in a cocoon, trapping her arms. I rolled her twice and left her faceup, straddled her, and looked into her eyes—vicious, evil eyes, devil's eyes—the eyes of a black widow spider.

"You killed Jeri," I said quietly. "You murdered my love."

She tried to cry out, but couldn't make a sound. Ma got a plastic bag from her purse and handed it to me. I pulled it over Julia's head, twisted the open end around Julia's neck, and held it there.

Then we waited.

Julia squirmed. The thin plastic huffed in and out a little. She made muffled animal noises.

At first I felt sick, then elated. Finally I felt nothing.

Julia struggled, tried to kick, but the duvet had her wrapped like a spider might wrap a fly. I sat on her as she rocked from side to side, but it didn't take long before her squirming grew less intense.

"You got her?" Ma said. Her voice was hard, not a tremor in it. Her eyes were like shiny black stones in her face.

"Yes."

"I'll go run the water."

She went into the bathroom. Julia was almost still, no longer making any sound. I heard water pouring into a bathtub in the other room.

Ma came out and watched. I was still straddling Julia, keeping her pinned. She was quiet now, inert. I could see her mouth, a wide oval where she'd sucked the plastic in half an inch trying to get air.

Murderer.

No. I was a garbage collector with a black crust around his heart, that was all. Murderers kill innocent people. Garbage collectors get rid of trash.

Ma watched the water level in the tub, turned it off when it was half full. We left the bag on Julia's head another ten minutes to be certain, then I got off and unrolled her. I put the duvet back on the bed while Ma stripped Julia down to nothing. I got Julia under the arms while Ma took her feet, and we carried her into the bathroom, set her gently in the tub. Ma wrapped Julia's fingers around the hot- and cold-water taps, ran a little more water into the tub, put her hands on the sides of the tub in a few places, then laid Julia back, closed her eyes. We backed away and looked at the scene.

Ma said, "Good riddance," and we turned away.

In the bedroom, Ma put the bed back together. She laid Julia's clothes neatly on a chair and put Julia's shoes side by side beneath it. She took Julia's purchase out of the bag—an expensive scarf—spread it out on the duvet as if Julia had taken a moment to admire it, then Ma and I looked around. The place looked pristine. Julia's purse was where she'd left it, money, credit cards, everything she'd had was untouched. No one would be in here for at least twenty-four hours. By then, we would be out of France. The room didn't look like a place where murder had been done. The truth might eventually come out, but finding the murderer or a reason for the crime might never be known. We hoped.

"So," Ma said. "We good here?"

"I am."

"Me, too. Let's go."

She opened the door to the hallway an inch, listened a moment, peered out, then left. I followed quickly. Wearing gloves, Ma put a sign on the door, French side out, *Ne pas déranger*—Do not disturb—then we walked away.

Hours later, at Orly Airport, Sarah and Ma flew west toward America. I caught a different flight and went east.

CHAPTER TWENTY-FIVE

Borroloola, Australia.

I dug holes beneath a blazing sun.

That was what I did. I didn't think about the past. I dug holes three feet deep in tough red dirt then used what came out to make a kind of slurry of dirt and water in a wheelbarrow, then poured it in around a nine-foot fence post centered in the hole, held up by diagonal braces clamped to the post and to stakes pounded into the ground. In two days the slurry would harden like concrete and that fence post would be there forty years later. Then I dug another hole and did it all again and the whole thing was like a kind of immortality marching across the land at a rate of forty feet a day. In a little over four months I'd dug nearly six hundred forty holes and put up the same number of fence posts. My work stretched fifty-one hundred feet the last time I'd measured it. Somewhere along the line it felt as if the fierce summer heat had burned away that black crust that had formed around my heart the day Jeri died.

"I brought you some water, Steve," Sally said. She was in dusty boots and a sleeveless cotton dress of some indeterminate sun-bleached color. She'd driven up in an ATV with a thermos in back. We were half a mile from the main house, a dark, low place beneath half a dozen gum trees. Sally was sixteen years old, starting to fill out. Cute kid. Another few years and she would be a knockout.

"Thanks, kiddo."

"I've got bread baking. Ma told me to tell you." She looked at my chest, probably at the little round scar where Winter had run her foil entirely through my body. It looked like a .22 caliber gun-shot wound in my sunbaked hide.

"Good deal," I said.

"You should eat more."

"Don't want to get fat."

"You're not fat. Ma says you're skinny. Well, not skinny, but she thinks you're gettin' awful thin. She'd kill me if she knew I told you, so don't."

"Told me what? Shoo."

Sally smiled and turned away. Ma was Kate Hardy, mother of Sally—and Matt, age twelve. Kate was a mile away in an old Ford pickup, wrangling sheep or whatever they call it when they run them around. I didn't do sheep. I dug holes and put up fences to keep sheep in. Or out. Sheep in a flock or in pens stink. Bad. I'd rather dig holes.

Kate was a tall, good-looking woman of thirty-seven with dark brown hair and skin that had seen too much sun, calloused hands that had done too much work. She'd lost her husband three years ago. I was working for room and board, nothing else. Everything I'd known before was either a million miles away or gone forever.

The temperature had topped out at a hundred four degrees that day—about typical for Borroloola in February. Above the waist I was getting as brown as an aborigine.

I was down to two hundred four pounds. I'd lost twenty-six in four months, and I'd put on pounds of muscle, so I didn't look much like the guy who'd rolled a woman in a bedspread and snuffed out her lights like someone stepping on a roach.

My shower was outdoors. It worked off the well system. It was meant for cleaning off the worst of the crud folks around here get into, sheep stuff you didn't want to bring into the house. There was a shower inside, but I only used the one outside. I looked askance at it when Kate said I could use it or the indoor shower. I didn't want to make myself at home, but the outdoor shower didn't come with a curtain of any sort. It was just a showerhead, a single valve, no hot water, and a kind of wooden platform to stand on. Water ran off into the dirt and that was that.

"We . . . things are pretty natural around here," she said when she saw me eyeing the house, thirty feet away.

"You've got kids."

She shrugged that off, but the next day I put up two posts and strung a wire between them, clipped a bed sheet between the shower and the house, and called it good. Three months later I was showering, shampooing my hair, which I did on Wednesdays and Sundays. It was evening, dusk, about nine o'clock. When I was finally able to open my eyes, Sally was six feet away, watching. "Ma says she's got apple pie in the house, if you want some."

"How long've you been there?"

"Not very."

"I'll be in soon. Now shoo."

She went, and that was that. Natural, I guess.

*　*　*

Sunsets in Australia are as good as anywhere else. Not better, but as good. I was in a chair leaning back on two legs against the shed that had become my home in mid-October as I watched the sun burn its way down into the land in a blaze of orange and rose. It was getting toward the end of February. I'd been in Borroloola almost four and a half months. Stars would be out and bright before the temperature dropped into the eighties.

The shed used to hold garden stuff. It was eight by ten feet. I had a bed in there now and a small chest of drawers and a tiny bookcase holding a dozen worn paperbacks. The place was sixty feet from the main house and stood beneath four gum trees. It had a wooden floor with a threadbare rug on it that Kate had given me. Good enough.

Kate came up the path from the house. "Hi, Steve," she said.

"Hi, yourself."

"Mind if I sit awhile?"

"Nope."

She pulled up a second chair and leaned back on two legs like I was doing, tucked her feet into the rungs, and watched the sky go purple and gray with me.

"Long day," she said after a while.

"Aren't they all?"

Another minute went by, then she said, "I don't know what I'd do without you."

"You'd get by."

"I don't think so. I've needed that fence for years. Jase bought all those posts and was fixing to do it when . . ."

She fell silent and the night settled around us. An hour ago I'd eaten dinner at the house. Fish this time, a change from lamb chops, mutton stew, all the things you can do with sheep. Sally's bread was good. Better than good.

Kate rapped the side of the shed. "This . . . it doesn't seem like enough room to stay in. I mean, for anyone." Her voice was soft in the dark. "If you want, I'm sure we could make some sort of a, well, an arrangement . . . in the house."

"Out here suits me, Kate."

Maybe not what she wanted to hear. This was about as close as she'd come to what might be an invitation to . . . what? Stay? Come over to the main house and share a bed? I looked out at the scorched flat earth as it gave up heat and felt Jeri, watching over me. Or maybe just watching, waiting, trying to tell me something.

"The kids really like you," Kate said.

"They're great. Really good kids."

"Sally's gettin' older."

"You're gonna have your hands full in another year or two."

After a while she looked over at me. "Why are you here?"

That was a huge leap forward. She'd asked me something like that when I'd first arrived in Borroloola, asked around, and was told Kate Hardy could probably use some help at her place, and I'd walked over, two miles south of town, asked, and she told me she couldn't pay anyone to work on the place, and I told her I didn't want pay, just a place to stay and hard work to do. She hadn't mentioned it since.

"Gotta be someplace," I said.

"That's not an answer."

"Only one I've got."

Still not what she wanted to hear. A few minutes later, she let out a little sigh and stood up. "Well, good night, Steve."

"Night."

She left.

I sat there another hour until the world was black and silent, then went inside and fell asleep so I could get up in the morning and dig more holes in the sun.

* * *

Six hundred forty holes. I chipped them out a fraction of an inch at a time with an iron bar that weighed sixteen pounds. One day I counted the number of times I lifted that bar and slammed it back down as I busted my way down three feet. I came up with four hundred twenty. So I'd lifted about 4.3 million pounds up two, two and a half feet, and drove it down into that hard red sonofabitchin' earth. I'd wanted hard work and I'd gotten it.

The day after Kate's visit I was on my third hole and it was a hundred two degrees in the shade when a Ford Explorer boiled up from the south, lifting a rooster tail of rust-red dust as it rolled past the driveway to the house and went north into Borroloola. Half an hour later, it came back and turned into the yard in front of the house. I'd never seen it before. Maybe it was special mail delivery, maybe a package, maybe Australian National Police with a warrant and I was about to take a ride, end up in France or back in the States.

I was pounding stakes into the ground, using a level to get the fence post vertical, when I looked up and saw her, a hundred yards off, walking toward me. She was blond and tall and slender and her stride was purposeful. She had an unconscious undulating sway to her hips. She wore running shoes, white shorts, a yellow sleeveless blouse that hugged her waist and accentuated her curves. A bolt of pain shot through me, as if someone had punched a hole in my chest with a railroad spike.

She stopped ten feet away and looked at me. "Hi, Mort."

"Hi, Sarah." I could barely speak.

"I turned twenty-five in January. I'm old now."

"Old, hell. You barely look twenty-one."

"The girl back there at the house said you were out here. She called you Steve, though."

"She would. It's on my passport."

"What're you doing?"

"Building a fence."

"I see that. What're you doing *here*?"

"Don't have a good answer to that."

"It took Ma nearly four months to track you down. She knew you were in Australia because of your passport, but she didn't find you here in this place until the middle of this month."

"She's good. This'd be a hard place to find anyone."

"She needs you. *I* need you. It's time for you to come home."

"I've got another hundred twenty feet of fence to put up."

"I'll wait."

"It'll take three or four days. Probably four."

"I've waited a lot longer than that. There's a pub in town. I got myself a room there. When you're done, I'll be there. I won't leave this place without you." She looked at me a moment longer, then said, "I have missed you *so* much. We both have, but I'm just goin' crazy."

* * *

Like I thought, the fence took another four days, during which time February slid into March. I didn't go into Borroloola, didn't see Sarah. I dug holes and put up fencing.

The second day, Sally came out. "She's gonna steal you away, isn't she? Miss super sexy?"

"She's not stealing."

"I hate her."

The morning of the fifth day I put my clothes in a plastic bag and left. Kate knew I was going. I'd said good-bye the night before. I saw her watching, half a mile away. She was standing in the back of the pickup, shading her eyes, watching. She didn't wave. I was glad I couldn't see her face up close.

I was almost to the main road, fifty yards from the house, when Sally ran up behind me. I heard her footsteps and turned.

"You're leaving?" she said. "Really?"

"Yup. Fence is done. I gotta go."

Tears formed in her eyes. "Ma's been crying. Mostly at night. Bet she's crying right now."

I didn't know what to say to that.

"You shouldn't leave."

"Got to, kiddo. Be good. Take care of her." I turned and headed toward town.

"Two minutes," she called out.

I stopped and turned. "Huh?"

"You had shampoo in your eyes. I watched you for two whole minutes that night." Then she turned and ran back to the house.

Kids.

* * *

Sarah and I drove to Cairns on Australia's east coast, nearly fourteen hundred kilometers away, eight hundred seventy miles on National Route One, which was mostly hard-packed rust-red earth crossed by little rivers without bridges. Sometimes the Explorer was up to the floorboards in water as we eased through. The land was flat and hot and harsh—gum trees as far as the eye could see. A typical sign would read: *Next Gas 341 Kilometers*. A mound of earth four hundred feet high was cause to stop and take photographs.

Borroloola to Burketown was 492 kilometers of slow going. We stayed at The Burketown Pub. Printed on the side of the pale yellow two-story building were the words: "*Australia's Greatest Outback Hotel.*"

"Outback, huh?" Sarah said. "I never would've guessed." The Explorer was theoretically blue, but it was rust-red from all the dust. I didn't know how vehicles survived more than one season out here.

The sun was low. The next decent-sized town was Croydon, three hundred seventy kilometers away. We ate at the pub and stayed the night in a room with a bed that wasn't a queen.

"Looks like we got us a double bed," I said, staring at it.

"It's a full."

"Looks double to me."

"Trust me, it's a full."

"Are we talking terminology or size?"

"Who cares?" She did her thing—sat on the bed and bounced a few times. All of her. Then she did her other thing—slowly took off her clothes and invited me into the shower.

I took her up on it. It wasn't sex, but it was damn nice anyway, and the view, as always, was something else. Spectacular, actually.

* * *

"Mort?"

"Yup."

"You asleep?"

"Yup. I talk in my sleep a lot."

"And make sense, too. That's amazing."

"Uh-huh. It's a knack."

She snuggled against me. "How're you doing? I mean, without Jeri?"

"Not great, but better than I was five months ago."

"Me, too. But it's still . . . really lousy."

"It is that."

She was quiet for a while. Finally, she said, "There was that gifting thing, back then."

"Uh-huh."

"I guess it's not necessary now . . . is it?"

"Guess not."

"I was wondering if we could do that again. When we get back to Reno. Sort of on a regular basis, like Tuesdays?"

I tightened an arm around her. "I have been inside myself for a long time, Holiday. It's been a quiet place, not always good, so the answer is yes. Any time."

She kissed me. "Thank you." She tucked herself in closer. "These past months . . . I've been so . . . so *empty*."

"Whenever you want."

She kissed my shoulder. "One other little thing?"

"What's that?"

"It's March already. We've got a bicycle ride coming up."

"Aw, jeez. You gotta be kidding."

"Nope. Just thought you oughta know."

CHAPTER TWENTY-SIX

THE OFFICIAL COUNT that year was one thousand seven hundred thirty-two riders. About half of them were women so you might say it was a unisex sport, not that it looked unisex to me.

The World Naked Bike Ride was about to begin. Everyone had crowded into a wide area to one side of a sidewalk, facing the bay, northwest of the Ferry Building, between a Farmer's Market and a Starbucks. The water was less than thirty feet away. Traffic slowed on the Embarcadero as it went by hundreds of naked people. Half an hour ago the word had been passed that there were enough of us in the group to strip down as far as we wanted, "as bare as you dare." The police didn't have any way to arrest that many. If no one strayed from the group, the police were okay with naked people protesting whatever.

Holiday and I were crowded against a four-foot concrete wall that kept us from being bumped into the water. Nude and seminude people milled about, talking, laughing. Bicycles lying all over made it difficult to walk around. I could turn my head and see a hundred dicks, a hundred pairs of breasts. Not everyone was naked, but most were. Holiday and I were in a warm patch of sunshine. She had a pot of red body paint and a brush and was kneeling on the grass in front of me, about to paint the stuff I didn't want the entire world to get a good look at, for all the good a little paint would do. She was gloriously naked, not a stitch on, still sporting a three-quarter Brazilian. But the ride was supposed to be a protest or some sort of celebration, so she had "4 Jeri" written on her back in red paint, as did I. It wasn't a protest, but it was enough to stay within the spirit of the event and keep the police happy.

"Paint you up when you're done?" I said. Standing there with everything hanging out wasn't as embarrassing or weird as I thought it would be back in September. In fact, it was sort of fun. I thought I was starting to understand Jeri better—and Holiday.

"Nope," she said. "I'm goin' like this. Totally in the buff."

"Well, I'm not, so you might want to hurry up with that brush," I said, looking around.

She pursed her lips and checked out her canvas, then looked up at me. "You sure? Lots of women out there with cameras would kill to get a shot of this. In case you hadn't noticed, there's a few hundred women within sixty feet of us and at least half of them are checking you out. You look really good after all that work you did in Borroloola—very *Thunder Down Under*."

"Guys're checking you out, too, sugar plum, now paint me."

"I would, if you'd hold it still instead of swinging it around."

"I'm not swinging it around."

"So you say."

She started in back at my waist. My idea was for her to produce something like a body-paint jockstrap, a *cache-sexe*, something for me to hide behind, more or less. She painted the back strap and the sides, working her way toward the front. She stopped before she got to what I considered the most vital region. Crouched at my feet, she looked up at me again. "Sure you want the rest of this painted?"

"Yep."

"Well, let's see." Gently, she moved things around.

"What the *hell* are you doing down there, woman?"

"Trying to figure out the best way to do this."

"What's to figure? Just slap it on."

"Did anyone rush Michelangelo? I don't think so."

I looked around. "Will you please hurry the hell up?"

"Mort?"

"Yeah?"

"When this ride is over and we're back at the hotel, things might get a little . . . interesting. At least I hope so. So I'd like to, well, fix you. It doesn't seem right to leave you all worked up. And, me, too. Not *sex* sex, but . . . we need to figure something out. Is that okay with you?"

"Uh . . ."

She looked up at me. "Was that a yes?"

"Having that in my head isn't helping anything right now. In fact, it could get me arrested."

"Just thought you oughta know. You okay with it?"

"It's not gonna happen if I'm in jail for indecent exposure."

"Is that a yes? What I'm looking for here is a yes before I slap on this paint."

I looked down at my blackmailer. "Yes. Now if you'll get on with it before I end up in the back of a police car."

Not three feet away, a girl in her twenties giggled and gave me a wink.

Well, shit. We were packed in there like sardines.

"Sounds like we have a deal," Holiday said. "I'll hold you to it." She dipped the brush in the pot and slapped on body paint, producing something that might have been mistaken for a jockstrap at a hundred feet.

She stood up. "There. How's that?"

I took a deep breath. "Better. Sort of. How about you? Sure you don't want your tits painted red?"

"Wow, Mort. The things you say. And, no, the sun feels really nice. My tits are just fine the way they are."

"Fine, or magnificent?"

She laughed. "I'll fix you for that." Her eyes went below my waist for a moment. "Like I said."

Minutes later, the ride began. That morning I'd learned that the thing was going to last nearly four hours. We were going to tour the hell out of the city, flash fifty thousand people. We got on our bikes and joined the laughing, colorful crowd as it started rolling along the Embarcadero, headed toward Pier Thirty-Nine. At first the pack was dense and I concentrated on not running into other riders. We went past good-sized crowds lining the street, watching, and it occurred to me that this was not only a celebration of freedom and life—which it was—it was also exhibitionism and voyeurism in the cloak of a First Amendment protest. If a thousand fully dressed people had gone by on bicycles, there wouldn't have been a dozen onlookers. But thousands were out watching, and they were there to check out not just riders, but naked riders. And for every one of us riding, five hundred or a thousand of them were wishing they had the courage to ride along with us.

Half a mile into it, there was Ma Clary with her cell phone, about where we'd told her to watch for us. Holiday and I got off our bikes and posed while she got a few pictures.

"I ain't seen so many shlongs in my life," she said, watching a few riders go by.

"Shlongs, Ma, really?" Holiday said.

"I calls 'em like I sees 'em, and I've seen a lot of 'em today. Okay, Mort, I want one of you alone. Something for my wall." She moved in for a close-up.

"Aw, c'mon, Ma."

"C'mon yourself. Relax and smile. Give an old broad a thrill."

So I struck a pose, tried to smile.

"Got it," she said. "I'll have it made into a poster." She gave me a critical look. "Wish you hadn't painted it red though."

Sonofabitch.

Holiday and I got back on our bikes and took off again. The day was terrific, warm, almost no breeze. I tried to relax, tried to settle into the ride, then, in a matter of seconds, everything changed and it was as if I'd ridden out of a dimly-lit tunnel into an ethereal light. I sat up straighter, taller, and steered with one hand as I looked up at the bright blue sky. Tears filled my eyes as I felt Jeri up there, looking down at Sarah and me, smiling.

"This one's for you, kiddo," I whispered to her.

She was watching, happy for us. I knew it and she knew I knew it because . . . she was the glow around my heart.